Living In Arcadia

Molly Moynahan

LIVING IN ARCADIA

All of the characters in this book are fictitious, and any resemblance to
actual persons, living or dead, is purely coincidental.

A BANTAM NEW FICTION BOOK 0 553 40509 8

First Publication in Great Britain

PRINTING HISTORY
Bantam New Fiction edition published 1992

Copyright © Molly Moynahan 1992

The right of Molly Moynahan to be identified as the author of this
work has been asserted in accordance with sections 77 and 78 of the
Copyright Designs and Patents Act 1988.

Extract from 'Hope I Don't Fall In Love With You' reproduced by
permission of Warner Chappell Music Ltd.
Conditions of sale

This book is set in 11/13pt Monotype Plantin by
Phoenix Typesetting, Burley-in-Wharfedale, West Yorkshire

Bantam Books are published by Transworld Publishers Ltd.,
61–63 Uxbridge Road, Ealing, London W5 5SA, in Australia by
Transworld Publishers (Australia) Pty. Ltd., 15–23 Helles Avenue,
Moorebank, NSW 2170, and in New Zealand by Transworld Publishers
(N.Z.) Ltd., 3 William Pickering Drive, Albany, Auckland.

Made and printed in Great Britain by
Cox & Wyman Ltd., Reading, Berks.

Molly Moynahan's
PARTING IS ALL WE KNOW OF HEAVEN

Also by Molly Moynahan
and published by Bantam New Fiction

Parting Is All We Know Of Heaven

To Jules & Lizzie, Mum and Dad,
from the Bison

Et in Arcadia ego

Inscription on a tomb in a painting (1623) by Guercino

Living In
Arcadia

I

For days after Matthew had left, the dog had whispered in his sleep, moaned in the early morning, finally waking up completely to howl and scratch at the door of her room. She turned over in bed, disturbed by the sound of a creature in pain, waking up to lie in the dark listening, moved beyond words. The dog had been his completely, unswervingly loyal and focused intently on his needs. The dog ignored her. At night the dog slept on the floor by the side of the bed and often licked Matthew's fingers which hung down from the edge. Sometimes when she and Matthew made love moments before the alarm went off she would be in a state of ecstasy, her head thrown back, her eyes opening and closing, her throat exposed, and she would catch the eye of the dog watching them in the half-light and she could feel his disappointment in his master and his absolute dislike of her. It was an unsettling feeling causing her to pull Matthew down deeper, hold him tighter, wrap her legs around his waist and kiss his neck so she could hear him gasp with pleasure and mutter 'Ah God, Lillian, you feel so good!' And she'd close her eyes and forget about the dog. She was a cat person temporarily bereft of feline companionship. She knew how to communicate with cats, the sort of noises they liked, how to purr them to sleep and the exact spot to stroke on the underside of their necks. She liked cats for their silence and their self-containment.

The day Matthew left, the dog had awakened her howling and when she'd turned over to tell Matthew to get up, his side of the bed was empty. Cold. Untouched.

She was suddenly awake and aware of being alone, in the room, the apartment, the city. She could feel that he was gone. His complete occupation of her life had ended with no warning. Without looking she knew his clothes were no longer in the drawers, his suits had been removed from her closet, his toothbrush was missing from its hook. All that he had left was his dog.

She began to sob, the dog bayed at the sound of her voice, the two of them howled, aware that his departure was total. She left unopened the note she found on the kitchen table and took the dog for a walk. She was in her bathrobe and an ancient pair of clogs. The sky was barely light and she walked the street in her undressed state without self-consciousness. The dog was subdued and almost affectionate. He did not stray far from her side. They clung together like children forgotten and left behind at a gas station.

Before she read his letter she opened the refrigerator and reached for a bottle of Heineken although it had been two years since her last drink. It was rarely beer she thought of when she considered giving up. Rather a perfect martini, gleaming silver in a lead crystal glass; or chilled French champagne, sipped from thin-stemmed flutes; or a Bloody Mary, a perfect companion to Eggs Benedict and intelligent conversation. Her drinking had always lacked glamour. When it was finally time to identify herself as an alcoholic, her memories consisted of endless nights spent fighting with her ex-husband, waking up sick, ashamed and full of fear, sometimes without any memory of what had transpired the previous evening. Getting sober had been the only way to regain her belief in herself. Now, after all this time, it seemed perfectly natural to reach for a beer. Instead she shoved a piece of cheesecake in her mouth and put the kettle on to make coffee. She gave the dog a milkbone but he merely gummed it, allowing the biscuit to dissolve in his mouth without chewing.

Dear Lillian, (it said)
I have decided to leave you before I become like all the other men in your life that have hurt you. It's not that I don't love you. I do. But I can't give you the sort of affection and security you deserve. Anyway, I don't want to. You were looking at me the other night as if you had finally decided I was the one who wasn't going to disappoint you. I can't handle that expectation. I've accepted a transfer to our Boston office and I'll be up in the mountains for a week before I start the new job.

I've left Thomas Wolfe. He's a good dog.
Matthew

She tried to remember how she'd looked at Matthew. Probably it was the night he had done the dishes and given her a back rub. The dog licked her bare toes. For a moment she was comforted by his rough tongue on her skin, but then the touch became unbearably painful and she took the note to bed, and the T-shirt which said 'ANDOVER' and smelled like Old Spice, and she cried until her eyes swelled closed and her cheeks broke out in a burning rash. She screamed things at her stuffed animals and smashed several glass-covered photographs of him, removing the pictures to tear them into tiny pieces. Later, she gathered up the fragments and put them in a cedar box with other pieces of old boyfriends and a snapshot of her as a bride feeding wedding cake to her ex-husband. She had thrown away the professional portraits but she thought that some-day someone might want to know what her first husband had looked like and she wouldn't remember. She appeared to be extremely drunk in the photograph and her eyes were unfocused. Not happy or sad, just empty. With the smell of the cedar, Matthew too became a part of the past.

Afterwards she collected his remaining belongings: a Ouija board, aftershave, weights, cuff links, neckties and socks and put them in the closet. She was left with the dog who had retreated to a corner of the living-room with the disintegrating milkbone now between his paws. It seemed particularly terrible of Matthew to have left behind this dog who had done nothing wrong except love him too well. She felt she was exactly like the dog and did not imagine it would be possible to be anything but kind to him. But she resented her sense of obligation and the dog sensed her resentment. He did not respond to her questions ('Is the doggy-woggy hungry?'). His dog chow remained uneaten. He lay, barely moving, in the corner by the window while she dozed, still clutching the T-shirt and trying to feel flu symptoms. At some point, footsteps approached the door and the dog went mad, jumping in the air, running from the bedroom to the bathroom, through the living-room and finally flinging himself against the door, barking loudly. The footsteps retreated and the dog turned to stone.

She'd taken the dog to the class out of the desperation caused by the embarrassment suffered when he'd run away from her in Central Park, trailing his leash. No matter how loudly she shouted his name or quietly crooned endearments, the moment she was close enough to grab his leash he had dodged and dashed away. Finally, a little boy helped her to corner the dog by the Delacourte Theater and then, of course, he had sat down allowing himself to be easily captured, pretending to be bored by the entire affair. He stared at her with sad brown eyes that said: 'So what? What difference does it make? I don't like you.'

The class met at the top of the path on the corner of 69th and Central Park West. Thomas Wolfe responded to this change in his normal routine (consisting of lying on the living-room floor, chewing on one of Matthew's old wingtips) by behaving as if he were being taken to the dog pound. Lillian dragged so hard on his leash he started making little choking noises and passers-by were staring at her with hate in their eyes. When they finally found the class, Thomas Wolfe promptly bit the thin back of a large Doberman standing next to them. The Doberman let out a yelp of pain and its owner gave Lillian a stunned glare.

'I'm so sorry,' she said, yanking on T.W.'s chain so that his paws went in different directions, 'He's not my dog.'

'It's OK. Camus's just a bit insulted. What's his name?'

'Thomas Wolfe. It's not OK. It's terrible. I hate this stupid dog!'

She shouted this loudly enough for the rest of the class to hear. Their group consisted of a middle-aged woman in a tweed coat with a golden retriever, a Korean girl with a collie and an old man with an ancient sheepdog. They were staring at her with disgust.

'She hates her dog,' the tweed woman whispered to the young girl. 'The poor baby.' The girl nodded and smiled at Lillian. It seemed probable that she didn't understand much English.

'She said it wasn't her dog,' the old man suggested hopefully. 'Maybe that's why she hates it.'

'Nonsense!' The woman adjusted her coat and glared at the old man who smiled at the Korean girl who smiled back despite her temporary alignment with the owner of the golden retriever – who looked at her watch and made some sort of remark about the class beginning. Their teacher was nowhere in sight. The man with the Doberman got down on one knee to talk to Thomas Wolfe. He had beautiful hands, long fingers and strong wrists. Lillian looked down at the top of his head and the man's scalp, the straightness of his parting and the little cowlick at the front, caused her to flinch at the memory of the first clear picture she'd had of Matthew, down on all fours trying to convince Thomas Wolfe to give him his paw. 'Slap me five' he had said to the dog who had simply lifted his heavy foot and dropped it again, landing on Lillian's ankle as she was waiting for the light. Her stockings were badly ripped.

'Jesus!' Matthew had leapt to his feet, yanking the dog hard on his leash, 'Sorry! He's really ruined your things. Let me buy you some new ones. Where could we get something like that?'

'It's OK.' Lillian didn't want this handsome man to look so miserable.

'Can we get some in there?' He was pointing at a Dunkin Donuts. Lillian laughed.

'At least let me buy you a cup of coffee.'

'OK. Coffee sounds better than L'EGGS.'

'Than what?'

'They're a brand of pantyhose. They come in little plastic eggs. Never mind.'

She could tell this man did not have a real girlfriend. A guy with a real girlfriend would have known what L'EGGS were just as he'd have understood the importance of a bad haircut, how to run the delicate cycle and what sort of Tampax to buy. Women ceased to be enigmas to men with real girlfriends. They smiled understandably when you mentioned PMS and were often able to recommend certain designers who made clothes in which women could feel comfortable. Men without girlfriends stared into windows featuring faceless models wearing black lace corsets. They hadn't been exposed to the fact that most women prefer to wear big T-shirts or long flannel nightgowns and men's athletic socks on cold winter nights. Men with real girlfriends or wives acted distant around most women. Neutral. Vaguely guilty.

This man was smiling and asking her questions about the neighbourhood. He bought four doughnuts which he was forced to eat by himself. Men with real girlfriends would have assumed Lillian was on a diet or, like most women, didn't eat anything but salad in public. He had just moved from the West Coast. He liked New York, but it was hard to make friends. Lillian smiled and patted his dog, who didn't seem at all happy about her talking to his owner. His body trembled under her fingers. She pretended to know people. She assumed he would be shocked if she told him she had not spoken to a single human being since she had done her laundry two days earlier. And that was only to buy fabric softener from the man who emptied out the quarters from the machines. Her life was narrowing down gradually to something she observed through the raised slats of a Venetian blind. Living without alcohol, the occasional drug, eliminated the distance between Lillian and the rest of the world. She had always liked that air pocket, the blurring of the sharp corners which life seemed to consist of. People were difficult to understand. They had expectations Lillian couldn't satisfy. At parties she tended to drift away towards bookshelves where she could read the titles aloud, attempting to seem engrossed in someone's library, hoping it would be late enough to leave without being rude. Until she stopped drinking she hadn't understood she was shy, awkward, a normal person. If someone attempted to speak to her she would inform them of their mistake, or pretend not to understand English. 'I'm boring,' she'd warn them kindly. 'I'm French,' she once told someone who immediately began to speak that language fluently. Mostly she stayed home. 'I'm having a life crisis,' she would tell herself as she stopped at the Korean grocery store to buy ice cream. Every time she noticed a woman standing silently in a window she thought it was her own reflection and she had to touch herself to believe she was not behind glass.

He called her. She had written her number down on the back of a matchbook. Late for work and full of regret for having allowed herself to be drawn out, she shook his hand quickly and ran for the bus. By the time she got home her machine was blinking. It was him.

He took her to clubs downtown where she saw people she'd read about in gossip columns. They were surprisingly unattractive. Matthew had the sort of look doormen liked. They were often summoned to the front of lines, allowed to pass in front of people who were considered too 'bridge and tunnel' to mingle with the trendsetters. They regarded Lillian with suspicion.

Lillian had no idea how to behave in such surroundings. She spent a great deal of time sitting in the ladies' room eavesdropping while Matthew effortlessly made connections. She borrowed glossy magazines from the bathroom attendants and tried to imagine herself as having style. They went dancing at Roseland, rode the Staten Island ferry and listened to Bobby Short sing Cole Porter at the Carlyle. Brunch in the Rainbow Room, late Sunday afternoons at the Cloisters, the Cyclone at Coney Island and high tea at the Plaza. They attended mass at St Patrick's and recitals at St John the Divine. New York was transformed into some sort of fairy kingdom filled with wonderful people and delicious things to eat. She stopped seeing rats in Central Park. Even the squirrels appeared healthier and well dusted. She handed out spare change to the homeless and allowed people to steal her dryer in the laundromat.

One morning she woke up at dawn to find him sitting by the window smoking a cigarette, staring at her. His expression was difficult to read. He did not seem affected by the sight of her. She sat up quickly, afraid of the way she must look. He seemed to be getting ready to say something difficult. She was filled with a nameless terror. 'Go,' she wanted to tell him. 'Just go now.'

He put out his cigarette, sat down on the bed and took her in his arms. 'I want to move in,' he whispered. 'I'm tired of leaving you.'

He was subletting a furnished studio on a dingy block near Columbia University. They had stopped there once to pick up some of his clothes. The hallway smelled of people cooking soup. He did not bring her in but she glimpsed an unmade sofa bed, a suitcase lying open on the floor and very ugly green-and-brown curtains. It gave the impression that the person living there had just arrived or was packing to leave. T.W. stood by the window, staring out at the street. The room was very narrow.

'Why do you live here?' she had asked him then. 'It's like a prison.'

Matthew's job at the bank involved trading foreign currency. He was considered by the management as being on the 'fast track'. He could afford a much nicer place to live.

'It's not home,' he had told her. 'It's just a place to sleep and hang my suits until—' he had stopped and laughed.

'Until what?'

'Until I find what I'm looking for. Look, it's a guy thing. Girls like sofa pillows and throw rugs. Guys don't need much. Furniture is too demanding.'

'What about Thomas Wolfe?'

'Dogs are like guys. They have to settle for what's available.'

Six months after moving in, Matthew was gone and she was the guardian of a very depressed dog. Her old ways did not fit so well. She had abandoned the routine and it felt strange to return to the cloistered life, to weekends without any plans, days where she spoke only to people to whom she was giving money. She didn't remember which shows she used to watch on television. Her health-club membership had expired. Her job writing ad copy for Bloomingdales did not provide any relief from the isolation. She worked alone in a cubbyhole and the office buddies she had previously gossiped with had somehow moved on. She was not part of anyone's life. Her attendance at AA meetings had nearly stopped altogether. About a week before Matthew's departure he had called to her while he was shaving and she was standing naked in front of her closet trying to decide what to wear to work.

'If I died,' he asked, 'do you think you'd drink?'

She could not decide between the linen skirt or the cotton dress. Part of her job requirement was to dress better than the store's customers. One of the sportswear buyers had suggested to Lillian that her image was not 'fashion forward' enough. This woman was wearing fuchsia bicycle-pants and a T-shirt with a five-inch-wide leather belt. Lillian didn't like clothes. She failed to understand how anyone could actually enjoy shopping. She always froze in the dressing-room, appalled by her own body in the green fluorescent light. She would pull her own clothes back on and go somewhere to grieve over her loss of presumed beauty. Her ex-husband had loved to shop and often suggested a trip to Macy's as a wonderful way to spend a Sunday afternoon. He liked to dress Lillian, and she allowed him his pleasure as it was a relief to settle for his wardrobe choices.

'No,' she said, shutting her eyes and grabbing at the garment in front of her, 'nothing would make me drink again.'

Matthew had begun to whistle then, a Warren Zevon song about a guy who killed his girlfriend and everyone called him 'an excitable boy'. He told her she looked lovely in the cotton dress and kissed her goodbye in front of the store. No-one commented on her clothes and an assistant buyer in small leather goods said she liked her make-up.

After the first dog-training class Lillian was surprised to find herself walking into a liquor store. She had gone out to buy milk.

'That will be $5.99.' She handed the clerk ten dollars and picked up the bottle of wine, its shape a familiar weight in her hand. Before she remembered she didn't drink. He gave her back the money without saying anything. When she returned to the apartment and sat down on the couch, Thomas Wolfe came over and leaned against her legs with a sigh.

'Hi T.W.' It was nice to talk to someone. His body was soft and warm against her legs. 'Hi, you stupid, miserable dog.' T.W. made happy sounds as she patted him, and as she tried not to imagine what might happen if she began to drink again.

Matthew liked staying up late. He often went out by himself, returning as a grey-blue light was slanting across the floor of their room. She would wake up to the feel of his cool body pressed up against her, shaking slightly, exhausted, smelling of smoke. 'Hold me,' he'd whisper. 'Don't leave me.' She couldn't understand why he seemed so unhappy. He always emptied his pockets out on the dresser. Sometimes there were matchbooks with telephone numbers written inside them. She didn't want to become the sort of person who searched other people's pockets. There was no point in her offering to accompany him. On the rare occasions she had visited his favourite bars, the smoke and the noise made her feel breathless and tired.

'You don't belong here,' he'd whisper tenderly into her ear as he ordered another vodka and a club soda for her. 'You should be home reading Jane Austen.'

On the nights he didn't return until dawn she would wake up to flowers on the dining-room table and a note saying he loved her. For days afterwards, he behaved like a man being punished for a crime he didn't commit. He played Zevon's quieter songs and called in sick to work. He talked about the homeless and the end of the world – which he predicted for the year he turned forty, the year he claimed the ozone layer would be burned away completely and all human beings would roast like chestnuts. He took endless baths and then would emerge draped in towels to lie on their bed in the semi-dark, his hands crossed on his stomach, his eyes closed.

'Talk to me,' Lillian would say, sitting on the edge of the bed. 'Tell me what it is.'

'What it is,' Matthew would repeat sarcastically. 'What it isn't, sweetheart, that's the answer. What it isn't.'

And Lillian would leave him alone, his headphones drowning out the sound of her voice, secretly relieved that he could not articulate his misery.

The Chinese laundry left a threatening message on her machine.

'Come get these shirts! We no longer responsible after thirty days!' They were his shirts. Seventeen hand-finished Pima Cotton button-down Oxfords with French collars. His mother believed a man could never own too many nice shirts. They were pink, cream, sky blue, mauve and navy pin-striped. They had been paid for in advance as Mr Chang, the laundry's owner, trusted no man.

She did not want Matthew's shirts in her apartment. On their way home from the cleaners, Thomas Wolfe had barked at a homeless man painstakingly folding a piece of blanket. Lillian handed him two shirts, a pink and a blue. He immediately hid them under his knapsack. The next was presented to a young man who requested a quarter for a phone call outside CHARIVARI. He put it on over his torn Grateful Dead T-shirt and went off looking elegant from the waist up. She gave two to a couple who were sitting on a bench in the middle of Broadway and 72nd Street holding hands. They were dressed like Raggedy Ann and her brother Andy. After a brief squabble, he took another blue one and she chose the mauve. And so on. By the time Lillian and Thomas Wolfe reached their street, the shirts were gone.

She then took out the box which contained what remained of Matthew's possessions and distributed books, neckties, tennis balls, aftershave and cuff links around the city. She gave the super his set of free weights. When she opened the door that evening she finally felt free of him. She no longer slept with the ANDOVER T-shirt and she allowed herself to sleep stretched across the entire bed, not scrunched up so as to leave his side empty. She gave the T-shirt to T.W. who began to chew it.

They attended the second obedience class and T.W. learned to heel and sit. He was not enthusiastic about fetching anything and he still refused to come when Lillian called. His sitting on command made this less crucial, as she could slowly approach him repeating the command 'Sit' over and over again until she was close enough to slip his leash over his head. It seemed deliberately stupid of him to fail to learn how to come, and Lillian felt her classmates did not respect her. Except for Sam, the Doberman's owner, who insisted Thomas Wolfe was a non-conformist with a 'Dadaesque' view of the world. Thomas Wolfe tried to bite his dog again, but she shouted 'Sit!' just in time and he sank to his haunches, teeth bared.

In late July her front buzzer sounded and she pressed the button without checking who it was. Her super was supposed to install a new smoke detector. When she opened the door and saw Matthew standing in the hallway she felt sick. He was wearing a light grey linen suit and his hair was cut very short. T.W. stood behind her, the ANDOVER T-shirt, a rag, hanging from his mouth. She tried to close the door again but her fingers were trembling too violently to turn the knob.

'Hi Lillian,' he said brightly. 'Can I come in?'

'No,' she said, wondering when T.W. would push through her legs and fling himself on his beloved master.

'Look, I'm really sorry about how I handled things. I didn't know how to explain anything. OK?'

'No. Go back to Boston.'

'I want to talk to you. I tried calling you at work—'

'I got the message.'

'There's some stuff here. My shirts—'

'I gave them away.' Matthew blinked. 'I gave your shirts to the homeless, your weights to Fernando, your tennis stuff to the bagel guy and your cuff links to Mrs Anastasia's son as a graduation present. He graduated from the John Jay School of Criminal Law. I said they were from you. She said to thank you.'

'Fuck!' Matthew said, his fist hitting the door frame. 'Those were solid gold. Where's T.W.? Where's my dog? I suppose you had him auctioned off to a dogmeat cannery!' Lillian moved slightly so Matthew could see T.W. 'Hey! There he is! There's the fella!'

T.W. looked everywhere but at Matthew. He opened his mouth to yawn and the T-shirt fell out. He picked up his head and gave his previous owner a long cool glance. His eyes were filmed over. He licked Lillian's hand and walked back to the bedroom. Matthew straightened up.

'I want my dog back,' he said.

'He's my dog,' Lillian replied, firmly closing the door.

Thomas Wolfe was at the window, his front legs on the sill, watching Matthew walking down the street, trying to hail a cab. His whole body was trembling. Lillian stood next to him, her hand resting lightly on his head. They watched as Matthew turned around to stare at her window. He stood with his hands at his sides, his head flung back. If she opened the window and called to him, he would come back to them both. Lillian closed the curtains.

She walked to the bedroom door and paused. 'Come,' she said, without hope. After a moment's hesitation, the dog obeyed.

2

Thomas Wolfe was not a gifted dog. Lillian was so humiliated by his lack of progress, she began to find reasons for missing the dog-training class. In August the leader asked her to remain after the others had left the park. It was an extremely humid, still evening. The sort of night that made you miss the ocean with an almost physical sensation, a longing for the sharp edge of salt air and a relief from the oppressive heat which blanketed Manhattan. The leader was a young man who never seemed to lose his temper or confidence in the animal's ability to obey instructions. Lillian thought he was close to being a saint. She couldn't remember the name of the saint who blessed all the animals, but she thought Paul would look well in a monk's garb rather than the cut-off jeans and T-shirts he wore.

'Lillian,' Paul said, 'how come you keep missing the class?'

'I'm sorry,' Lillian replied humbly, trying to get T.W. to stop walking around in circles so that his leash wrapped around her ankles, 'I've been terribly busy.'

She was lying. She was lying to a saintlike animal trainer. Since she had quit her job she had done practically nothing. Quitting her job had seemed easy after refusing to allow Matthew into the apartment. The head of the advertising department didn't seem very surprised. 'Retail was never your life,' he said very gravely. 'Without that commitment, you get nothing but a headache and a lousy paycheque.' She watched as he took a hearty swig from a pink bottle. 'And an ulcer.' Lillian packed up her desk with the feeling she had never actually been there.

Without a place to go, she had found herself spending large amounts of time beginning projects only to abandon them at their most crucial stage. Spackling the ceiling inspired her to start painting the bathroom tiles on the hottest day in July. There was now a patch of pink surrounded by a sea of blue.

She signed up for a course on closet organization offered by her local hardware store, but then began to meditate with a group of recovering overeaters who said as long as she had a problem with something she was welcome.

'What's your relationship like with T.W.?'

Lillian smiled but Paul looked serious. 'Well, it's sort of relaxed, I guess. I mean, we don't pay much attention to each other.'

Paul was listening to her very carefully. Lillian began to feel uncomfortable. She looked down and met the accusing eyes of Thomas Wolfe. 'You don't spend quality time with me,' they seemed to say. 'You're a selfish bitch.' Paul was still staring at her.

'You think that's why he can't learn anything?'

'Indifference kills iiving things, Lillian. Show him his performance matters to you.' He had nice eyes, she thought. She wondered if he were gay.

'You mean give him extra milkbones or something?' she asked, trying to be witty. 'More positive reinforcement?'

'Just love him, Lillian,' Paul said, patting her shoulder. 'He's a lovable dog.' The park was almost cool so Lillian sat down on a bench and tried to imagine what it would mean to love Thomas Wolfe.

'I love you,' she said, just as a jogger ran up the path towards 69th Street.

'I love you too,' he shouted, dashing across Central Park West before the light changed.

She got up early the next morning and was very nice to T.W. She brushed his coat and played an incredibly dull game of find-the-ball with him. After nearly an hour of saying 'nice dog' and 'good boy', she tested his progress.

'Sit,' she commanded. Thomas Wolfe left the room. 'Fuck you,' she said as the phone began to ring.

After the fourth ring she realized the answering machine was off. The tape was almost worn out and she'd been trying to re-record her message. She had been screening her calls to avoid: 1. Her mother 2. Matthew on drugs calling to lie 3. A straight Matthew calling to lie 4. Her ex-room-mate calling to urge Lillian to join her newly formed Women-Who-Love-Too-Much Support Group 5. The Macy's credit department requesting immediate payment of her overdue bill. On the ninth ring she picked up the phone but did not speak.

'Hello?' She held her breath.

'Yes?'

'Lillian?'

'I'm not sure.'

'You're not sure if this is Lillian?'

'Who is this?'

'Is this Lillian?'

'I asked you first.'

'No you didn't.'

'Is this Lillian who owns the dog who won't sit?'

'I'm hanging up.'

'It's Sam. Camus's owner.'

'Oh. Hello.'

'You gave me your number. You were going to recommend a masseuse. For my lower back.'

'Right. Hold on. I'll get my Roladex.'

'Well, if you weren't busy I thought we could have a cup of coffee or something.'

'When?'

'I'm in a coffee shop in your neighbourhood. The Broadway Donut Shoppe.' Lillian lived above this restaurant.

'I'm sort of busy.'

'What were you doing when the phone rang?'

'Trying to relate to Thomas Wolfe. I mean . . . trying to give him positive reinforcement.' Sam giggled. 'It's not funny. My dog won't sit because I don't love him.'

'You love him.'

'I don't think I do. He reminds me of my old boyfriend—' Lillian wondered if she should be having such an intimate conversation with a near stranger. She saw that Thomas Wolfe was eating one of her flip-flops. The thong was hanging from his mouth.

'I'll see you in ten minutes.' Sam hung up.

Lillian hated the Donut Shoppe. Her greatest secret fear was that someone would notice her sitting in there alone on a Saturday night and say: 'I know that girl. She lives upstairs. How pathetic.' The owners were friendly and always waved at her and Thomas Wolfe when they went on their morning walks. Matthew had practically lived on their sticky buns. But on Saturday nights she saw the place as a resting place for old men, the homeless, each sitting alone, nursing a cup of Sanka and staring out at the street.

Sam was better-looking than she'd remembered. His hair was streaked with blond light and he was wearing a soft cotton T-shirt the colour of the Adriatic. She hadn't studied him very closely during the dog-training class. It was easier to recall Camus's face and body than his owner's. He was eating a sesame bagel and studying the diner's twenty-page laminated menu. Lillian ducked into the doorway of the copy shop next door and tried to breathe.

She had hung up the phone and sat motionless, staring out of the window until she realized she had three minutes left to dress if she were planning on meeting him in ten. She was wearing one of Matthew's old rugby shirts and sweatpants. She took off the shirt and stood naked in front of the hall mirror. Her skin was barely touched by the sun.

Her body looked indefinite, under-exercised, unfucked. She pulled on a pair of jeans that had fit once after a severe bout of food poisoning. They closed when she used her yoga breathing and lay flat on her back with her head hanging over the side of the bed. Thomas Wolfe came over to breathe in her face. His breath smelled of rubber. He had eaten her second flip-flop. As she attempted to force the zipper, he watched her with an expression that suggested contempt for the human race.

'Leave me alone,' Lillian muttered, trying to get off the bed without bending. 'We have a lousy relationship.'

Finally she took off the jeans which were too tight for a hot day and put on a sundress which cruelly exposed her pale shoulders. She added a pair of Matthew's after-a-coke-binge sunglasses and left the apartment without make-up. Her reflection in the copy-shop window told her she resembled an ageing drug addict except she lacked the requisite gauntness. She felt like crying. Why couldn't she be better adjusted to life? Why hadn't she spent an afternoon lying in the sun with all the other New Yorkers not too proud to get a tan in Central Park? She wondered how she could possibly pay her bills without a job. She wondered if she should stop hanging up on Matthew.

'Hey there! Lillian. Great shades. Want some breakfast?'

'Oh, no. Just some coffee.'

'Decaf?'

'Regular. I mean caffeinated. Real coffee.'

'No food?'

'No.'

'Do girls eat?'

'No. Personally I live on art. Music. An occasional opera.' Lillian took her sunglasses off.

Sam smiled. He seemed delighted to be sitting with her and she couldn't help wondering what was wrong with him. Perhaps he was a member of a religious cult or that group founded by a shrink which devoted themselves to group sex. Their headquarters was, according to the papers, on the Upper West Side. Or maybe he was married. She tried to sneak a subtle look at his left hand to see if there was any sign of a missing ring. He caught her eye and beamed again. Without thinking, she smiled back.

'What a pretty girl you are,' he said, 'I—'

'Don't.' Lillian reached for the ashtray. She looked around for a 'No Smoking' poster but seeing none, she lit her cigarette. The woman at the next table glared. Lillian glared back. Her coffee was put in front of her. She blew smoke in the direction of the disapproving woman. Sam continued to smile at her. Lillian resisted the urge to put her sunglasses back on. 'That was nice. What you said.'

'Just the truth.'

'I'm sort of angry and it's hard to accept compliments graciously. It's hard to accept anything, actually, but compliments are impossible. The newsman next to my building told me he liked my sneakers and I scowled at him until he apologized . . . "I'm sorry," he said. "Was that too personal?" I've seen this guy every morning for years and I make him feel like a slime ball . . . Oh, I got you that masseuse's card.'

'Terrific. It was nice of you to bother.'

Lillian sipped her coffee. She felt exposed. Why hadn't she stayed home? She believed her life was becoming a series of social disasters. She began to twist her hair and chew on her lower lip. Habits that were alien to her. Horrible physical behaviour she had always pitied in others. It would be terrible to begin to scream in a restaurant she lived above. She thought about bolting, but she felt Sam's hand lightly touch her wrist.

'Do you go?'

'Where?'

'To this masseuse.'

'Oh. No. I used to go. Mostly when I was a writer. Well, sort of a writer. I was mostly a waitress. And a writer. Except I didn't sell anything so I don't know if I could call myself a writer. I made a lot of money being a waitress. I should have kept on, but I didn't and now I'm really poor. I mean, relatively. I just quit my job.'

'Good for you!'

Lillian looked up from the pile of Sweet-and-Low packets she was busily constructing. It was a nice thing for him to say. Other people had quickly changed the subject or mentioned their own financial problems or immediately said they'd let her know if anyone they knew needed to hire someone. As if she'd asked.

'Thanks. People think I'm crazy. New Yorkers seem to believe anyone not working is automatically in terrible trouble. I hated my job.'

'What was it?'

'Writing ad copy for Bloomingdale's. Ten lines of adjectives describing slipcovers and sixty-dollar-an-ounce eye-wrinkle cream. Satin. I always used the word satin. Everything began to sound the same.'

'God, I hate Bloomingdale's!'

'Everybody does. I mean, normal people. Hollywood directors like to shoot movies there and some people get off on being insulted by cosmeticians. They think it's a genuine New York experience. But I used to work there. You'd come out of your cubicle at lunchtime and you'd be trapped in this store! Tall women trying to spray you with perfume named after exits on the LA freeway. Make-up artists offering to resculpt your face—'

'I had to buy a tie there once. Some aunt gave me a gift certificate. The man behind the counter criticized my haircut. "What a shame," he said, "You have this hot tie and that really pathetic cut." Then he smiled at me and winked. It was really unpleasant.'

Lillian nodded and they were both quiet. She knocked over the Sweet-and-Low tower. When she glanced out the window she saw a man across the street who looked exactly like her brother, Edward.

'Edward,' she screamed, sliding open the glass window. 'Hey! Edward!'

The man was someone else. Not her brother. Certainly not named Edward. A panhandler came over and tried to shake her hand.

'My name's Frank,' he said hopefully. Lillian slid the window closed.

'Who's Edward?'

'Not him.' Sam looked like he expected more. 'My brother.'

Edward was probably somewhere strange like Michigan or Fiji. He didn't like New York. He enjoyed a good stroll and he said he felt New Yorkers were pushing at his heels, trying to hurry him up.

'It's the land of Lillian clones,' he had told her. 'People are always leaping into the silence, trying to catch up with something slightly out of focus.' It was the closest he had ever come to telling her she wasn't living the sort of life he could enjoy. Lillian's feelings were hurt.

Edward had been the one to tell her she drank too much, that she couldn't stop drinking, that she was, in fact, dying of alcoholism. It was two months after her wedding, enough time for Lillian to have realized she had made a terrible mistake. She stood alone in their kitchen night after night, Anthony asleep in the bedroom, the refrigerator door open, drinking what was left of the wine or the whisky. Her body was breaking down. She could actually feel the cells dividing, crumbling, waking before dawn, her heart pounding so hard it hurt, screams caught in her throat, sweat-soaked.

She had auditory hallucinations, the sound of a baby crying, a kitten screaming, she was constantly searching their apartment for small, injured creatures, finding nothing.

Edward had walked into the apartment one Sunday afternoon. They had been fighting and the door was unlocked. Anthony had just hit her. Lillian was lying in a heap on the floor, her head ringing from the force of the punch. Edward had not spoken to Anthony but he had asked Lillian: 'Do you want to leave?' and Lillian had nodded. He had taken her coat from the closet and when she moved towards Anthony, her husband had put his head in his arms and began to sob. Edward stood between them. 'No, Lillian,' he had said. 'No.' She had never gone back.

'Did this happen before?' Edward asked as they drove through the Lincoln tunnel.

'Yes.' Lillian's head ached. She wanted something to drink. She had her face pressed against the glass of the window.

'Why didn't you tell us?'

Lillian looked at the grey expanse of the Hudson. Anthony had thrown her out of the car once on the Brooklyn Bridge. She had sat on the edge all day trying to muster the courage to leap.

'Because I thought I loved him. It was hard to believe this was happening to us. It was humiliating.'

'Why did he hit you?'

'Edward—'

'I want to know why anyone would hurt my little sister!'

She looked over and saw that his eyes were full of tears. For a second she wondered if he were using this to prepare for a character. She thought he must understand how people could behave under difficult circumstances. Even he had hurt her before.

33

'Maybe because I drank so much. He said it made him feel lonely. Like I was shutting him out. And I didn't love him.' Lillian's head filled with air. 'I wanted to get away from him. I want to get away from everyone.'

'You have to stop drinking.'

The following day she went to her first AA meeting with a gay friend of Edward's who told her she had a brother designed by Olympian gods. He held her hand all through the meeting.

'This will keep the wolves away,' he whispered to her. 'And remember, all these people used to throw up in their shoes.'

It had been enough then. Not to drink and not to be pushed around by her husband. It had seemed like enough just to wake up without feeling that her head was banded by steel and not to lie next to a man she feared. Why did she stop being grateful? Matthew's presence had forced her to accept how little she had changed. She was sober and alone but still aware of herself as flawed, without value. It had never been comfortable with him but she accepted his ambiguity. When he left her there had been an odd sense of relief, the thrill of the inevitable. Now, as she looked at the man sitting across from her she felt a great wave of exhaustion wash over her body. Sam was offering her a piece of his doughnut.

'Have you noticed recently how gross everyone is?' she said.

'Gross?'

'Selfish. Greedy. Not hiding their greed. I was on the subway last night and there were these two Wall Street guys – kids – discussing playing golf. Like it was some sort of incredibly cool thing. They sounded like corrupt government officials – like those guys who are always being busted for bribing people – and it was just fine. Just fine to wear a Rolex and two-hundred-dollar loafers and complain about your co-op as long as you made sure

34

you had absolutely no shame! Like, this is capitalism, man! If you can't handle the karma, if you can't step over the beggars without flinching, then give it up!'

'What about car phones?'

'Exactly. Car phones. Breast augmentation. Retin-A. Power breakfast. I was on the elevator going to my shrink – this is a shrink story which is probably bad but I see her because I'm crazy. Well, relatively. The doorman never says hello and I've been going there for nearly three years! Maybe I should have tipped him at Christmas, but what sort of relationship do I have with my shrink's doorman? He thinks I'm a compulsive crier and I don't like the way he treats the messengers. I'm in the elevator and this guy gets on wearing a camel-hair coat and very expensive shoes. I know how expensive the shoes are because my ex-husband used to be a shoe freak and every time we had a big fight we made up by going to Barneys and buying him shoes. This guy keeps holding the "door open" button but no-one's coming and he gives me a look. So I smiled and then he moved to the back of the elevator and he just kept staring at me like I was selling something. I opened my mouth but I didn't know what to say and then this woman got on wearing spandex and she started to stare at him while he stared at me. It was like being trapped in a cage with wolverines or coyotes or something. And I couldn't say anything to either of them. I felt like we were in a porn movie and the camera was above our heads and the scene where we all got naked was coming . . . '

Lillian stopped. She had forgotten why she had started. She also didn't know how the story really ended.

'They got off on the same floor and I felt almost as if I should have followed them. But then I had this attack of insecurity, like maybe he didn't really like my body. And this man was horrible! Why should I care what this wolverine thought about me?'

'I think you have a beautiful body.'

Lillian blushed and stopped talking.

Sam patted her hand. 'Sorry. That wasn't really the point.'

'It doesn't matter. I was babbling about nothing. I can't believe I told you that story. It's utterly pointless.'

'I like listening to you. You're very vivid. Filled with insights.'

'Crazy.'

'Maybe.' Sam shrugged. 'Unhappy perhaps.'

The man on the sidewalk who introduced himself as Frank was still staring through the window. He seemed to be enjoying himself, as if he were watching a movie. Lillian nodded at him, and he gave her a look that somehow indicated pity. She wondered if he had targeted her as a future loony, if this prolonged eye-contact were a form of networking. After another second the man winked and nodded. Lillian's heart skipped a beat. She thought she might pass out.

'I'm sorry,' she said to Sam, standing and picking up her cigarettes. 'I'm not well. I'm much too neurotic for anyone who's not related to me. I'll see you at the next dog class.' She ran out of the restaurant and into her building certain that someone from the Mayor's office was going to throw a net over her.

She watched a special on PBS that ended with the commentator saying: 'We will finish with rare footage showing the Chinook salmon swimming upstream in the Oregon river. They are returning to their place of birth, to lay eggs and die, worn out by their own biology.'

Lillian watched as the impossibly large fish (this was the source of the lox she bought in Zabars?) fought the swift current, the water eddying around their fins while they hung suspended in the middle of the river. 'Look at this,' she said, poking Thomas Wolfe with her foot. 'What a fucking tragic miracle instinct is!'

T.W. opened one eye and blindly contemplated Lillian's afghan before falling back into his dream of chasing fat pure Persians across wide open, treeless fields. The cats were all his and their eyes were filled with terror as he approached them, jaws open wide.

Lillian turned off the television. 'I want to spawn,' she announced to her empty kitchen. 'I want to build my nest.' She opened the refrigerator and took out a jar of crunchy peanut butter, raspberry jam and some rice crackers. She sat down at the table and continued to read an article which claimed that eighty per cent of the married women in America were having affairs.

'No wonder I can't meet anyone,' she commented to T.W. 'These married sluts are screwing all the available men.' The same paper had recently printed a survey which claimed ninety per cent of the men in America preferred chubby women. A few days later it was revealed that only thirty men had been questioned and all of them were overweight.

What had possessed her to tell Sam that ridiculous story about the man in the elevator? He would think she was more disturbed than charming. There's a fine line between being attractive and eccentric, and psychosis, she told herself grimly, staring at her reflection in the peanut-butter knife, her face pale and difficult to recognize through the peanut-butter streaks. And what about him? she thought to herself, realizing he had told her nothing significant about himself. 'Self-absorbed neurotic seeks masochistic nebish,' she chanted.

She dug a rice cracker into the jam and then into the peanut butter. What she was doing would have so disgusted Matthew he would have left their apartment after confiscating his preserves. Perhaps it was better to be alone. It was time to take stock of her present circumstances. She had no job, no savings, no boyfriend, no valuable possessions, no insurance, a $1000 debt on her

Visa card, an outstanding Macy's bill of unknown amount since she refused to open their letters but simply mailed them a cheque for fifty dollars each month to extend her credit and, finally, she had an inexplicable and ridiculous desire: an actual physical craving for a baby, a helpless, demanding, expensive, tiny, smiling baby.

'Oh God,' she prayed, screwing the lid back on the peanut butter, 'please God, remove this obsession. Make me ambitious again. Make me want alligator pumps. A compact disc player. A leather mini.' It was no use. All she could see was tiny figures zipped tightly into baby buntings. All she could hear was gurgling and baby giggles, and all she could feel was the touch of small fingers: the skin of a baby's belly when you kissed its stomach, the velvet texture of the back of a baby's neck. She thought she needed help. Baby Cravers Anonymous? A programme for financially insolvent, unmarried would-be Madonnas?

Perhaps it was simply the late Sunday afternoon malaise, the panic that appeared after the best parts of the paper had been read and one's coffee limit reached. She was due downtown at the Unemployment Office to sign a piece of paper that said she had not worked for two weeks and to be informed she was still not getting a cheque. They were considerate enough to schedule her appointment at 9 a.m. so she could pretend to have a job. Thomas Wolfe wandered into the kitchen.

'Sit,' Lillian said, as she stretched to put the peanut butter back on the top shelf of the cupboard. Thomas Wolfe sat.

'Oh my God,' Lillian whispered, kissing his ears and rubbing her face against his neck. 'You are the smartest dog in the world.' Thomas Wolfe stood and sat again without being told.

'I love you,' Lillian murmured. 'Don't ever tell anyone, but I love you.'

3

The day after their coffee date Sam called and suggested a movie. Lillian had seen it. She had spent the morning in line at Unemployment. After an hour, the counsellor had informed her she would not receive any money for two more weeks.

'I knew that already,' Lillian said. 'Why did I have to stand in line?'

'You giving me attitude, lady?' the man had replied, throwing her papers across the counter. 'How come all you losers think you can give us attitude?'

Sam had been gratingly cheerful. 'Bowling,' he'd suggested, 'walk in the park, Soho galleries, breakfast, lunch or dinner, tea, brunch, tapis, dumplings. Theatre, symphony, jazz, ballet, rock-and-roll, trendy downtown boite . . .'

'What's wrong with you?' Lillian asked. 'I'm morbidly self-absorbed and unemployed.'

'Your melancholy is temporary. I want to be around when you cheer up.'

She agreed to a walk in the park the following Sunday. They wandered in silence for nearly an hour, stopping to watch a man juggling fruit and some bicyclists finishing a long race. Sam held her hand and whistled parts of *Aida*. Lillian felt inadequate and decided she had nothing interesting to say. She began to tell her Unemployment story but she stopped, afraid it would sound like whining and that her description of the man behind the counter might appear racist. Whenever she glanced over at Sam he swung her hand and raised his eyebrow. She started to get a small headache.

They went to the Boathouse Café and ordered lemonades. Sam asked for a dish of chocolate ice cream. The pond was flat, glassy with the heat. An exhausted-looking couple lay in their rowboat, their toes in the water, their hands limp over the boat's sides. Lillian was happy to be silent. It was too hot to talk. When Sam leaned forward, presumably to kiss her, she shrank back against the seat.

'I thought,' he said and paused.

'It's OK,' Lillian said. 'I'm just not available.'

'Will that change?' he asked, taking her hand, turning it over. They both stared at her palm as if the answer were there.

Lillian's headache returned. She drew a deep breath. It seemed largely folly not to keep this nice man on ice for a future date, a time when she didn't feel quite so awkward. There were certain shortages in modern urban life and hoarding was always an option. On the other hand, she never condoned such behaviour.

'No,' she replied, 'at least not until I completely alter my present existence.'

'The new job?' Sam asked politely.

'Yes. And I want to get my hair cut in a really severe geometric style and finish painting my apartment and wash my Venetian blinds and lose weight and start a freelance business.' She thought for a moment. 'Oh, I'm thinking about motherhood.'

Sam looked startled. 'Motherhood? In theory or practice?'

'Oh, practice. Well, theory right now. But I want to have a baby before I'm forty.'

'Ah,' Sam said. He looked at her, let go of her hand and motioned for a waiter. 'Quite a full agenda,' he said as he accepted the cheque and stood up.

She had found a new job in publishing. The company was large, but she worked for a senior editor who bought new fiction and the editorial decisions were done as a group. Writing copy at Bloomingdale's gave her the advantage of being able to come up with excellent copy for the cover and inner jackets of their books. The salary was ridiculous, far less than she was paid to turn out bad puns at Bloomingdale's. When the woman in Personnel told her the starting salary she had laughed. The personnel woman had laughed also.

'Are you serious?' Lillian had gasped.

'I'm afraid so,' the woman said, giggling.

However, the benefit package included a generous rebate on college tuition, free books, and an excellent medical and savings plan. She had an expense account on which she could charge lunches with minor publishing friends and lesser authors. By choosing wisely from the menu (all four food groups) she managed to eat her main meal of the day on the company and cut her food budget to almost nothing.

Also, there were parties. Publishing parties were easy to crash. Despite their lavish settings and splendid refreshments, they seldom employed security people and Lillian frequently recognized marginal people eating expensive hors d'oeuvres, people who had nothing to do with publishing. Perhaps it was intentional, a way to compensate for the fact that their employees were paid slave wages and expected to be grateful for their jobs. Perhaps it was necessary as many of these parties were frequented by distinguished literary bores and the presence of hungry young people made them seem slightly livelier.

The most lavish party of the year was held in early September at the Metropolitan Museum of Art. The party was given by an advertising firm named Ludlow, Stuart and Fox. The firm had made a movie deal on a project based on one of the books Lillian's company published. Most of the important members of the publishing world were invited.

The event was held in the gallery which housed the

Temple of Dendaur, the museum's most valued piece of art, an authentic ancient Egyptian temple. Lillian was rather shocked at the museum's agreeing to allow gold-painted models to pose on the stones, frozen in attitudes which replicated the detail on the ancient wall paintings. These models were so skilled at appearing inanimate, Lillian dropped a stuffed cherry tomato when she caught an Egyptian High Priestess scratching her nose against a heavy gold bracelet.

Lillian went to the party with Lizbeth, a contracts assistant with a deadly eye for style. She had been a singer in an all-girl punk band and neatly combined the sensibility of a rock star with the fashion instincts of a Parisian. Accessories never failed her. Staples were key, Lizbeth told her. One should own five basic elements: a black cashmere sweater (pearl buttons), a grey wool pleated skirt, a linen A-line dress, straight black trousers and expensive shoes, pumps and flats. Lillian's wardrobe was far larger, but she rarely managed to wear anything different to work. Lizbeth would add a belt or a scarf and look like a fashion model. On their first meeting she had walked up to Lillian and asked: 'Kamali?'

'No,' Lillian replied. 'Jordan.'

Lizbeth looked puzzled. 'Jordan? You mean Jordan Marsh?'

'No. Lillian Jordan. Me.'

'Oh. No, I'm sorry. I meant your dress. It's a Norma Kamali.'

'Is it?'

'Sure. Let me look at the label.' Lillian turned around. 'It's been cut off. Loehman's, right?' Lillian nodded. 'So there should be a code number. Here it is. Yup, it's a Kamali. What did you pay?'

'Twenty-nine dollars.'

'Good girl!' Lizbeth beamed at her which made Lillian feel savvy and stylish. The two women began to eat their salad bars together in a plaza across from their building when the weather was decent enough to sit outside. Sometimes Lillian cooked them both stir-fried vegetables and rice and they rented a movie. Lizbeth doted on Thomas Wolfe and was shocked when she heard of his owner's abandonment.

'How could he leave this perfect angel?' she cooed at T.W. who was on his back, waving his paws while Lizbeth scratched his belly. Lillian laughed. 'Oh God, Lil, you too! It's just that I think all men are incapable of loyalty except where their mothers or their dogs are concerned. I would just assume he could leave you. But his dog?'

Lizbeth's ex-husband was a drug runner in Miami. She had left him when she discovered a cache of weapons under their bed. Despite her low opinion of men, Lizbeth was an accomplished flirt. Because of her style and her ability to put people at their ease, she was an excellent person to bring to parties.

When the two women entered the room where the party of the year was in progress, they heard a chamber orchestra playing Debussy and watched as waiters glided past bearing silver trays laden with bowls of caviar, chopped egg, baskets of crisp bread and vodka frozen into blocks of ice. 'Oh my,' Lizbeth breathed. 'La te da.'

On the far side of the gallery a harpist wearing white chiffon stroked her harp, while a mime dressed in black pretended he was trapped in a box. 'Ugh,' Lizbeth said loudly. 'Mime makes me puke.'

Lillian overheard people discussing the probable price of the party. 'That waiter told me the caviar is Beluga,' a woman whispered to a man who handed her a drink. 'If Beluga was selling for seventy-eight dollars an ounce last week that means this party cost them about a hundred thousand.'

Lillian walked over to the food table next to the harpist and helped herself to three portions of caviar.

'No calories,' the man carving an entire roasted lamb told her. 'Those fish eggs make your cheeks pink and your hips slinky.'

She listened to a woman describing the commercial she was planning to pitch to an account. 'There's a voice-over. This guy sounds sort of shy and unhappy. You know, desperate. "Will you call me?" he says. Then you see this beautiful woman shrugging a fur coat over her shoulders. Very cool. She spritzes herself with POWER—'

'Power?' The man she was speaking to paused with a forkful of shrimp halfway to his mouth. '*Power?*'

'That's the name of the scent.'

'Power? A perfume with such a hideous name?'

'It's very state-of-the-art, darling. Post-modernism and all that. Andrew, you design book jackets. You deal with a semi-literate population. Let me worry about what to name products. So you hear this fellow again. "I don't understand," he says. "How can you fly to Paris with no warning?" Then we see the woman again sitting behind this huge mahogany desk. She's nodding to her secretary. A man, of course. Then we hear the man again. The nerdy one. "The roses were beautiful," he says, "but I miss you." We see her sitting in a hotel room, talking to him. Then the door opens and this gorgeous hunk comes out of the bathroom. She hangs up slowly. Then a close-up of the bottle. What do you think?'

'Emasculating and insulting to men. Perfect. But get rid of the name, Harriet.'

Lillian was exhilarated by the party's choreography. Groups of people moved around the gallery, their numbers shifting, heads raised each time a new person entered the space. She wandered counter-clockwise, smiling at top executives from her company who smiled back, looking vaguely puzzled, probably wondering who she was. She stopped at the dessert table to survey the assortment of cheesecakes, chocolate truffles, flaming cherries jubilee, ice cream shaped like fruit, tarts covered with whipped cream and a huge basket of chocolate-covered strawberries. She was about to put one into her mouth when she saw Sam across the room, with his arm around a tall woman who appeared slender until she turned to profile and was noticeably pregnant.

'Eat that,' Lizbeth said. 'The chocolate's melting all over your fingers.'

'Do you see that man over there?' Lillian pointed at Sam.

Lizbeth nodded.

'Do you think he's married to that woman?'

Lizbeth took a strawberry and nodded again.

'How can you tell?' Lillian asked. 'Is it because of the way he's holding her arm? Because he's acting like a husband?'

Lizbeth laughed. 'Acting like a husband? Silly girl! My husband hid Uzzis in the freezer and yours used to hit you. I know that's his wife because he's the managing director of a PR firm I temped for. And most guys aren't into pregnant women. I mean alien pregnant women. God, what a great name for a horror movie: Alien Pregnant Women!'

Sam waved at Lillian. She could barely raise her hand.

'Oh, look, he's waving at me,' Lizbeth said, smiling and waving. 'What a nice guy. I was just a temp—' She looked at Lillian. 'No, he's waving at you. Did you have an affair with that guy?'

'No,' Lillian said. 'I'm going home.'

'It looks like he's coming over here.'

Lillian saw Sam move away from his wife. She grabbed Lizbeth. 'Lizbeth, I don't want to talk to him.'

'Come on.'

As Sam circled the room, the two women headed in the opposite direction. They ran through the gallery of armour, giggling and sliding on the shiny floor in their high heels. 'Ladies,' a sedate guard called to

them and they exploded in giggles. When they got outside the air felt fresh and cool.

'Let's walk,' Lillian said.

There were limousines parked outside the Pierre, and
a homeless woman had put up a tent directly across the
street at the entrance to Central Park. They headed west
on 59th, and watched as young girls in satin dresses
wafted into the Plaza escorted by short-haired young men
in tuxedos.

'God,' Lizbeth said, 'what's happened to the youth of
today?'

'Did you go to your prom, Lizbeth?'

'No. Nobody went but the worst social misfits. We had
an anti-prom and roasted a pig. Did you go?'

'I dropped acid and ruined the evening when I told
my date he reminded me of a little rat, no . . . a mole.
I kept going on about his teeny little eyes and stuff. He
got insulted. I ended up with the boy I wanted anyway,
because I just wandered out of this party and ran into
him. He was sitting on top of his car drinking a bottle
of Jack Daniels. It was love at first sight.'

'You loved the guy?'

'Oh, no. I loved his Jack Daniels. He wasn't smart
enough to get out of the eleventh grade. But he drank
more than I did and I needed someone like that. But
even he told me I was an alcoholic. Like his mother.
They had to cut off her legs.'

'God,' Lizbeth said. 'God, I'm glad I left my husband.'

'So am I.'

'And I'm glad you left your husband.' They walked in
silence for a minute. 'Did you have an affair with that
guy?'

'No,' Lillian said, breathing deeply. 'Almost.'

Lillian called Edward. She told his answering machine
about the party until it hung up on her. Seeing Sam had

made her feel terrible. Thomas Wolfe seemed to sense her sad mood and he hovered around her chair, his nose moist, quivering with concern. 'Oh Lord,' she whispered into his neck, 'the only thing I have in my life is a stupid dog!'

The phone rang. She was afraid it was Matthew. He called infrequently and she had refused to say more than a few words but now she felt weak, as if she might agree to something completely wrong. After the tenth ring, she picked it up.

'Oh, there you are darling!' Her mother possessed a knack for calling when Lillian was having difficulties. She was always complaining about Lillian's telephone manners.

'Hi, Mom.'

'You sound tired.'

'I'm fine.'

'Did I get you out of the shower?'

'Yes.'

'You want to call me back?'

'No.'

'You sound hoarse. Are you getting strep?'

'No. I don't know. Maybe.'

'Do you have a thermometer? Take your temperature. Are you getting enough sleep?'

'Mom—' Her mother made her feel as if she were being cross-examined. Edward said he often banged the receiver against something hard until she stopped asking questions.

'Daddy's here. Shall I put him on?'

'No.'

'Hi honey.'

'Hi Daddy.'

'How's the dog?'

'He's OK. He's finally learned how to sit.'

'Isn't that something? And how are you doing? Is the job working out?'

'Sure.' Maybe he could tell her how men were able to lie so easily. There was a long silence.

'You want to talk to your mother?'

'No, Daddy, don't go—' She heared him gently replace the receiver.

'What's the matter, Lillian? Is there something wrong?'

'No. Maybe I'm just a little sick.'

'You want to come home?'

'No.'

'You never want to come home.'

'I'm just very busy.'

'When you were little you said home was better than Heaven and you were never leaving.'

'Mom—'

'Maybe Edward said it.'

'I'm coming home in a few days.'

'How's work?'

'Great. Everything's great.'

'Be careful now.'

'I'm always careful.' There was a pause. 'Mom, I'm going to see if I have a fever, OK?'

'We love you darling. He wasn't what you needed.' Matthew.

'I don't want to talk about it. Goodbye. Tell Daddy I said goodbye.'

'Of course. I always give him your messages.'

She paced the length of the apartment, stepping carefully as if to avoid land mines. She felt it was important not to make noise or to occupy much space. Thomas Wolfe followed her for a few minutes but then he stopped, sat down and watched her suspiciously. She went into her room and lay down on the bed, holding herself, her hands caressing her own shoulder blades. She missed Matthew. It was all very well to recognize his limitations, to resolve not to allow the relationship to continue, to purge her house of all traces of him, to take aerobics and avoid chocolate. She still missed him. His voice, his body, his smell, the sound he made walking on her floors, his male presence in her life: all seemed to be irreplaceable, priceless, lost for ever. His dog wasn't a fit substitute. If he knocked on her door, she would let him in. Instead, T.W. put his head on her stomach and let out a long, loud, dog sigh. She stared into his bloodshot eyes, laughed and went to bed.

She woke up very early the next morning. Dressed in a pair of white athletic socks, an ancient pair of hightop red sneakers stained with bleach, her father's flannel nightshirt and wrapped in Edward's old silk cape (a stolen wardrobe item from a production of *Uncle Vanya*), her head covered by a grey fedora bought by her grandfather with his first paycheque in the New World, she went to walk the dog.

On their second lap around the area of Central Park that T.W. claimed as his own turf, Camus bounded up the path.

'Go away!' Lillian shrieked at the dog who was frisking around T.W. 'Go away, you ugly mutt! You hound from hell!'

Thomas Wolfe and Camus were by now fast friends. Lillian threw a tree branch at the Doberman which missed, but the dog was frightened and shrunk back.

'Lillian—' Sam was standing at the top of the path, a leash hanging from his jacket pocket, his hands empty.

'You go away, too!' She picked up a rock heavy enough to hurt her arm. 'I never want to see you again, you liar!'

'Let me explain—'

'I don't want an explanation! You told me you weren't married!'

'I said I was unattached.'

'Unattached? Your wife is going to have a baby! What's the matter with you?'

Sam held out his hands. 'I just wanted you.'

'Well, you can't have me! No-one lies to me any more! I won't accept it!'

She saw them, two people standing in Central Park, early fall. The woman was just thirty, wearing a nightshirt, holding a rock, screaming. The man was a bit older, nicely dressed for Sunday brunch, calm. There is nothing very important happening here, Lillian thought. It reminded her slightly of the way her own marriage had ended. Bad timing. Inappropriate clothing. Lillian sank down to her knees in the dirt and beat the ground with the rock.

'Sam,' she begged, 'just leave me alone. Please. Just leave me alone.' When she opened her eyes he was gone.

The phone rang. Her machine clicked on.

'Hey! Pick it up!' It was Edward.

'Edward—'

'What happened?'

'How's the movie?'

'Lillian, I didn't call you on a portable phone on the set of a desert alien flick to discuss my karma. You sounded weird on the machine last night.'

'I'm fine.'

'You're never fine. What's wrong?'

'I'm fine sometimes.'

'Are you still in therapy?'

'Why does everyone keep asking me that?'

'Because you're crazy.'

'I am not crazy.'

'What does your therapist think?'

'That's none of your business.'

'What does she think of me?'

'I don't talk about you.'

'Of course you talk about me. I'm your brother.'

'Do you talk about me?'

'That's none of your business.' Edward laughed. 'So what's wrong?'

'Nothing. I almost went to bed with a married man with a pregnant wife.'

'So?'

'So . . . I didn't. But I feel terrible.'

'Why? You wish you had?'

'No!'

'Are you drinking?'

'Edward—'

'What are you doing now?'

'Lying on my couch.'

'I meant with your life.'

'Lying on my couch.'

Edward sighed. 'Just pay closer attention to the signs.'

'What signs?'

'If the guy keeps looking over your head or slightly to the left, watching the door, like that Matthew creep, get rid of him. And the married signs.'

'I looked for a ring! Anyway, it doesn't matter. I'm never having another boyfriend.'

'Good idea. I like that idea. As your older brother I fully sanction that concept. Get your virginity back.'

'How's the movie?'

'Sweltering. I play an alien brain-eater in a rubberized costume. It's like having all the liquid slowly squeezed from your pores. Really glamorous. Be careful, little sister.'

'I will be. Drink lots of water. Bye.'

Lillian went to the AA meeting across the street. There was a crowd of people around the cookie tray. She saw a woman who had sponsored her during the first ninety days that she didn't drink. Lillian used to call her in the middle of the night when she thought she heard her ex-husband out on the fire escape.

'Lillian,' the woman said, smiling, her arms outstretched, 'what a wonderful surprise.'

'Yes,' Lillian said, picking up a cookie, 'I thought I needed a meeting.'

'Always a good thought,' the woman said, putting her arm around Lillian. 'So, how are you doing?'

'Just fine,' Lillian said, waving the cookie. 'I got a new job. In publishing. It's great. And my boyfriend left. That's great too.' She began to cry.

'You need to remember you have a fatal, incurable disease,' her old sponsor whispered into her ear as the meeting began.

Lillian nodded. 'Thanks,' she said, drying her eyes. 'I'd nearly forgotten.'

The speaker introduced himself. He was an elderly man who'd been sober for a long time. He used to be a judge, and he told them funny stories about conducting trials after drinking a quart of vodka. She had trouble concentrating on his story. Her mind wandered from the room she was sitting in to other places. For some reason she had a vision of the room that Matthew occupied before he moved into her apartment. It occurred to her that he had needed to leave that room. Had he pretended to love her merely to escape those sad green walls? She realized it was impossible to live without getting hurt. Her old sponsor sat quietly next to her, still holding her hand, listening intently. When the speaker finished talking and the meeting was opened up, her sponsor nudged her.

'Raise your hand,' she said. Lillian raised her hand.

'Hi,' she said. 'My name is Lillian and I'm an alcoholic.'

'Hi Lillian,' the room answered.

Lillian swallowed. Her throat was closing. The speaker nodded and smiled. 'I don't know how to live,' she whispered. 'I'm still such a victim.' Most of the women in the room were leaning forward and nodding. The men stared at their shoes. The person sitting to her left patted her softly on the shoulder. 'If I start to drink again, I know I'll go insane. Or kill myself. My boyfriend moved out in the middle of the night and left his dog behind. I almost took one of his beers. It was like I'd just forgotten I was an alcoholic and there was this stuff I could use to keep the pain away. And . . . ' She'd forgotten what else she meant to say. 'The dog won't sit.'

The room filled with the sound of people laughing.

The speaker said: 'That dog's probably an alcoholic and resents being told what to do. Don't be a stranger, dear. You belong here.' During the coffee break, before anyone could speak to her, Lillian ran away.

Her phone rang. When Lillian picked it up she heard Matthew's voice. Replacing the receiver, she unplugged the telephone. On a tablet of yellow paper she began to write:

THINGS TO DO
1. Plan the baby.
2. Lose ten pounds.
3. Tell them and find out all genetic possibilities.
4. Go to more AA meetings.

4

Her parents lived on a boulevard that was once canopied by massive Dutch Elms. Sunlight rarely pierced the front of the houses and most families spent a great deal of time in their backyard gardens. Dutch Elm disease had decimated the trees, sparing a few short maples and a massive fir that grew at the side of her parents' house. When the trees began to fail, her father had organized marches and raised money to bring down a Canadian tree expert who confirmed the fatal diagnosis supplied by the local tree surgeon. He was joined in his crusade by their neighbour's son, Alf, who raised bees and was mildly retarded. Alf and Mr Jordan had made the front page of the *New York Times* (the Jersey section) under a headline that said: DEDICATED DUO DENY DEADLY DUTCH DISEASE.

Her father had looked much older than she'd remembered him being. Not long after that she had visited them and her father had shown her the scrapbook which documented the gradual decline of his elms. He had wept. When she gently touched his shoulder, he had seized her hand and pressed it against his cheek. Edward had warned her their parents were acting rather oddly. For a moment neither of them moved. Then Lillian looked up to see her mother glaring from the hallway and she slowly moved away. Neither of them said anything.

That night she dreamed of a cradle, a cradle rocking in the middle of an empty white room. Her father was ancient, sitting on the edge of a rusty bed, waiting for someone to visit him. He had become her responsibility. He expected Lillian to take care of him. She saw his arms raised to her like an infant. The cradle kept rocking back and forth as if pushed by an invisible hand.

She woke up to the sound of coffee beans being ground, the sound came from two floors below and echoed in her ear almost like a cat's purr. Her room was in the attic, sparsely furnished but still somehow crowded as each object held the weight and volume of her memories. The bed she slept on had first belonged to Edward. On her tenth birthday she had hinted around for a canopy bed, leaving cut-out pictures from *Seventeen* magazine in places where her parents would find them and be sensitive enough to provide their little princess with an appropriate place to sleep. She was given a typewriter. 'I wanted a canopy bed,' she had howled at her surprised parents. 'How will I ever learn to be a woman?'

There was an old oak desk handed on by her grandmother, a woman who seldom said anything kind or encouraging to anyone, especially her daughter, Lillian's mother. She had presented the desk to Lillian on her thirteenth birthday with the command that Lillian 'maintain standards'. Lillian was glad her grandmother had died before her wedding. She knew the old lady would have spotted her ex-husband as a liar and would not have hesitated to share her opinion.

The walls were covered by books. Books that Lillian and Edward kept claiming as their own, writing over one another's inscriptions: 'Lillian Jordan: My Book.' Or, 'This book is the property of Edward William Jordan.' In the end they had left most of them behind. Edward's nomadic life did not invite his carrying around all the volumes of the Narnia chronicles and Lillian was reluctant to reveal her love for *The Five Little Peppers*

And How They Grew which featured two sets of disgusting twins: Flossie and Freddie and the older ones whose names she had forgotten.

'Lillian?' Her mother's voice floated up the stairs.

'Yes?'

'Boiled egg?'

'OK.'

'It's from the hen next door.'

'Great.'

'Toast?'

'Sure.'

'It's homemade bread. Three minutes?'

'Four. But don't start it yet. I'm getting up.'

She found an old pair of jeans and was amazed that they still fitted. Was I fat? she wondered. Or am I thinner? She looked in the mirror hanging on the closet door and saw that she didn't look at all as she'd imagined. She was almost as pretty as she'd ever been in her life. Her skin was clear and her eyes weren't puffy and her body was slender and well exercised. She pulled up her shirt and looked at her breasts. They were quite nice. It was odd, she thought, she had expected to be marked, to have a glowing 'S' on her forehead for stupid.

'You're so beautiful,' Matthew had told her over and over again. 'Just perfect. Lovely, lovely Lillian.'

'Asshole,' Lillian muttered, pulling her hair back with a piece of string she found under the bed. 'Lying, fucking asshole.'

She sat down at the dining-room table and her mother put down a plate. It was one of her own wedding-present plates, containing an egg cup which held a boiled brown egg, and two pieces of toast spread with butter and raspberry jam. There were three pieces of orange artistically arranged along the rim.

'Mom,' Lillian said, biting into an orange slice, 'how LA! Where's my sushi?'

Her mother smiled and went into the kitchen. Lillian wondered if she had given her mother this set of china, or whether her mother had simply decided to spare her the trauma of owning china which had been meant as a symbol of wedded bliss. In any case, she thought, admiring her plate, it would be nice to have some dishes.

Mrs Jordan came out of the kitchen with two mugs. 'Tell me about work,' she said, sitting down in the chair across from Lillian, her eyes filled with concern.

'It's fine. I might buy a book about how to keep your dog from attacking your baby.' Lillian took the top off her egg.

'Really? Should people with babies have angry dogs?'

'No. But they do. And sometimes they like the dog more than the child. It's pretty terrible. This guy, the guy with the book, is a famous dog trainer. And people kept calling him up to ask how they could get their baby to behave so they don't annoy the dog!' She dipped her spoon into the egg. It was perfectly cooked.

'Umm.' Mrs Jordan put her hand against Lillian's forehead. 'Is your fever gone?'

'Yes. I mean, no. Actually, I wasn't really sick. I just feel . . . ' she groped for the right word. 'Ineffectual.'

'How can you say that? Every time I introduce someone to you they always tell me later that you are the most impressive person.'

'Why?' Lillian was holding her egg spoon in a death grip.

Her mother shrugged. 'Because you have this energy—'

'Yeah, like static electricity. I attract men with pregnant wives and my brother: the man who can't commit.'

Her mother was smiling.

'Why do you look so happy, Mother?'

'I don't know. Of course I'm not happy that you're upset, but you don't tell me about your life very often.'

57

'I try not to think about it. It depresses me.'

Mrs Jordan shook her head. 'I think you're making a great deal of progress.'

Lillian snorted. Her mother had a habit of being completely supportive and optimistic when things were terrible. During the months following her separation from Anthony, her mother had constantly suggested activities like House Tours and trips to Flea Markets. Once she had signed them up for mother-daughter knitting classes which Lillian boycotted. Her shining moments came with the utter defeat of her daughter.

'Are you still going to AA?'

'Yes.' Lillian hated the way her mother referred to AA as if it were some sort of vitamin.

'Is it fun?'

'What?'

'AA.'

'No.'

'There's a new TV show with a character on it that goes to AA. I think it's AA. Maybe it's group therapy. Anyway, I think it looks like fun.'

Then why don't you go to AA? Lillian thought while she grimly bit into her toast.

Her mother patted her hand and pushed the newspaper across the table. 'Eat your breakfast,' she said fondly to her daughter.

Lillian walked downtown. She went into Woolworth's where she used to spend hours reading the dirty paperbacks which had covers featuring bosomy young women in bondage. The idea of having sex against your will seemed like a good solution to the guilt problem when Lillian was a teenager. She didn't consider the issue of rape, but saw it as a way to satisfy the intense longings she felt in her body without being held responsible for the act itself. Shoplifting had provided a suitable diversion. In those days she was the possessor of every lipstick Yardley produced, shiny pink stuff her mother described as 'obscene'.

'Lillian?' There was a woman waving at her from the sewing section; a woman wearing a baby. Lillian couldn't place the face but she waved back. The baby was totally passed out, hanging from its mother like a giant pink piece of lint.

'Oh Lillian,' the woman said, 'I haven't seen you in nearly ten years.'

It was Suzanna Benson, her ex-best friend. Suzanna who everyone said was a lesbian. She had controlled Lillian through guilt and accusations of disloyalty mingled with slavish devotion and lavish praise. Like a lover. Suzanna who always invited Lillian on expensive vacations with her family, who wrote terrible obsessive things about her in her journals and told Lillian's mother that Lillian needed to be psychoanalysed.

'I think' Mrs Jordan had replied, 'you are consumed with jealousy.'

Suzanna wasn't pretty. Men found her difficult and didn't want to sleep with her. They wanted to sleep with Lillian. Lillian was demanding, but relatively pleasant. She drank too much, but she was pretty. Suzanna was dependable, but nobody wanted to fuck her. Everyone wanted to fuck Lillian. Suzanna made a movie and cast Lillian in it as a deaf-mute. She bought several bottles of wine and gave them to Lillian. Lillian was instructed to take off her clothes. She took off her shirt and stood in the harsh sunlight, a cold breeze covering her skin with goosepimples, staring into the glass eye of Suzanna's camera. When one of her boyfriends saw the movie he said: 'Can't you see how much that dyke hates you?' Lillian thought her breasts looked too small. She found Suzanna exhausting, but it was difficult to find a reason not to be her friend. It was difficult not to feel sorry for Suzanna and guilty for her lack of success with people. 'She's my best friend,' she would reply. 'Don't be mean.'

Where had Suzanna, the probable lesbian, found this baby?

'Suzanna,' she said, 'whose baby is this?'

'This is Edward,' Suzanna replied.

'Edward?' Suzanna had also been in love with Lillian's brother.

'Not your Edward. That's his father's middle name.'

'Who's Edward's father?'

Edward woke up and began to cry quietly. Lillian made a face like a fish and he started to laugh.

Give me that baby, she said silently.

'Remember Chucky Weatherford?'

'No.' Lillian put her finger out and the baby grabbed it. 'Eddie,' she murmured.

'You know . . . Chucky. He could eat glass.'

'Oh. Oh, right. Chucky. How nice.' Lillian didn't remember. Her finger was now the prisoner of a perfect baby.

'Do you have time for coffee, Lillian?'

Lillian looked at Suzanna and found herself feeling strangely angry. Then she remembered that Suzanna had refused to allow her to spend the night on her couch once when Lillian had called her from a subway station because Anthony had threatened to kill them both. She had known Suzanna lived nearby and had obtained her number from Information. Dialling Suzanna's number she had begun to cry with the relief of remembering her friend.

'Are you drunk, Lillian?' Suzanna had asked her after she explained why she'd called.

'No,' Lillian had whispered, 'I'm just afraid.'

'How can you be afraid?' Suzanna asked. 'How can you be afraid of a man?'

'I don't know,' Lillian said. 'He hits me.'

'Go home,' Suzanna had replied. 'You married him.'

Lillian had pressed the receiver down. There was no-one else to call. Edward was shooting a commercial in Bermuda.

'I'm divorced,' Lillian now said, picking up a ball of bright purple yarn. Suzanna looked uncomfortable.

'I heard. I'm really sorry it didn't work out. Maybe you were looking to be punished.'

'What?' Lillian couldn't believe what Suzanna had said. The baby hung between them like some sort of protective barrier. Lillian wanted to slap her face.

'It's just women like you—'

'What do you mean "women like me"?'

'Oh Lillian,' Suzanna said, smiling, 'you know what I mean.'

Lillian steadied herself on the edge of a counter which displayed packets of knitting needles and crochet hooks. She remembered how easily Suzanna had said 'no' when she had asked for a place to sleep. She had stood in the subway station watching the trains rumble through, trying to get up the courage to jump.

'Let's go sit down somewhere,' Suzanna suggested. 'You can tell me everything.'

'I don't have to tell you anything,' Lillian said. 'You have a beautiful baby. God help him!'

On the way home Lillian found herself feeling very happy. She began to sing a song about an IRA gunman who leaves his lady waiting on the banks of the Liffey. He's dead, of course, and she just keeps waiting. The song was written before the IRA became a bunch of thugs who trained children to steal cars and to murder for profit. She couldn't remember the last two verses so she whistled. The air was clean and clear. The houses looked freshly painted and open, unlike the shuttered windows of Manhattan. It was nearly Hallowe'en. She stopped at a farmstand and bought a pumpkin and some crisp apples. She jumped into someone's carefully raked leaf pile. Her life was changing.

Old grievances slid off her shoulders and blew away. As she ran down the street she felt her breath filling up her body so that she was light and strong. When she walked into the kitchen her parents were listening to National Public Radio and eating radicchio salad.

'I'm having a baby,' Lillian announced, putting down the pumpkin. 'I'm going to have a baby without a husband. I just met Suzanna Benson in Woolworth's with the most beautiful child and if that bitch who won't admit to being a lesbian—'

'Suzanna's married to Chucky Weatherford,' her mother murmured.

'If that closet dyke can have a baby, I can.'

'Chucky Weatherford's father has a seat on the New York stock exchange,' Mrs Jordan said. 'Lunch? There's more radicchio.'

'Lillian,' her father said, putting down his fork, 'where will you live?'

'In New York. I'll partition off part of the apartment.'

'I wish you'd be more patient,' her mother said, putting down a plateful of radicchio. 'You haven't really tried. There must be someone perfect for you.'

'What happened to that fellow with the dog?'

Lillian glanced at her mother who shrugged. 'He moved to Boston.'

'Nice dog,' Mr Jordan said.

'Thomas Wolfe stayed. I'll bring him down the next time I come.'

'Good. That dog had a lot of presence.' Lillian's father picked up his newspaper. 'I believe you'll make an excellent mother. You are full of good ideas.' He leaned over to kiss her.

'Thank you, Daddy.'

Mrs Jordan let out a deep sigh.

'We'll get you a better major medical. I'm going to find our policy.' Mr Jordan looked cheerful. He loved projects.

Left alone with her mother, Lillian began to shred her salad into thin strips of red and green.

'I want to know everything about our family. I want my baby to have a clearly defined gene pool.'

'A what?'

'Genes. Who went bananas? Why? Is anyone else an alcoholic? Who's a manic-depressive? Are we prone to cancer or diabetes or heart disease?'

'I don't understand.'

'Our family. There's a way to plot out what happens to someone by avoiding certain combinations. Edward has the perfect hereditary mix. He never gets sick, his body is great and he's very stable. If Anthony and I had had a baby it would probably have been depressed, drunk, a brooder, guilty and paranoid. I don't want my child to be affected by some horrible inter-generational thing.'

Lillian's mother exhaled loudly.

'Mom, why are you so pale?'

'I'm . . . Let me get your father.'

'What's the matter? Does someone have something terrible? Haemophilia? Is there a latent deadly disease? A recessive gene?'

'No. No. It's . . . Walter!'

'Mom—'

Lillian's father came into the dining room holding a file full of papers.

'Walter, Lillian wants to know the family medical history so she can plan this child.'

'Ah.' Mr Jordan sat down heavily.

Lillian thought she was going to faint. 'Tell me what's wrong! Tell me why you both look so sick!'

'Lillian—' her mother's voice broke and then stopped altogether.

'We can't tell you your medical history,' her father said slowly. 'There are many things that happen in a family that are difficult to explain.' Lillian tried to calm herself. She nodded at her father. 'I can't explain about times that I've failed you.'

'I don't think you failed me,' Lillian whispered, her eyes searching her parents' faces for an answer to the mystery.

'All parents fail their children. It's part of the job. A child isn't equipped to accept limitations so it thinks the parent is perfect. Until he fails that child. Then they think that parent is a liar.'

'Daddy—' Lillian looked at her mother.

'What your father's trying to say has to do with before you came here.'

'Came here?' She suppressed the urge to laugh. It sounded as if she had arrived in the mail.

'We don't know about your genetic history, Lillian, because you're adopted. We aren't your genetic parents.'

She looked around for the hidden camera. The silence in the room continued. Tears stood in her mother's eyes. Her father was unbraiding his place mat, his long, slender fingers trembling. She wanted to say something, but her mind was blank. Outside a small boy was delivering evening papers from a wagon.

'Where did I come from?'

'Maine.' Her father's answer was unexpectedly clear.

'*Maine?*'

'Walter!' Her mother leaned across the table, putting her hand on Lillian's arm. 'We wanted you,' she said, 'more than if I'd had you.'

'Why Maine?' Lillian saw herself like some sort of product. Maple syrup. Lobsters. Unwanted babies.

'That's where your mother lived.'

'Who's my mother? Why did she give me up? Why didn't you tell me? Who else knows?' Lillian's mother began to cry. Lillian looked at her father. 'This sucks,' she said flatly.

'Yes,' he replied. 'I know.'

Her parents sat in their chairs, in the places where she always imagined them when she thought about her family. Everyone in their proper position. Each of them belonging. But she came from somewhere else. Maine. The room grew dark and still they sat until Lillian turned on a light.

Sometime around midnight, alone in bed, she began to cry. They were strangers, she thought. Edward had always claimed to have been left behind by Martians, but it was Lillian who was the alien. Did he know he wasn't her brother? She could marry him. She wanted to kill him. After them. Downstairs in her parents' bedroom she heard the soft murmur of their voices. They were in pain. She wrapped her arms around herself, putting her icy palms between her knees and rocked herself to sleep.

5

Someone was outside, throwing something. The clock said 12.57 a.m. Edward stood in the street, his right arm raised. She opened the window.

'What the hell are you doing?' she asked crossly.

'I rang your buzzer for twenty minutes.'

She pressed the door release and pulled a sweater over the cotton nightgown she had been sleeping in.

'Hello.' Edward was tan. He was dressed in faded Levis, cowboy boots and their father's old leather bomber jacket from college. His hair had been streaked for the alien movie. He put his arms out but she remained motionless, her hands hanging at her sides. It no longer seemed an automatic response to hug him. They weren't related. He wasn't her real brother.

'What are you doing here?'

'Mom called.'

'You came all the way back for this?'

'Yup.' He bent over Thomas Wolfe. 'Hey fella! You look marvellous! How's dog-training class?'

'We quit.'

'Jeez, Lillian! Your dog's a dropout?' He glanced at her unsmiling face. 'Oh yeah, I forgot about the creep. Sorry.' Edward rested his hand on Lillian's shoulder. 'You started the summer with a midnight flit and now this. Been having a bad time, kid?'

'I don't want to talk about it. If you came to New York for this conversation, you've wasted your money.' She folded her arms against her chest.

Edward shut the door. 'Well, can I come in?'

66

'Of course.'

He sat down on Lillian's couch and lit a cigarette. Thomas Wolfe went back to sleep, his head resting on Edward's boot. 'Can I smoke?'

'Certainly.'

'Thank you. Boy, this movie is proving to be some bust! The writers gave up and never finished the screenplay. We're inventing it as we shoot. Whoever has the first idea, not the best, gets the writing credit. The director's on ups and the producer's on downs so one's peaking while the other one's beginning to crash. It's either gonna be the biggest cult film since *Attack of the Killer Tomatoes* or useless garbage. Probably the latter.' Edward stopped talking abruptly. T.W. yawned and then dropped back into a dream. The apartment was so quiet, the hum of the kitchen clock echoed. Somewhere uptown, a siren wailed. 'What the hell, Lillian? What the hell? You angry?'

She took one of his cigarettes and lit it, avoiding his eyes. Nodded.

'Good. That's good. I think you should be angry. Good.'

'Did you know, Edward? Did you figure it out?'

'I guess so.'

'How?'

'I was looking for my birth certificate and found some papers. You were nearly seven.'

'Why didn't you tell me?'

'It never came up.' Edward shrugged.

'Fuck you!'

'What do you want me to say? You never told me that sleaze was beating you.'

'That's not the same thing.'

'Sure it is. Sometimes we just can't wrap words around things. You don't think I lived in mortal terror of blurting it out some night when you wanted to watch *Gilligan's Island* instead of *The Outer Limits*? You were such a pain in the butt! You don't think it's every boy's fantasy to discover his stupid sister's adopted?'

He was nearly two years older than Lillian. There was never a time during their childhood that she didn't feel inferior to him and yet he had always made sure that before he climbed higher, she was safe. 'You aren't my brother.'

'What?'

'I said you aren't my brother.'

'Yes I am.'

'No. I come from two entirely different people. They're your parents. You're their son. I don't belong.'

'Ah, Christ!' Edward put his head in his hands and tugged at his streaky hair. 'Mom and Dad are going nuts. They think they've ruined you because you're the sensitive one. How do they know I'm not sensitive?'

'I don't care how they feel.'

'Great. Terrific attitude, Lillian. Do you think you had some perfect deal with whoever it was that put you up for adoption?'

She jumped to her feet and waved a finger in her brother's face. 'I don't have a family! Don't you dare allude to my past as if it were some sort of case history! Why should I be grateful to them? I don't even know who I am. Someone didn't want me—'

She held herself as if she might break. It had been essential not to cry alone. She believed those tears would kill her, burning away the fragile skin she still retained as protection against this new version of her life. Edward was a witness. Now she could grieve.

He let her sob while he made tea, stopping once or twice to wrap a blanket around her, once to push the tangled hair out of her face, another time to hold her tightly in his arms.

'Lillian,' he whispered, 'what about the ones that did want you?'

'I can't . . . ' she choked. He made her blow her nose on his handkerchief.

'Breathe,' Edward murmured, rocking her gently back and forth. 'Breathe deeply.'

'I don't know who I am.'

'My little sister.'

'Edward,' she stared at him, her eyes burning from the tears, 'we could be lovers now.'

He hastily unwrapped himself from around her, moved to sit at the end of the couch, handing her a pillow.

'Lillian—'

'Yes. You must have wonderful genes. Why not? It wouldn't matter now. It wouldn't be incest. Not technically. I remember how you kissed me once with your mouth open . . . '

'I was practising! You said it was disgusting!'

'Just give me the baby.'

'Jesus!' Edward rose to his feet and stood in front of the window. 'What in hell's name is this about?'

'I want my own baby and I need to choose someone to be the father.'

'You don't ever think, Lillian!'

'You don't love me!' But he did. That had never been the issue between them. Why was she doing this? Pushing him hard enough to send him away hating her.

'I'm your brother.'

'No!'

'You can't always decide things. Sometimes, I simply can't deal with this will of yours. Our least important bond is sharing the same parents. What do you think makes a family?'

'How should I know?'

'You do know. Time and faith and trust and forgiveness. You've been my little sister for thirty years. I took you to your eighth-grade dance and you came to all my plays. I was class president because of you.'

'You saved my life—'

'Because you are my history, Lilly.'

'But you aren't my brother.'

'I consider that betrayal. I consider that abandonment.'

'I don't feel connected to anything!'

'That's no-one's fault. You don't allow people just to love you. You're attracted to men that have nothing to offer. You've suffered, but I wonder at the power you give people who have no interest in making you happy.'

'That has nothing to do with this.'

'Yes it does! You felt like this before you found out about the adoption.'

'You can't possibly understand how I feel!'

'No. But I'm here and I want to help. I'm not saying you have no right to be angry, Lillian. I think you've been dealt a rotten hand. But you can't give up. Life will continue and you need to decide what you want.'

'To find my parents.' She spoke without thinking. It was not something she had consciously decided.

Edward sighed. 'I think Mom and Dad know where your mother is. Mom said I should tell you she'd give you the information if you want it.' He sat forward, his arms resting on his knees. 'I need to get some sleep. I flew the red-eye from LA.'

'I'll get you sheets.'

At dawn he came into her room and sat down on the side of her bed. She had been crying, sobbing quietly into the pillow.

'Lillian,' he whispered, 'don't hate us.' She sat up and put her arms around him, her head resting on his shoulder. He was her brother. She loved him.

'I'm sorry,' she sobbed. 'I'm really sorry.'

'Sorry for what?'

'Everything. Being an alcoholic. For being adopted and having terrible boyfriends.'

'OK. Well, I'm sorry for being so handsome and talented.'

'What?' She stopped crying.

'It must be hard for you. And naturally charming. That's probably the worst.'

'*Charming?*'

'*People Magazine* called me "charismatic".'

'Was that in the piece which referred to Sylvester Stallone as an intellectual?'

'Yup.'

'Edward?'

'Yes?'

'If I wasn't your sister, would you want to marry me?'

Edward laughed. 'No,' he said, tucking in her covers. 'You are far too much woman for this cowboy.' He leaned over and kissed her forehead.

She met her mother for lunch near the station. Approaching the restaurant, she watched as a waiter put down a bottle of Perrier and a glass of white wine at her mother's table.

'For my alcoholic daughter,' Lillian imagined her saying. 'For my adopted, bad-taste-in-men, divorced, alcoholic daughter.'

Her mother's face was finely etched with lines as unfamiliar to Lillian as the loose skin under her chin and the dark spots on her hand. Watching her mother glance around the restaurant, sip her wine and then chew on a breadstick, Lillian felt the stone heart she'd carried since discovering her parent's deception melt. What was the point of staying angry? How could they know the right thing to do? They were old. Soon they would die. Lillian didn't want to believe herself incapable of mercy.

'Hi, Mom.'

Mrs Jordan smiled. 'This is my daughter,' she said to the waiter who nodded politely. 'My only daughter.'

Lillian rolled her eyes. 'You look pretty, Mom.'

Mrs Jordan picked up her butter knife and checked

her reflection. 'It's such a shock,' she said, 'getting old. I think I'm too old to be pretty.'

'Old is in,' Lillian said. 'People over fifty are the trendsetters.'

The waiter brought over their menus and then opened his mouth to recite the specials.

'Are they written on the board?' Lillian asked before he could begin.

'Yes, but—'

Lillian waved her hand. 'It's OK. I eat here all the time. I'll tell her what to order.' She lit a cigarette, cherishing her last bad habit. 'You want pasta, Mom?'

'Your father put together the information about your biological mother.'

'Edward told you?'

'About your wanting to find her?' Lillian nodded. 'Yes. I think it may be difficult—'

'Why? And what about . . . him?'

'Who? Oh.' Mrs Jordan frowned. 'The father was never in the picture, dear. I don't know what's happened in the past twenty years.'

'She never wrote?'

Mrs Jordan shook her head.

'Did she ask after me?'

'Sweetie—'

'Why did she give me up?'

Lillian's mother sipped her wine. 'Adoption doesn't mean you comprehend what is happening in the other person's life. There was a lawyer dealing with most of the details.'

'Weren't you curious?'

'No, dear. In fact, I didn't want to know her very well. She was young and unhappy and I wanted a happy baby.'

Lillian grimaced. Her mother shook her head.

'You were a happy baby. Nothing ever upset you. You

liked everybody. People called you Little Miss Sunshine.'

'Mother . . .'

The waiter returned, his expression clearly indicating the certainty that because he was barred from doing his job properly, they had failed to select their entrées.

'Ladies?'

'We'll both have the pasta with seafood. OK, Mom?'

Mrs Jordan nodded. 'She was the happiest baby,' she said to the waiter as he picked up their menus. He winked at Lillian and then disappeared in the direction of the kitchen.

'I think there were problems.' It seemed very hot in the restaurant. She watched her mother's lips moving but there was no sound. 'Speaking of money,' her mother said. 'We were going to give you this for Christmas,' her mother slid an envelope across the table. 'It's not that much, but we thought if you were going to Maine . . .'

'Mom—'

'It's not much. You should put most of it in the bank. Get a CD. You've been very independent. Edward owes us three times that amount. You were always good about budgeting.'

'Just a happy, budget-conscious baby, eh Mom?'

Mrs Jordan blinked. 'There are books about this.'

'About what?'

'Finding adopted parents.'

Lillian laughed. 'There are books about everything. Men who hate women who love men who love men who hate women . . . I should write a book.'

'That short story you showed us was wonderful. It reminded me of Emily Brontë.'

'Thanks.'

'I mean it. Boy, those Brontë girls had a miserable relationship with their father, didn't they?'

Lillian looked at her mother sharply. 'In what way?'

'Oh,' Mrs Jordan said vaguely, 'he was a brooder and

they were obsessed with trying to please him.' The waiter put their plates down. 'This looks divine,' Mrs Jordan said, picking up her fork. 'I'm starving.'

They ate in silence for a moment.

'Have you heard from Matthew?'

'I don't take his calls.'

'Ah,' her mother put a huge shrimp on Lillian's plate. 'You're very strong,' she said tenderly.

Lillian snorted. Her lovers became so quickly taboo, cast-out, history. She barely had time to confide in her mother about her ex-husband before he began to act like a monster. Matthew had only met her parents once and felt they disapproved of him.

'There will be someone right for you, darling.'

Lillian watched as her mother transferred half her lobster tail to her plate. 'Do you want dessert?' she asked.

'Oh yes,' Mrs Jordan said, beaming. 'Something chocolate and covered with whipped cream.'

They kissed goodbye on the street. Mother and daughter. It was hard not to think: I did not come from this woman. In the past, Lillian had considered her heartbeat as an echo of her own. She thought she could recall the sea rhythm of the womb, the connection of that fragile life-giving cord. When she had raged at her mother, despised her as an adolescent, there had always been the belief that this woman had given her life, had experienced pain to bring her to the light. But in whose arms *had* she been laid, bloody and screaming? How could anyone have willingly given her up?

'Mother,' she whispered into the sweet-smelling hair. 'Mother, I love you.'

Lillian's mother stood crying on Seventh Avenue as her only daughter walked north.

*   *   *

When Lillian asked to see her boss and explained the situation, the discovery of her status as an adopted child and the search necessitating her departure to Maine, she found herself being questioned intensely by the woman.

'How do you feel about this?' her boss asked her.

'Fine,' Lillian said, looking out of the window, admiring the view of downtown Manhattan.

'I wouldn't have to keep paying a shrink if I found out my mother adopted me. I know there's something missing, but I can't identify what it is.'

Lillian nodded and smiled. She hoped her boss wouldn't continue. The atmosphere in the office was uncomfortably close, like a sauna where naked, sweating women told each other secrets.

'You never suspected?' her boss continued. 'Not even when you were a child?' Lillian shook her head. 'Well, we must keep in touch,' her boss said. 'I bet there's a great book in this. You write a bit, don't you?' Lillian nodded. 'That's good. Keep a journal. Well, I'll miss you. Now I'll probably have to hire one of those moronic publishing college kids. A boy would be nice.' Her boss leaned forward. 'Demographically there are lots of men in New England.'

Lizbeth wanted to throw her a party, but Lillian refused to come. 'It's inappropriate,' she said stubbornly. '*Bon voyage* isn't what people should be saying to me. I don't think family skeletons deserve a wheel of brie.'

She was going to Maine. Her apartment was sublet from month to month by someone who knew someone from work. She had located an apartment in the town where her mother lived from an ad in the local paper which her father tracked down. His success with that project caused him to visit the Maine Tourist Board, obtaining an extraordinary number of pamphlets on the state's natural attractions and historic renovations. It was as if

Lillian were simply embarking on an extended vacation. He helped her buy a new car, or rather an extremely used one. A 1973 Pontiac which was as long as two generous New York City parking spaces. But the engine was strong, and somehow Mr Jordan seemed to feel a large car would increase the safety factor in his daughter's life. She patiently listened to him list the reasons for her driving the monstrosity, and agreed that the price should come down and allowed him to handle the details. Whatever feminist rules were violated by her father's behaviour, she ignored. The car gave them something to discuss which wasn't full of emotion. They stood staring at it, kicked the tyres and somehow felt less unhappy about what had occurred. Owning a car after so many years helped her to recognize the step she was taking. The apartment was the top half of someone's house. She had an idea for some writing projects, but nothing was definite. It was important to leave New York, to find her real parents, to be somewhere different. This much was clear.

On the night before she left for Bangor, Edward arrived at her door again. He was in town to test for a pilot of a new television series. When she opened the door he handed her a portable coffee cup with the words 'DESERT ALIEN PUNKS FROM HELL' printed in capital letters. Underneath: 'The Movie'. He showed her how to attach the cup to her glove compartment. He also gave her a beautiful leather jacket: it was black and lined with fur.

'If you don't come back by late spring, you'll miss the world premiere. And you're my date. They're serving haggis and sheep's eyeballs afterwards.'

'I'll be there,' Lillian said. 'Sheep's stomach is something I crave at least once a year.' She picked up the leather jacket. 'This is unbelievable, Edward. How much did it cost?'

'Put it on.'

'Why did you do this?'

'I don't know. Giving you nice presents is almost as much fun as exploratory surgery.'

She tried on the jacket and jumped up and down in front of the bathroom mirror.

'Why don't you have a full-length mirror?' Edward sighed, sitting down on her couch.

'How does it look?'

'Much better. You had the shape of a quarterback in that down thing. I can't bear to have a sister who's as wide as she is tall.'

She stuck her tongue out.

'Your tongue looks weird. Why don't you stay here?'

'Don't,' Lillian said. 'I'm nervous enough.'

'Remember,' Edward whispered into her ear as he left, 'we're much nicer than those people. Direct descendants from the original Mormons.'

'Goodbye. I hope you get the part.'

'It's a terrible part.'

'So what? You're an actor. Work is work!'

'Goodbye, you alien baby from Maine.'

When she reached the border of New Hampshire, she began to feel terrible. Deciding to check into a cheap motel, she spotted a Red Roof Inn and settled Thomas Wolfe in front of the TV while she went to the 7–11. There she bought taco chips, Pepperidge Farm cookies (Mint Milanos), Diet Coke, caramel corn, a local paper and an old copy of *Vanity Fair*.

Rod Stewart sang 'Forever Young' to a child the VJ on MTV identified as not his son. Rod kept hugging the little boy, and Lillian wondered how the child managed to look so calm while this man (who was not his father) stared lovingly down at him, singing at top volume. Rod looked suspiciously healthy.

'I bet he's had his face lifted,' Lillian remarked to

T.W. 'I can't believe plastic surgery is so acceptable these days.'

George Harrison sang a duet with Bob Dylan and Tom Petty. Dylan looked old and cross. A young John Lennon sang a love song to Yoko Ono who managed to look bored, stoned and possessive all at once. Eric Clapton rasped a love song to a model. A model sang a love song to another model. Both models appeared to be women, but Lillian was pretty sure one was a man. She finished the caramel corn and opened the package of cookies. Thomas Wolfe rolled over on his side and fell back asleep. Lillian lay on her stomach watching music videos filled with an unidentifiable longing. She didn't want to drink. She didn't want to die. She wanted to go back. She wanted to know far less than she knew. She wanted to have never experienced a single New Year's Eve. She wanted to be the girl in black underwear dancing with Prince.

She opened *Vanity Fair* and in the 'People' section there was a picture of Edward with his arm encircling an actress who had a small rôle in a new sit-com. Edward looked perfectly at ease. He was talking to someone just beyond the picture frame.

'Look,' she said, to T.W. 'Our brother. With a bimbo.'

T.W. had managed to bite into the bag of taco chips. They were sticking out of his mouth and his coat was dusted with little specks of orange. Lillian pulled the remaining chips away from him. She watched another video. A man and a woman were standing on the top deck of the Staten Island ferry. The song swelled around them. The man kissed the woman's swan-like throat. She was obviously a model. Tears fell from her eyes like rain. Her head fell back and the light from the sun reflected off the skyscrapers of New York.

'Come here.' Lillian brushed Thomas Wolfe's coat. He put his face in her lap and pushed hard against her thigh with his nose. She took out the map. They would be in

Bangor tomorrow. The adoption agency had provided her with the name and address of her mother. 'Helen Carter'. She lived in a town forty miles north-west of Bangor. She thought it would be best to meet her mother after she was settled. Perhaps she could do some freelance editing or proof-reading. An article about her search would probably sell to one of the women's magazines.

She turned off the light and waited for T.W.'s breathing to quieten. Sometimes it was hard to sleep with a dog. After a few moans, he settled. She ran her hands over her stomach and up to her breasts. They had all liked her breasts. Or they said they did. So many compliments, Lillian thought as the tractor trailer's headlights traced against the far wall, so many fucking compliments. She thought of a story Edward had told her about when they were small.

'You had a crush on this retarded kid from next door,' he said. 'Dicky Miller. And he used to tell you to close your eyes and he'd kiss you. Jesus, no-one wanted Dicky Miller's lips on them but you. Every time you closed your eyes, he'd push you down the hill. And then he'd laugh like a nut because he was the smart one. And you'd get up, this fat little girl, maybe three years old, all covered with dirt, smiling like something great had happened. And you'd run back up the hill and close your eyes again.'

Lillian loved that story. She loved being that smiling, hopeful girl. Who cared if Dicky was retarded? She had loved him. Maybe she liked rolling down the hill. At least she'd taken risks.

She pretended to be someone else. A stranger. She pinched her nipples slowly. A shiver went down and across her body. She paused and then began again, lightly stroking between her legs, her thighs parted. The silence darkened. She heard the television from the neighbouring room. The news was on. Many people had gone down in a jet. Their bodies were strewn across the water off the coast of Ireland. Where was Dicky Miller now? Had he died without ever kissing anyone? There were tears on her face. She tasted salt. Snow was predicted for the New England states. The New England states where she had been born. Fear came from nowhere and she stiffened. What was she doing? Who would take care of her? She stroked herself again and then she prayed: 'Oh God, don't let me be alone for the rest of my life.' She imagined being undressed by someone, the clothes cut from her body like in a James Bond movie. No-one ever had sex in them, but God did she dream about that man! A spy come in from the cold. She continued stroking until her back arched and she came hard, the pillow clenched between her teeth. Then, almost on command, she fell fast asleep.

She dreamed about her father. He was sitting next to her watching a Disney movie. The movie became horrific with small animals being hunted and a child dangling over a ravine. Lillian had to find her father. She was alone in the theatre, strangers all around her. She ran up and down the aisles trying to see him between the rows of seats. She started to scream and then her father appeared.

'Lillian,' he whispered softly, 'I was right next to you. Why did you run away?' He held her in his arms, she was just a little girl and he smelled like soap and his shirt was very, very soft.

The room was still dark when she woke up. Thomas Wolfe stood by the bed, his leash hanging from his mouth. They walked around the edge of the parking lot and T.W. peed on each tyre of a black Corvette parked in front of the motel. It was already very cold. She tied T.W. to the newspaper dispenser and went into the coffee shop to buy them breakfast. She ordered sausage links for him and a bagel and coffee for herself. She turned to pay the cashier and saw a man sitting at the counter who so resembled her ex-husband she nearly ran out of the restaurant, afraid that he would see her. But it wasn't Anthony. This man's eyes were set closer together and his jaw was less sculpted. He didn't look as if there were something inside him which hurt.

Anthony had proposed to Lillian on the New England freeway. They were driving to Cape Cod in a lashing rainstorm and he was, as usual, exceeding the speed limit. The car hydroplaned across the road into a ditch. Lillian had looked into the lights of the approaching cars and thought it was unfair that she would spend her final moments on earth in a skid some place south of the Cape Cod Canal. When the car stopped spinning, she found herself unharmed, in Anthony's arms.

'I love you,' he said feverishly, kissing her eyes and the inside of her elbow. Anthony was the new floor manager of men's accessories at Bloomingdales. They had met during inventory, a time of high emotions in major department stores. Assigned to small leather goods, Lillian counted while Anthony filled out the forms and listened to her complaints about copy-writers having to perform menial tasks. They made a good team. He barely said a word, just watched her and laughed at her attempts at humour. Small leather goods meant thousands of key cases and men's wallets. They became giddy with boredom and went out for dinner. After two bottles of good red wine and a small amount of food, she found herself naked on her living-room floor with Anthony explaining how many times he had come up to the advertising department in the hope of seeing her. 'You wrote the ad for the Italian leather portfolios,' he told her. 'We sold out in a day.' Lillian didn't know how to respond to him. She laughed and he put his hands on either side of her face and looking deeply into her eyes, he continued. 'And then when I met you . . . I couldn't believe how beautiful you were.' Her last boyfriend had told her she had 'limited appeal' and set rules about the degree of intimacy he would allow.

She had forgotten what it was like to be desired.

'I love you, too,' Lillian had answered, meaning she loved him for not crashing into the other cars.

'Marry me,' Anthony asked, kneeling on the floor of the car, his chin resting on her knees. He pulled a jeweller's box out of his pocket and slid a diamond ring (it was too big) on to Lillian's finger.

'I'll have it made smaller,' he whispered, kissing her knuckles. 'Marry me.'

'OK,' Lillian said, her mind almost blank but still aware of what she was doing. The lights from the police car flashed across her finger. She had never liked the cold white light of diamonds, but the weight of the ring seemed significant.

She married him in a state of semi-shock, the same state she'd been in when he'd proposed; heart pumping, short of breath, dizzy. The thing was, she'd expected someone to stop them, to interrupt the ceremony, to announce: 'This has gone far enough!' She had told him she loved him because he'd said it to her. To remain silent would have caused pain. How was she to know the next thing would be a marriage proposal? How did you stop something once it was moving? His relatives sat together, the women clutching their purses, the men watching from behind dark glasses, pacing the lawn as if to record its exact dimensions. Edward loved the look of them. As each black Cadillac pulled into the Jordans' driveway, he whistled the theme from *The Godfather* and turned on his video camera. She wanted to stop him, to slap him and say: 'This isn't a movie!' In every frame of the film, Lillian was holding a glass of champagne.

She had made a mistake. Anthony was insanely jealous and insecure. He resented her position in the store and was constantly visiting her cubicle while she was trying to finish a deadline. After a few months he suggested she stay at home and have a baby. When she pointed out the smallness of his salary, he slapped her across the face. He kept hitting her. Sometimes for talking back to him, sometimes for refusing to answer. She never believed it was happening. The moment before his hand would contact some part of her body, she would think there must be some sort of mistake and fail to protect herself.

Drinking made the fear diminish. 'I never loved you,' she told him one night. 'I married you because I felt guilty. I thought I'd done something to make you think I did.'

Anthony had leaned across the table and hit her hard enough to knock her off her chair and up against the couch. Then it was over. He rarely beat her for any length of time. Just powerful blows that made her breathless with pain and left her living in fear of the next one. It went on and on, not so long but long enough.

She was drinking to escape from anything that would connect her to the pain. Leaving Anthony had meant admitting to alcoholism. All of it had felt like dying. Sometimes she missed the idea of him. Her husband, a man who tried to make her happy.

She untied Thomas Wolfe and fed him sausages while they watched the morning news. Bodies were being airlifted out of the Irish Sea. The camera panned the ocean and framed what appeared to be a floating child. No, the obligatory plastic doll. She had once loved a palomino pony and a green-eyed cat with rabbit fur around its ears. Lost.

As they pulled on to the New England freeway, they passed a car full of blonde children who waved at T.W., laughing at his hanging tongue, sticking out their own and then going into fits of giggles, disappearing completely, presumably to roll around on the floor of the car. Lillian was impressed by the impassive calm of the driver until she passed them and saw that the young woman was wearing a Walkman and was oblivious to what went on behind her back. She was tapping on the steering wheel, shutting her eyes and singing. Lillian tried to get her attention by beeping her horn, but the woman ignored her.

'That's criminal,' she fumed to Thomas Wolfe. 'There are five children in that car.' The dog seemed unimpressed by Lillian's moral indignation. 'I'll never act like that,' she told him. 'I'll never neglect my child.'

6

'You'll be wanting to rent by the week?' Lillian and Thomas Wolfe stood next to the car while Mildred White walked slowly towards them, her hands shielding her eyes against the dazzling reflection off the high-piled snow.

'Yes, please,' Lillian said, her hand resting on T.W.'s head in case he decided to impress Mildred with his uncanny imitation of an attack dog. 'But we'll probably stay longer.'

'Vacation?' Mildred looked a little baffled by the prospect of anyone deciding to spend their leisure time in Ceylon, Maine. The air was rigid with chill. Lillian could feel her facial muscles stiffening as she spoke. A slight breeze pushed the temperature even further below freezing.

'Not really,' Lillian said. 'Family.'

Mildred looked pleased. 'You have family in Ceylon? Well, that's just wonderful. Who's your relation if you don't mind me asking?'

'No, of course not. The Carters.'

'You don't say! Which ones? There's a mess of them.'

'Helen Carter.'

'Ah.' Mildred looked slightly less happy. 'Helen. Well dear, let's get you settled and find some extra blankets. It's already dropped a few degrees since this morning. Is that dog friendly?' She leaned over and looked Thomas Wolfe in the eye. The dog responded by yawning widely.

'Oh, yes. His name's Thomas Wolfe or T.W. He's just never been in the country before.'

'Good. Welcome to paradise, T.W.' Mildred straightened up. 'Dog paradise, that is. I'm not sure humans see it that way.'

The apartment was on the third floor of Mildred's house. The living-room had a breakfast nook and the kitchen was larger than Lillian's bedroom in Manhattan. A huge claw-footed bathtub filled one side of the bathroom. The depth was at least three feet. There was a hose attachment on the shelf above it.

'No shower,' Mildred said. 'But you could live in that tub.' Lillian nodded. She imagined herself neck-deep in bubbles or wrapped up in a cosy bathrobe, watching the snow fall from her window. The bedroom was up a short flight of winding stairs. An attic room, the roof slanted down to meet the wall, a skylight above the bed framed a patch of blue sky. The bed was brass, pushed into the corner of the eaves, covered with a home-made patchwork quilt. There was a desk built into the opposite corner with a window overlooking the backyard and woods. Another wall was covered with bookshelves.

'This is a wonderful room,' Lillian said.

Mildred looked pleased. 'My daughter lived up here before she moved to Paris. Her boyfriend built the shelves and put in the skylight so she could look at the stars. You said on the phone you might do some writing, so I'll find you a better lamp for the desk.'

'Thank you. Your daughter moved to France? You must miss her.'

'Maine, honey. Paris, Maine. That's about twenty miles as the crow flies. I see her all the time. I miss her a little, of course, but she's got two children and it was certainly time for her to move out.'

Thomas Wolfe had his front paws on the windowsill and was barking at someone outside. They walked over to him and watched a cross-country skier schussing across the far end of the yard. His skis left a trail which resembled punctuation marks. His face was covered with a scarf and a pair of goggles. He wore a large leather backpack. The speed at which he moved across the snow was extraordinary.

'That's Steven Woodruff. He must be delivering.'

'Mail?' Lillian asked, watching as the skier moved with graceful swoops across the snow, more animal than human.

'Babies. Steven's a midwife. He's delivered nearly all the babies in this area during the last five years. Skis work better than cars in this weather.' Lillian watched as he disappeared into the woods. 'You know he was Emily's husband.'

'Emily?'

'Helen's daughter. You must have heard about Emily.' Mildred was taking blankets out of a large cedar chest and putting them at the foot of the bed.

'We haven't been in touch for a long time. The family's not close.'

'Emily was Helen's only child.'

'Oh. Yes, of course.' Lillian looked down at the floor and followed the line of grain to where the stairs began.

'She drowned nearly two years ago. Two years ago this summer, I guess. A boating accident in the Penobscot. Hit on the head by something, probably the mast, while Steven was down below trying to get the engine going. He almost died diving for her. That water's too cold to swim in. Helen's never been the same. There's something missing. Well, I can't imagine. Burying a child has to be the worst nightmare for any parent.'

'God,' Lillian said, leaning her hand on T.W. 'I didn't know.'

'You never met Emily?'

'No.'

'Wonderful girl.'

'What's Helen like?'

'I admire Helen Carter a great deal. She's always spoken her mind, and if someone was in trouble she'd do anything in her power to help them. But she could be difficult. When Emily was an infant there was some kind of scandal about her drinking and other talk . . . Helen never bothered making too many friends.' Mildred stopped. 'I don't mean to gossip. I guess I think a family ought to know the same as other people.'

'Right,' Lillian said, trying to smile. She sat down on the easy chair. There was a faint yet distinct ringing in her ears.

'Her only daughter,' Mildred continued. 'Smart as a whip. Made Dean's list at Yale and the *Law Review*. The sort of person who's always being written about as an example for other young women. Terrible things can happen in a family.'

'Yes,' Lillian murmured, 'that's true.'

'Well, I'd better stop running my mouth and let you get settled. There's a Shopwell about six miles back towards Bangor. They're open until six, but you might want to run down there pretty quick and pick up some dog food. It gets dark here early. I left some breakfast things for you.'

Mildred patted her on the shoulder and then went downstairs. Lillian sat down on the edge of the bed and stared at her hands. She had a sister, she thought, a dead sister. None of the books she'd read about adoption contained the suggested etiquette for dealing with the death of previously unknown siblings. The situations were mostly on the topic of dealing with other relatives. This list did not include dead children. Other children. Before she left New York, she had mailed a short letter to Helen Carter stating who she was and her intention to visit Ceylon. There was no implication of her staying. She'd simply said she was 'passing through' and would contact her when settled. Things were already complicated.

Still, it felt wonderful to have left New York. The apartment was cosy and smelled of pine. She went down the attic stairs followed by T.W., who kept bumping his nose against her leg. He wasn't used to stairs. There was a basket full of kindling and logs in the fireplace. She turned on the kitchen light and marvelled at the size of the refrigerator. Inside was a carton of milk, some eggs, butter and an orange. On top was a package of English muffins. A Post-it sticker on the range read: 'Oven lights with match!' She peered into the oven. It was very clean. And for the first time since she'd left Anthony, she had a freezer that actually worked.

Why had her mother not told her about Helen's daughter? Was Lillian given away because of some failure to charm or fascinate? Emily had graduated from Law School and married a doctor. Lillian wondered if promising behaviour could be detected in a baby. What might have happened if she'd been the one to have stayed in Maine? Probably teenage pregnancy, alcoholism and a home in one of the trailers she had passed on her way to the Shopwell. The houses along Highway 101 were nearly all mobile, set up on concrete blocks with plastic goblins in the front yard. Some of the decorations spun or twisted in the wind. There was an abundance of satellite dishes and a wide variety of rusting cars parked in the backyards. Good television reception must be important, Lillian thought, as she drove along the deserted highway humming 'Onward Christian Soldiers' slightly off-key.

The Shopwell was empty except for two cashiers and a young woman with a toddler who kept running away from her. 'Trixie!' the woman screamed from the paper-goods aisle. 'You get your little behind over here!' Lillian met Trixie in the frozen-food section. She had managed to get the door of the ice-cream case open and half her little body was wedged inside.

'Trixie,' Lillian whispered, opening the door and touching her shoulder, 'your mommy wants you.' Trixie slowly inched her way out, a half-gallon of fudge ripple clutched to her chest.

'Ice cream,' she proudly announced to Lillian.

'Trixie Tiffany Tyler, if you don't come here right this minute—' The sentence remained unfinished. Trixie shoved the carton into Lillian's shopping cart.

'I'm going to put this back in the freezer, OK?' Trixie nodded mournfully. Lillian took her cold little hand and smiled down at her. 'Come on, Trixie Tiffany Tyler.' The little girl had a head full of spiky brown hair and large grey eyes. When she smiled her entire face disappeared into cheekbones and eyes. They met her mother in the dairy section.

'Great smile,' Lillian said, handing over the kid to her mother.

'Just like her daddy.' Trixie's mother looked about seventeen. 'He loves to make trouble.' She bent over and picked up Trixie. 'Say "thank you" to the nice lady.' The child buried her face in her mother's neck and wiggled her behind in Lillian's direction. Both women laughed.

'You're welcome,' Lillian said.

'Now she's Little Miss Shy. In two minutes she'll make another break.' The woman pushed her heavily loaded cart towards the cash registers. 'Bye now.' Trixie picked her head up and made a fist which she uncurled and waggled her fingers at Lillian. Lillian crossed her eyes which caused the child to scream in delight. The store manager announced the Shopwell would close in ten minutes and Lillian went off to search for dog chow.

There was a fire burning in the fireplace when she opened the door and Thomas Wolfe was sleeping on the rug. He looked like a different dog, more relaxed and somehow more doglike. There was a loaf of home-made bread on the kitchen counter with a note from Mildred.

'Nice to have you. Turn on your electric blanket before you go to bed.'

'Oh,' Lillian said, picking up the bread and pressing her nose against the crust. 'Divine!'

She lay beneath the skylight, dazzled by the number of stars visible in the northern sky. There were more stars than she'd ever seen in her life. More than the Planetarium. It felt like a foreign country instead of Maine. New York seemed to represent a stage of her life that she'd left behind. Now things would be different. She'd learn how to quilt and make jelly. Perhaps she'd take a job at the Shopwell where she'd noticed a sign asking for cashiers. Or she'd clean houses. Except the mobile homes of Ceylon didn't look like they needed maid service. It wasn't necessary to contact Helen Carter immediately. It would be a good idea to get some rest. The electric blanket was very warm. She started to count the stars on the right side of the sky. She could see T.W.'s head resting on his paws where he slept on the chair, curled up like a cat.

'You are the silliest dog,' Lillian said sleepily. She thought about her real mother and how she would introduce herself. 'I'm sorry about your daughter,' she could hear herself saying. 'How are you now? Did you ever wonder about me? When she died did you hope I'd come back to you?' Gradually the stars dimmed and she fell asleep.

In her dream she was standing in the kitchen when someone, a man, came up behind her, encircled her waist with his arms and kissed her neck. She leaned back, felt her weight supported and what she thought was: *Who is this man?* There was no answer to her question. A feeling, a sort of burning sensation, came over her body and then she stared out of the window (there was a window in her dream) and outside people were going to work, buying newspapers and wearing clothes while she was idle and naked in her kitchen with a stranger. And it was over. Whatever it was that brought this man into her life was finished, and if she turned around he would tell her either with words or just the blind look in his eyes that he wasn't going to help her be happy, that he didn't want to stay and that he'd never really experienced anything close to what she thought he had. So, she continued to stare out of the window, refusing to turn around, delaying the inevitable, hoping for a miracle.

Thomas Wolfe was barking. It was morning, although the light was very dim, diffused. The sky in the frame of her skylight was light grey with faint streaks of pink. T.W. stood on his hind legs, paws on the windowsill, his ears forward, tail stiff, barking.

'Shut up!' she said, crossly. 'Shut up.' Thomas Wolfe looked over his haunch at her and she saw that he'd had a previous life, a life full of hunting and blood. A life that did not include her. He had been waiting for this, his quivering nose told her. His ears were erect, pricked forward, listening to something mysterious, high-pitched, a dog noise. She shivered.

'Sit,' she suggested feebly. 'Sit and be quiet.' But his body was electric, his tail contained the energy of an anticipated chase. She lowered her bare feet to the floor. It was freezing. Her soles automatically lifted from the icy wood, the toes curling with shock. The air hung in the room, solid. Frost formed on the inside of the skylight. During the night, the boiler had ceased to hum. She plugged in a space heater Mildred had left in the closet and found her socks at the bottom of the bed. She looked up to meet the yellow eyes of Thomas Wolfe, his leash hanging from his mouth.

There was a family of rabbits scattered across the field. The buck and his mate were nibbling on grass which had pushed its way through the snow's crust. Their babies were in a tangled heap of furry paws and long ears. Thomas Wolfe had gone back to the window to watch them, his body quivering with anticipation. When Lillian touched his leash, he bared his teeth slightly and growled.

'Bad dog,' she said severely, tapping him hard on the head. 'You can't eat those innocent bunnies.' At the word 'bunnies', T.W. snapped the air and barked.

'Fiend,' Lillian muttered as she pulled on her Chinese silk underwear, wool tights, two sweaters, jeans, hiking boots and the leather jacket Edward had given her. When she opened the front door, she paused for a moment, overwhelmed by the silence, the cold and the stillness. She could hear the distant sound of the pond-ice shifting across the field.

'What do you want to do today?' she asked T.W. as she unsnapped his leash. It was an idiotic question. The dog gave her a single look, an almost human stare and then, like a black streak, he attacked the family of rabbits, snatching a baby in his jaws, its blood staining the snow while the others rapidly retreated. He ran into the woods with his captive and the sounds which issued were those of a mad wolf feeding on its catch. She had screamed his name but to no effect. His Central Park training did not translate to the Maine woods.

'I have a monster dog,' Lillian thought as she poured water through the Melita for coffee. She could see snow flying where T.W. was burrowing, searching for more fresh blood. 'Everybody in my life has a secret identity.'

She dialled Helen Carter's number but hung up. Once, before the phone rang at all, and the second time just as someone picked up the receiver. Her throat was closed with nervous tension and her fingers had shaken as she'd dialled. After she slammed down the phone she walked around the kitchen swinging her arms, breathing in great gulps, tears streaming down her face. She decided it would be better to wait. For three mornings she followed this pattern, but always put down the phone before it rang in case Helen Carter began to wonder who was calling her. The bone-shaking terror she felt about contacting her mother took her by surprise. What was she going to say to this woman? Had coming to Maine been such a good idea?

On the fourth morning she opened her eyes and felt something missing; a pain which had once seemed inevitable was gone. She felt lighter, more flexible and strong. While her coffee brewed, she stretched to the floor and found herself able to put her palms flat, her back completely relaxed. She had no desire to return to New York. The air which touched the tip of her nose promised another cruelly cold day, but a thin light slanted down from the skylight and a small bird was singing outside. Her most pressing problems were deciding when to drive to the Shopwell for T.W.'s dry food and how to exercise in sub-zero temperatures.

The previous afternoon she had tried running. In addition to her regular layers, she added a hat and a scarf to filter out the cold air. She started very slowly but then became enchanted with the white silence of the wooded trail and after nearly forty-five minutes of running she found herself on the far side of the lake, the sun dropping rapidly, a huge red ball of fire.

Everything changed. The temperature plunged and shadows sprang up around her. The trees groaned and creaked with the wind that sprang up and blew across the lake. Sweat froze on her face, her hair was covered with tiny pieces of ice. She felt the inside of her nostrils begin to freeze and fear made her tremble. Nature's power was always a shock. Living in a city had diluted the intensity of every season. The concept of freezing to death had always appealed to her. It seemed as if you were given the opportunity (until the spring thaw) to remain forever perfect, young, unspoiled by time. Her favourite fairy tale had been about the Snow Queen, an exquisitely beautiful woman who lived in a frozen wasteland and prepared small children for Heaven.

But Lillian didn't believe in Heaven. 'Oh God,' she cried as she jogged, her muscles knotted, the blood leaving her fingers, 'I don't want to die! I don't want to die now! It's not fair. I need more time. I haven't done anything interesting.'

She heard herself begging and stifled the impulse to giggle. Hysteria would probably further deplete her precious body heat. She imagined a voice answering her pleas for mercy.

'This isn't a rehearsal,' the voice would thunder in a Charlton-Heston-playing-Moses tone. 'This is your life!'

'I know that,' Lillian whined. 'I'm going to do something. I'll get a job.'

When she saw the sign 'Waitress Wanted' outside the Flaming Hearth Grille, she decided to apply for the job. She would tell anyone who questioned this career choice that it was 'God's will'. When she opened the heavy wooden door, there was a man reading a paper behind the bar.

'Hello,' Lillian said. 'I'm here about the waitress job.'

The manager rubbed his eyes and yawned. Finding a reasonably attractive cocktail waitress in the middle of a brutal Maine winter had proved difficult. He told Lillian he had almost hired a chubby, fiftyish mother of five the previous day.

'She's the type who'd tell you to go home and take a hot bath rather than sell you a drink. Not good for business.'

'I'm not sure how long I'm staying, but if I leave I'll give you plenty of notice.'

'You a writer or something?'

'Sort of.'

'You're renting Mildred's apartment? Lillian, isn't it?'

'Yes.'

'Good person, that Mildred. A bit of a mouth, but nothing mean about her. You don't find many who aren't lockjawed in these parts. I'm from Winthrop, Mass. It's my wife who has people around here. I thought she was quiet before I met her family. Bunch of clams! Why don't you start tonight? The shift's from six to twelve. Come in at five-thirty and have some supper. Light bar menu, fried zucchini, onion soup, that sort of thing. Your basic drinks. Know them?'

'Yes.'

'Good. Until it warms up you'll probably get nothing but shots and beer. There's a ladies' night and they like their "Sex on the Beaches". Thursday nights are slow, but we have a hot band so it heats up around ten-thirty.'

'Thanks.'

'Can you wear a short skirt? I know it's not the weather for it but you can change here. You got a white shirt?'

'Yes. Are sneakers OK?'

'Sure. My name's Bill. Did I tell you that?'

'No. Hi Bill.'

'See you later, Lillian.'

As she drove home she realized that working at the Flaming Hearth was an odd thing to do. Her reason for being in Ceylon was to find her biological mother and to discover the circumstances of her birth. Instead she was working as a cocktail waitress and had no idea when she'd get the courage to call Helen Carter. It occurred to her that she was now much closer to Matthew. He'd sent her a postcard from Boston, a black-and-white photo of Greta Garbo glaring into the camera. There was one sentence on the back: 'You're more beautiful than her.' Maybe she'd invite him to visit and then take him to the far side of the lake, hit him over the head and leave him there to freeze to death. She began to laugh and turning on the radio she listened to a man explaining the correct method of sealing a chimney. 'Plenty of grout,' he kept repeating in a nearly unintelligible Maine accent. 'You can never git enough of that stuff.'

When she got home there was a message from Mildred to call her father.

'Daddy?'

'Lillian, hello.'

'You called?'

'I just wanted to be sure everything worked out with the car.'

'Oh, fine. The car's fine. And the apartment is great.'

'Good. That's good. Do you need some money?'

'No. Mom gave me that cheque.'

'Sure. So, have you contacted Mrs Carter yet?'

'No. Well, she's out of town I think. I got a job today.'

'A job?'

'In a restaurant. A nice place. I'm sort of a waitress.'

'Is that good?'

'Yes. I need something to do.'

'You're thinking of staying?'

'For a little while. It's so beautiful here and safe. I was tired of feeling afraid all the time. The air is really clean and cold, and I feel much healthier and stronger and I sleep so well. I don't know how to describe it. I go outside and it's like when I was little.'

'Well, you deserve a break. The city's very tiring.'

'Daddy?'

'What?'

'Do you think it has anything to do with my being born here? I mean, feeling so safe?'

There was a short pause. 'I don't really know, Lillian.'

'That's silly, I guess. Don't tell Mom or Edward about my job, OK?'

'Why, honey?'

'I don't think they'd understand. You do . . . I know you do. We think like each other. I like to work, no matter what sort of work it is. You're like that.'

'I see.'

'Thomas Wolfe loves it here. He slaughtered a rabbit on our first morning. I think he may actually be part-wolf.' Mr Jordan chuckled. Neither of them spoke for a moment.

'Well—'

'I'll write.'

'Be careful of frostbite.'

'Are you OK?'

'Sure. Your mother's fine, too. Her back was acting up but it's better.'

'Bye, Daddy.'

'Goodbye Lillian. I love you.'

She held the phone until it began to make beeping noises. She realized this was probably the first time her father had ever called her since she'd left home. It was always her mother on the line, asking her questions, telling her what they had eaten for all three meals, describing their lives. Often she would hear him in the background, murmuring suggestions, adding things that she couldn't hear until she became impatient with her mother, causing herself to despise the voice that kept on telling her things she didn't care about. She wanted to scream loud enough so he would hear her through the receiver. 'Talk to me!' she'd say. 'Tell me what you're saying.' But she never dared. 'Your father sends his love,' her mother would add at the end of their conversations. Lillian never believed her.

7

The band didn't arrive until nearly eleven. By then, Lillian had about twenty customers, quiet, steady drinkers who tipped on each round. The work had been easy to remember. How to order drinks (twist, rocks, up, JB dark or light, no olive), how to set up the glasses, the right attitude. Her approach was to be friendly to the women and act slightly distant to the men. If there were several men, she cultivated the nerd, the fat one, the one who never got anywhere with the cocktail waitress and lavished attention on him. If all the men were handsome she was businesslike and cool. If it was an older couple she was a sweetly attentive daughter; an older man, a slightly seductive nurse; a single woman, a supportive friend.

'You are some diplomat,' Bill commented when Lillian had persuaded a table full of retired teachers to try their special Irish coffee. 'Those geezers always have seltzer, heavy on the lime juice. They look as happy as frogs in mud. You ever study psychology?'

Lillian shook her head and declined to reveal how many years she had spent in bars, both working and getting drunk. She felt a bit guilty about her superior knowledge of how to manipulate drinkers. Bill was pretty corny but he was a nice man, an ex-divinity student who'd dropped out of Yale after tasting his first puff of marijuana.

'Don't get me wrong,' he said, wiping down the counter. 'I wasn't all that dedicated anyhow. I was getting laid every weekend and trying to figure what my chances were for not being celibate and remaining straight.' While he loved Maine, he didn't like living so close to his in-laws. He told

Lillian that when a black friend of his visited from Boston, his wife's mother nearly called the police.

'She calls up Donna, my wife, and starts whispering into the phone: "There's a gentleman of colour, a gentleman of colour just walked into your house, Donna! He let him in." I'm "he" of course. So Donna says: "Ma, you mean that big black guy? He's my old boyfriend. The one you never got to meet because Dad got an attack of the shingles over Memorial Day Weekend and then Fred went to England because of some dumb scholarship he won for being the smartest person at Yale. You wanna talk to him?" And Donna puts Fred, that's my friend, on the phone and Fred does an Amos and Andy act with her, and tells her how grateful he is to be allowed in to the great white state of Maine and how good all them people up at Yale were to a poor, ignorant black man that everyone called "boy". She gets all fluttery and tells him that she considers Bill Cosby a genius and that she'd cried when they shot Martin Luther King and she could tell he was a really good negro, too. And Fred keeps saying: "Lordy, lordy, you gotta point there, ma'am!" The guy's a Rhodes scholar, a full professor at Harvard. She comes over later with fried chicken. But that's typical. People around here can be pretty racist. Frightened.'

When the band arrived Lillian was in the kitchen trying to persuade the cook to steam some vegetables for her. The drummer began setting up his kit on the stage while the lead singer leaned over the bar, drinking a bottle of Bud, showing Bill a picture of his new car.

'It still looks like a Honda to me, Vince,' Bill was saying, squinting at the photograph.

'What? How can you say a BMW looks like a fucking Honda?'

'Don't swear in front of my new waitress. Lillian, come and meet the next teen idol of the music world. Lillian's a refugee from the Big Apple.'

'Vincent Delacroce,' he said, wiping his hand on his pants and then holding it out.

'Italian,' Bill said, winking at Lillian. 'Vinnie the Guinea from Bangor!'

'Lillian Jordan,' Lillian said, putting down a bowl of steamed broccoli, wondering what her face looked like. Vince was extremely handsome. His thick brown hair was pulled back into a ponytail. He wore a black T-shirt, the sleeves rolled up to show off strongly defined muscles and a tattoo of a rose. The shirt was tucked into tight black jeans.

'So,' Vincent said, taking a swig of his beer and handing her a Polaroid picture of a shiny red car, 'what kind of car is that?'

'A Honda?'

Bill hooted. 'All right!'

'Whattya mean, a Honda? It's a fucking BMW!' Vincent looked deeply offended.

'Watch your mouth, stud!' Bill snapped his dishcloth at Vincent and then moved to the other end of the bar.

'You're from Manhattan? Not Brooklyn or Queens or the Bronx or Hoboken or Staten Island or Jersey City or Bayonne or Union City?'

Lillian laughed. 'I'm from the Upper West Side.'

'The Upper West Side of what? Secaucus?'

'Manhattan. The Upper West Side. The neighbourhood where John Lennon was shot.'

Vincent choked on his beer. 'Nice. That's a nice way to identify your home turf. The place where they plugged the greatest musician in the world. You live in the Dakota?'

'No.' Lillian glanced around the room. Everyone had a drink and looked content. Vincent patted the seat next to him.

'Park your rear, Lily,' he said. 'It's a Thursday night in Ceylon. If you're waiting for the rush, you just had it. Isn't that right, Bill?'

She didn't sit down, but observed this man who viewed himself as irresistible. She had never trusted musicians.

Bill looked up from the book he was reading, *How to Be your own Banker*. 'Yup. I warned Lillian that business was slow in the winter. It's going to pick up though.' He pointed at Lillian. 'You should see this girl. She could sell real estate to Donald Trump!'

'I believe it.' Vincent touched the inside of Lillian's elbow. 'I'd buy anything she'd sell me.'

Lillian picked up her tray. 'Why don't you practise your charm on someone else?' she said.

Bill frowned. 'You'd better watch yourself, Vincenzo.'

Vincent sighed and rolled his eyes. 'I'd rather watch Lillian, Father William. Now leave me alone. I'm trying to score points with your new employee.'

Bill picked up the wooden barrier and headed towards the kitchen. 'You guys mind the bar for a second. I gotta see a man about a horse.'

Lillian went behind the bar and lowered the barrier. She hunched her shoulders and rolled her head slightly. Her neck was stiff. Vincent leaned forward and putting his hands on her shoulders he pressed down hard. She let out a small cry.

'You're pretty tight,' he said, fingers moving across her shoulder blades, massaging her neck. 'You work out?'

His hands felt too good to pull away. She dropped her head and breathed deeply.

'I did when I lived in New York. I tried to run, but it's too cold.'

'I'll bet you look hot in spandex.'

Lillian glared at Vincent. 'Didn't anyone teach you manners?'

'Didn't anyone teach you how to flirt?'

'Didn't anyone tell you when to give up?'

Vincent laughed. 'So,' he said, 'this is a nice surprise.'

'What?'

'You. First thing I said to Bill: "Who's that babe in the mini?"'

'Babe?'

'You're a babe.'

'I'm not a babe.'

Vincent looked deeply into her eyes until Lillian couldn't return his stare. 'You can't run in the winter around here, sweetie. Anyway, running sucks. You pound the shit out of your knees and it doesn't do a thing for your upper body. You lift weights?'

'A bit. I belonged to a club. I did some free weight stuff. I didn't like the way everybody stared at their bodies.'

Vincent laughed. 'Oh yeah? Whatsa matter with liking what you got? Huh? You don't enjoy being looked at?'

'It's not that. I didn't think those people were really seeing each other. They were staring at their own muscles and it was yukky.'

'*Yukky?*' He raised an eyebrow. She couldn't believe how long his eyelashes were, the way they seemed to shadow his cheeks.

'Narcissistic.'

Vincent laughed and leaned forward so she could feel his breath against her skin. 'Not sexy?'

Lillian shrugged. Of course it was sexy. It was sexy watching herself watch all those men in the mirror. The ones who weren't watching each other, watching her. It was sexy seeing her muscles ripple. It was so sexy she'd stopped doing it immediately, preferring to jump up and down to the Pointer Sisters singing 'Jump!' with all the other women in her aerobics class.

'I got a gym set up in my house and a treadmill. Why don't you come over and work out? We can be narcissistic and yukky together.'

Lillian snorted.

'Hey, you're an extremely pretty woman which I believe you already know, but maybe you don't since most of the pretty women I know rarely seem to understand what it is that makes men like me, real men—' Lillian banged her tray against the bar. '—look at them. But that's not what I'm offering you. It's hard to keep your head straight in Winter Wonderland and your body suffers even harder. You get over the cold and the white by having an intimate relationship with your VCR and a box of Mallomars. In my business it matters how you look in your spandex. I gotta hustle to keep the pork off.' Vincent pounded his seemingly flat stomach. 'Hey, aren't you going to tell me I look like Jon Bon Jovi?'

'You look like Jon Bon Jovi.'

'Yeah, I know. So, how old are you, Lillian Jordan?'

'Thirty-one.'

'Umm.' Vincent licked his lips. 'That's a great age,' he said quietly, one finger touching the edge of her earlobe. 'I mean you're fucking peaking . . . '

'And you've peaked. What a shame.' Lillian picked up her tray again.

'I might be eighteen,' Vincent said. 'It would be like *Clash of the Titans*.'

'You aren't eighteen.' One of her customers seemed to be looking for her.

'I didn't know what to do with a woman like you then. It would have been a total waste. Anyway, that sexual-peak stuff is bullshit. Research has proven, in fact it was in the science section of the *Bangor Daily News*, that the perfect mate for a red-hot thirty-one-year-old female is a muscular, brilliant twenty-six-year-old male. Especially if he's in the music business.'

'Twenty-six? Aren't you too old to be a teen idol?'

'I'm perfect. I can be a teen idol *and* your trainer—'

'I don't want a trainer.'

'Or your lover.'

'I don't want a lover or a trainer or a teen idol.'

'I can be your friend.' Vincent put his hand out slowly. Lillian held her tray up against her chest. 'Come on, Lillian. Has New York made you unfriendly?'

'No.' She shook his hand.

He held it lightly, then interlaced his fingers with hers, staring, his grey-blue eyes reflecting her face, the features missing. 'We're anthropologically fated to lift weights together. Come over tomorrow?'

'To work out?'

'Yeah. To work out. Of course, you'll get one look at my sweating body, my perfect pecs and be my sex slave—' She unhooked her fingers and started to walk towards the table. 'Just kidding!'

He was very arrogant but somehow gentle. There didn't seem to be many people to make friends with and she longed for some company.

'What time?'

'How about noon?'

'OK.'

'So . . . I'll see you then.'

His voice was low, hard-edged. The band did cover versions of several Springsteen tunes and some blues. She watched him from the shadows by the kitchen door. When he started a ballad by Tom Waits, she sat down at the bar and lit a cigarette. The room was silent. This was a song she used to listen to when she drank alone. A picture of herself nearly ten years previously, sitting in one of her apartments – totally fucked-up, an empty bottle of wine on the floor, another one waiting, while the gravel-voiced singer wailed about being broken and busted and alone and afraid – formed in her mind. Bill was talking to his wife on the phone. Vincent had sat down on the edge of the stage and when she looked up he was looking back at her. The song was about falling in love with someone in a bar because you're afraid to be alone.

'I hope that I don't fall in love with you.
Falling in love just makes me blue.
Well the music plays and you display your heart for
me to see—'

The black leggings looked better than the grey ones. They elongated her legs and went well with the royal-blue leotard she put over them. She was pleased by what she saw. Her skin was clear, the cheeks glowed pink without make-up. The purple circles under her eyes had disappeared and her hair had finally grown past her shoulders, curling nicely around her face. She braided it and put on a headband, wiped off most of her lipstick and decided against mascara. Sitting on the edge of her bed, she tried to visualize herself in a calm blue place, a room that was quiet and safe. She didn't feel particularly safe.

Vincent wasn't a logical companion for a woman who'd ceased to trust men. He was a musician. A very, very handsome man with an image that she thought required his attempting to seduce all available women. When he sang to her she had felt as if she would do anything to secure that attention for herself. In high school she had refused to attend the practice sessions of the bands that her girlfriends followed. The idea of sitting in someone's basement or garage, listening to boys pretending to be rock stars made her want to throw up. Instead she went climbing with a guy who was raising his own pig. She had standards musicians did not satisfy. As she picked up her car keys, she saw T.W.'s tail wag hopefully and realized she hadn't given him much of her time.

'You want to come?' she asked him. 'You want to protect my virtue?'

Vincent lived in a house at the edge of town. There was a red BMW parked in front. The licence plate said 'VINNIE'. He opened the door after two rings, wearing a sleeveless T-shirt and shorts. His hair was standing up on end. He'd obviously just got out of bed.

'Linda—' he said yawning.

'Lillian,' she corrected him sharply.

Vinnie laughed. 'Duh,' he said, pulling her in the door. Before he could hug her, Thomas Wolfe pushed between them. 'And Marmaduke,' Vincent said.

'He's trained to rip the throat out of any man who touches me before I make the secret sound.'

Vincent bent over T.W. 'What a dynamite puppy! Sit boy.' T.W. sat. 'What's his name?'

'Thomas Wolfe.'

'Figures.'

'What would you have called him? Iggy? Elvis?'

'Nah. Leon or something. Gimme your paw, Wolfe.'

'He doesn't do that.' T.W. gave Vincent his paw. 'Fuck!'

'Lillian! What a mouth!'

'He never did that! He's never done that for anyone. He didn't do that for the dog trainer or me. He didn't even do that for Matthew.'

'Who's Matthew.'

'My ex-boyfriend.'

Vincent straightened up. 'I bet you have a lot of those.'

'How many groupies do you have?'

'Dozens,' he said, yawning, walking down the hall, Thomas Wolfe at his heels. 'I have magic powers. Dogs, children, angry black people, elderly Jews and over-hyped career women fleeing from their miserable urban existences are silly putty in my hands.' In the kitchen he went to a cupboard and removed a box of dog biscuits. When the biscuit was held aloft, T.W. begged. Lillian sighed and sat down.

'Roll over.' The dog rolled. 'Play dead.' He flattened. Lillian groaned and giggled.

'Hey,' Vincent said, 'I can teach you how to beg, roll over and play dead. It's very easy. You just have to follow directions.'

'So women are like dogs, eh Vinnie?'

'Nope.' He put the biscuit in T.W.'s mouth. 'You're pretty angry, aren't you?'

'You're very handsome,' she said. 'You make me nervous. I don't know if I'll sleep with you ever. I'm not going to sleep with you today. If you aren't patient you should give up because—'

Vincent kissed her. Without effort he moved across the kitchen and pushed her back against the kitchen table so that her head rested on a box of Corn Flakes. He kissed away her breath. She kissed him back. He kissed her eyes closed. He kissed her from her brow to the top of her leotard – which he tugged down to kiss, slowly and carefully, each breast. He held her face between his hands and waited for her to open her eyes. When she did he put his lips against hers and kissed her again, deeply, his tongue moving inside her mouth. When he stopped, she was limp. He pulled her to her feet and then put her down in a chair.

'Was that necessary?' Lillian asked him when she was calm enough to speak.

'I thought so,' Vincent said, putting water in the Mr Coffee. 'It was kinda like letting the air out of a tyre—'

'How dare you—' Lillian began, jumping to her feet.

Vincent held up his hand. 'I wanted to kiss you since I saw you last night. So, maybe I jumped the gun.'

'You are the most conceited human being I've ever encountered.'

'Possibly,' Vincent said, 'but I'm showing you the worst part. I have all these charming parts too.' He took out the coffee filters. 'We're gonna be great together,' he said. 'As for waiting, I'm great at that, darling. We just had to get the kissing part out of the way. We'll work out and then I have a rehearsal. What's on your agenda? Do you have a Filofax?'

Lillian shook her head. She felt dizzy. 'I need to buy some wool. Mildred, my landlady, offered to teach me how to crochet.'

'With a hook? Come on, Lillian! Whattsa matter with you? Chicks don't crochet!'

'I'm not a chick.'

'You want some toast, Grandma Moses?'

'Sure.' T.W. had fallen asleep under the table. Vincent loaded up the toaster with raisin bread.

'Hey,' he said, his eyes lighting up, 'I bet you know how to bake bread!'

Lillian slowly shook her head.

'You're lying to me.'

Lillian nodded. Vincent looked hurt.

'How come nobody wants to bake me bread?' he asked T.W., poking him with his foot. T.W. snorted and went back to sleep. It started to snow.

When breakfast was over they went into the gym and Lillian began to run on the treadmill while Vincent did sit-ups. He gave her a Walkman and after a few minutes she pulled the headphones off her ears and asked him whom she was listening to.

'Me,' Vincent replied, his teeth clenched with the effort of sitting-up on an extreme angle.

Lillian laughed and shook her head. 'I don't believe you.'

'Like it?' Vincent paused on the way down, his hands crossed in front of his chest. His stomach muscles were quivering.

Lillian shrugged.

Vincent frowned. His position looked uncomfortable but he managed to smile. 'What's that mean?' he asked, his voice flat.

Lillian shrugged again and smiled slightly.

Vincent lowered himself and then quickly sat up. 'Would you explain the smile, Mona Lisa?'

He was angry. She could hear it in his voice. There was this unexpected flash of memory: Anthony holding her shoulders, his fingers hurting, digging, his face very close to her own, trapped and bullied like a kid. She took off the headphones and tried to get off the treadmill. Vincent moved towards her, touched her arm and she screamed.

'Hey!' He was looking at her, his face full of concern and kindness. The treadmill slowed down and stopped.

'I was only kidding,' he said quietly.

'I know. I . . . it's not you.'

'Who?'

'Just someone.' Lillian walked over to look out of the window. The snow was filling in all the traces left by man and animal. Vincent came up behind her and she flinched.

'What happened?' he asked tenderly, not touching her. 'Did someone hurt you?'

Lillian nodded. A group of deer appeared at the deer lick and bent their heads to taste the salt.

'I'm sorry,' Vincent murmured. 'I wish I could have helped you then.'

She put her hand out behind her back and he took it. And there, holding hands, she glimpsed the possibility of joy.

8

In all her life Lillian had never seen so much snow. It was ploughed into deep trenches through which cars passed and people scurried on their way to work or school, heads bowed to the bitter wind. The headlights illuminated a world which was white, smooth, flat. On waking up she had learned to expect the shock of being underneath an electric blanket in an icy room. After a single experience with frozen hair she no longer went to bed until it was thoroughly dried. The amount of clothing required simply to cook breakfast – long johns, socks, a sweater – no longer seemed bothersome. She could better understand why so many Maine women were fat. It was a rare occurrence to be naked and, if you were, you seldom felt inspired to attempt a meaningful inventory of your body parts. In fact, Lillian learned how to dress after a bath in a mere five seconds.

Vincent took her on a shopping spree to Sears where he advised her to buy chains, rock salt, flashers and a portable battery-operated heater for her engine. He explained the rôle of anti-freeze, checked her brakes and picked out the best buy on snow tyres. He kissed her behind a towering display of motor oil in front of a family dressed in their Sunday best. Not wanting to neck in public, she had pulled away from him, frowning. Vincent had given her an angry look and walked off to stare at a display of very unattractive ties. From the back, he looked like a fifteen-year-old deadhead.

Having someone behave like her high-school boyfriend was unnerving. She wondered if it were such a good idea for them to do things together. Eating lunch in the pizzeria at the Ceylon Mall, she saw Vincent was a local celebrity heart throb. When he went to fetch their pizza, the girls behind the counter dissolved into giggles and asked him if he was appearing on MTV soon.

Lillian sat at their table feeling self-conscious, listening while one woman told another exactly what she'd eaten for a week.

'OK, I had a bagel with cream cheese which was all my fat calories for the day, and then I had another half with butter which took up all the next day's fat calories. So then I had a pint of ice cream.'

The woman was showing her friend a pamphlet from Weight Watchers, profusely illustrated with coloured photographs of what appeared to be extremely rich food. Her friend was thin. They were sharing a large pepperoni pizza.

'My fans,' Vincent said on his return, setting down her Diet Coke.

'Uh huh,' Lillian said tonelessly.

'I was on MTV last month,' Vincent said, sticking out his lower lip.

'Not to change the subject, Vincent, but let's talk about my car,' Lillian replied. 'What do I do if I hit a patch of ice?'

'Steer into it,' Vincent said, his hair in little braids all over his head. 'If you twist suddenly, the wheels will lock and you'll start spinning. Doesn't it snow in New Jersey?'

'It used to. Before I could drive. But I don't have a car in New York and the winters aren't snowy any more. Just cold. It's got something to do with the ozone layers.'

'What does?'

'Why it doesn't snow.'

'What's the ozone layer have to do with snow?'

Lillian thought for a moment.

'I don't know. Something about the greenhouse effect. That's what people say.'

'What people? New Yorkers?'

'I guess. People say it in New Jersey too. I heard someone say it on the morning news.'

'They said: "Good morning. It isn't snowing because of the ozone layer."?'

'Not exactly. Why does it matter?'

'Because it's so New York! This "I'm an expert" act. I get sick of it. Everybody does. That's why people around here keep their mouths shut. We know what we know and the rest of it's up to the experts.'

'What experts? The ozone-layer experts? Who are you? The thought police? Maybe I'm quoting Pee Wee Herman!'

'Listen to me, Lillian. I know music—'

'Classical music?'

'Yeah, but that's not what I'm talking about.'

'What about jazz and blues?'

'I know more about music than ninety per cent of the people in this country.'

Lillian snorted.

'I went to Berklee School of Music, bitch!'

Lillian was surprised. 'You did?'

'Sure I did. A full fucking scholarship! What did you think? Two years of community college?'

'High school,' Lillian snapped back. 'Or maybe just an equivalency diploma like the back of a matchbook.'

He grabbed her wrist hard. 'Stop it,' he said quietly.

'Let me go,' she hissed. 'Immediately.' She stood up and walked blindly out of the pizzeria and out of the mall. The air hit her face like an undeserved slap.

'I'm sorry,' he held his hand out to her, his face full of concern.

'I was in a bad marriage. He beat me.'

'Christ . . . I'm sorry, Lillian!'

'Did you get your pizza?'

'No. It's OK. I'll take you home.'

They drove in silence for a few minutes. Lillian counted the cars which had bumper stickers identifying their inhabitants as 'real Americans'.

'Why do you have your hair in all those little braids?' she asked him.

'To make it ripply. We're playing a wedding in Ellesworth and I wanna look pretty.' Vincent preened.

'I'm sure you always look pretty, Vincent.'

'Not as pretty as you.'

'Well, I am the girl.'

'I wanna be the girl.'

'Who'd change my tyres?'

'Hey, this isn't a custom or anything, babe. It's your job from now on. I just showed you how. Now you know how to use a jack.'

'I wasn't paying attention.'

'So, I'll show you again. You gotta learn how to do the things you want done. *Capisce?*'

'What about men getting women to sew their buttons on?'

'What about it?'

'They could do it themselves. I could change tyres. But who wants to?'

'I fail to follow. Your logic is always so skewered!'

'Why should I bake you bread?'

'Bake me bread to make me happy.'

'Why should I make you happy?'

Vincent didn't say anything for a moment, then he smiled. 'So I won't tell anyone about your ozone-layer snow theory.'

'I don't care. I'd deny it. Anyway, how do you know it isn't true?'

'That's not the point. You should always know what you're talking about. Hey Lillian, what do you want to do with your life?' Vincent was leaning forward, the tone of his voice was serious, his clear eyes were full of concern.

'For God's sake, Vincent!'

'I'm serious.'

'You don't plan things that way. It's too disappointing. It's better to decide what you don't want.'

'OK. Tell me that.'

'I don't want to bake you bread,' she said, hunkering down in the seat, turning on the radio.

When they got to her house, she put her hand on the handle but Vincent turned off the ignition. 'Can you tell me what happened with your ex-husband?' he asked her quietly.

Lillian cleared her throat. She felt ashamed. 'It's pretty complicated, Vincent. Maybe sometime—'

'A friend of mine hit his wife once and broke a bone in her face. I took her to the hospital. They never could be with each other again. I hated him for a long time and then I tried to understand it. She had a lot of support. Nobody talked to him.'

Lillian nodded. 'I just . . . when someone touches me in a certain way, I feel sick.'

'Maybe I could ask you this and you wouldn't think it was an accusation?' Vincent stopped. Lillian nodded. 'Why did you stay? I mean . . . couldn't you just walk away?'

She felt a heaviness in her chest and thought that if she still drank, this conversation would be just fine over a bottle of Wild Turkey. Then it would be possible to be dramatic and intense. Now she just felt tired and hopeless. 'Maybe it's sort of like being in a bad accident,' she said slowly. 'You don't always react to what's happened until you're already home or in the hospital.' She drew a deep breath. 'Some time has passed, you try to remember what he did to you but now you're walking down the street hand-in-hand and he's like your dream come true and you just forget.' She exhaled and shook her head.

Vincent put his hand out. 'You left him and that's a miracle. I won't ask you any more questions but tell me if I don't respect you.' Vincent paused. 'You tell me when I'm being a jerk and I'll tell you when you're wrong.'

She smiled and took her mitten off. They shook hands solemnly.

Mildred was teaching her how to crochet. Lillian found a store which sold unwashed wool, thick masses of heather-coloured yarn, dyed with natural dyes. The lambs were raised organically and the woman who ran the store was wearing a crystal and told Lillian she had a brilliant aura. Despite her heavy Long Island accent, Lillian felt this woman was selling her something precious which helped justify the outrageous cost of the yarn. Mildred found the material odd for a blanket, but agreed it would be very warm.

'Not just warm,' she said. 'From the smell of this I'd say it was waterproof. Who's it for?'

'A baby.'

'Any particular baby?'

'I'm not sure yet,' Lillian said, yawning. 'There are many possibilities.'

It was cosy and cramped in Mildred's living-room. Their rockers were pulled up by the fire and the television was on although neither of them ever looked at the screen. The room was full of antiques. When Mildred's daughter had married she hadn't wanted her brand-new house to be furnished with old pieces. Her husband was a junior executive with a paper company. He liked modern furniture. She wasn't interested in polishing wood and her tastes were rather modern and feminine. Most of the Maine furniture was heavy, wooden and uncomfortable. There was a huge old-fashioned grandfather clock on one side of the room with an ornate face and a tone like some sort of harbinger of doom. Lillian loved it. There was a tapestry wing chair, a handmade wood-based couch and a low wooden table on which was piled their wool and pattern books. On the far side of the room was a glassed-in cabinet containing pieces of Maine pottery and the old silver which Mildred had inherited from her grandmother. She had been cleaning out a drawer that morning and now sat with a book on her lap, obviously eager to show it to Lillian.

'Look what I found,' she said. 'My high-school yearbook.'

Lillian glanced at the year and was surprised. Mildred seemed older than sixty-two.

'You know I was in Helen Carter's class,' she said, unexpectedly. 'We were in the future writers' club together. Helen was so sharp. Boys were afraid to ask her out.'

'Because she was so smart?'

'Partially. Helen was always intimidating. Angry.'

'Why was she angry?'

'Oh, her Dad was the town drunk. Her mother never managed to leave him and Helen helped raise half the kids. She didn't have much of a childhood. And other things—'

'Like what?'

'Well, she was very outspoken and a passionate friend of underdogs. People around here didn't like to hear stuff about foreign politics. Or Jews. Helen had a pen pal in Poland who wrote about what the Nazis were starting to do. She tried to tell us. Nobody listened. She tried to raise money, but we were only interested in our boys. We were knitting socks for Americans. We didn't want to hear all that bad news.'

'Cassandra,' Lillian murmured.

'Exactly,' Mildred nodded, counting her stitches. 'Things became so terrible over there and Helen knew and nobody cared. That's a very heavy thing for a young girl.'

Mildred opened the book and began to hunt for her picture. Lillian felt herself drawn across the room to watch the portraits of young women dressed in white sailor-blouses and boys in dark suits flip past.

Mildred stopped. 'Here I am. My maiden name was "Fork". Can you believe it? What a curse!'

The photograph was of a rather plain girl with a high brow and a shy, sweet smile. 'Our little Millie,' the caption read. 'Still waters run deep.'

Mildred sniffed. 'Gladys Potter was the yearbook editor. I couldn't stand her.'

Lillian swallowed. Her lips were dry. 'You were so pretty,' she said. 'Is Helen in there?'

'Oh yes. Helen was the class beauty. She looked like Myrna Loy. Let's see . . . here you are.'

Mildred handed the book to Lillian who took it over to the light by the couch. The eyes were the first thing that caught her attention. They were almost almond-shaped, fringed with thick lashes, hooded. She had a wonderful bone structure, the cheeks high and a strong chin. Her lips were full, but rather stern. Unlike the others, Helen didn't smile. Her hair fell to her shoulders in unstyled waves.

'What colour was her hair?' Lillian asked, unable to take her eyes from Helen's face.

'Oh, reddish. Auburn I guess you'd call it. Is she like the rest of your family?'

Lillian looked up. 'Sort of.'

'You know,' Mildred said, walking over to where Lillian sat, 'you look an awful lot like her. Something about the eyes.'

The caption under her mother's name said: 'A fountain of knowledge is our Hel'.'

'Umm,' Lillian said, shutting the book. 'Can you show me how to join the pieces again?'

Later that night, lying in bed, Lillian saw that unsmiling face in front of her eyes. She hadn't been prepared for seeing her mother like that. How she had been when so young. She didn't have Lillian until she was nearly thirty-two. How could she have cared so passionately about those people in Poland and not want her own baby? Why couldn't she have kept her? In her dream she and Helen were both eighteen years old, sitting on a park bench. The girls were whispering. Lillian, the dreamer, was too far away to understand what they were discussing. She was grown-up, excluded from their secrets. Lillian, the child, turned to stare at her with an expression of betrayal on her face.

'Why didn't you take care of me,' she seemed to be saying. 'Why didn't you protect me?'

The dreamer attempted to argue and found that she was mute. Her wisdom, the understanding gained in years of living, became worthless. Her teenage mother and teenage self bent their heads again to whisper. Lillian, bad mother to them both, wanted to hear what they were saying. As she moved closer, they gradually faded away. She was alone, a child, lost in the woods. While she waited, the stone cold against her legs, she tried to sing. She had no voice. From the smoke, the dream smoke, emerged a figure. It was a man. Her ex-husband. He was the one who would take her home and give her back her voice. If she obeyed.

When the alarm went off she felt as if she were hungover. Her room was still dark but T.W. was awake, his yellow eyes watching her, waiting for a signal that their day had begun. Her throat was raw, as if she'd been yelling. In the bathroom mirror she recognized her mother's eyes. There had never been someone with her features before. The reflection dissolved as her eyes filled with tears and she sat down on the edge of the tub, her head between her legs, weeping.

9

Lillian didn't think of Vincent as a suitable boyfriend. In fact, she tried to rid her mind of him, tried to consider him as a pleasant, albeit inappropriate, new friend. His image, a tight-jeaned rock-and-roller, his age and his indifference to the things she viewed as important – a career, a family, committed relationships – all served to encourage her to dismiss him as an object of passion. However, there were several factors which worked against indifference. In the first place, Lillian was disgusted by her own narrow-minded and mundane set of values. When had she become so rigid about family life? It wasn't as if anyone were calling her up to appear in a *Glamour Magazine* article about career success.

'I can't sleep with you,' she imagined herself saying. 'Cocktail waitresses have high standards.' As an adopted, divorced, single, future mother of an illegitimate child she had no right to toss gravel, let alone a single stone.

Added to this was the fact that Vincent was so attractive. While his physical beauty was beyond question, there was something else which completely disarmed Lillian, who tended to keep her distance from very attractive men. It was his enthusiasm, his total embrace of all that life offered, his unqualified optimism. Of course, she told herself, he'd probably had a happy childhood. Lillian believed people who considered themselves happy children capable of massive self-delusion. Still, in her experience with others, a cheerful disposition was a rarity. The common mood amongst the men she had previously been involved with was gloomy. They had bad mothers or cruel fathers or uninspiring jobs. Her task was to make them happy.

There was also the question of Vincent's vanity. She had never met anyone so enamoured of his own reflection. Edward had fought against self-consciousness and remained aware of other people and the possibility of their requiring his attention or having needs different from his own. Lillian's chronic low self-esteem had produced a sort of modest narcissism in her that, while schizoid, almost passed for a healthy lack of conceit. Matthew disliked everything including himself. But Vincent could spend an entire evening playing his guitar without paying any attention to the mood of his listeners. He had organized an evening around viewing videos of himself performing in various clubs in the North-east and made no apologies for forcing his guests to sit in the darkened living-room watching him play 'Light My Fire' to enraptured co-eds born after Jim Morrison had soaked himself to Heaven in Paris. There were times when Lillian was dumbfounded by his belief that everything he did was fascinating. One Saturday afternoon she found herself sitting in a fancy new-wave hair salon listening to the colourist describe how she planned on streaking his hair. Vincent was listening intently, his arm around Lillian's shoulders.

'What do you think, babe?' he had asked her after the colourist had described all the options.

'I'm going to the movies,' she said, ignoring the hurt look on his face when she leaned over and murmured 'good luck'.

After Vincent's band played on the Thursday before Christmas, Lillian turned around from the bar to see a very thin girl in extremely tight faded jeans and a black T-shirt standing on tiptoes, her face strained upwards to receive Vincent's lips on her own, his hand pressing on the small of her back. Lillian gasped, the pain sharp and unexpected. When she turned around to pick up the tray she realized her eyes had filled with tears.

'You wanted something, honey?' Bill was smiling kindly at her.

She shook her head, unable to speak.

'Why don't you take a break then,' Bill said. 'Everybody's taken care of.'

She nodded and put down the tray. The cook had set aside a piece of chicken and some salad for her. She sat down at the far end of the bar with a copy of the *Bangor Daily News* and tried to eat.

'How's the car?' Vincent took a tomato from the salad, sitting next to her with his back to the bar, impossibly long legs stretched out.

'Fine.' She started reading the classified ads. Snowblowers were being sold at an alarming rate.

'No problem getting it started in the mornings?' He began to take another tomato, but stopped when she moved her plate.

'No problem.' Someone had written to 'Dear Abby' about the best way to discourage unwanted guests. The suggestion was to tell people your entire family had lice. Lillian wondered why it was considered so difficult simply to ask someone to leave.

'You've been using the heater?'

'Yes.'

'You want to work out tomorrow?'

'No.' She turned the page. A major celebrity had just come out of a famous drug rehab.

'You should work out every three days or nothing happens. It won't do any good.'

'I don't care,' Lillian said miserably. 'I don't want it to do any good.'

'Ah,' he twisted around in his seat, trapping her legs between his own, removing her fork. 'She's just an old friend.'

'Who is?'

'The blonde who was eating my face.'

'Oh for God's sake—' She tried to get out from between his legs, but his thigh muscles were very strong.

'You went completely white,' he said, touching the tip of her nose, 'then pink and then slightly green . . . '

'Go fuck yourself!'

'Don't talk like that.'

'I'll talk any way I please.'

'Does this mean you're interested?'

'Interested in what? No.' She turned the page. Another major celebrity had just come out of another famous drug rehab.

'No?'

'No.'

'No?'

'*No!* Believe it or not Vincent, how your hair gets streaked means absolutely nothing to me!' She waved the paper in his face. 'There are things going on in the world you completely ignore! We're probably invading Panama next week!'

He released her and jumped off the bar stool. 'I'm not turning myself inside out for you, babe.'

'Don't call me babe!'

'Jesus, woman! Chill out! You'd think someone committed a capital crime! Does it upset you to admit you find me irresistible?'

'Oh, leave me alone! It might be impossible for you to believe that there is one female in the state of Maine who isn't waiting for you to smile at her! Just remember, I'm from New York. Women from New York don't like men like you! Women from New York like men who know whether the current administration is pro or con increasing the military defence budget!' She screamed loudly enough for the people sitting at the other side of the bar to look up. He left her alone.

*　　*　　*

'Thomas Wolfe!' She'd already called him for nearly ten minutes before she heard the whimpering. It was very cold, the air seemed to crackle and felt solid against her skin. Her breath hung in front of her face as she beat her gloved hands against her legs in a vain attempt to keep them warm. She was becoming numb and the anxiety she felt was causing her to shake, further sapping the warmth from her body. She noticed that the back door had not been shut properly.

'Thomas Wolfe! Here boy!'

The whimpering was an odd noise. At first she thought it was some sort of bird in the forest until she crossed the road and when she called his name she heard it again, accompanied by a feeble bark.

He had dragged himself into a small pit where he lay, his face and chest matted with blood which also stained the surrounding snow. When he saw her, his tail wagged and he tried to get up. Since that was impossible, he put his nose down and tried to pull himself forward.

'Oh my darling,' Lillian cried. 'Oh T.W! My doggy! My poor, hurt doggy!' She sat down on the ground sobbing, put his bloody head in her lap and tried to see what was wrong. He was very cold. When she touched his jaw, he gently put his teeth against her skin as if to warn her that this was painful.

Once she began to talk to him, he grew quiet. 'I'm getting a blanket,' she told him, 'and then we'll go to the vet.' She leaned over to kiss his broken head. 'I love you.' She took off her coat and covered him with it and then ran back to the house to warm up the car.

Mildred was away visiting her married daughter in Paris, and Lillian had already pulled into Vincent's driveway before it occurred to her that he might not want to have a visitor and her bloody dog at 2 a.m. She didn't know how to find a vet. There was nowhere else to go. T.W.'s breathing sounded shallow and too quick, and her tears kept falling on his head where it rested in her lap.

'Lillian,' Vincent said, scratching his head, 'what's going on?' He was wearing nothing but a pair of old sweatpants.

'My dog—' Lillian said.

'Why the fuck aren't you wearing a coat?' Vincent asked.

'It's over T.W. He's been hit by a car.'

'Shit!' Vincent grabbed a sweatshirt that was hanging on the coat rack and two coats. He stuffed his bare feet into a pair of sneakers. 'Where is he?'

'In the car.'

'There's a twenty-four-hour animal shelter with a vet in Bangor. You got enough gas?'

'Vincent,' Lillian wailed, 'my dog's going to die.'

'Nah,' he said, zipping her into his coat, 'don't talk shit.'

They drove in silence for a few minutes. All three of them sat in the front seat, T.W. next to Lillian. He seemed to fall asleep. His breathing was quieter and more regular. Vincent put his arm around Lillian, drawing her closer.

'OK?'

'Yes.' His coat smelled like motor oil.

'I had a dog once. The dumbest dog in the world. This dog was so stupid he only chased parked cars. He'd run up to them and start barking and growling until he was satisfied. Never blinked at a cat. Never chased a squirrel. Just those goddamned parked cars.'

Lillian didn't say anything. Vincent leaned forward and turned on the radio, but turned it off before any sound came out.

'So what happened?'

'I don't know. He got out somehow. Mildred's visiting her daughter and I was late for work this afternoon. I had to put the garbage out. I didn't shut the back door properly. He doesn't know anything about roads and cars. I shouldn't have an animal. I can't take care of anything.'

'Hey, he's a city dude! This dog could ride the subway! No problem. Listen, I know the night vet at this place and he's really good. A friend of mine had a horse with seizures. Unbelievable mess. An epileptic horse. There's a lot of blood, but he still has all his legs. He doesn't seem to be in shock. He'll be OK. Won't you, boy? Hey, T.W?'

The dog's eyes opened at the sound of Vincent's voice saying his name and he wagged his tail slightly.

'Hey, rock-and-roll! There's my hound!'

Lillian was thinking about Edward. When they were children, he'd had a dog the rest of the family barely tolerated because of its slavish devotion to Edward and its habit of barking in the middle of the night. After Edward went to college, the dog developed a horrible, obscure disease that gradually destroyed its vision, its ability to walk and finally its appetite. The vet had decided it would be kinder to put him to sleep.

Edward was devastated.

'Binky,' he kept saying as he dug the dog's grave, 'you were my best friend.'

'For God's sake, Edward,' Lillian finally snapped. 'How can you be so stupid about a dog?'

'You don't understand,' Edward said. 'Animals break your heart.'

The surgery was empty but the vet was there, a young-looking middle-aged man with gentle hands and a soft voice. T.W. accepted his handling him and only nipped gently when the pain was severe.

'He's got a broken jaw and a dislocated shoulder, a few broken ribs and a smashed right foot. He was hit in the front. I'll operate after we get his body temperature up to normal, set the jaw and the shoulder. He should be here for about ten days. Why don't you call me late tomorrow afternoon when he's alert and I'll give you all the details.'

'You don't think I should stay?'

'No. He's going to be fine. I'll call you if anything weird happens.'

'Great. Thanks, Carl.' Vincent shook the doctor's hand.

'You're welcome. Hey, I hear the band's really cooking. We saw your video. My kid thinks you're God.'

'Yeah? Well, that's a start. Things are finally happening.'

'This guy's incredible. You ever see him play?' he asked Lillian.

She nodded.

'I've known him since he was playing in my grandmother's garage. I taught him how to roll joints. You're from New York, Lillian?'

'Yes.'

'How do you like the frozen tundra?'

'She loves it,' Vincent said, putting an arm around her shoulders. 'Where men are men and women are fat.' Both men laughed.

Lillian kissed T.W. and she and Vincent went outside. The sun was rising in a riot of violet and rose. The faded moon and diminishing stars were still visible. Bangor shone like a golden Egyptian city.

'Come here,' Vincent pulled Lillian into his arms. 'Hey, you're shaking.' He put his coat around them both and buttoned her inside. 'You're still shaking, sweetheart.'

'There's so little I feel connected to,' Lillian whispered. 'My childhood's finished and it wasn't the one I thought I had. My dog—'

'Let's go home.'

When they reached Vincent's house, he leaned across her and opened the door. Then he came around the other side and pulled her from the car. She was still wearing her waitress uniform. In the hallway he took off his coat and then hers and then led her upstairs where his bed was just as he'd left it, the blankets and sheets in a tangled heap. He opened up a drawer and pulled out a pair of sweatpants, socks and a large cotton sweater.

'Change, honey,' he said. 'I'll make some breakfast.'

Lillian sat down on Vincent's bed. He had a nice room. The walls were painted white and there were some interesting black-and-white photographs matted and framed in steel. The furniture was sparse but the pieces were well chosen: an old brass bed, an antique roll-top desk, an old captain's chair and a faded but lovely Oriental rug. It was not what she'd expected of him. Her fantasy ran more along the lines of a fur-covered water bed and life-sized posters of himself and 'the Boss' on the wall.

She changed into his clothes, brushed her hair in the bathroom, noticing the deep purple circles around her eyes. She opened the medicine chest and saw a spray container of Chanel Number 22 on the shelf. She sprayed some on her neck and wrists. The rest of the cabinet was full of Vincent's skin and hair treatments.

'Umm,' Vincent said, turning the bacon, 'what smells so good?'

'Bacon.' Lillian drifted around the kitchen, her feet small in his large wool socks.

'Bacon doesn't smell like wood nymph,' Vincent said, putting down his spatula, starting towards her. 'I smell wood nymph.'

Lillian put her hands up. 'Someone's Chanel Number 22 I found in your bathroom.'

Vincent shook his head. 'Skittish little filly, aren't you?'

'This isn't an episode of *Bonanza*, Vincent. Be normal.'

He went back to the frying pan. 'You want fried or scrambled?'

'Scrambled.'

'Rye or wholewheat?'

'Rye.'

'Orange or apple juice?'

'Apple juice.'

'Before or after breakfast?' He moved behind her chair to kiss her neck, his lips softly nipping along her bare shoulders.

'After,' she murmured.

'Sure?' He pulled her hair gently so her head tipped back and kissed her hard, his tongue deep inside her mouth.

'Before.'

Vincent turned off the stove and then lifted Lillian out of the chair, his hand pushing up the sweater while his mouth remained on hers, his hands holding her breasts, their lips opening and closing. Lillian's head was bent backwards, Vincent's mouth moved slowly from her own, along the inner line of her neck and then gradually enclosed each nipple in turn. She shut her eyes and then felt herself being led from the kitchen to the living-room where they sank down in front of the fire and despite being so closely wrapped around one another, finished undressing.

Vincent took her hand, kissed each finger and then pressed it against his crotch so that she felt him, felt him growing hard and long in her hand.

'Touch me,' he hissed into her ear. 'Don't stop touching me.' She kept her hand on him, and she began to open, her response to his lips which were moving from her shoulders and then down her sides, across her stomach, between her legs. He put his mouth against her, inserted his fingers inside and all the while he muttered: 'Don't let go of me, Lillian.' And she didn't although she began to feel close to losing the ability to concentrate.

'Do we need—?'

Lillian nodded and Vincent replaced his fingers with her own and reaching behind him he pulled a rubber out of his jeans.

'No problem,' he said, waving it like a flag.

Lillian laughed. 'Thank God,' she cried, climbing on top of him, lying down so that her breasts were flat against his chest, sitting up to wrap her legs around him. 'Thank God,' she whispered again when he entered her, deep inside so it hurt. She screamed slightly, and Vincent pulled her into his arms and kissed her face so tenderly the pain left and all she felt was heat. As their bodies gleamed and reflected in the fire, their image in the mirror was of some sort of outrageous two-headed animal, dancing, moving in rhythm.

'Tell me I'm the best you've ever had,' Vincent whispered in her ear as he turned her around to enter a third time. She was so wet he kept slipping out.

Lillian remained silent, concentrating on the sensation that she was experiencing, the knowledge that she was going to have an orgasm with this man the first time she fucked him.

'Tell me,' Vincent groaned, his strokes becoming faster and deeper.

'What?' Lillian gasped.

'That I'm the best.'

'The best what?'

Vincent slapped her ass lightly. 'Bitch,' he hissed.

'Shut up!' Lillian snapped. They both came, their bodies covered with sweat, Vincent kissing her back while she was still face down, her body shaking with passion.

She lay in his arms afterwards, her hair tangled in his, listening to his even breathing. She was wide awake. When she tried to slip out from under his arm, he held her tighter and she saw he wasn't asleep any more.

'Where are you going?'

'Nowhere.'

'Good.' He vaguely opened one eye. 'You OK?'

'Sure.'

'That was great.'

She nodded, but didn't speak.

He opened both eyes and pulled up on one elbow, his other arm holding her tightly. 'What's wrong, Lillian. Your lower lip seems a bit fragile.'

'I'm thinking about T.W.'

'He's fine. Think about me.'

'You do that enough for both of us.'

Vincent sat up. '*Touché!* Is that a complaint?'

'I'm not used to giving reviews in the middle of things.'

'*Things?* Don't you mean performances? Is that what you think?'

'I don't know what to think.'

'Did you have a good time?'

Lillian nodded.

'I thought so. Unless you're an incredible actress. So why does it require so much analysis? Just let me be your lover.'

'Are you my lover?'

Vincent frowned. 'Excuse me,' he said in a fake English accent, 'have I just been jerking off? How terribly rude of me! Please allow me to introduce myself, I'm—'

He stopped abruptly when he saw her tears.

'I'm sorry,' she said, sniffling. 'Things haven't been very easy.'

'Come on! Does feeling intense pleasure make you suffer? Do you miss your shrink? Would you like to call her and find out if I'm capable of treacherous be- haviour? I know all the lingo, Lilly. I'm not some hick from down east who's going to come for you with a shotgun and a pick-up truck!' When he saw she wasn't smiling, he pulled her back into his arms. 'It's OK. I mean, aren't things getting better?'

'I don't know. How can a man own so much mousse?'

Vincent looked bewildered. 'Hair matters in music.' He addressed an imaginary audience. 'This deluded female just had sex with one of the hottest dudes in rock and roll and the jury's still out on whether she had a good time! You came didn't you?' Vincent growled.

'Yes,' Lillian said sullenly. 'Sort of.'

'Oh come on! You came like a goddamned dam bursting! Jesus!' He drew a deep breath. 'You want some breakfast, little girl? Some nice scrambled eggs? I think you're just hungry.'

'No,' Lillian said. 'I don't want anything. What am I doing here?'

'Ah,' he said, kissing her. 'Don't.'

'I'm sorry,' Lillian sobbed.

'I'm not,' he whispered. He kissed her belly and the inside of each thigh. 'Mmm, you taste like maple syrup.'

'No I don't.'

'Yes you do.' He licked each nipple. 'Like vanilla ice cream and maple syrup.'

She stroked his back and thought about Edward's dead dog.

'What are you thinking about?'

'My brother's dead dog.'

Vincent jumped up. 'Fine! That's just fine! It's definitely time for breakfast!'

'Hey!' Lillian called to him before he left the room.

'Yes?'

'You have a gorgeous ass.'

Vincent looked over his shoulder, checking his reflection in the mirror. 'I do, don't I?' he said happily. He turned around and looked at himself, smiling with such pure delight that Lillian couldn't help loving the way he reminded her of a toddler.

10

When Lillian told Mrs Jordan about Thomas Wolfe her
voice grew very soft. 'Honey,' she said, 'that must have
been terrible.'

'It was. But he's expected to be fine.'

'Have you decided anything about Christmas?'

'Oh God! Is it next Thursday?'

'Yes. Your brother's stuck on location.'

'Mom—'

'Are you spending it with them?'

'Who?'

'Your . . . the other—' Her mother's voice died away.

'No. No, Mom. I haven't even called her yet.'

'But you have her number.'

'I know. It's just hard.'

'Would you like to come home?'

'No. I mean, it's a bad time now with T.W. and
everything.' Lillian paused. 'I really need to talk to her,
Mom.'

'We've been invited to the Grays for Christmas dinner.'

'Would you mind?'

'No. We've had Christmas apart before.'

'Not very many.'

'Are you afraid to call her, Lillian?'

'Yes.'

'Why?'

'Mom—'

'If my daughter was like you, I'd feel like the luckiest
woman in the world.'

'Your daughter is like me. Jesus, Mother!'

133

Mrs Jordan laughed. 'What do you want for Christmas?' she asked.

'Electric socks. Cashmere underwear. A space heater.'

'OK. We'll call you on Christmas Eve. If you change your mind you're welcome at the Grays'.'

'Thanks, Mom.'

The meeting began. Lillian looked around the room and saw a man waving at her. It was one of the cooks from the Flaming Hearth.

'Hey there,' he said, 'far out.'

She saw someone else, the girlfriend of a steady customer. And then another woman, a friend of Mildred's, leaned forward and smiled.

The speaker was introduced and when she sat down at the table in front of the room, Lillian saw the face from the yearbook, slightly more lined and somewhat less sharply featured but still the same perfect cheekbones and almond-shaped eyes. Stern lips. She felt herself stop breathing and then she began to count, using the numbers to stop herself from hyperventilating.

'Hello,' the woman said, 'most of you guys know me. I'm Helen C and I'm an alcoholic.'

'Hi, Helen,' Lillian said in dumb chorus with the rest of the room.

'I've been sober nearly twenty-five years. I drank badly. I stopped drinking because I couldn't do it any more. I got sober because being a dry drunk was as close to being dead as I'll ever come. I couldn't drink any more because I'm an alcoholic and that meant if I didn't stop I'd die.'

Lillian looked down at her feet. She thought there was very little she wanted to know about this woman but she also felt herself wanting to stand up, to stand up and tell all the people in the room that the woman they were listening to with such interest was actually her mother.

Little phased an alcoholic. The meeting would simply continue. People would nod and smile.

'When I was first married I used to hide my bottles from my husband. It didn't make any sense. He knew I was drinking. He didn't drink so I wasn't protecting my liquor supply. I just didn't want him to see those bottles.'

Lillian nodded. She looked into the eyes of her mother, trying to make her stare back. Helen's eyes scanned the room and then dropped. Lillian felt rage grow in her belly. All around the room people's heads were going up and down. She stifled an impulse to laugh. *Liar!* she felt like shouting. *Hypocrite.*

'When my child was born, I tried to stop drinking. Emily was such a good baby and I wanted to try and be a good mother. When I got drunk around her she could tell there was something wrong. She was too quiet. She tried to be a good baby so her mother would feel better.' Helen's eyes filled with tears.

Lillian looked around for an escape route. She was sitting towards the front, in the centre of the row. There were too many feet.

'I controlled my drinking. My husband and I were having problems. I began an affair with his best friend.' Helen took a deep breath. 'I had always loved this man. He and my husband had shared an apartment together in college. After Larry went to bed, John and I used to sit up and talk about all the things we wanted to do with our lives: travelling to Europe, moving to New York, writing books. But we were stuck. His wife had MS. She would never walk again. He was the kindest person I've ever known. A good artist. But he couldn't save me. He knew I was a drunk and he wanted me to stop. Something happened that changed everything.'

I was born, Lillian thought.

'My husband left me. John wanted to tell his wife about us, but I couldn't stand to hurt another person. Anyway,

I didn't believe anyone could love me that much. Emily missed her daddy. I made a terrible decision. It was necessary for the survival of our family, but it never stopped hurting. In the end, it ruined all the good there was.'

You gave me away, Lillian thought.

'I started drinking around the clock. John couldn't get me to stop. I told him I regretted everything that had happened between us and that I didn't love him. I told him I'd given birth to a baby girl, our child, and abandoned her. I invented other lovers and I described having sex with them. Once or twice, I hit him. He kept trying to get me sober. I told him I preferred to die rather than stop drinking. I thought all of this would make him stop loving me. Perhaps it did. One night, after a violent argument, he shot himself.'

You gave me away, Lillian screamed inside. *You killed my father.*

'Sometimes I look back and I want to change everything. I didn't pull the trigger that killed John. He had his own higher power.' Helen paused and took a deep breath. 'Most of you know about Emily's accident. I see myself from before, full of dreams and unspoken ideas and I want to hold that young girl, that hopeful, brave person and tell her she's going to be all right, that I love her. I want to explain to my daughter that she had nothing to do with my anger and my disappointment.'

Me, Lillian thought. *You should tell me!*

'But I can't go back. I can't save him. I can't pull Emily out of that cold water. I can't return the breath to my own daughter. I can't drink. I don't understand why some people seem to have happy lives. But I do understand that I'm not very important. When Emily died I thought there was no good left in the world. Sometimes I still feel that way. I don't know why I stayed in this town, but something made me not run away. I have a life. Not the one I'd always expected, but the one I have. When people ask me what I am, I think, no matter what I say, *I am an alcoholic.*'

Lillian started crying. The woman sitting next to her handed her a Kleenex.

'I'm going to stop now. Thank you all for my sobriety.'

She followed her into the parking lot. At the touch of her hand, Helen turned around. She looked shocked.

'Yes?'

'I'm Lillian.'

'What?'

'I wrote you a letter.'

'A letter? Who—' Helen swayed. She put her hand against the truck to steady herself. 'Oh my God.'

'I'm sorry. I didn't know you were speaking.'

'What are you doing here?'

'I come to meetings.'

'Ah,' Helen's face saddened for a moment, 'of course. How long have you been sober?'

'Over two years.'

Helen smiled. 'How wonderful. Was it very bad?'

'Yes,' Lillian said. She couldn't believe how easily this woman was speaking to her. She felt dizzy with anger. 'Could we see each other?'

Helen stared at Lillian. Her hand came forward tentatively to touch her hair. 'You look like both of them,' she said, almost to herself. 'Your half-sister had freckles . . . '

'Emily? I'm very sorry.'

'When I first saw you—' she stopped. 'He had beautiful hair.'

'My father?'

'Yes.' Helen touched her forehead.

'Why did he kill himself?'

'There were many reasons.'

'Did he ever see me?'

'Look—'

'Did you tell him about the adoption? Did he want me?'

137

Helen shook her head. 'The answers were lost, dear.'

'He might not have killed himself.' Helen reached forward but Lillian shrank back. 'He might have lived if he knew he had a daughter.'

'Lillian, you'd better come and see me. Why don't you come for lunch tomorrow?'

'OK.'

'I live in the old Tucker house. It's on Mill Pond Road. The last house on the left. Twelve-thirty?'

Lillian nodded wordlessly and watched as her mother unlocked the door of her car and drove away. Back in her own car she sat with the engine running, the radio blasting, crying until the church lights were switched off. For the first time in her life she had seen in person where her features came from. Helen's face told her there was no mistake.

'Hey.' Vincent opened the door, the sound of a bass guitar filled the hallway.

'I should have called,' Lillian said. 'You're having a party.'

'Nah. I'm just listening to the new basic track we did last week. I'd invite you to my party.'

Lillian started to back out of the door. 'Well, it's really late . . . '

He pulled her gently into the hallway. 'Why do you act so weird?' he asked her kindly. 'Don't you feel like you belong anywhere?'

'No,' she said, holding herself tightly, 'I mean, I don't know. I should have called.'

'If you had I would have asked you to come over.'

Lillian sighed. 'There are some things I should tell you.'

'You want to take your coat off and come in? I'm not all that fond of the hallway.'

'I don't know.'

'Trust me,' Vincent said, taking her hand and kissing the palm. 'You don't have to tell me anything.'

'I—' Lillian stopped.

'Come and listen to this new song I just wrote.'

It saved her from talking.

Vincent's living-room was full of equipment. A bass guitar leaned against the couch. She sat down stiffly on the edge of a chair.

'You want a beer or something?'

'No,' Lillian said, 'I don't drink.'

'Oh yeah,' Vincent called from the kitchen. 'Tea?'

'Sure.' She followed him into the kitchen. 'I really don't drink.'

'You mind?' He held up the beer. 'I should cut down.'

'No! It's not like that. It's me.'

'Uh huh.' Vincent leaned against the refrigerator. 'So? That's no big deal.'

'Yes, it is a big deal. I don't drink because I'm an alcoholic.'

Vincent looked shocked. 'Oh, come on.'

'What?'

'Aren't you a little young?'

'Do you know any alcoholics?'

He thought for a minute. 'My drummer.'

'Your drummer? Have you ever asked him about it?'

'Nope.' Vincent took a swig of his beer. 'Do people want to discuss stuff like that?'

Lillian shook her head. 'No, I guess not.' She stood up. 'I can't talk—'

Vincent put down his beer and held out his arms. 'Come here,' he said.

Lillian walked towards him slowly. He unzipped her coat, turned her around and pulled it off.

'Can I ask you a question?' he asked, pushing her hair back on her forehead.

'OK.'

'When did you stop?'

'Nearly three years ago.'

'I admire you very much for that.'

'Thanks.'

'Is it hard?'

'Sometimes. Not the drinking part so much. I miss *not feeling*. Nothing is as hard as drinking. You're in pain whenever you sober up enough to feel. It's terrible.'

'You would like not to feel anything?'

'Maybe.'

'Do I make you feel too much?' Vincent was staring straight into her eyes.

She put her head against his shoulder. 'Probably,' she whispered, 'but I want to try.'

'You go to AA meetings?'

'Yes.'

'My drummer's in the group for drug addicts. But sometimes he goes to AA. He says the people aren't as crazy. You want me to come with you?' The kettle began to whistle.

'To AA?'

'Yeah. I could keep you company.'

'No, Vincent. You'd get really bored.'

'Peter said some really screwed-up women go to those meetings. I could be a positive male figure.'

'Jesus—'

'It's a joke!'

'Why do you think you're so perfect?'

Vincent shrugged. 'I dunno. Is it a problem? Should I go to therapy to find out I'm really pond scum?' He put his arms around her in a huge hug. Her body was rigid. 'What's wrong, Lillian?'

'Something happened.'

'Something bad? Is T.W. doing OK?'

'It just feels like my heart's been broken.' She drew a deep, shuddering breath. 'I'm sorry I didn't call. The vet told me T.W. is a born survivor.'

'Well, Lillian, humour me, OK? Make me think you don't need continuous positive-reinforcement.'

'I don't. It's just—'

'Be normal! It will turn me on!'

When she got home that night she took the yearbook off the shelf and opened it to Helen's picture. She walked over to the mirror and held the book up next to her face. Her mother could have been her younger sister, the eyes clear of pain, the face unlined. She wished it were possible to protect that serious-eyed girl. She saw her own suffering for what it was, the darkness of an unresolved past overwhelming the present. Her ears filled with a curious noise, a sort of flat humming, and she wept – rocking back and forth on her bed, a pillow cradled in her arms like a sleeping baby, an image of a man without hope walking down a dark street filling her mind. If she could tell him how much she loved him he would forget about the other things, the disappointments and the worries he felt. She saw him standing at the end of the garden, looking up at his sick elms, his face suffused with grief. 'Look at me!' she wanted to scream. She dialled her parents' number but hung up before the phone rang. It was very late and her father never answered. Before she fell asleep she saw Vincent's handsome face smiling at himself in the mirror.

II

Helen's house had been easy to find but Lillian was still ten minutes late. She'd kept changing her mind about how to dress and gone back and forth between a skirt which was completely impractical for the frigid weather and jeans. It was an excuse to postpone her departure. Her clammy hands and the difficulty she had breathing told her she was frightened. Edward used to give her advice about how to overcome fear.

'Try and imagine the worst possible scenario,' he had told her when she was terrified about the prospect of being fired from a job. She had. She imagined being called into the office and her boss saying: 'You aren't what we imagined when we hired you.' That was exactly what happened. Somehow, having already imagined it, reality wasn't that painful. She managed to retain her composure and negotiated a generous severance package. Her boss offered to write her a glowing letter of reference. By the time the interview was finished it was unclear why she was being fired. When she called Edward she felt triumphant.

'I got fired,' she said. 'Thanks.'

'Oh my God,' Edward groaned. 'That wasn't supposed to happen. The point of a worst-case scenario is that it never happens.'

To you, Lillian had thought grimly, *to me, it happens*. Edward's lovers didn't leave in the dead of night, he was rarely the recipient of bad news. Edward was someone few chose to disappoint. If he failed to get a good part, he was usually offered something with less status but equal pay. He was always being bumped into first class, provided with free dinners, taken care of by strangers. He wasn't adopted.

'Come in, Lillian.' Helen wiped her hands on the apron she was wearing and put her hand out. Lillian shook it.

The two women walked into a high-ceilinged entrance with white walls and a polished wooden floor. Along the wall hung a sequence of photographs. Emily, Lillian assumed. The pictures began with a smiling baby and ended with a serious-eyed, dark-haired woman standing next to a taller, smiling man. Behind them was a large sailing boat.

'That's Steven,' Helen said. 'Emily's husband.'

'How sad,' Lillian murmured. 'They look so happy. I'm really sorry.'

'Come in the kitchen. Steven's probably going to drop by. He'd like to meet you. I thought we'd eat in there. It's the warmest room in the house.'

The kitchen was large and full of books and plants. There was a smell of cooking vegetables.

'Ratatouille,' Helen said.

'Oh, lovely! I adore ratatouille.' Why am I talking like Eva Gabor, Lillian wondered to herself.

There were several loaves of freshly baked bread on the counter. Lillian picked one up and put her nose against its crust.

'My mom bakes bread,' she said. 'I never have the patience any more.'

Helen smiled.

'Do you know my parents?'

'Not really. I know their names. I guess I met your dad once or twice. Your mother sent me a couple of pictures.'

'Really?' Lillian wanted to hear more.

Helen shrugged. 'It wasn't worth the misery. I felt it was better to let go.'

Lillian nodded. She felt a sharp stab in her stomach and resisted the impulse to break the perfect loaf across the edge of the counter. She looked up and Helen was watching her intently.

'You want some coffee?'

'OK.'

The kitchen table was set for three people with place mats and cloth napkins. Lillian sat down.

'Do you have a picture of my father?' She unbraided the fringe of the woven mat.

'I have several I can give you. I made copies.' Helen took down one of the books and removed an envelope from its pages. 'I'm going to check the furnace for a second.'

He looked too young to be a soldier. The jacket he wore was absurdly long, the pants too short on his long legs. He held his gun awkwardly. His expression indicated mild confusion.

'Oh.' Her father as an angry young man. T-shirt sleeves rolled up on muscular arms. Slim-hipped, he smoked a cigarette and glared at the photographer.

Then the two of them. Helen's face reflected a quiet joy which made her eyes appear full of light. He held her hand carefully. They were both about thirty. He smiled like someone about to say something important. Helen came back into the kitchen.

'What's his name?'

'John Moore. Scots-Irish.'

'Did he drink?'

'No,' Helen said, pouring a cup of coffee. 'Certainly not like me.'

'Like us,' Lillian said, raising her cup.

'He wasn't self-destructive until he met me. The thing with his wife's illness hurt, but he managed. It wasn't so important to be happy. He had faith.'

'Church?'

'Yup. Then he met me and I introduced him to gin-induced honesty. The passion of infidelity.' Helen's voice was flat.

'Didn't you really love him?'

'I'm an alcoholic, Lillian. Now that I don't drink any more I can tell the difference between love and obsession. We breathed each other's air. It was unhealthy.'

'Oh.'

There was a long silence. Helen watched as her visitor unbraided another mat. 'It's very hard . . . ' She faltered and began again. 'You have his eyes and I've missed them so terribly.'

My eyes, Lillian thought, remaining silent. *Eyes you turned away from.*

Helen stood at the window. Lillian felt sick. She hadn't imagined a mother like this. Her fantasy had run along the lines of a plump Maine housewife who grew vegetables. But instead she was reminded of a passionate, doomed heroine. Like Cathy in *Wuthering Heights*. There was an energy source, her pupils seemed to reflect a smouldering fire. Lillian had never expected to identify with this woman so closely.

'I'm not sure I understand anything about love either.'

Helen turned around. Her face softened. 'I'm sorry,' she said, sitting down. 'I'm not sure how we're supposed to act.'

'Someone's probably written a book: *Etiquette For Totally Bizarre Family Reunions*.'

Helen laughed. 'You know what I did? I wrote to "Dear Abby". I sent a letter to the *Bangor Daily News*.'

'Did they print it?'

'Confidential. She said to get therapy. That's what she tells everyone. Nothing practical. I'd hoped she'd tell me how to dress and what to serve for lunch.'

'I was married.'

'No! When?'

'A few years ago.'

'What happened?'

'I don't know. He had a horrible family and I think he wanted to escape from them. Just before the ceremony I was upstairs drinking wine and trying to find a way to get out of the whole thing. His mother and all his aunts were outside sitting on folding chairs, clutching their purses as if they were afraid of thieves. His father pacing off the garden.'

'What did your parents think of him?'

'I don't know.'

'Well, didn't they say anything?'

'Oh . . . no. Of course not.' Helen raised her eyebrows. 'We don't say much about those sorts of things. It's mostly about work. Grades when I was in school. Current events.' Lillian saw her father sitting in his chair. Her mother asking questions. Questions which illuminated Anthony's unsuitability. Questions which prompted her to marry him. *Leave him alone,* she had thought to herself, *he's good enough for me.* She knew something terrible was happening to her. Sometimes if she couldn't drink until she passed out, she believed she would simply die from the pain.

'I never belonged,' Lillian said. 'Something was always missing. And my mother knew that. She wouldn't admit it, but she knew.'

'Of course she knew,' Helen said, crossing to the stove and stirring the ratatouille. 'It's impossible not to know when your child is suffering. That doesn't mean you do anything. You just know it.'

'He beat me.' Lillian ripped off a piece of bread. Helen nodded. It was a relief to talk to someone who didn't wince.

'Is that why you left him?'

'Well, no. It was as if someone else was having our fights. Edward got me to leave.'

'Edward is your older brother?'

146

'Yes. He's two years older.'

'Ah.' Helen turned off the stove and began to slice the bread.

Lillian swallowed. 'Did you look at me before you gave me away?'

'I didn't give you away.' Helen's tone was sharp. 'Putting a child up for adoption isn't some sort of auction.'

'Then what was it?'

Helen turned around. She was holding the basket of bread. 'It's life, Lillian. I was married to a man I didn't really love but who sanctioned my life. I had always been an outsider, too. In my family, this town, maybe in this country. I loved a man with a sick wife who was willing to give it all up for me. I couldn't accept the burden of his sacrifice. I had no faith in the idea someone could love me that deeply.'

'But he shot himself.'

Helen's face darkened. 'Yes. He wanted us to start a new family. When I refused to agree to his fantasy about us, he shot himself. And I no longer consider that my fault.'

Lillian jumped to her feet. 'I don't think I should know this,' she said loudly. 'I don't think you want me to know any more!'

Helen put down the bread. 'You made the decision to come here. You said you wanted to know what happened. Your father shot himself because he was a miserable man. An angry man. But he also shot himself so I'd keep you.'

She's my mother, Lillian kept repeating to herself, *no matter what she says or does, she's my mother*.

'It didn't work but he meant to have the last word. And he got it.' Helen's face looked like a mask.

'My God,' Lillian sobbed, 'that's not fair.'

There was a loud knock on the back door and then Steven Woodruff walked in, stomping snow from his feet on to the mat. He looked different from the man in the pictures; thinner and less boyish. 'Hey,' he said.

147

'Are you two having some sort of meaningful confrontation? Should I come back later?'

Helen sighed. 'No. Perfect timing.' She walked over and kissed him. 'This is Lillian, Steven.'

'Hi, Lillian.' Lillian smiled and blew her nose on the paper towel Helen handed her. 'I admire your courage.'

'Thanks. I'm very sorry about your wife.'

Steven nodded. 'Yeah. Life sometimes doesn't give you much to laugh about, does it?'

There was a silence filled by the sound of Helen putting ratatouille in bowls. Lillian thought about her real father. Would *he* have been able to look at her without turning away as if a father admiring his daughter was somehow wrong? Would they have been able to tell each other things without the endless silences, the awkward pauses? Why couldn't Helen have accepted his love? She laughed.

Steven smiled at her. 'A private joke?'

'Well, it's strange to realize you may have inherited something from someone you didn't even know existed.' She looked at Helen. 'Besides alcoholism.'

'I delivered the Montgomery twins last night,' Steven told Helen, hanging up his coat. 'Both over nine pounds. Nathan was drunk as a judge. He kept making Wonder Bread sandwiches with iceberg lettuce and Miracle Whip. Dozens of them. Like an army was going to descend or there was going to be some sort of food shortage. Drinking Jack Daniels and whooping: "Ooeeh! We're having babies!" Grateful Dead music turned up till you went deaf.'

'How's Martha?'

'Just fine. Totally cool and calm. She kept asking me to check on Nathan.'

'You're a midwife?'

'Yup.'

'It's very fashionable not to go to the hospital these days,' Helen said, pouring water into their glasses. 'Why

148

not stay home and have this hunk ski over and deliver your baby?'

Lillian laughed. 'Are you very busy?'

'Christ, yes! Every seventeen-year-old girl in Maine seems to think she's going to be responsible for the Second Coming. They don't understand that a child completely alters reality. The little booties are so cute and they figure they can leave it with Ma, like a cat, if it's too much trouble. I try to explain to them that they won't ever be young again but . . . ' Steven shrugged. 'What do they care? They're young now.'

Lillian glanced at Helen. Her face was blank. She was looking into her bowl as if it contained something fascinating. 'I want to have a baby,' she said.

'That will be nice,' Helen commented. 'Something to do while you decide how to make a living.'

'I can make a living.' Lillian snapped. 'I've always taken care of myself.'

'Your parents had nothing to do with that, I assume,' Helen asked, her tone quiet, yet sharp.

'They never noticed their teenage daughter was a raging alcoholic,' Lillian replied, staring into Helen's eyes. 'They didn't enjoy anything that wasn't part of their own perfect world.'

'Wait until you have a child, Lillian,' Helen said.

'Don't you tell me about the meaning of motherhood,' Lillian snapped, her hands shaking with anger.

'I'm not trying to suggest I didn't fail,' Helen replied, her voice trembling.

Steven laughed. 'You sound like her mother,' he said. Both women stared at him. 'Sorry. I guess this wasn't the time for mother jokes.'

'Not at all,' Helen said. 'It's one of the few species you can hunt every day of the year.'

'I didn't come here as a hunter,' Lillian said. She picked up her coat. 'You did something thirty years ago that you think made sense. I see it as an act of ultimate selfishness. You owe me an explanation.'

'Don't,' Helen said as her daughter went out of the back door. 'Don't go!' She called across the driveway as Lillian ran towards her car without pausing or looking back.

Lillian drove home recognizing what she had done in coming to Maine. Now she had a biological mother who was emotionally frozen and a lover who believed himself one of the world's natural resources, a martyred father who could displace Mr Jordan as the unavailable man in her life and a job as a cocktail waitress in the local gin mill. She looked at her watch and realized it was time for the local radio show that had lately become important to her. It was a call-in programme where Maine residents discussed how they felt about current events. She had become very fond of an ancient man named Ben who was always griping about 'wimmin libbers burning their long johns'. It wasn't much, but it certainly beat listening to New York intellectuals complaining about the theatre.

12

Vincent wrote Lillian a song for Christmas. She had given him a framed painting he'd admired at an art show they'd attended and a badly crocheted scarf in his favourite colours, a T-shirt with a picture of John Lennon on it and a tin of his favourite home-made cookies.

'I wrote you a song,' he said after kissing her for each gift, putting on the scarf and the T-shirt, hanging the picture and eating a cookie.

'I have other things for you,' he said, walking over to the tape machine, 'but this is the big one.'

The words were simple. It was about falling in love with someone you don't really understand. Beginning to understand that person and loving her more. Wondering what she thinks of you although you're pretty sure she loves you too.

'You used my name,' she said when the tape was over.

'It's about you.'

'It could be about someone else.'

'But it isn't,' Vincent kneeled at her feet, putting his arms on her knees.

'Can you play it again?'

'Sure.' He picked up his guitar and sang along with the tape. This time she heard the sadness.

'It's beautiful,' she said after the music ended. 'I don't know what to say. Thank you.'

'I sent a demo of it to my agent and he's including it in the package.'

'The package?'

'The package is how I'm being marketed. You know
. . . the image. And they think the image is sensitive but
totally male.'

She sighed. 'That sure sounds like you, Vincent. The
caring macho man. What's the song called?'

' "Lillian".'

'What? You can't call it that!'

'Why not?'

'Because . . . because people will think it's about me!'

'It is about you.'

'But it shouldn't be.'

'Why not?'

'Because it's not accurate.'

'It's a song!'

'The girl in this song is gentle and girlish and
frightened.'

'Yup.'

'I'm none of those things!'

Vincent put down his guitar. 'I disagree. Anyway, it's
my fucking song!'

'Well, call it something else!'

'Like what?'

'I don't know. Name her after your mother. John
Lennon wrote a song about his mother.'

'Lennon's mother was run over by a bus.'

'So?'

'My mother's fat and sixty and living in a trailer park.'

'What's her name?'

'Trudy.'

'Oh.'

'Look, songs are a composite. Some of this is about you
and some of it's—' Vincent paused.

'About other women?'

'Sure.'

'Then name it after one of them, you vulture!'

'Vulture? Jesus, why are you so goddamned fucked-up?'

'Because I am! You seem to find it inspiring.' Lillian stood up. 'This is too much.'

'What's too much? Have I broken some sort of boyfriend rule? Was it time for me to start acting like a creep?' Vincent went into the kitchen and came out with a beer. 'Why do I choose the only chick on the eastern seaboard who doesn't want a song written about her? I mean, you are weird, Lillian.'

'It's just . . . ' She stopped and ate one of his cookies.

'What?'

'It's so . . . historic. When we stop being together there will be this song about how you once felt about me. This moment in time frozen in eternity.'

'Why do we have to stop seeing each other? We just started.'

'I didn't say that!'

'You implied it! Maybe we'll get married. Maybe you'll have my children.'

Lillian stood up again. 'If we're going to fight,' she said, 'I'm going home. I don't like this talk about children. It's too depressing.'

'I don't fight with anyone. This is like totally alien.'

'I'll bet it is. Passive aggressive types never take responsibility for how they affect other people.'

Vincent put down his beer. 'Stop it. I can't compete with Jung. Not tonight. Not on Christmas Eve. I'll write a sequel, OK? How about: "Now that she's gone" or "Big City Woman". The video can show you on the subway in Brooklyn with me crying over my guitar in Bangor. Would that make you happy? Huh?'

Lillian smiled.

'Let me give you the rest of your presents.' Vincent went into his bedroom and came out with a stack of lavishly wrapped gifts.

The first box contained an antique white nightgown she had noticed hanging in the window of a store in

Stonington. Its bodice was embroidered with insets of lace and pink ribbon.

'I remembered how much you liked it,' he said kissing her.

The second box was smaller. Inside was a turquoise and silver necklace.

'Vincent,' she said, tears filling her eyes, 'what's happening here?'

He picked up his guitar and then put it down. 'Put that stuff on for me, OK?'

She stood in the bathroom staring at her reflection in the mirror on the door. How would she look in a video, she wondered. The models in the ones she'd seen seemed slightly bored or they overacted, tears like raindrops standing in their huge, blank, beautiful eyes. The nightgown dropped over her head and hung on her shoulders smelling faintly of lilacs, clean and sweet. The necklace was lighter than she'd imagined. She brushed her hair and put on some perfume. She sat down on the lowered seat of the toilet and tried to feel happy. She wanted a drink. If she got drunk she would have the courage to call Helen Carter and tell her exactly what sort of monster she was. And Helen would feel responsible for her losing her sobriety. 'You made me drink,' she could tell her. 'Everything bad that's happened to me is your fault.'

Vincent was standing in the centre of the living-room with his shirt off. The only light came from the fire. He looked sad.

'I'm sorry,' she said quietly.

'You're beautiful.'

'These are the nicest presents anyone ever gave me.'

'I wanted to make you happy,' he whispered. She saw she had hurt him.

'It's a wonderful song,' she said. 'I'm just neurotic.'

'Yeah,' he said, 'you sure are. Come here.' Vincent held out his arms.

Lillian dreamed. She dreamed she was climbing a mountain with Thomas Wolfe. They were almost at the top when it began to snow. The storm blinded them and T.W. disappeared. She had put her hand on his collar, but lost her grip when the snow started. She kept hearing him crying for her, but the direction was impossible to follow. She woke up to find Vincent kissing her breasts. She had fallen asleep while he was brushing his teeth.

'I want you,' he said.

She started to get up to insert her diaphragm but he held her down.

'I need—'

'No,' he said. 'Let me take care of everything. Just close your eyes again. Pretend you never woke up.'

His lips covered every inch of her body until she thought she'd go mad with wanting him. Her thighs opened and he put his fingers inside her, kissing from her knees to her upper thigh, his palm stroking her until she began to buck, to moan and shake.

'Relax,' he whispered. 'This should last a long time.' He turned her over and licked the length of her spine, along her inner thigh, each foot, massaging the heels and each toe. He took her own hand and put it between her legs.

'I'm coming back,' he said. 'Keep yourself happy.'

His hands seemed to touch her everywhere. Lillian fell into some sort of a dream. Many men were fucking her and she was insatiable, completely without shame, open to all of them. She heard nothing but encouragement, compliments, approbation. There was no parental condemnation or image of herself as some sort of whore. She was very good and she was getting fucked.

Vincent turned her back over and spread her legs wide apart. He put his mouth on her and she pressed his head hard so that he was deep inside. She began to come over and over again, the waves were never quite finished before the next began. On the third or fourth she watched him put on a condom and then he lifted her up, putting her legs around his waist and he thrust himself into her. It went on and on, both of them making noises, moaning and growling and he was her lover, he told her that he loved her, he said he would always want her and she thought her head was going to explode. No drug had ever had that effect.

She woke up to the sound of Vincent practising scales in the shower. His voice was very strong, rich and deep. Rock lyrics rarely called for his using the full range of his voice. When he came out, he was already dressed. She felt unexpectedly disappointed. Abandoned.

'Hey, sleeping beauty,' he said, jumping on the bed to kiss her.

'Why are you dressed?' she asked him, tugging at his shirt.

'Rehearsal, babe.'

'Oh.' Lillian attempted to smile.

'What are you doing today?'

'I'm not sure.'

Vincent took her hand. 'You want to call your parents?'

'My parents live in New Jersey,' she said sharply.

'So what? I don't care if you use my phone.'

'No,' Lillian said, climbing out of bed. 'Will you be gone if I take a shower?'

'No. I'll wait. Hey, Merry Christmas, angel.'

'Umm.' Lillian walked towards the bathroom.

'You want some breakfast?'

'No.' She began to cry.

'What's the matter now?' Vincent said as he took her into his arms.

'I don't know,' Lillian sobbed.

'Do you hate Christmas?' He sat down on the edge of the bed and pulled her onto his lap. 'Lots of people hate Christmas. What did you do last year?'

'On Christmas Eve Matthew snorted cocaine and gave me a leather corset and then we went to a party at a club and he tried to pick up the bartender who turned out to be a transvestite. The next morning we went to my house and he never took off his sunglasses and Edward called him Eurotrash and my mother decided he was horrible.'

'She was right.'

'How do you know?'

'Because he treated you badly. I think you're just too happy.'

'Am I happy?'

'What else? You just spent a night of bliss with an about-to-be-incredibly-famous rock star. And now he's making you breakfast.'

She jabbed him in the ribs and slammed the bathroom door in his face while he went downstairs singing 'Deck the Halls'.

'What happened to that corset?' Vincent asked her while he was heating the waffle iron.

'I'd never wear it!' Lillian said. 'It was black leather and covered with studs.'

'I was thinking about me,' Vincent replied, putting a plate of waffles down on the table. 'I need something to go with my red jodhpurs.'

'I'm calling my mother,' Lillian said, going into the living-room, clutching a warm waffle. 'This is not an appropriate discussion for Christmas morning.'

13

When she got home, there was a note from Mildred saying that the vet had called to say T.W. was well enough to leave the animal hospital.

With his hair shaved in front, he looked like a much smaller dog with a punk haircut. When she walked into the vet's office, T.W. wagged his tail so hard his whole body shook. She got down on her knees to hug him.

'You're my dog,' she whispered into his ear. 'I love you more than anything in the world. I slept with Vincent,' she told him on the way home. 'He's a teen-idol dolt.'

When they walked into the house he rushed around smelling all his favourite toys. She made him an especially nice dinner and let him watch an old episode of *Lost in Space* so that he could bark at the robot.

Her parents called at eleven and said Edward was planning to visit her.

'He's still stuck on the set,' her mother said. 'They don't seem to know how to end the movie.'

'When the movie ends, the investors have to be paid off,' her father suggested, 'Eddie said there's no money. Did you have a nice Christmas?' he went on, talking to her directly for once. 'Did you sing carols?'

'Yup.' It didn't matter if she lied to her father. He was easily deceived.

'"God rest ye Merry Gentlemen?"'

'Uh huh.'

'"Silent Night."'

'Of course.'

'"Little Town of Bethlehem."'

It was a game they had played since Lillian was little.

'Lillian Town of Bethlehem, you mean? Daddy?'

'Yes sweetie?'

'I found her.'

'Helen Carter?'

'Yes.'

'Is everything all right?'

'I don't know. I found her speaking at an AA meeting. Her life turned out to be tragic. She had an older child that drowned last year. She gave me up and then her other child died. And my real father's dead.'

'I know, honey.'

'He killed himself because of me.' She waited for her father to say something. They almost never talked to one another like this. Why had her mother hung up? 'She said he was very angry about not being able to marry her.'

'You can't wonder what his reasons were, Lillian. People don't tell the truth if they're afraid other people won't accept it. He was probably desperate and angry and he couldn't see a way out.'

As she listened to her father she heard something else in his voice. Empathy and understanding.

'Are you unhappy sometimes, Dad?'

'No.' He cleared his throat. 'You make us very proud.'

That's not what I meant. She wanted to scream: *Tell me how you feel.* Instead she murmured, 'Thank you.'

'Would you like to come back home, Lillian?'

'I'm not sure what I want to do.'

'Bowser all healed?'

'Yes.'

'Good. I like that dog. And I love my daughter.'

'I'm glad you're my father,' Lillian whispered. 'You're good at it.'

'Bye, darling.' He hung up. As she was about to drop the receiver, she heard a second click. Her mother.

'Mother?' she screamed. The phone was silent and then the signal which indicated a disconnection came on. How many times had she tried to push aside everything that obstructed her view of her father? How long had she been running after him attempting to catch hold of his hand, to pull him away from the edge of something terrible? How long had she felt like the parent, the one responsible for taking care of everyone, failing miserably, succeeding only in creating chaos?

Falling asleep, she heard T.W.'s regular breathing and realized how much she had missed his company. She didn't want to go home. It had become something else. She was in some sort of corridor and had to keep moving.

'So, was Santa good to you?' Bill was wearing a bright-red tie covered with embroidered holly. It was tacky enough to be chic.

'Powerful tie,' she said. 'You could raid a corporation wearing that.'

'Hey,' Bill said, 'I don't need to raid anything. I'm perfectly incorporated.'

'Are we still selling Heineken for one dollar forty-five?'

'Shit! Why do I have to deal with mundane details?'

'You're the boss.'

'Umm. Whattya think?'

'Raise it to one dollar seventy-five. People keep leaving me fifty-five cents instead of a dollar.'

'You get tips?' Bill raised his eyebrows.

'Can I have tomorrow night off?'

'Why?'

'I have plans.'

'What sort of plans?'

Lillian sighed. 'I don't have to reveal my personal life to you.'

'What's so personal about dinner with Vinnie's parents?'

'How did you know that?'

'It's in the gossip section of the *Ceylon Daily News*. "New York Mystery Woman Eats at Home of Rock Idol". Did you like the song?'

'What song?'

'Your song. "Lillian".'

'He told you about that?'

'Sure. There was a bit in there about you . . . I mean the woman being kind of . . . hmm.' Bill stopped. 'Well, that's not important. I told him to take it out. I'm like Vincent's priest. How do you think you two ever got together?'

'Kind of what?'

'You two got together because I told him you were the best thing that ever walked into this place.' Bill shrugged. 'Of course, you don't get much quality around here.'

Lillian threw a lime at him. 'Oh, be quiet!'

'His folks are born-again Christians.'

'I know.'

'They worship Elvis, too.'

'I realize that.'

'They have very strange ideas.'

Lillian walked into the kitchen. She didn't want to hear any more details about Vincent's parents. She'd already been warned by Mildred, and by Steve Woodruff who had called to invite her on a hike with him. She wasn't used to living in such a small town. In New York you only met your neighbours during disasters like fires or floods. As soon as possible, you disappeared back into your apartment and double-bolted the door. People here were obvious about their interest in your personal life. She kept wondering what had happened to the famous Maine reserve.

'Oh, we save that for real strangers,' Vincent said when she asked him about it. 'You're Helen's kin and you've hooked up with a local legend. Now you're part of the community. People can stab you in the back.'

'Yippie ay yeah!'

Vincent's parents sounded like a problem. They *were* born-again Christians, lived in a trailer park, were very fat and had never finished high school. Helen had supplied most of this information. 'Trudy was three years behind me in school. You never saw her without the Bible and a chocolate bar. What I can't fathom,' she continued, putting down her crochet hook, 'is how those two weirdos produced such a miracle.'

'A miracle?'

'Sure,' Helen nodded. 'You should have seen Vincent when he was a little boy. An Eagle Scout. First in all his classes. A soloist in the choir and a real kid. Not spoiled at all. He used to come over here and hang around Emily and we'd discuss the war in Vietnam. He always knew what was going on and was full of opinions.'

Lillian wasn't sure she wanted this picture of Vincent's boyhood. It would have been more helpful to hear he was some kind of obnoxious juvenile creep who was mean to old ladies and tortured animals.

This was the second time she had seen Helen since their lunch. On the day after Christmas she had come over with a sweater she had knitted for Lillian, and a box of fudge. They hadn't fallen into one another's arms but they managed to agree not to fight over whether or not the adoption had been necessary. Then Vincent had invited her to a family dinner and she had called Helen asking for advice. She was confused about meeting his parents. It was unlikely there was a single thing about her of which they would approve. She worked in a bar; she was divorced; she had premarital sex and was contemplating single motherhood. And she didn't like Elvis.

'They'll love you,' Vincent said as she raised these points. 'Don't worry.' He put down his guitar. 'You're kidding about Elvis, right?'

She worried. She lay awake until she fell asleep and dreamed of saying: 'Hello, I'm Lillian. An alcoholic, atheist, feminist neurotic.'

'You look great.' Vincent was standing on her steps dressed in a button-down shirt, corduroy pants and a sports jacket.

She had borrowed a proper winter coat from Mildred, fearing her leather jacket would not convey the correct attitude. A long, black wool skirt, tights, flat-heeled pumps and a pink sweater completed her outfit. 'Are you sure this is OK?' she asked him anxiously.

'Come on. Mom wears polyester pantsuits and I don't know where my father finds his clothes. They just seem to appear on his body.'

Lillian understood what Helen meant when she called Vincent a 'miracle'. There was something special and completely graceful about him, while his parents reminded her of prehistoric creatures trapped in clay. The trailer was quite large, mounted on a concrete foundation. All the furniture was slip-covered with plastic except for one large Easy-boy recliner which belonged to Vincent's father.

'Nice to meet you, Lillian,' Mrs Delacroce said, shaking her hand limply without making eye contact. His father mumbled something and offered her a seat on his crushed-velvet chair. She sat on the plastic sofa. They were very shy. Lillian noticed whenever Vincent opened his mouth they leaned forward slightly, their eyes growing brighter and their large bodies filling with energy. He was the focus of all their attention. And he accepted their worship without any self-consciousness. Lillian would not have been surprised if his mother had suddenly kneeled down and started washing his feet. It made her feel sick.

'Who do you think you are?' she whispered to him as Mrs Delacroce brought him a second beer and Mr Delacroce searched the cupboards for his favourite mixed nuts. 'The infant Jesus?'

Vincent looked hurt. 'It's not my fault,' he whispered.

When his mother urged a third helping of roast beef on him, he refused. Instead he took the platter away from her and gave her a big hug. Lillian almost started crying. She couldn't remember ever having that sort of spontaneous affection for her parents. She stopped being nervous. She felt invisible. After the dishes were cleared, she followed Mrs Delacroce into the kitchen and picked up a towel.

'So,' Vincent's mother said, handing her a wet plate, 'I understand you're a writer?'

'Well, I haven't really begun. I'm still deciding what to write.'

'You read the Bible?' Mrs Delacroce was holding a glass, smiling, her eyes blank.

Lillian thought hard. She'd read the Old Testament for a Milton course in college. 'Yes.'

'You can't go wrong then.' Vincent's mother opened a cupboard door. 'Split a Twinkie?'

'Sure.'

When they rose to go, Vincent's mother presented Lillian with a Bible. 'Take care of my boy,' she whispered into Lillian's ear.

'Why did you tell your mother that I'm a writer?'

'Aren't you?'

'I don't know.'

'I looked at that short story you put on my computer. It was powerful, Lillian. I can't write like that.'

'Thank you.'

'You know Helen is the features editor of the *Ceylon Times*. You should see if you could do something for her.'

'Maybe. Did your parents like me?'

'They sure did. My dad said you were quite a girl. That's high praise.'

Lillian snuggled up under Vincent's arm. The truck's headlights illuminated the road. It was snowing again.

'They look at you and their eyes glow like you were some sort of energy source.'

'No shit,' Vincent said grimly. 'I feel like the fucking eternal flame around them.'

'Was it always that way?'

'Yup.' Vincent turned into her driveway. 'My mom used to bring my lunch to school at noon. Everything just cooked. Everybody else got bologna on Wonder Bread.'

'Why didn't you ask her to stop?'

'It made her happy.'

Lillian snorted. 'Well,' she said, 'I wish it were that simple.'

'Maybe it is,' Vincent said, pinching her cheek lightly. 'Why don't you try it for a while?'

'Why don't you?'

'Because you hate people being nice to you.'

When they drove up to her door, she wanted to ask him in but as he leaned over to kiss her he said: 'Sweetness, I gotta be up at seven tomorrow to work construction. I need to write some stuff tonight, OK?'

'Oh. Sure.' She ducked under his arm and opened the car door. 'I'll just read the Bible and practise worshipping your picture.'

He grabbed her arm. 'Hey,' he said quietly, 'I really liked introducing you to my parents.'

'Thanks,' she answered shortly. She shut the door and stepped into a pile of newly ploughed snow. As she stood knee-high in the whiteness, her feet gradually getting soaked, tears filled her eyes. Something in her chest hurt. She felt sick and dizzy. She needed to tell Vincent who Helen really was. Her reason for waiting had never been fully realized and now everything appeared very complicated.

'I love you,' she heard herself saying into the still night. 'Oh God, Vincent, I love you!' A vision of herself staring at him with the same hungry look as his mother appeared. She saw herself eating dozens of Twinkies while he made teenage women writhe in passion. And she saw herself bringing him hot meals, accepting his affectionate pats on the head, staring up at him with the same expression as Thomas Wolfe. He had written her a song and she had told him it was too much. She held herself in the cold and thought about going home. But was New York still home? As she went into the house, T.W. met her at the door. She dropped to her knees and buried her face in his warm fur.

'I love Vincent,' she told him, forgetting she had once promised the dog her exclusive affection. At the sound of Vincent's name, T.W. began to wag his tail and wiggle his rear end. The phone rang.

'Lil?' It was him.

'Yes?'

'I forgot to tell you sweet dreams.'

'That's OK.'

'Do you think I'm spoiled?'

'Uh . . . Possibly.'

'So, straighten me out.'

'Vincent.'

'Yeah?'

'I—' Lillian stopped. She was still wearing her coat in the dark. Her feet were freezing. The words stuck in her throat.

'What is it, babe?'

She wished he'd stop calling her that. 'I like your parents.'

'They liked you. Good night, darling.'

'Night.'

Lillian sat on the side of her bed and thought about how little she knew about seeing things through. Somehow disaster had usually struck, choices were obliterated, decisions were made by others on whom unhappiness or dissatisfaction could be blamed. But this time things were different. She'd decided to find her real mother and whatever the results of that action, no-one else could be held responsible. The feeling she had was one of extreme discomfort. Lying back on her bed, she rested her head on T.W.'s flank. The skylight displayed a starless patch of sky while the dog sighed and shifted in his sleep.

14

'Why don't you write something. If it's suitable, I'll see if I can fit it in.'

Lillian could tell Helen wasn't enthusiastic about the idea of hiring her as a freelance reporter. She wished she'd never brought the subject up. 'I'm actually pretty good,' she replied defensively. 'I wrote all the ad copy for the cosmetics department at Bloomingdale's.'

'Good,' Helen said. 'Let's talk after you write the article.'

Lillian hung up the phone and hit the wall with her fist. Ever since the night of the dinner with Vincent's parents, she had been thinking about New York. She called Lizbeth and left a message on her machine. Vincent had a gig on New Year's Eve and Lillian declined his invitation to go. It was a huge private party in Boston with many important music-industry contacts expected to show up. She didn't feel like trying to amuse herself in a room full of strangers. Anyway, Mildred was giving a small dinner party.

Helen was invited but she had the flu and called to say she was staying in bed. She invited Lillian to dinner the following week. At midnight Lillian found herself dancing with Steven Woodruff. He had come to the party alone and asked her to dance several times.

'May I?' he asked, as the bells began to ring, leaning over to kiss her. Lillian nodded and raised her lips expecting a brotherly peck. Steven pulled her hard against him, bending her back from the waist, his mouth pressing against her with such force she opened her lips and Steven's tongue went deep inside her mouth, his hands holding her hips so that their bodies were tightly joined. She tasted the brandy on his breath and after a moment during which she found herself kissing him back with equal intensity, she broke away, looking around the room quickly to be sure no-one had been watching them.

'I want you,' Steven whispered, grabbing her hand and kissing her knuckles.

'No you don't,' Lillian said primly. 'Everyone feels needy on New Year's Eve.'

'I don't feel needy,' Steven said, beginning to nibble on the inside of her wrist. 'I feel great!'

'Can I write an article about you?' Lillian asked, snatching back her hand, moving so there was a foot of space between them.

Steven laughed. 'What for?' he asked.

'The *Ceylon News*. A lifestyle article about what you do. Your midwifery.'

'For Helen?'

'She suggested I do something on spec.'

'How are you two doing?'

'What do you mean?'

'I mean, the natural mother thing. Are you glad you found her?'

'Yes. I mean . . . of course. Why?'

'Why don't you write about that?'

'Helen and me? I couldn't.'

'Why not?'

'I don't have any distance. It's happening now. I don't have an idea of what really matters . . . ' She looked at him. He was shaking his head.

'It's pretty weird. Of course, everything's pretty weird. Emily and all.'

'I'm so sorry.' She noticed for the first time how deep the circles were under his eyes.

'Yeah. Well, we had our problems. Emily and I. Yes. Well, sure.'

'Sure what?'

'You can write me up. You want to come on a delivery?'

'I guess so.'

'You might have to help.' Steven sat down on the steps.

'I'll boil water.' He reached up and pulled her down next to him.

'I'm going to bed,' she said.

She quickly found Mildred in the kitchen and wished her a Happy New Year. As she mounted the stairs to her apartment, she heard someone following her.

'Can I have some tea, Lillian?' He looked miserable. The holidays had to be hard on a person with a dead wife.

'OK.'

When they were sitting at her table, the teapot between them, Steven put down his cup and looked at her.

'What the hell are you doing here?' he asked.

'I came to find Helen.'

'You found her. Why do you stay?'

'That wasn't enough.'

'What about Vincent?'

'What about him?'

'Did you come to find him, too?'

'I don't know. What do you mean?'

'Isn't that every fucked-over woman's dream?' Steven asked, watching her over the rim of his mug. 'To find a truly good man?'

'Why do you assume I've been fucked over?'

'Haven't you?'

'Well, yes. But I don't understand why you just assume it's true.'

'That's all women talk about these days. Don't you want to find a truly good man?'

'Maybe.'

'Emily thought that was what she wanted. When I first met her she was all tear-stained and shaken by the big bad world. Law school. Screwing professors. Married men. Scum.'

'Were you the good man?'

Steven laughed. 'Of course.'

'Are you still?'

'You tell me.'

'I don't know you that well.'

'Hazard a guess.'

'I think you've had too much brandy.'

'Don't be so fucking evasive. Lillian.'

'Yes.'

He shook his head. 'Wrong. I lied to her. It's easy to lie to women. They're such eternal optimists. If a man wants to fuck you, he'll tell you anything you want to hear.'

'You think Vincent's a liar?' She wished he would stop staring at her.

'You tell me, babe. Is Mr Rock-and-Roll some kind of twentieth-century saint?'

'No.'

'Ma and Pa Kettle think so.'

'What about Emily?'

'Emily? She was a spoiled brat. Helen saw the sun rising behind her big blue eyes. Nothing like a reformed drunk to destroy a kid. Helen's guilt was Emily's reward. She was such a manipulator.'

'Why did you marry her?'

'I loved her. When the accident happened we were filing for divorce. I mean, discussing it.'

Steven kept staring at her. She didn't know what to say. Her fantasy about Steven and Emily was now proven completely false. The photograph of the two of them had made her think they worshipped each other. She had imagined Emily as perfect: compassionate, brilliant, kind.

She had a brief vision of Vincent leaning off the stage to kiss a beautiful, thin blonde. Steven leaned forward and put his hand on her cheek.

'You remind me of her.'

'Emily?'

'Yes. The way your face moves when you speak. But you have so much more heart.' He moved around the other side of the table, bending to kiss her neck. She felt his hands go down the front of her dress, his hands holding her breasts. She let him pull her to her feet, turn her around, his hands pushing the dress down her shoulders so she was naked to the waist. His lips touched each nipple, softly. She looked down at his head and thought about Vincent. There is ice in my veins, she said to herself, nothing but ice. The phone had rung several times before she pulled away.

'Yes?'

'Hey! Is this my little sister?' It was Edward. She pulled her dress back up, turning away from Steven.

'Hi! Happy New Year.'

'You too, sweet thing. How are you doing?'

'OK.' She heard Steven pick up his cup and put it in the sink. When he picked up his coat, she said, 'Hold on a sec, Eddie.' Then, with her hand over the receiver, 'It's my brother.'

'I understand. So, you still want to come on a delivery?'

'Yes.'

'I may have one early this week. I'd just have to call or come get you.'

'That would be fine.'

'Happy New Year.'

'You too.' Steven closed the door quietly behind him.

'Sorry, Edward.'

'No sweat. You want I should call back?'

'No. He's gone.'

'New boyfriend?'

'No. He's Helen's son-in-law. The daughter was killed in a sailing accident.'

'Your half-sister is dead? Jesus. So things are pretty grim?'

'Not really. Complicated.'

'The fucking movie's finally wrapped.'

'Is it good?'

'Are you kidding? Everybody's in rehab. The director, the first camera man, two of the stars . . . forget it!'

'I'm sorry.'

'Hey! God grant me the serenity . . . you know the rest. I thought I'd come visit you.'

'That would be great!'

'For two weeks?'

'You better bring a lot of warm clothes!'

'I was packing my Bermudas!'

'There's not much to do here.'

'I just want to see you.'

'I'm fine.'

'You sound fine. Going to meetings?'

'Yes.' Edward's interest in her meeting schedule irked her. It was as if he were always asking her how much she weighed.

'I'll leave on Thursday so you should expect me some time on Friday.'

'There's a key in the stump to the right of the door if neither of us is here. Just go straight up the stairs to the second apartment.'

'It's a wrap! Bye, babe!'

'Bye.'

She dreamed she was in a white storm. There were others wandering around, but they were all blinded by the snow and the light. She could hear first her father and then Vincent calling but there was nothing she could do. Then she saw two people standing a few feet apart. Steven and

173

Emily. Emily was hunched over, crying. Emily looked exactly like Lillian. Helen was somewhere in the background. Steven was punishing Emily. He held something in his hand, a stuffed animal, and Emily kept reaching for it and Steven kept refusing to let it go. He didn't hold it properly because the animal changed into a baby and Emily was down on her knees and Steven held the child high in the air as if he would drop it and then, of course, the baby would die. Because Emily/Lillian was a bad mother.

The phone was ringing. Her clock said it was seven a.m.

'Hey.' It was Vincent.

'Hi.'

'Sorry to wake you up.'

'That's OK.'

'I just wanted to wish my girl Happy New Year.'

'Am I your girl, Vincent?'

'You better believe it.'

'How was the party?'

'We just got back. I met a lot of important dudes. The "Lillian" cut's getting really hyped in LA. You want to come over and cook some spaghetti later?'

'Yes. Vincent—'

'Yeah?'

'I missed you last night.'

'Who'd you kiss at midnight?'

'Steven.'

'That was meant to be a rhetorical question. That snake!'

'Who'd you kiss?'

'Our manager's wife. On the cheek.' She could tell he was speaking the truth.

'You're a better kisser.'

'See you later?'

'Yes.'

* * *

When she told Helen her idea for the article, she sounded surprised.

'A piece on Steven? Why?'

'I thought people would be fascinated with the story of a male midwife. How he relates to his patients. The delivery . . . ' Her voice dwindled away under Helen's silence.

'Maybe in New York,' she said sharply.

'I think in Maine, too. It isn't common at all. He's the only one in the state.' Lillian had already done some research in the public library.

'So you'll just interview him?'

'No. I thought I'd go on a call. Cover a delivery.'

'Well,' Helen said grudgingly, 'that could be interesting. Of course, one can't tell until reading it.'

'Of course. Helen, my brother Edward's coming to visit.'

'You must bring him to dinner.'

'I'd really like that.'

'I heard your visit with Vincent's parents was a resounding success.' Helen's voice dropped. 'Did you tell Trudy you were born-again?'

She had stopped wondering how news travelled in Ceylon. 'Of course not. She just entrusted me with the care, if not the feeding, of the Messiah.'

'Now, now . . . '

Lillian hung up the phone with the sense that her relationship with Helen Carter was improving. Talking to Helen she felt like an adult, a feeling she seldom experienced with her own parents. She wondered if Helen had any idea of the state of Emily's marriage. With a slight jolt, she realized she was rather pleased to hear about Emily's defects. The brilliant, dead, beloved, beautiful Emily was a bitch.

15

'What are you doing here?'

'Get up.' Steven's face was an inch away from her own. She looked up at the skylight and saw that the glass was black.

'It's night.'

'It's three o'clock in the morning. Sandy Truitt's in labour.'

'Oh.' Lillian jumped out of bed before she realized she was wearing nothing but one of Vincent's old Iron Maiden T-shirts. She didn't like sleeping in underwear.

'Turn around,' she snapped at Steven who was standing in the middle of her room wearing a quilted parka over his jeans.

'I'm a doctor,' he said, sitting down in a chair. 'Women's bodies mean nothing to me.'

Lillian snorted. She went into her closet and found some thermal underwear and, pulling her jeans over it, she quickly took off the T-shirt and put on two long-sleeved undershirts followed by a flannel shirt and a sweater. When she came out, Steven was standing by the door holding her boots. As she put on her socks he bent down and put each boot on, lacing them up quickly.

'Thank you, Doctor,' Lillian said.

'Let's go,' Steven answered gruffly, pulling her to her feet. 'It took ages to wake you up.'

'How long were you here?'

'Twenty minutes.'

'How did you get in?'

'There's a key under the porch.' Steven handed her his coat. 'You sleep well.'

She glared at him. 'What's that supposed to mean?'

'You don't drool.'

The truck had been left running. It was so cold the air stung her cheeks. As she went down the steps she almost slipped and Steven caught her, pulling her into his arms.

'Steady,' he said. 'My assistant can't break her leg on the way to a delivery.'

Her sleepiness had been shocked out of her. 'I'm not your assistant,' she replied, gently removing his hands from her waist. 'I'm an impartial observer.'

'No-one's impartial at a birth,' he told her as they pulled on to the deserted road. 'That's where you discover what sort of human being you really are.'

Lillian put her head back and closed her eyes. Steven switched on the tape deck and Mozart played. The motion of the truck lulled her slowly back to sleep.

'There's coffee in the thermos.' She poured them both a strong, milky cup. Steven lit a cigarette. In the glare of the headlights she saw a deer gallop across a snow-covered field.

'Nervous?' Steven was looking at her closely.

'A bit. Sorry.'

'Hey, I'm the scared one.'

'But you're the midwife.'

'That's why I'm scared.'

The Truitts lived in a small green framehouse at the end of a long driveway lined with the rusting shells of several American cars. Steven knocked at the door but opened it without waiting for an answer. There was a man sitting in a Lazy-Boy recliner, a pair of stereo headphones clamped over his ears, a bottle of beer between his legs. The room was draped with drying laundry but otherwise was quite clean. The television was on and

Annie Lennox, wearing black leather, was singing a song to a bored-looking cheetah. They both heard a groan from upstairs.

'I'm going to get started,' Steven said, handing Lillian his coat. 'Tell Sandy I'm here, introduce yourself and bring the coffee up.' Lillian nodded. 'How do you feel?'

'Weird. Excited. Is Sandy her husband?'

Steven laughed. 'Uh huh. Being supportive in Maine means you cancel poker night.' He gave her a quick hug and went upstairs with his bag. After Lillian had hung up their coats, she waited for Sandy Truitt to indicate he was aware that the midwife had arrived. His eyes stayed closed. He was playing air guitar to silent chords. Lillian began to fold the laundry. There was a pile on the couch when she realized Sandy had opened his eyes.

'Hi,' she said. 'I'm that friend of Steven's who's writing the article.' Sandy nodded. He had his hair pulled back in a long ponytail. He looked younger than she'd expected.

'My wife's having a baby,' he said after a minute. 'You want a beer?'

'Oh, no. We brought some coffee. Actually, I think I'll go upstairs.'

Sandy shrugged. He put his earphones back on and closed his eyes. As Lillian walked up the steps she heard Steven telling Sally Truitt a terrible joke. The punchline coincided with her need to groan.

'Hey,' he was saying, as Lillian opened the door, 'I can't help it if people tell me cruddy jokes.'

The lights were low and there were several candles lit on the bureau. There was a nice smell of lilacs and Steven had set up a portable CD player which was playing New Age meditation music. Sally Truitt looked tired but surprisingly serene.

'Hi, Lillian,' Sally said, 'you want to interview me?'

Lillian laughed. 'The camera crew's outside.'

'Where's the reporter who wants to hear about what a bastard I'm married to?' Sally gasped between contractions. Lillian moved to hold her hand. 'You want to hear about my lousy life so far?' Sally asked through clenched teeth.

Sandy Truitt appeared in the doorway, a bottle of beer in his hand, his Walkman earphones around his neck.

'Everything all right?' he asked vaguely, looking at Lillian.

'You fucking creep,' the future mother of his child screamed. 'You selfish, cowardly bastard!'

Lillian watched as Sally's stomach began to contract. She moved to the end of the bed and saw that the child's head was visible.

'Oh my God,' she said.

'You ever see anything get born?' Sally Truitt gasped.

'Just kittens,' Lillian murmured.

'Kittens are nice,' Sally screamed.

'I hate cats,' Steven said. 'Bear down, Sally.'

There was a great deal of blood. Sally's face was contorted with pain. The child seemed reluctant to move. Lillian felt there was something she should do, but Steven and Sally weren't asking for help. She walked to where Sally's head rested on the pillow and finding a damp washcloth in the basin by the bed, she wiped Sally's forehead.

'That feels wonderful,' Sally gasped. Lillian held her hand. Sally's fingers seemed to dig inches into her flesh.

Steven had his hands ready for the baby.

'Push down Sally,' he said. 'Come on!'

Lillian watched the baby slide out of its mother's body. It still seemed reluctant to leave. Sally's husband sat down in the armchair and took a swig of his beer. When the afterbirth arrived, he left the room again. The baby boy was wrapped in a soft white cloth and placed on Sally's chest. They both seemed quite happy just to lie there.

Lillian took a deep breath and realized the reason she felt ready to pass out was simply a complete lack of oxygen.

It was full morning when they walked out of the house. Lillian felt intoxicated. She had witnessed something indescribable. On her pad she had written down several things.

1. Mother in divine isolation
2. Husband as scumbag
3. Cry of life
4. Blood
5. Steven's hands

The rest was indecipherable.

'I don't know how I'll write this article,' Lillian said on the way back, shutting her eyes.

'Just tell what happened.'

'Umm. I'm not sure if I could do it justice.' She fell asleep for a few minutes. When she opened her eyes they were pulling into a strange driveway.

'Where are we?'

'My house.'

'I'm—'

'You need breakfast. I need breakfast. You need more information for your article.'

He got out of the truck and left her sitting, dazed still with sleep. After a minute, she followed him inside.

Steven lived in a small wooden farmhouse, painted white with black shutters. The hall floors were stripped and polished. Along the wall hung photographs. Many of the pictures were the same ones that Helen had. A tribute to Emily. Lillian stared at her half-sister and wondered what it would have been like to meet her. They might have hated each other. Everything would have been more complicated. She could hear coffee being ground. Steven was standing in the middle of a large, light-filled kitchen. The walls were lined with spices, jars of preserved fruit and chutney. There was an arsenal of expensive state-of-the-art kitchen equipment.

'You cook?'

'Emily did.'

'Oh.'

'I'm not a fan of the food processor. Everything looks and tastes like coleslaw.'

She was still wearing her coat, scarf and mittens. The kitchen wasn't very warm.

'Why don't you get undressed?' Steven asked.

'What?'

'Take your coat off.'

Lillian sat with her belongings piled in her lap. When Steven put down the cup of coffee, he removed them.

'I make you nervous, don't I?'

'Yes.'

'Why?'

'You kissed me on New Year's Eve.'

'I'd kiss anyone. I'd kiss Mildred or your mother.' He paused and then pointed the knife he was holding at her. 'I also felt your tits.'

'Right.' Lillian pulled a cookbook off the shelf. It was called: *Cooking for Crowds*.

'You let me.'

'I wasn't quite conscious.'

He laughed. With his head thrown back, Lillian noticed how white the skin of his throat was compared with that on his face. His hair was thick and full of highlights.

'Vincent—'

'I know about Vincent.'

'No you don't.'

'Of course I do. Vincent's my buddy. He's a great kid.'

'I love Vincent, I think.'

'Not possible.'

'Why not?'

'He's beneath you.'

'No he isn't.'

'No-one loves Vincent like Vincent loves Vincent.'

'OK, his ego's a bit . . . '

'Enormous? Let me tell you something. What that man expects from a woman is his mother's devotion in the body of a lingerie model with a brain the size of a spring pea. Trust me.'

Lillian stood up. 'I don't trust you. I'm not letting this happen again.'

'What?'

'This.' She waved her arm around indicating the entire room.

'My kitchen?'

'No. That's just a . . . metaphor or something. Men like you. I'm tired of letting things like this happen. You aren't going to do anything for me.'

'What are you talking about?'

'You just want to fuck me because I'm Vincent's girlfriend. Why don't you just hit him and leave me out of it?'

'Are you his girlfriend?'

'Yes.'

'His only one?'

'I don't know. It doesn't matter.'

'Have you told Vincent who Helen is yet?'

Lillian started. She wondered how Steven knew that Vincent still thought Helen was a distant relative. 'No.'

'I didn't tell him,' Steven said, watching her closely. 'It's just an odd thing not to tell someone you claim to love.'

'There hasn't been time.'

'Don't you think he loves you?'

'Why should he?'

'Don't underestimate your own power.'

'I'm not. I could sleep with you but I don't want to.'
'Are you sure?'
'Take me home.'
'Fine.'

They drove back to Lillian's house in silence. Steven didn't seem angry nor did he fail to offer her more information for her article. 'Don't give up on this idea because of me,' he said kindly. 'I'll still do an interview.'

'I'll call you if I need more information.'

Thomas Wolfe ran to the door, his tongue hanging from his mouth. She patted him, hooked on the leash and took him across the yard to the wood trail. Unhooking the leash, she watched as a flock of Canadian geese skimmed across the frozen pond. It was still better to have come, she thought. She had never felt so serene even with all the turmoil around her. When the baby had blinked in the light and Sally had reached out her arms, the simplicity of nature had seemed absolute. They walked the entire circumference of the pond in an hour. At first Thomas Wolfe kept trotting back, his gait awkward because of his injured paw. When he realized they weren't turning back, he went forward, barking fiercely at imaginary foes and making feeble attempts at catching squirrels. When he was far enough ahead, there was nothing but silence broken by the clear creak of the branches, her footsteps and the sound of the wind blowing across the ice.

It was only when she sat down that she realized how deep the ache in her chest was. She breathed deeply, the air's coldness a sort of pleasure in her lungs. She had been thinking about her dead father. He had never seen her after she was born. Did anyone come to the hospital to look at her while she lay in the cot? Helen had signed the adoption papers and gone home. How long was it before the Jordans came to pick her up and kiss her? How many days passed before she was aware of human love? Was this the reason for her lack of faith in Vincent? It was wrong not to have told him the true nature of her relationship to Helen Carter. But everything seemed so complicated. And her natural father was always standing a bit too far away for her to see the expression on his face. She was always guessing, hoping he was smiling. And hoping she had done something to make him feel the world wasn't such a bad place, like looking at him when he'd knocked on the nursery glass and making him think: *There she is. My perfect baby daughter*. 'Daddy,' she muttered to herself as she walked on. 'Daddy-daddy-daddy-daddy.'

16

She interviewed Steven Woodruff over the phone. She asked him about his education, his previous jobs, his medical training and his belief that all medical services should be provided free to people with the government picking up the bill. He felt doctors should be educated for free and not expect to become wealthy.

The article took nearly a week to write. Mildred lent her an old but excellent electric typewriter and she delivered a copy to Helen three days before the suggested deadline. It didn't seem possible to impress Helen with her talent so Lillian thought promptness would at least make a positive statement. There was no immediate answer to her knock so she'd slipped the article under the door. When she got home after stopping at the grocery store, the phone was ringing.

'Hello?'

'Lillian?' It was Helen.

'Yup.' Lillian clutched the top of the table for support. She steeled herself for being told the article was terrible. She tried to think of some sort of witty response to whatever criticism Helen would voice. Why had she done this? It was going to ruin everything.

'This is very, very good.'

'It is?'

'Don't sound so shocked! You told me you were good.'

'I didn't mean it.'

'Well, surprise! I think the whole thing is quite extraordinary. I felt as if I'd just delivered that baby. Did you clear everything with the Truitts?'

'Yes. A different name was enough for them. You really liked it?'

'Yes. Now, I'm going to have to do some cutting. The details about Steven's political ideas go on for too long. Also, I think we should omit the stuff about his marriage.'

'Why?'

'He sounds too cynical.'

'Ah.' Lillian breathed deeply. 'Thank you for letting me do this.'

'I expect one of the larger papers might want to buy this. The *Globe* is very concerned about alternative forms of medicine. I'll send a copy to their features editor.'

'You think it's good enough?'

'Yes. Why didn't you tell me you were a writer?'

'I'm not sure I knew.'

'There's a lovely sense of the environment in the piece. Do you really like it here that much?'

'Yes. It feels like home.' There was a pause. 'Oh, my brother Edward's visiting next week. You said you'd like to meet him.'

'Would you bring him to dinner on Saturday?'

'Sure.'

'With Vincent. Bring Vincent. I'll invite Steve and we'll have a house full of men.' There was a pause. 'Don't run away if there's no answer to your knock. Come in and wait for me. The door's never locked.' Helen paused again. 'You're my family, Lillian. My house belongs to you, too.'

Unable to speak, Lillian drew a deep breath.

Helen rang off, saying, 'OK. That's all. I'll see you Saturday.'

On her way to Vincent's she pulled over into a scenic area (there was nothing to see but a picnic table and several garbage cans) to put on some make-up. On the seat next to her were two loaves of just-baked bread. Her palms were so sweaty, it was difficult to steer.

When she arrived, he was underneath his car trying to locate the reason for a mysterious noise the engine had recently begun to make. 'Hey,' he yelled, 'hand me a thingamajig.'

She handed him a socket wrench from his collection. It always seemed to be the tool that people wanted. There were several loud banging noises and then he came out from under the car.

'Howdy,' he said, leaning forward to kiss her. 'What's with the warpaint?'

'I wear make-up. I always wore make-up in New York.'

'This isn't New York.'

'Vincent, don't state the obvious to me. I know this isn't New York. Edward's coming today.'

'Ah! The divine Prince Edward! Now I get it!'

'Get what?'

'The red lipstick, the blue eyeshadow.'

'Eyeliner.'

'Kiss me you slut!' They kissed. She opened the door to her car and took out the bread.

'I baked some bread,' she said, holding tightly to the still-warm loaves.

Vincent laughed. 'What?'

'I baked some bread.'

'For your brother?'

'For you.'

'Jesus,' he said, looking at her closely. 'What did you do?'

'Nothing. Can we go in the house?'

She put the bread down on the table and took off her coat. Vincent washed his hands. She lit a cigarette. There was a prolonged silence.

'You want some coffee?' He was holding up the pot from the sink.

'OK.' Lillian cleared her throat. 'I'm adopted,' she said.

187

Vincent turned off the water and leaned against the sink. 'Really?' he asked softly. 'Well, that's OK.'

'Yes, I mean, I know it's OK. It was always OK. It's just . . . I'm really adopted.'

'Spit it out, Lillian. This is the part I don't enjoy.'

'I came here to find my real mother.'

'We're not related are we?'

If she didn't feel so badly, she would have laughed at the expression on Vincent's face. 'No!'

'So?' He held his arms out. 'I don't get it.'

'It's Helen Carter.'

'What is?'

'She's my mother.'

'Jesus!' Vincent hit the counter hard with the flat of his hand. 'God help me, I'm an idiot!'

'Why?'

'You two are so fucking alike!'

Lillian stiffened. 'I don't think so.'

'That's a compliment, kid. You'd better accept it.'

'In what way?'

'She's the bravest woman I've ever known. Her life should have killed her and she just kept going forward. I think she's one of the most intelligent people I know. And she's beautiful. Like a woman in a Titian painting. And you look like her.' He paused. 'This isn't much of a relationship, is it?' he asked, looking straight into her eyes.

'Vincent—'

'You don't trust me yet. We sleep together. You let me inside of you, deep, deep down inside of you and you keep a secret like this as if I wasn't capable of understanding!'

She had never seen him so angry.

'She must have assumed I already knew. I mean, we've been sleeping together and everything. It's not like that's any big secret. She said something about a "situation" and I just nodded. What an insensitive jerk she must think I am! By the way, I'm not like either of your daddies, my darling. I didn't blow my brains out and I don't spend all my time avoiding my daughter! Damn it, Lillian—'

'Hey, stop yelling at me!' She had picked up a loaf of bread as if to throw it at him. 'Is this all about you again, Vincent?'

'That's not the point.'

'Yes it is! You're upset because of how you look? Your parents didn't give you away. Your father didn't blow his brains out! What does this say about our relationship? It says I think you're totally selfish and I don't trust you yet.' She ran out of breath and sat down, still clutching the loaf.

'I think you'd better leave me alone for a while,' he said quietly. 'I need to think.'

As she put on her coat she thought it wasn't the time to tell him she loved him. Perhaps it never would be.

'Thanks for the bread,' he called out as she opened the door.

'Stinky!'

'Dork Brain!'

'Thunder Thighs!'

'Bongo Rear!'

Brother and sister fell on each other at Bangor airport. Edward was wearing a massive, elegantly tailored overcoat. He had on calfskin gloves and a cashmere muffler. Lillian's work boots were muddy and her quilted jacket hung down to her knees.

'Hideous coat,' Edward whispered in her ear as they hugged.

'Listen, Sherlock Holmes, where did you get that outfit?'

'It's a present from a desperate admirer.'

'Male or female?'

'The wife of a movie producer. She has no bones in her cheeks and terrible lips.' Edward leaned over and kissed Lillian. 'Not like yours. Take that pillow off for a second. I can't see you.'

Lillian stood with her arms full of the coat until Edward took it away.

'You've lost weight.'

'A little.'

'A ton! Honey, that is some body. And your face! Where did you buy the peaches-and-cream complexion? You want to be in the movies?'

'No!' Lillian reached for her coat. 'Give me my pillow back.'

Edward stared into her eyes. 'I know what it is,' he announced melodramatically. 'You're having intercourse!'

Several lingering passengers looked in their direction and shook their heads.

'Edward—'

'Are you having sex?'

'God . . . '

'Tell me.'

'Yes! OK? *Yes!*'

'With someone normal?'

'I don't know.'

'Is he married?'

'No.'

'What does he do?'

Lillian picked up her brother's bag and began to walk towards the exit.

'Now listen, Miss Thing,' he said gently as they were sitting in the car, waiting for the engine to warm up, 'I just want to know what he does.'

'He's a musician. A rock musician. And sometimes a construction worker.' Lillian barely avoided a sheet of ice. 'At the moment, he despises me.'

Edward looked closely at her profile. 'My God,' he whispered dramatically.

'What's wrong?' she asked anxiously, scanning the horizon for a possible moose.

'You're in love with this man.' Lillian made a face, but Edward shook his head. 'I didn't think it was possible. He isn't retarded, is he?'

Lillian punched her older brother hard on his cashmere-covered shoulder.

As they drove towards Ceylon, Edward described the gradual descent of the cast of *Space Aliens* into paranoid schizophrenia. They'd begun to hoard food and steal each other's make-up until there was so much tension people wandered off into the desert to scream at tumbleweeds.

'A real experience,' Edward said, staring out of the window at the snow-covered mobile homes. 'A real, fucking cosmic trip. Where are you living, sweetness? The frozen K-mart tundra? Does your house have wheels on it?'

'No.'

'Why is there so much snow?'

'Winter.'

'Where's the mall?'

'We'll go tomorrow.'

'Goodie. Now, where was I? Oh, what about this rock idol you're boinking?'

'Boinking?'

'It's very LA. For example: *Boink you!*'

Lillian laughed. 'His name's Vincent Delacroce. We're having dinner at Helen's tomorrow. She wants to meet you.'

'Ah.' Edward inhaled. 'This is quite a little human-interest story, isn't it? Is this the genetic match to produce your unborn saviour?'

'I don't know. He's written a song for me.'

'What's it called?'

' "Lillian." '

'Oh. Subtle.' They both laughed.

'So, when are you coming home?' His voice had become serious. She glanced at him and saw that he was staring at her.

'Is there something wrong?' she asked.

'Not really. It's just they think they did something terrible to you.'

'Why?'

'How you found out about the adoption.'

'That's not the point,' she snapped. 'It shouldn't have been a secret.'

'Mom said all the adoption experts recommended waiting—'

'She always finds a way to reinterpret history. There's no point in discussing how people feel. I'm sick of feelings. Vincent's furious at me.'

'Why?'

'Because I didn't tell him about Helen. I don't know why . . . I just didn't and then you were coming and he doesn't think I trust him.'

'Do you?'

'Of course not. I don't trust anyone. And he's so pleased with himself. It's very difficult.'

'What is?' Edward looked baffled.

'Mom's such a hypocrite! I learned this from her!'

'What?'

'Not being able to tell people things.'

'I'm not arguing with you about Mom. When are you going home?'

'I don't know what that word means.'

'Back to New York.'

'I'll never live in that city again.'

'Lillian—'

'Leaving Manhattan made me recognize that I hadn't taken a deep breath in five years. People aren't meant to feel as if a guillotine is about to swish down twenty-four hours a day. That's how I always felt there. It's the greatest city in the world. I leave it to the hopeful, the homeless and the mega rich.'

'I'm not about to defend New York,' Edward said, looking out the window. 'I think it's like living in a pinball machine. But that doesn't mean you belong here.'

'It means a lot to be getting to know Helen.'

'What's she like?'

'Like me. An alcoholic. So like me it's almost repellent. Powerful, angry.'

'How did her daughter die?'

'A boating accident.'

Edward shivered. 'Life is so sad sometimes,' he murmured. 'You think you know the meaning of tragedy and then someone comes along and reinvents it.' He leaned back in his seat. 'If you've found someone more self-involved than you, I'm impressed.'

She leaned over and grabbing a handful of thigh skin, pinched hard.

Getting used to Edward's presence in her apartment was difficult. He made a great deal of noise in the morning, singing in the shower and playing loud rock music while he shaved. She had grown accustomed to waking up at seven, writing for an hour before she got dressed.

Edward was an early riser who wanted something to eat as soon as he got out of bed. He consumed doughnuts and made fruit-based yogurt milkshakes for breakfast. On the first morning, Lillian had set the table for him and written a note describing all the choices he had for breakfast. She had bought four varieties of doughnuts at the Shopwell the day before. When he wandered into her room carrying a mug of coffee she looked up with poorly concealed annoyance.

'Sorry,' he said quickly, sensitive to potential disapproval. 'Do you want a doughnut?' He waved his hand in front of her face, a half-eaten doughnut flashed past her nose.

Lillian shook her head.

'What are you doing?'

'Writing,' she snapped, ideas vacating her mind while her brother stood above her.

'Is it something you can tell me about?'

'Edward,' Lillian said slowly. 'Leave me alone for an hour!'

'Sorry! What should I do? Shovel snow?'

'Take T.W. for his walk. There's a beautiful lake at the end of the path. He'll love you for ever.'

'Will you?'

'Yes.' Lillian looked up to see her brother gazing down at her fondly, white sugar from the doughnut covered part of his nose. 'Why are you looking at me like that?' she asked.

'I'm so proud of you, Lilita.'

She sighed. 'Remember when I told you I didn't believe you were my family?' Edward nodded. 'I should never have said that. It wasn't true.'

He kissed the top of her head and shut the door behind him.

When they arrived at Helen's shortly after seven, they found Steven washing lettuce in the kitchen and heard Vincent playing the piano in the living-room. Thomas Wolfe headed directly towards the music, to Vincent.

'Welcome to Maine,' Steven said, wiping his hand on his jeans and then offering it to Edward. 'I guess we're almost related.'

'In a non-existent sort of a way,' Edward agreed.

'Beer, wine, Perrier?' he asked.

'Perrier, please,' Lillian said.

'Wine.'

Vincent was playing a Mozart sonata that turned into jazz and then ragtime. Edward looked at her.

'Is that your boyfriend?'

'I guess. He's never played classical music for me.'

The piano stopped and Vincent appeared in the doorway, T.W. leaning happily against his leg. He looked slightly nervous, wearing a corduroy jacket and new jeans.

His long hair was pulled back into a ponytail. 'It's nice to meet you, Edward,' he said.

'Likewise.' Edward raised his glass slightly.

'Would you care for a brewsky, Mr Delacroce?' Steven asked, wearing Helen's apron to wash the dishes.

'Don't mind if I do, Woody, my old boy,' Vincent replied in an excellent British accent. He kissed Lillian lightly on the lips. They avoided each other's eyes.

'Where's Helen?' Lillian asked.

'Changing.'

The kitchen became silent. Steven began to whistle off-key. Edward lit a cigarette. Vincent beat on the counter with a wooden spoon. T.W. yawned and fell asleep.

'I think we'll get more snow,' Lillian remarked feebly after nearly a minute of whistling and tapping interspersed with Edward's inhaling and clearing his throat. 'There's a thick cloud-cover.'

'Yup,' Steven said, opening the refrigerator and putting the salad inside. Silence returned.

'Edward plays the piano,' she remarked to Vincent.

'That right?' Vincent sipped his beer. 'Did you know Helen was her mother?' he asked Edward. Edward nodded. Vincent looked at Steven. 'What about you?' Steven nodded. There was a long silence.

'I don't play very well,' Edward said modestly, pouring himself more wine.

'Let's get shit-faced,' Steven suggested.

'Do you think I'm selfish?' Vincent asked Edward.

'I don't know you,' Edward replied. 'But my sister has poor judgement so you're probably a monster.'

Steven tapped Vincent on the arm. 'Why not ask me that question?'

Vincent nodded. 'OK.'

'Completely,' Steven said. 'Your ego knows no bounds.'

'Does an ego actually know anything?' Edward asked leaning forward. 'Did you ever consider that?'

Lillian decided to see what Helen was doing. The door to the bedroom was ajar but no-one answered her knock. As she walked in she saw Helen sitting in a chair by the window.

'Hi,' she said, pausing.

'Hello.' Helen looked tired.

'Do you feel all right?'

'Yes. Do you?'

'I don't know.' Lillian sat on the edge of the bed. 'Men are so screwed up.'

'Why?' Helen stood up and walked over to her dresser. She opened her jewellery box.

'They aren't equipped. They spend all their time grabbing each other's toys and then they grow up and try to impress each other and it's just pathetic.'

'What do women do?'

'Who knows? Steal each other's boyfriends? Empathize. Share . . . I think it's hopeless.'

'Is it nice to see Edward?'

'He doesn't belong. I feel like he's part of another life.'

'You're living your life, honey.'

'He thinks I'm hurting my mother. He thinks I'm too hard on her.'

'Are you?'

'I doubt it. She doesn't hurt easily.' Lillian stopped. Her tone of voice sounded too harsh. 'I mean . . . I don't think I understand my mother.'

'That's normal.' Helen selected a pair of silver earrings. 'I'm nervous about meeting your brother.'

'Why? He's a dope.'

'Your brother is an excellent actor, Lillian. I saw the PBS production of *Hamlet*. He was wonderful.'

'Well, Mr Wonderful and his pals are getting trashed in your kitchen.'

'Are they?' Helen laughed. 'That's not a very nice thing to do in my house.'

'Vincent knows who you are.'

Helen looked puzzled. 'Vincent has always known who I am.'

'I didn't tell him I was your daughter until yesterday.'

Helen sat down on the edge of the bed. 'Why not?'

'I don't know,' Lillian said, sitting down next to Helen and beginning to cry. 'People used to expect me to do inappropriate things. I'm not used to all these great expectations.' Helen snorted. 'I thought . . . I assumed we'd never really be a couple. When it seemed time to tell him it was too late.'

Helen put her arms around Lillian. 'Don't worry,' she said gently. 'He'll forgive you. Everybody's still alive. As long as people are still alive you can tell them things.'

They sat in the room quietly. Helen kept her arm around Lillian. Neither of them moved.

When they walked into the kitchen, Edward was juggling two peppers, a tomato and a zucchini. He was an excellent juggler. Steven was using a jar full of beans as a maraca and Vincent was playing the comb.

'Edward,' Lillian said sternly, 'here's Helen.'

He caught the vegetables, put them down and then bowed low. 'What a pleasure,' he said smoothly. 'I'm very happy to meet you.'

Helen extended her hand but Edward leaned forward to kiss her.

'May I?' he asked.

'Of course,' Helen said, blushing.

Lillian had forgotten how handsome Edward was. She turned to Vincent and put out her hand.

'I'm sorry,' she said.

'Me too,' he answered, pulling her into his arms.

'Hey, you guys! Look!' Steven was juggling two peppers, an apple and an egg.

Edward dropped Helen's hand and standing next to Steven, he caught the juggle and then sent it back. The two men were evenly matched in skill. Vincent let go of Lillian and made an apex of the triangle. Thomas Wolfe woke up and began to bark.

'I hate boys,' Lillian said, watching the vegetables fly around the kitchen. 'They're so immature.'

Helen looked at her sharply. 'Why don't you just learn how to juggle?' she suggested quietly. Lillian made a face behind her back.

17

Helen sat at one end of the dining-room table and Steven sat at the other. Vincent and Lillian were seated across from Edward. Lillian felt sick, the feeling clung to her like a spider web. Each time she'd brush it off and feel better, it would return. Vincent tried to hold her hand underneath the table but she shook off his fingers. Steven brushed his foot up her leg and she kicked him. Edward kept smirking at her and wiggling his eyebrows so that she stared at her plate. The men continued drinking and discussing the merits of four-wheel drive jeeps. They finished three bottles of wine.

Finally, Lillian got up from the table and went into the living-room. The silence and the dark made her feel better. She put her head against the smooth wood of the piano and thought about home.

She had always believed her mother loved Edward more than her. Once she had asked her outright.

'I won't answer that question,' her mother had replied angrily, her chin quivering. 'You have no reason to think that. It's incredibly selfish.'

When Lillian told her parents about her alcoholism she directed her words to her father. She would always remember the startled, frightened look on her mother's face. She couldn't bear to look at her. Finally Mrs Jordan had burst forth.

'It's Anthony's fault!' she had screamed. 'That abusive little creep! He frightened you and bullied you and you couldn't make him stop! That's why you drank too much.'

'Mother, I started drinking when I was fourteen. Didn't you listen to what I just said?' Lillian asked, calmly.

'No you didn't! We never let you drink.' Mrs Jordan looked at her husband. 'Did you ever let her drink!' Mr Jordan shook his head and patted his wife's hand.

'I stole it. Edward bought it for me sometimes. I put water in your whisky and you thought the maid did it. I couldn't stand how I felt. I wasn't able to be normal.'

'You were normal! You are totally normal! Look at you – you're perfect!'

'I want to die,' Lillian said quietly. 'Do I have to show you that in a way you can never come back from?'

Mrs Jordan had inhaled sharply while Lillian's father put his hand on his daughter's shoulder.

'You have to stop telling her what she feels,' he said quietly to his wife. 'It will kill her.'

Mrs Jordan rose to her feet. 'Oh,' she said, her voice heavy with sarcasm, 'now I understand. Mommy as murderer.' She looked at her daughter. 'Was he ever around when you needed someone to talk to?'

'I didn't need anyone to talk to, Mother.' Lillian's head ached so terribly she wondered if she were developing a brain tumour.

'I see,' her mother said. 'Well, the mother is always responsible, isn't she?'

This isn't about you, Lillian remembered thinking, *Not you! Me!*

'I'm sorry,' she said, facing her mother. 'I'm sorry I'm an alcoholic and I want to die. I'm sorry for not being normal. I'm sorry I feel as if you're suffocating me to death.'

And her mother had left the room followed quickly by her father.

Vincent opened the door. He walked over to the piano bench and sat down next to her. He smelled of wine and some sort of lime soap.

'What's wrong, kid?'

'I don't know.'

'I think I understand what kept you from telling me about Helen. This whole situation is very difficult to explain. We haven't made things that clear between us.'

She took a deep breath. 'I'm sorry.'

'Your brother's something.'

'Yeah.'

'You think he's better than you?'

'Sometimes.' The vague pain in her stomach became a sharp ache.

'He isn't.'

'Right.'

'Lillian?'

'Yes?'

'If I told you I loved you, would you disappear?'

'Probably.'

'What if I take away your ruby slippers?'

'I still have a charge card.'

'I—' She put her hand over his mouth.

'Don't say it.'

'Why not?'

'It will be terrible.'

'For Christ's sake! Everyone else knows it already! My manager, Bill, Mildred, Helen, the girls at Pizza World, your fucking brother – Mr Personality! "You love my sister." That's what he just said while you were in here. "You love my sister and if you hurt her, I'll rip your lungs out."'

'Brilliant. Nothing nicer than male bonding! That really makes me feel warm all over.'

'So, can I tell you?'

'Do I have a choice?'

'No.'

Lillian nodded, her nose against the piano keys. Vincent stood up and pulled her to her feet. He put his hands on either side of her face and looked down into her eyes.

'I love you,' he said.

'I love you, too,' she replied.

They both began to giggle.

'I didn't know that,' Vincent said. 'Are you sure?'

'Aren't you Jon Bon Jovi?' Lillian asked, sitting in his lap.

'Nope.'

'Uh oh. I love him. You, I just like.'

Steven and Edward decided to go out drinking. Vincent offered to be the designated driver. After they left, Helen began to clear the table.

'Let me do this,' Lillian said, taking the plates out of her hands. 'Come and sit down and have some tea and talk to me while I clean.'

'Your brother is afraid of losing you,' Helen said, after the tea was made and Lillian was up to her elbows in soapy water.

'What do you mean?'

'He thinks you're going to drift off and allow time and distance to erode everything.'

'Oh,' Lillian said, pulling the cookie jar down from the shelf. 'Can I take a cookie?'

'Sure. Vincent's afraid of losing you, also.'

'Helen—'

'You don't make it easy for him.'

'Everyone else does.'

'Those aren't easy parents.'

'I know.' She had a vision of Vincent's mother watching her son move, her eyes shining. 'He told me he loved me tonight.'

'He wants to marry you.'

Lillian put down the plate she was washing and bent her head for a minute. 'What makes you think that?'

'He told me.' Helen laughed at the expression of disbelief on Lillian's face. 'We went outside to inspect my tomato plants and he told me. You aren't the only *femme fatale* in this town, my darling. Vincent's been my special pal since he was six years old. I used to drive him all the way into Bangor for his jazz-piano classes. His parents didn't drive and his music teacher knew how important it was for him to study. We've been close friends for a long time.'

'This is too fast.'

'He's a decisive person.'

'No.' Lillian turned around to look at Helen. 'He thinks there's no possibility of my refusing. So why not go for it? Damn the torpedoes!'

Helen shrugged. 'Is that so bad?'

'I should leave,' Lillian said, spooning tea into the pot. 'I didn't come up here to find a husband. I don't understand how this could have happened so quickly.'

'What do you want to do?'

'Live,' Lillian said abruptly. 'Try writing more articles for the paper and getting used to feeling reasonably happy. I'd like to take care of myself better. Before I start taking care of Vincent.' She sat down at the kitchen table. 'Mother—' she paused. 'Tell me more about my father.'

'He was a very brave, kind man who read D.H. Lawrence and Nabokov when no-one was reading anything but *Time Magazine* and *Gone With The Wind*. His wife was sweet. Limited. She became addicted to the pain-killers she was given and they didn't have any sort of life together but he was devoted to her. Or to the memory of who she had once been. We were both movie fanatics. In those days the local pictures changed every two weeks. We kept meeting at the same movies. The *Thin Man* series, Fred Astaire and anything with Katharine Hepburn and Spencer

Tracy. One night we danced on the empty street. We both remembered a combination that Fred and Ginger had done around a bale of hay.'

Helen laughed, her eyes were shining. 'We kissed. All the years disappeared. Nothing else mattered. My husband was like a shadow in my life. John felt completely torn. I believed his education would save him. We had seen the pictures of the death camps. All of our young friends, the young men, had died or been crippled. It seemed wrong not to take what joy was available. I didn't know how much he suffered. I never thought anyone would love me that much.'

'Did your father love you, Helen?'

'My father was a raving alcoholic,' Helen said shortly. 'He beat your grandmother and he beat me and my sisters. One day he went up to Canada and we ran away. I never saw him again. For years I dreamed he would walk back into the house. His arms full of presents. Changed. I was the president of my high-school class and I said the whole speech to him; I imagined he was somewhere in the back of the auditorium, whispering to the people next to him that I was his daughter. He died in some small town in Canada. With a new wife, several new children.'

The kitchen became quiet. Outside there was a vast expanse of white, the stars seemed close enough to touch. Helen stood up and opened the back door and both women drew in huge breaths of clean, cold air. Down at the end of the garden, a stag raised its heavy antlered head to stare at the two women. Its powerful silhouette was thrown across the snow.

She was pulled from sleep by the sound of someone singing. 'When I'm calling you-oo-oo' in a slightly off-key false soprano. Then a baritone voice carried on. Steven and Edward were outside her window. They had their arms around each others shoulders in the snow. It was nearly two a.m.

'What light from yonder window breaks?' Edward bellowed as Lillian opened the window.

'It is fair Lillian,' Steven shouted in a very bad English accent.

'Shut up,' Lillian hissed. 'You'll wake up Mildred.'

'Hard-hearted cow,' Edward intoned in his best Laurence Olivier tone.

'Trollop,' Steven added.

Vincent came up the path and stood next to Edward.

'You want me to take these nuts away?' he asked.

'No. Leave Edward.'

'I'll call you in the morning,' Vincent said. Lillian blew him a kiss.

'I'm her brother,' Edward said, turning towards Vincent. 'Who the fuck are you?'

'Her friend,' Vincent said quietly. He tapped Steven on the shoulder. 'Come on, buddy.'

'I'm her friend, too,' Steven said, dropping on one knee in the snow. 'Am I your friend, Lillian?'

'Yes,' she said. 'Go away.'

She filled the kettle and lit the stove. Edward was sitting at the kitchen table, his head resting on his hands.

'This place reminds me of a movie about small-town life in America,' he said, making a great effort to appear less drunk. 'It's very surreal.'

'It is small-town life in America.'

'I love you, Lillian. You're so coherent.'

'Stop it.' Lillian put a box of doughnuts down in front of him. 'Have a doughnut.'

'Don't marry that guy, Lil,' Edward said, trying to sit up straight. 'You can't marry that guy.'

'Why not?'

'He's too young for you. He's from fuckin' Maine.'

'Those aren't very good reasons.'

'Remember Anthony!'

'I'm nothing like the woman who married Anthony. And Vincent is nothing like Anthony.'

'He could be.'

'All men could be. And who are you to tell me how to manage my affairs? You've never had a relationship last longer than a movie.'

Edward sat up. 'Yes I have,' he said quietly. 'I've been off and on with someone for over a year.'

'Who?'

'She's married.'

'Oh. I'm sorry. Do I know her?'

'No. She's married to one of the studio heads. It's a real mess. She won't leave him.'

'Damn,' Lillian said, putting the teapot on the table. 'I'm sorry, Edward.'

'Shit. Life is shit.'

'No it's not.'

'Are you still having your baby?'

'I don't know. I saw one getting born.'

'Babies!' Edward shuddered. 'God, babies can be an incredible bore. There are these highpoints they show on television: the first word; the first smile; birth. But then you have to put up with the utter tedium of watching the thing spit up milk.'

'It was quite a spectacle.'

'Bloody?'

'Yes. But also perfect. Exactly how it should happen. Inevitable.'

'Everything's inevitable. Birth, death, misery.'

'You aren't miserable, are you?'

'I'm not happy.'

'Then change.'

'Thanks.'

'It's not as hard as it seems.'

Edward stretched his arms over his head and flexed his

biceps. 'It is for the successful. Unless you really fuck-up big time.'

'Like me?'

'Like you. No-one expects successful people to change. They think you're fine the way you are and prefer you to carry on behaving in a predictable fashion. It's easier for other people. They don't have to adjust.'

Lillian poured the tea. Edward stood up.

'I'm pretty drunk,' he said apologetically. 'I'd better just go to bed.'

'Were you warm enough last night?' Edward nodded. 'There are extra blankets in the linen closet if you get cold.'

'When are you coming home, Lillian?'

'I don't know.'

'Mom asked me to ask you. Dad said you'd come home when you were ready.'

The tea was too strong. She poured more hot water in her cup and went to stand at the window. It had begun to snow. Thomas Wolfe pushed next to her, fitting his snout into her hand, licking her palm.

'You love it here, don't you, T.W? This is where you belong.'

Edward came out of the bathroom. A toothbrush in his mouth, his pyjama bottoms on. 'I don't mean I hate babies,' he said, his mouth full of toothpaste. 'I think it's being the oldest and having something take away your parents' attention.'

'Good night, Edward.'

'I'm sure your baby would be very charming.'

'Shut up.'

As she climbed the stairs to her room, he called out to her.

'Lil?'

'Yes?'

'You can marry Vincent if you want.'

'Good night.'

'But he has to get his hair cut.'

In the patch of sky above her bed, she watched the first streaks of dawn appear. Far away, she heard a rooster cry out a warning of the day to come.

18

When Lillian finished her first short story, she immediately submitted it to a small magazine which published new writers. The mere act of composing a cover letter, xeroxing her pages and mailing the package made her feel connected to the literary world. Being a waitress became part of the process which led to an understanding of the real world. She was too efficient and made Bill nervous. Accustomed to her lack of motivation, he enjoyed having a cocktail waitress who stood at her station reading *Moby Dick*.

A letter from the magazine arrived during the final days of Edward's visit. They wanted to buy her short story and enclosed a contract. She was to receive seventy-five dollars. The editor said he was looking forward to reading more of her work. It had been an exhausting two weeks. Steven was constantly dropping over, using Edward as an excuse to hang around Lillian. Edward treated Steven like some sort of long-lost brother, constantly suggesting what Lillian dubbed 'repulsive male-bonding activities' such as getting drunk and attempting to pick up unresponsive Maine women. They undermined Vincent by telling pointed stories about the sexual habits of famous rock stars and suggesting to Lillian she bleach her hair, wax her entire body and invest vast sums of money in serious lingerie and spike heels.

Often she felt as if she were living in the middle of a television sitcom based on a depressing Russian novel. She seemed to spend an inordinate amount of time brewing pots of tea and ministering to the needs of all three men. Edward insisted she take him on a tour of old Maine houses. His fondness for seeing the inside of other people's homes was, in her opinion, unnatural. During their visits, he embarrassed her by opening closets and peering underneath beds. He enjoyed observing the inventory of people's medicine cabinets and refrigerators. When she protested that he had no respect for people's privacy, he correctly pointed out that people who offered house tours were not overly concerned with keeping secrets. Finally, she handed him the keys to her car and a list of historic residences, suggesting he drive himself.

Steven had been asked to write an article for a medical journal about natural childbirth and Lillian was helping him edit the piece. He called or dropped by nearly every day and discovered that Edward was obsessed with Claude Chabrol's early films, a passion he claimed to share. The two men rented a VCR and soon there were non-stop screenings in Lillian's bedroom, the sound of French being spoken while they bickered over filmography.

Vincent's song-writing contract was in negotiation. The record company loved his music but wanted to use the performers they had under contract. Vincent was frustrated by their lack of interest in developing him as a performer. When he came over, tense and angry about the lawyer's behaviour, she gave him back rubs, agreeing that the record company lacked vision. But when he referred to himself as a genius, she laughed at him. To change the subject, she told him about the magazine buying her story.

'What are they paying you?' he asked as they lay soaking in the bathtub. She could hear Steven and Edward discussing the symbolic meaning of the colour red in Chabrol's movie.

'Almost nothing,' she said, 'it's symbolic.'

'The money's symbolic? Like the colour red?'

'Yes. Well, no. But it's almost nothing.'

'What? A couple of hundred?'

'No. Seventy-five.' He didn't say anything but she could feel his stomach shaking with laughter. She rose out of the water, her hair streaming in coils like Medusa, dripping and furious.

'You don't understand,' she yelled, throwing Edward's rubber duck at him. 'Why can't you ever appreciate anything I do?'

'Babe, I loved the bread—'

Lillian turned the overhead shower on, cold, and stomped out of the bathroom only to find Steven, Edward and Thomas Wolfe lying on her bed, the men's feet on her pillow, a bowl of popcorn on the floor in front of them as well as several open beers. She was wearing nothing but a towel. The two men began to whistle. T.W. barked and snapped at the air. When Vincent appeared in the doorway wearing her bathrobe, the din became unbearable.

'Go home, Steven,' Lillian said, 'and take my brother.'

'And Claude,' Edward interjected, grabbing the VCR.

When the apartment was finally quiet, Lillian sat down on her bed feeling angry and sad at the same time. Why should she expect Vincent to comprehend what it meant to her to have changed her life so completely? He was preoccupied by his own interests. She had kept the truth about Helen from him for precisely this reason, she told herself. It had nothing to do with a lack of trust.

'Well, that's fine,' she said, as he came back into her room drinking a beer, bringing her a seltzer, dressed in sweatpants and a sweater, Edward's favourite sweater, she observed.

'What's fine?' Vincent asked, sitting down in the rocker after handing her the drink. 'You started without me.'

'I have my stuff and you have your stuff. It's better that way.'

'What's better, what way? What stuff?'

'Us. Separated.'

'You want to be separated?'

'We are already. This just clarifies things.'

'What things?'

She knew he was being deliberately stupid but it seemed too hard to give up and laugh. The ice was so thin, she could see the bottom, dead leaves gathered in odd patterns underneath her feet. When he smiled and held out his arms she longed to cross that fragile surface, glide away from danger, accept exactly what he had to give and stop searching the woods for what was lost. But she couldn't.

'You don't care about what I do because I'm not that important to you and that's fine.'

Vincent sat back and sipped his beer. 'Don't tell me what I care about.'

'Why should you? I don't expect you to get involved in my issues with alcohol.'

'Do you want me to?'

'No!'

'Then why mention it?'

'Because—' Lillian stood up and began to feel as if she were in danger. Here we go again, she thought. Longing to tell him to leave, she simply stood and stared at him. He isn't perfect, she told herself, he's the most conceited person you've ever met. But she loved him and that was what made her burst into tears.

Vincent didn't move. He watched her cry for a moment and then he set down his beer. 'I'm not inside your head,' he said softly. 'If you tell me about your stuff, I'll try to understand.'

'Then don't be so selfish,' she sobbed.

'OK,' Vincent said. 'I guess seventy-five dollars is nothing to laugh about.' He put out his arms. 'Come sit on my lap, you crazy dame.'

The day before Edward's departure the rep from Jupiter Records, Vincent's label, came to Maine on his way to Boston to watch a brand new band with what he described as 'Major screaming potential'. Vincent asked Lillian to accompany him to the Bangor Airport to meet his plane.

'I could use your support,' he told her over the phone, his tone slightly defensive as if he expected her to say no.

Lillian sighed. She had been kept up the previous evening playing a combative game of Scrabble with Steven and Edward. Towards the end both men were using highly suspect words and the dictionary was constantly consulted. She had finally left them and gone to bed, waking at nearly dawn to hear them arguing over a word she knew that Edward had made up.

'Is this your old lady?' the rep from Los Angeles asked, pushing up his Ray Bans to reveal absolutely bloodshot, small red eyes.

'Yes,' Lillian replied. 'I am literally his old lady.'

'This is Lillian,' Vincent said, picking up his bag. 'Lillian Jordan meet Frank McKenzie.'

'Oh! Hey! You are the muse, babe! The spinner of dreams. Vincent's elusive white rose. I love that song!'

Lillian laughed.

Vincent shrugged. 'This is how it's done,' he said as they walked towards the exit, Frank trailing behind, his ear glued to a cellular phone. 'The whole thing is hype.'

'What whole thing?' Lillian hissed.

'Lillian,' Frank caught up with them in the parking lot, his Gucci loafers sliding on the ice, 'are you in the music business, babe?'

'No.'

'So, maybe it's a little difficult for you to fully comprehend what's happening to our boyo here.' Lillian smiled grimly while Frank continued. 'It's a little tricky but you see I think Vinnie's going over the top. A singer-songwriter. What could be more American?'

Lillian thought for a moment. 'Undeclared war.'

Frank looked stunned for a moment before he smiled. 'Hey! That's good! I really like that! You're smart aren't you? She's smart, Vinnie. Where you from? New York?'

Lillian shrugged. 'I was born in Maine,' she said.

'But you didn't stay here, did you?'

Lillian shook her head.

'I can always tell when people are from the City. See, I still call it "The City" even though I live in the canyon. You ever been to LA, Lillian?'

'No.' Lillian felt the manager's body quivering next to her as they piled into the front of Vincent's car. She wondered how much coke he had done.

'Well, when Vinnie's song gets recorded by Call Your Mother—'

'What's that?'

'You never seen Call Your Mother? Great band. Incredible hair. These guys have the best hair in the business.'

'They suck,' Vincent mouthed into her ear.

'When these guys do "Lillian"—'

'Can't they change the name?'

'Why?' Frank looked worried. 'You got a problem with the name?'

'Well, it's mine.'

'Hey, you can't copyright titles like this—'

Vincent interrupted. 'She knows that, Frank. It's OK.'

'You think it's OK that a band named Call Your Mother with major hair is singing a song you wrote about me?'

Frank laughed. 'I like this chick, Vin. She's sharp.'

Frank sneezed, lowered his Ray Bans and passed out. Vincent pulled Lillian closer to him, putting his right arm across her shoulder.

'Thanks,' he said.

'He's completely wacko,' she said under her breath.

'That's the music business, Lil.'

'I feel like I've been snorting speed.' They drove in silence for a moment.

'Lillian, I have to ask you something.'

She glanced at his profile and caught her breath. I have a handsome boyfriend, she thought, filled with self-satisfaction, wishing she could show him off to Lizbeth who had such an appreciation for quality. 'What?' She kissed the palm of his hand.

'Would you marry me?'

Lillian flinched. The movement disturbed Frank who let out a snort but then settled again, his head against the window. There was an endless minute of silence until Vincent continued.

'This wasn't how I meant to ask but you've been with Edward all the time and I had this contract to sort out.'

'That's OK.' She felt her throat begin to close. 'Vincent—'

'Don't say no, Lillian! I'll take it back!'

'Wait a minute.' She swallowed. 'Why do we have to get married?'

'We don't *have* to. I thought it might be something you'd like.'

'Marriage?'

'Do you have to say it like that? It sounds like an infectious disease. Just because you had a bad experience—'

'*Bad?*'

'Whatever!' Vincent raised his voice. 'Let me fucking propose, would you?'

'OK. Fine. Don't yell at me.'

'I love you, I respect you and we're good together. I'm going on tour and that means forty cities in five months.'

'You want me to go on tour?'

'Yes.'

'When?'

'It starts in May.'

'Vincent, I can't sit on a bus with your band for five months.'

'Why not?'

'I . . . well—' Lillian hated buses and motels and the idea of being on tour with a rock band. 'Thomas Wolfe.'

'We'll bring him.'

'He'd hate it.'

'That dog doesn't hate anything. He's too stupid.'

'Don't call my dog stupid!'

Vincent pounded the steering wheel. 'What is happening here?' he hissed through his teeth.

'You asked me to marry you,' Lillian explained with exaggerated calm, 'then you insulted my dog.'

'Look, the bus is equipped with everything. We'll get you a lap-top computer.'

'Vincent—'

'Goddamn it, Lillian! I listen to your stuff!'

Frank woke up with a start, banging his head against the window. 'What?' He sat up. 'Are we here yet?' He looked out the window. 'Jesus! Where the hell are we? Antarctica?' He looked at Lillian. 'Are you two fighting?'

'No,' Lillian said.

'We're getting married,' Vincent announced grimly.

Frank glanced at Lillian. 'Why is she crying?'

'She's so happy,' Vincent replied bitterly. 'She can't believe how happy she is.'

'Why won't you marry him?' Helen asked, shaking out a sheet she had just removed from the dryer.

'I don't know him well enough. I didn't come here to get married.'

'You came here to meet me and you did that. So why can't you do something else?'

'I want to write.'

Helen finished folding the sheet. 'What makes you think this will happen again?'

'What?'

216

'A man like Vincent asking you to marry him.'

'That's not a good enough reason.'

'You had better say yes, Lillian! You can't count on making a living from writing!'

She recoiled at the tone of Helen's voice. She didn't remember ever hearing such coldness, a disapproval that implied Lillian would fail completely. She had a flash of a woman turning over in a hospital bed, refusing to hold her new baby. Her hands began to shake.

'Rock-and-roll musicians are faced with lots of temptations,' Helen continued.

'So what?'

'What if he doesn't come back?'

'Then he was never mine to start with.' Lillian looked at Helen. Her face looked strange. 'What's the matter with you?' she asked. 'Why are you so upset?'

'I don't know what you expect from me,' Helen snapped.

'Nothing.' Lillian picked up her coat. 'I can't imagine why I've told you about this. You don't have to approve of me. It's all ridiculous.'

'Lillian—' Helen had sat down on the edge of the unmade bed, her arms were open.

Lillian shook her head. 'It started with a man disappearing in the middle of the night, because loving me upset him. He left his dog behind. I went home and told my parents I was contemplating single motherhood and they gasped and announced I'd been adopted. I come here and discover my real father's a suicide and my mother's exactly like me and someone I've just begun to love asks me to marry him because he can't bear the idea of touring in a bus by himself.'

Helen looked stunned.

Lillian put on her coat. 'By the way,' she said, 'a good magazine bought a story of mine.' She drew a deep breath. 'For seventy-five dollars.'

'Congratulations,' Helen said quietly as she shut the door behind her. Lillian stood outside the bedroom waiting for Helen to follow her. She wanted to go back and explain more about herself, to tell Helen that she couldn't bear the idea of leaving so soon after finding her, to explain about her father and the hope she still held that someday, if she discovered the magic combination, they would find one another. There was total silence when she put her ear against the door. She put her hand on the knob but then she let it go. A thought formed in her mind which brought a stabbing pain. She was going back to New York.

Edward needed a ride to the airport. As they drove towards Bangor, he inserted a tape and the opening chords made her reach to turn it off.

'Don't,' Edward said. 'I asked him for it.'

'Oh for fuck's sake.' She took her finger off the Eject button.

> You count your blessings every day,
> Down on your knees.
> Stay baby, stay, stay, stay.
> I'm the answer to your prayers.
> I'm the one you waited for.
> I'm the man your daddy hates.
> I'm the stranger at your door!
> Lillian, let me in. Don't bar your soul.
> Lillian, let me in! Can't you see I'm everything,
> You're everything, we're everything, you've waited
>   for.

She wanted a drink more than she had in three years. She wanted to swallow whisky until her throat burned, her vision blurred and she could tell Vincent to take his passion and strangle himself with it.

'I'd say that ditty is going to make your boy very famous.'

'No it isn't. It's going to make a band named Call Your Mother famous.'

'That's a great band. An LA original.'

'Oxymoronic, Edward.'

'I think Vincent's the best thing that ever happened to you.'

'Really, Edward? What about: "Lil! Don't marry that guy."?'

'I thought he was some sort of guitar jockey noodling around trying to nail my sister.'

'Well, he asked.'

'He did? When?'

'Yesterday.'

'And?'

'We had a fight. He wants me to tour butt-fuck America with four guys and the dog. I'm going back to New York.'

'Why? Oh honey—' Edward reached for her but she avoided his hands. She didn't want to be touched.

'It's fine. I want to go home. It's too cold here.'

'He loves you. Lillian, you love him, don't you?'

'Yes. But I think it's easy to say that and I don't know how we'll manage. Vincent's obsessed with his music and I'm obsessed by my obsessions. If we had a baby its life would be all about its narcissistic parents arguing over whose issues were more important.'

'So? The kid can see a shrink. You can all see shrinks. You can stay home and write. Or work and let Vincent stay home. Don't you want someone in your life who really cares about what happens to you?'

Lillian shook her head wordlessly.

'Why does it have to be so complicated, darling? What's the matter with that picture: Mom, Dad and our kid?'

She drew a deep breath. 'I'm not in it,' she said quietly. 'I'm just missing.'

His flight was delayed because of heavy traffic over Boston. Edward didn't want her to wait. He gave her a T-shirt that said: 'Don't Worry, I'm His Sister.'

'I love you, Edward,' she said.

He gathered her into his arms, kissing the top of her head. 'Go talk to Vincent,' he whispered. 'Tell him why you're afraid.' He held her for a minute and then let her go, giving her a gentle push in the direction of the Exit sign.

Guitar music was audible from the front yard. When she tried the door it opened. She followed the music to the basement. Vincent was sitting on a futon, moodily playing chords.

'Hi,' she said, walking across the room, leaning over to kiss him. He put the guitar down and pulled her into his lap. Burying his face in her neck, he moaned.

'Oh baby,' he said. 'I'm so sorry, baby.'

'No,' she answered brokenly. 'No-no-no-no-no. Don't be sorry. I'm wrong. I'm completely wrong.'

'No,' Vincent whispered, biting her ear.

'Yes,' Lillian murmured, as he undressed her, kissed her, touched her so that she clung to him and before she had a conscious thought, they were making love. It happened so smoothly and swiftly, neither of them remembered birth control. She was wet as soon as he put one finger inside and spread herself wide for him and he was hard and both of them were crying and claiming to be wrong. At one point she remembered, or part of her remembered and thought, *Don't let him come; pull away*. But it didn't seem possible to separate and she was gasping too hard to speak. He held himself above her waiting until she opened her eyes to stare back into his.

'Love,' Vincent whispered. 'I love you. I'll always feel like this. Don't leave me.'

Anthony had always said that to her after their fights.

She would be lying on the floor or hiding or locked in the bathroom and he would say it over and over again. '*Don't leave me.*' Wasn't that what we always thought as we held our lovers in our arms? '*Don't leave me.*' Matthew had whispered it into her hair, the night before he disappeared. High and awake, holding on to her hand, assuming she was fast asleep, Lillian had heard him murmuring that phrase over and over again until she couldn't bear it and had taken him in her arms, put his poor head on her bosom and soothed him to sleep. Those words were what she longed to say to Helen, to Edward and her father.

She lay in Vincent's arms, her head resting on his chest, his breath even in her ear, her other ear receiving the steady sound of his heart while his hand stroked her hair softly. Her own heart felt like a rock inside her. It pierced the area above her rib cage. She was ice-cold.

Vincent was washing her hair. Since she stopped cutting it, it had grown nearly to her waist and its wet weight bent her head backwards. His fingers were strong and steady in a massage along her skull and neck.

'I put some money down on a place,' he told her while he rinsed out the conditioner.

'Where?'

'Stonington. It's a beautiful town. I remembered you said you'd like to live there. I got one of those houses by the harbour. We can take it from next September.'

How sure he was of himself. 'What was the deposit?'

'Nine hundred. It's only six hundred a month and there are three wood stoves. There's an extra room for a study and the basement makes a perfect studio.'

'Vincent—' His hands stopped moving on her head.

'What?'

'I'm going back to New York.'

There was a long silence. He turned off the water. She closed her eyes and tried to breathe.

'When did you decide this?'

'I don't know. Yesterday.'

'So, you came here to tell me?'

'Yes. No, I came here to apologize.'

'Fine. You're forgiven. Now, get the hell out.'

Mildred didn't seem surprised but she was very sorry to lose Lillian.

'I can't say I blame you,' she said, wiping her eyes. 'You shouldn't settle for such a dull life.' She laughed. 'Not that your life is dull. It's more complicated than most soap operas!'

It didn't take long to pack. Any furniture she'd once owned was still in her parents' basement. After her separation and divorce from Anthony, she used to visit her past in the form of their bed and several chairs, boxes of old photographs and piles of books. Her mother allowed her half an hour of sitting on their bed, sobbing, before she'd call from the top of the basement stairs, her voice shrill with false cheer. 'Darling,' she would say, 'stop wallowing. You're well rid of him.'

What had Lillian thought after leaving Anthony? It was strange. She didn't blame men or the institution of marriage, or how alcohol affected her or the silence that seemed impossible to penetrate in the house where she had first observed people trying to love each other. She blamed herself. As if she had set out to create something wonderful, a perfect soufflé for example, and deliberately omitted a key ingredient.

'You failed,' she muttered aloud as she ran or stuffed another piece of cheesecake in her mouth depending on how she was coping with her shame at that particular moment. Why couldn't she forget how Anthony held her after their fights, filled the house with flowers, whispered that she was beautiful? Why couldn't she remember the feeling of his open hand branded across her skin, how he brought her to her knees in fear, the way she always felt herself choke as he crossed the room towards her while she cried and said over and over again: 'What have I done? I'm sorry!'

She drove to Vincent's with T.W. on his leash, a bag full of his toys, the 'Andover' rag and a scarf she'd knitted him, packed into a paper bag. When Vincent opened the door she put down the bag.

'Can you take Thomas Wolfe?' she asked, her voice shaking. 'He doesn't belong in a city.'

'Neither do you.' Vincent had his arms folded in front of him and his jaw was tight with anger.

'Will you take him, Vincent? He loves you. He can't go back to an apartment.'

He sighed and slowly shook his head. 'What's the matter with you? Can't you even commit yourself to a dog?'

'I want him to be happy.'

'Oh, bullshit! Don't give me that noble crap, Lillian!' He leaned against the door frame, his eyes cold. 'You really believe this garbage, don't you? I thought everybody in New York had a shrink. Why don't you go see one?'

'I might,' she said, biting her lower lip. 'Will you take T.W.?'

'Sure, fine. I'll take your dog. Why not? Jeb is house-sitting while I'm on tour, but he likes dogs.'

'OK,' Lillian said, nodding. 'Great.'

'Yeah, great.' Vincent took the leash out of her hand. 'Come on,' he said to T.W. 'She's got bigger fish to fry.'

'No, I don't,' Lillian snapped. 'I'm not a monster. I love you and I love him but I can't stay. There's something wrong with me.' Vincent didn't answer. Lillian got down on her knees and buried her face in the dog's hair. 'You're the best dog in the world. The only dog I've ever loved. The only dog I ever liked, even.'

She kissed his brow, his ears and the top of his head.

'I bet a lot of women in New York have cats,' Vincent said, picking up the bag full of T.W.'s stuff. 'Or birds.

Or goldfish. A goldfish wouldn't ask for much intimacy. And they're easy to kill.'

Lillian stood up. She touched Vincent's cheek for one second and then the top of Thomas Wolfe's head. 'I'm sorry,' she muttered.

Why don't you ask me why I'm leaving? The words formed in her mind. Didn't he understand marriage was too large a leap, that if he gave her time she would try to believe he loved her? Vincent knew what her ex-husband was like. Straightening, she opened her mouth to speak. But there were no words to describe her fear and his face was dark and closed. No-one had ever said 'No' to Vincent. He would not easily forgive. When she put her hand on his arm, the surface felt like iron.

'Come on, boy,' he called to Thomas Wolfe as the dog followed her part of the way down the path and then sat down, looking from one to another, waiting for a sign.

As she drove away she watched the man and the dog grow smaller in her rear-view mirror until the road dipped and they disappeared completely.

19

She met Lizbeth for lunch at a Japanese restaurant in midtown. The place was full of smartly dressed people consuming raw fish. When Lizbeth came in wearing what appeared to be a genuine Chanel suit, Lillian felt her shoulders stiffen. Her own straight black skirt and handknit sweater seemed hopelessly provincial.

'Chanel?' she asked after they had hugged and kissed.

'My perfume?' Lizbeth asked.

'The suit.'

'Oh, Lilly! What do you think? Would I be caught dead in something genuine? It's from this amazing place called Sam's Style Salon. A converted supermarket in Bayonne filled with designer spin-offs. You wouldn't believe the prices! Crazy shoppers getting naked in the aisles and listening for five-minute fire sales which they keep announcing over the loud-speakers. You'd love it!'

'I'd rather spend the day in Motor Vehicles.'

'We could do that. First Sam's, then Motor Vehicles and after that . . . let's get new passports!'

They ordered sushi and sat back to look at one another. Lillian thought her friend appeared very pale and noticed that her neck bones were far more prominent.

'But look at you,' Lizbeth said, pinching Lillian's cheek. 'You're like an ad for *Field & Stream*! You're glowing.'

'Fat?'

'No! Perfect. I mean, everyone can't look hungry all the time! But why have you returned to Sodom? Go back! One of the vampires is going to suck all this rich, red blood out of your veins!'

Their food arrived and Lizbeth described how she'd survived the hostile takeover of their company. She took out her wallet and gave Lillian an engraved card.

'Assistant Art Director? Lizbeth, that's wonderful!' Lillian noticed the deep circles under her friend's eyes, the brittle way she laughed. How exhausted she seemed to Lillian, bone-weary and falsely gay.

'Well, it's a completely bogus title but I don't care. They fired that monster I worked for and gave me her office! What a revenge. I found all these old copies of *Playgirl* under a pile of company reports. That woman actually liked staring at naked men! Anyway, the new honchos called me into the office and asked me if I had any loyalty to the old regime. I laughed and said I didn't have any loyalty to anyone but my second-grade teacher who taught me how to cross my eyes. Then I demonstrated. I assumed this was a prelude to their firing me. They offered me the new job.'

Lizbeth put a tuna roll in her mouth and drank some tea.

'What do you do?' Lillian asked, biting into sea urchin and instantly wishing she had not.

'Spit it out,' Lizbeth advised, handing her a napkin. 'Nothing. I read magazines and shop. But we're all on hold. No-one knows anything. My deep throat in the mail room was fired for dealing crack.'

'Are you happy, Lizbeth?'

'Happy?' Lizbeth thought for a moment. 'That's a completely separate issue, sweetheart. I never expect to be happy. You're the one with that idea. Did I ever tell you I was an abused child?'

Lillian shook her head and leaning forward, put her hand on her friend's arm.

'Well, it's not very interesting. My mother was crazy and my father couldn't handle things so he just let her be mean to me. In a way it was OK until Child Welfare got on the case because of the marks . . . '

'Oh, God.'

'I was really a good kid. She was sick, Lilly. It wasn't her fault. And I loved her. No-one really knew her like I did. When you told me about Anthony and how ashamed you were that sometimes you missed him, I understood. I was devastated when she died. That's where the compulsive-shopping thing comes from. I never had any clothes when I was little. Just my cousin's horrible cast-offs.'

Lizbeth stopped talking. Lillian was holding her hand and then, lacking anything else to offer, gave her the nicest piece of salmon.

'Why did I tell you that story? Oh, happiness. It's all relative, isn't it? But I have news!'

'What?'

'Guess who I met at an incredibly tasteless party?'

'Who?'

'Remember that Temple of Dendaur thing? This was much worse! The Rainbow Room. Doves in cages! *Doves?* I mean, what's the point? It was for this ridiculous novel written by an ex-Wall Street hotshot about the crash being caused by the Soviets and nuclear destruction . . . something like that. Anyway, I can't believe that I keep running into your ex-lovers at parties. Like that Sam guy.'

'He wasn't my lover.'

'You never fucked?'

'His wife was nine months pregnant.'

'So?'

'Lizbeth!'

'This party-god, it's a terrible thing to be born poor. You never quite get it. I should have been enjoying myself but I felt so angry! All the men there had gone to Choate or Exeter or Andover. *Andover.* Does that sound familiar?'

'Matthew?'

'He's no friend to Lassie.'

'You met Matthew?'

'We were talking about publishing. In fact, I was trying to pick him up. He was very morose. But otherwise, nice. I mentioned my company, he got all excited and said his ex-girlfriend once worked there. I got the giggles and all I could choke out was: "You scum!" over and over again.'

'Oh, Lizbeth.'

'When I could breathe again, I told him exactly what sort of low-life creep he was. He agreed. I said you were gloriously happy and totally in love with a very almost-famous rock star.'

Lillian felt sick. She didn't want any more raw fish. Her head ached and her feet felt swollen.

'How did he look?'

'Gorgeous. I said you might be coming back to the city and he made me take his card. He's taking a course for the bank. He seemed quite desperate about you.' Lizbeth reached into her huge leather bag. 'You want the card?'

'No.' Lillian took another bite of the sea urchin and felt close to tears.

'Here.' Lizbeth held out a napkin like a mother and Lillian spat out the fish. 'Why did you come back? New York is horrible.'

'No, it isn't.'

'Just wait, sweetie. Give it twenty-four hours. Ride the subway. Try to buy groceries and find yourself having a panic attack in the aisles of Food Emporium. Say, how's Jon Bon Jovi?'

'He wrote a song about me. Call Your Mother are going to record it.'

'*Call Your Mother?* They're an LA bar band. Post-nuclear punk, I think. What's it called?'

'"Lillian."'

'"*Lillian*"? Oh my God! Like "Layla" or "Roxanne" or "Suzanne"? Remember Leonard Cohen? The garbage and the flowers? It's like a fantasy. It's like . . . .' Lizbeth paused, a tuna roll halfway to her mouth. 'Does your mother know?'

'Why?'

'It would be funny to hear her reaction. I think those guys are head bangers.'

'Great.'

'What's the matter with you? You never appreciate how cool things are! What about MTV? Is there a video?'

'I think the budget's pretty low.'

'What's the song about?'

Lillian frowned. 'A neurotic, insecure idiotic chick who doesn't know how good she has it.'

Lizbeth nodded. 'That sounds pretty accurate. So, where is he?'

'Maine.'

'Are you going back?'

'He proposed.'

'Proposed what?'

'Marriage.'

'What are you doing *here*?' Lizbeth shrieked just as their waiter was refilling their teacups. The tea spilled as he jumped in response to the pitch of her voice. Lillian smiled apologetically.

'This woman's been proposed to,' Lizbeth said to the waiter who was attempting to escape. 'Go back, Lillian! This is the city of the damned! The undead. You already knew that. A man wrote a song about you. He wants to marry you. And you left him?'

Lillian tried to breathe. The glare from the sidewalk made it difficult to look through the windows.

'I thought you loved him.'

'I did. I do. Lizbeth, I just couldn't say *yes*.'

'What did you say?'

'I told him that I was coming back to New York. I gave him Thomas Wolfe.' Tears were rolling down Lillian's face, landing in her tea.

'Oh, Lillian. You left him with your dog?' Lizbeth's eyes filled with water and when the tears rolled down her skin, they streaked her pale make-up, showing pinker skin beneath.

'It was too soon.'

'What was too soon? Being happy?' Lizbeth handed Lillian a napkin from the neighbouring table. 'Why didn't he just give you more time?'

'He's going on tour.'

'Oh.' Lizbeth patted Lillian's hand. 'A steady groupie, eh?'

'Yes!'

Lizbeth arched an eyebrow. 'Really?'

'No. He loves me. *I* just don't love me.'

'Get a therapist. Go to couples counselling. Get an acupuncturist or someone to do shiatsu. Meditate. Fast. Don't be like me, Lil!'

'Lizbeth, are you unhappy?'

'In five years I'll be making six figures. There are nothing but sample sales in this city. But you're different, honey. You have no style.' Lillian stuck her tongue out. 'I've got a married lover and a summer share in the Hamptons. But I'm four years younger than you. I can afford to have more senseless, self-destructive relationships with men who can't love. I can still binge! You're too old and tired. I doubt I'll ever want a child.' Lizbeth smiled angelically at the waiter who put down a quartered orange and their bill.

'Nice girl,' he said shyly.

'No I'm not,' Lizbeth replied. She pointed at Lillian. 'That's a nice girl.'

As she walked up Fifth Avenue, Lillian felt that the armour she'd acquired during her years in Manhattan was now missing. There were so many people standing on each corner, their hands outstretched, begging. Living in Maine had meant learning how to look people in the eye, smiling and nodding as you made contact. Now, everyone she passed had their eyes on the ground. She winked and smiled at a little boy and his mother glared at her. She passed a marble entrance to a gleaming steel tower and saw a young man wearing nothing but dirty shorts slumped against the wall. The sign in front of him said he was homeless and had Aids. There were beggars opening the door to Saks until a security guard made them stop. Descending into the subway, she felt surrounded by angry, frustrated people. It was the beginning of the rush hour and the token line was very long.

'Goddamnit!' the man behind her yelled. 'Would you hurry the fuck up!' She turned around as he followed her through the turnstile and saw that he was very well-dressed in a silk suit, carrying an expensive briefcase. This was not what she had expected. The streets felt unsafe and her ability to move through crowds of people had disappeared. Her sense of direction failed her and she felt related to the bewildered visitors who were visible on each corner, furtively consulting street maps.

The tenant to whom she'd sublet had left the previous week. The apartment had much less space than she'd remembered. The kitchen was practically useless for making anything more complicated than microwave food, or coffee. The house in Maine had ruined her perspective, she thought. Moving from room to room had seemed normal. Now she was always in her bedroom as the living-room which had once seemed spacious was really just the outside of the kitchen and nothing more than a hallway. Opening a window, she blackened her hands with the soot and dirt on the frame. At night, people screamed at one another and the garbage trucks made an unbelievable din at three a.m. Police sirens were always audible, and there was the constant sound of glass breaking. Her pulse accelerated and she had a terrible throbbing in her head which seemed to echo the bass of her neighbour's stereo which was clearly audible through the wall. Wide awake, Lillian pined for the Maine woods, the silence and the calm.

Returning from her lunch with Lizbeth, she closed the door behind her and then sat down on the couch. The phone machine blinked.

'Darling? Mother. That's wonderful news about your short story. Chucky Weatherford's sister-in-law is a literary agent. What sort of book are you writing? Well, call us when you get in.'

'Hi. It's Matthew. I guess you know that. Uh – I met your friend Lizbeth at a party. She's pretty . . . uh . . . nice. So . . . I went to a rehab and I don't do cocaine any more. I told my counsellor what I did to you and I cried. Look . . . I just want to talk to you. If that's possible. Maybe it isn't. So, I'll try to call again.'

'Lillian? It's Helen. I want you to call me. Collect. I didn't mean to speak to you like that. I can't detach properly. You remind me so much of John and Emily . . . ' Her voice faltered. 'I really don't know how to explain your importance to me. After you were born, I went to the nursery and a nurse there let me hold you. I saw the prettiest baby I'd ever seen in my life. Looking into your eyes was like staring into the most perfect blue sky. My little Buddha. But . . . nothing seemed to work. Emily was already taking care of herself at six years old because her mother was a drunk. I was afraid I'd lose her. It was my idea to keep the adoption a secret. I was afraid I'd never get sober and you'd have this terrible drunken mother. Someone you were ashamed of. Please don't disappear, Lillian. I can't lose another child.'

*　　*　　*

She rewound the tape and listened again. In her book of family pictures she found one of herself as an infant. Edward was pretending to hold her hand gently but she could see he was pinching her. Her parents were displaying her like some sort of trophy between them. Clearly, a baby doesn't judge who is taking care of it, who picks it up when it cries and makes sure there is enough food and warmth.

But her eyes were those of an eighteen-year old girl who stared at the photographer without apology. Lillian had torn the photograph from Mildred's yearbook. Helen as her long-lost little sister, frozen at eighteen. If they had been classmates, would they have been best friends? If she had been Emily, would she have died or swum to shore?

The final call was a hang-up. Vincent? She already missed him. And she missed Thomas Wolfe who had provided constant company, the steady beat of a second heart. The enormity of leaving them both hit and there was an overwhelming sense of emptiness, her stomach felt sick with loss. She slept in the far corner of her old bed, expecting her dog, missing Vincent's arms. She dreamed of when she was little.

She was hungry all the time. Not eating seemed impossible. She visited her parents and when the house was still and silent, she went down to the kitchen in search of more food. In the morning her stomach felt so empty it was painful. As she steadily grew heavier she thought, with grim satisfaction, that Vincent would no longer proudly claim her as his lover.

Her parents were happy to see her although her father was uncharacteristically critical of her decision to leave Maine.

'You're not going back?' he asked her as they drove into town to buy groceries.

'No.'

'Why not?'

'It's better this way.'

'What's better?'

'It's . . . I mean, my life.'

'I thought you disliked New York.'

'I did. I do. But things were too complicated in Maine.'

She didn't understand this behaviour of her father's. It was her mother's job to interrogate.

'Edward really liked your boyfriend.'

'He's easy to like.'

'What about Mrs Carter?'

Lillian sighed and looked out the window. They were driving past the place where she used to smoke pot before school. She felt old, tired, fat. Her father was looking at her. They pulled into the parking lot of Shopper's World.

'What's the matter, Lillian?'

She couldn't answer him. She shook her head.

'Maybe you shouldn't give up so easily.'

Was he criticizing her? She tried to see his face but he was looking out of the window. Talking to him had always been so difficult. She nodded.

He began to say something and then stopped. He patted her shoulder awkwardly. 'Don't worry any more,' he offered finally. 'Everything's OK.'

As she watched him search for a shopping cart, she realized she had no idea what her father expected from life. He was much older than she'd remembered.

On the third night of her visit, her mother came downstairs and discovered her eating a grilled cheese sandwich. 'Was dinner too spartan?' she asked her daughter who was leaning against the refrigerator, shoving food into her mouth.

'No,' Lillian said. 'I think I've developed some sort of eating disorder.'

'You look fine.'

234

'Well, I'm not fine, Mother.'

'What's wrong?'

'I don't know.' Lillian saw the panicked expression on her mother's face. 'It's nothing. I'm not drinking.'

'I didn't—'

'You never believe I change.'

Mrs Jordan wrung her hands. Lillian stared at her.

'Don't, Mom.'

'I want you to go back to therapy.'

'Well, that's not possible right now.'

'We'll pay.'

Lillian slammed the refrigerator door so hard the bottles rattled.

'It's not our fault,' her mother said.

'No,' Lillian replied slowly. 'I'm not even your child. She's an alcoholic, too.'

Mrs Jordan's face collapsed. *What am I doing?* Lillian thought. *Don't!* She moved across the kitchen and touched her mother's shoulder. 'I'm sorry.'

Mrs Jordan nodded.

'Mom, there's someone in Maine . . . that rock musician. He asked me to marry him.'

'Really? Wasn't he very young?'

'Twenty-six.'

'You're thirty-two.'

'Am I? Thanks. I'm never quite sure.'

'Come on—'

'Why do you have to remind me of my age? Do you think I'm a moron?'

'No. Of course not. I'm sorry. Go on.'

'He wrote a song about me.'

'How nice.'

'No. I mean, it is nice but this other band's going to record it. A punk band.'

'What's the name of the song?'

' "Lillian".'

Her mother laughed. 'I'm not surprised,' she said.

'What's that mean?'

'Well, it's a compliment. You're very intense, dear.'

'Yeah. I inspire people to hit me and dump their animals on me.'

'Did he do anything wrong?'

'No.' She cleared her throat. 'I gave him T.W.'

'He wrote you a song and asked you to marry him?'

Lillian put her dish in the sink.

'Why did you give him Thomas Wolfe, sweetheart?' The softness of her mother's voice surprised her.

'I don't know,' she said. 'New York is bad for dogs and children.'

'You were very good with that dog.'

'Thanks.'

'Never mind. What does this have to do with your appetite?'

She shrugged. 'I'm not sure. Since I have every other trendy disease, I thought I might enjoy compulsive eating.' She abruptly changed the subject. 'Daddy seems muddled.'

'Old. We're both just old.'

'Could he take vitamins or something?'

'Yes. He could do that. Don't worry. You're meant to be having a life. Not worrying about your ancient parents.'

A life. Lying awake in her childhood bed, Lillian tried to remember what the future had meant when she was a child. There was always a vision of some sort of glamorous job: acting or politics, or just being gorgeous and mysteriously wealthy. The man was very handsome, devoted, quite often away on business trips. In fact he was nearly always missing from the picture, although he invariably called and sent massive bouquets of roses to his beloved wife. Or was she a wife at all? Mistress perhaps. Maybe the man was absent because he had another family and Lillian was the secret. She sat upright in bed, shaking. That was what she'd always been, first Helen's secret, and then her parents'.

'I'm going to change,' she promised, whispering in the dark. The words hung in the air. She did not know to whom they were addressed.

Lizbeth called. 'Turn on MTV,' she screamed. Lillian had been writing, her desk was covered with pages torn from a yellow tablet, she was still in her pyjama top and an ancient pair of sweatpants.

Call Your Mother were grinding out the opening chords of 'Lillian'. The band consisted of six young men, half of them shaved like Zen monks, the other three with hair nearly down to their waists. The extraordinary part was a short film that cut in at the end. There was Thomas Wolfe bounding through a snow bank and when Lillian saw him she burst into tears.

She picked up the phone to hang it up and heard a voice at the other end.

'Go back for your dog,' Lizbeth said.

Lillian didn't answer. Tina Turner was sashaying across the screen singing about lies.

'Is that how Vincent sings his song?' Lizbeth continued.

'No,' Lillian snapped.

'How's the book coming?'

'Why does everyone assume I'm writing a book?'

'What are you writing?'

'Nothing. Another short story but it's not going well.'

'Are you miserable about this?'

'No. I'm fine. I'll call you in a few days. Bye.'

She stood in the dark of her room looking out at the street. He had asked her to marry him and she had answered 'no'. It was her choice to be alone. Had she expected him to follow her, to ask her again and again until she finally believed in what he was saying, that he wanted her near him, that she was so special he couldn't imagine a life without her? Would she ever believe him?

Lillian dreamed. She was running after Thomas Wolfe. He was heading towards a huge super-highway and did not obey her commands to stop. He dashed across one – two – three lanes of traffic. She was screaming. Her body was too slow and heavy. Large. At the fourth lane he was hit hard and was flung to the side of the road. He died in her arms. Her dog was dead.

She dialled the number but when the phone was picked up, she slowly replaced the receiver. She didn't deserve to hear his voice.

20

'You're pregnant.'

'No I'm not.'

'Yes you are. I'd say about two months. Do you know when it happened?'

'Yes.'

'This wasn't planned?'

Lillian shook her head.

'Do you want to terminate?'

Terminate. That's what they had called it when she had the abortion in college. The sadness was unexpected, overwhelming.

'No.' Lillian felt the sickening pain in her stomach. 'Can you tell if it's healthy?'

'It's pretty early. We can order Ultrasound to look at the foetus.'

'Will that tell us if anything's wrong?'

'Most things. You aren't very old, Lillian. What are you worried about?'

'Alcoholism.'

Her doctor raised her eyebrows. 'I thought AA was going well for you.'

'It is. I'm just . . . this disease. It's so hereditary.'

'Yes, but there's always AA. And you can't assume your baby would be born with a predilection to addiction. Is its father an addict?'

'No.' As she was waiting for her appointment she had read the office copy of *Rolling Stone*. Call Your Mother had just signed a major recording deal. She wondered when Vincent's tour would begin.

'You shouldn't gain too much more weight.'

'OK.'

'My nurse will give you a diet. Do you intend to have the baby in a hospital or use a midwife?'

'A midwife.'

After the appointment she went to Häagen-Daz's and had a double-fudge ice-cream cone and a cup of coffee. She read her new diet.

'Avoid saturated fats and eliminate caffeine,' it advised. She patted her stomach. 'Excuse me,' she whispered. 'I'll begin this tomorrow.'

When she got home she sat down on the couch for a moment but then she immediately fell fast asleep. It was early evening when she woke up. Light was filtering through the layers of dirt on her windows, snaking across the floor. The building was very quiet. She watched part of a talk show which featured identical twins who claimed to be able to sense when their double was in pain or danger. Several videotapes were shown that seemed to prove their connection to be extremely shaky, if not completely fake. The siblings smiled and whispered to each other.

'It doesn't matter what anyone thinks,' one twin woman with teased hair said, smiling at her sister. 'We always communicate.' The next set of brothers said they'd been kidnapped by space aliens who were 'just like us, only smaller'. She switched off the TV. She didn't think she'd want to carry the burden of anyone else's feelings. She found an old AA schedule and located a meeting in her neighbourhood which was beginning soon.

'Hey! Lillian, you're back.' The speaker was a handsome, young black man who gave her a huge hug. 'Remember me? You talked to me when I only had two weeks. I was shaking like an old leaf! I got me six months now!'

'Alan, right?' He nodded. 'That's wonderful.'

'How you doing, girl?'

'I'm going to have a baby.'

'You don't look it, sweetie.'

'I'm not very pregnant yet.'

'Happy?'

'I don't know.'

'I like babies,' he said wistfully. 'I was a great baby.'

After the speaker qualified, Lillian raised her hand. 'My name is Lillian,' she said, 'and I'm an alcoholic. I'm going to have a baby. I love its father but I don't feel ready to marry him. And I'm afraid I'll raise an unhappy child.'

The woman sitting next to her leaned over and whispered. 'Dear, you have an obligation to love that spirit that is in you right now. Start immediately. If you love the father, let him help you. There's nothing wrong with asking people for what you need.'

Lillian wrote. The job at the Flaming Hearth had left her with plenty of money. Despite long and frequent naps, she managed to finish a second story. An editor from a women's health magazine expressed interest in seeing the article she'd written about Steven. With an occasional sugar binge, she stayed on her diet and even began swimming regularly. Each day she added two more laps until she was able to tolerate nearly an hour of going back and forth, watching the black line, thinking about the past, the present, and new ideas for articles – chanting baby names when all else failed.

'Bethany – Lydia – Rachel – Sarah – Margaret – Elizabeth – Siobhan – Aisling – Brendan – Luke – Matthew – Henry – Nicholas – Edward—'

She lived in New York as a recluse, rejecting the normal schedule of the city. During the rush hour or when the streets were apt to be crowded, she stayed inside. She no longer used the subways nor would she shop in crowded supermarkets after she'd noted the acceleration of her pulse whenever she entered the local Food Emporium. There was an AA meeting in the late morning and a meditation class which met several afternoons a week. In her fourth month she began to feel afraid of being a single parent. She called Vincent's number each night, hanging up as the last button was pressed. The books she took out of the New York Public Library claimed that children who grew up without a father lacked a male mirror figure which caused boys to lack confidence and girls to feel unattractive. Lillian lay awake at night, her hand resting on the peak of her belly and tried to decide what to do.

Lizbeth called and they met for tea at The Waldorf. It had not occurred to her to announce her condition over the phone. Arriving early, Lillian sat alone. She noticed how many women looked beautiful from a long distance but when they came closer it was impossible to ignore the hardness of their eyes and the humourless lines of their mouths. They gave off a feeling of exhausted bitterness. Glancing at Lillian, they recorded her pregnancy and then quickly looked away. Their attitude towards her wasn't a surprise. She used to regard pregnant women with a sort of condescending indifference which masked her own extreme jealousy. The only people that smiled at her were other pregnant women, or men who often seemed undone by a woman in her condition. A man on the subway had beamed at her stomach and said 'That's great!' before he got off the train.

When Lizbeth arrived wearing a short black linen dress and a white jacket, Lillian stood up and her friend's face drained of colour.

'Oh my God,' she said, 'you're pregnant.'

'Sorry,' Lillian said, sitting down again. 'I should have told you on the phone.'

'What do you want me to say?' Lizbeth asked. 'Is it good news?'

'Yes,' Lillian replied, feeling fat and stupid. 'Yes.'

'Did you meet someone?'

'This is Vincent's.'

'What does he think?'

'He doesn't know.'

'How are you going to do this alone?' Lizbeth asked loudly, checking her lipstick in the teaspoon.

Lillian shrugged.

'Will your parents help?'

Lillian picked up the menu.

'Should I shut up, now?' Lizbeth asked quietly. 'Am I being a bitch?'

Lillian nodded.

Her father called and asked her to meet him for lunch. She was six months pregnant and looked it. She began to explain over the phone but words failed her. He suggested a popular restaurant in her neighbourhood. Taking her credit card, she went to a store in the neighbourhood that sold designer maternity wear. Her wardrobe consisted of leggings and old shirts. She found a mauve linen dress, cut low in the back, that made her look quite stunning. She had her hair trimmed and got a manicure.

When she entered the restaurant, her father put down his menu, smiled, took off his bifocals, stared and then stood.

'Lillian,' he asked as she approached the table, 'are you having a baby?'

'Yes.'

He ran around the side of the table to hold her elbow. The people at the table next to them stared. 'I'm going to be a grandfather,' he told them, his face suffused with joy.

'That's wonderful,' the woman said, 'it's the best thing in the world.'

Lillian's father suddenly looked much younger. The vaguely lost expression she had grown used to seeing on his face was replaced. He looked the way he often looked when he talked about his trees: inspired and animated. Happy.

'I'm calling your mother right now.' He motioned to the waiter. 'Bring us a bottle of something sparkling and non-alcoholic and your best Beluga.' He leaned over and kissed his daughter tenderly on the forehead. She realized how alone she had felt, locked in the apartment, worrying about the future, trying to write something a magazine editor might find interesting.

Their waiter came over with a bottle of seltzer in a silver bucket and two champagne flutes. 'I think pregnant women are gorgeous,' he said, 'and that dress is simply divine.'

When her father returned to the table, he was beaming. 'She's delighted,' he said. 'She sends you her dearest love and she's going into the cellar to find your old bassinet. And she wants you to see some expert baby doctor.'

'I'm going back to Maine, Daddy,' Lillian said slowly. 'There's someone there, a midwife, I'd like to deliver my baby. And I want to talk to Vincent.'

'Are you sure?' her father asked, resting his hand on her arm. 'You don't have to do that if you're not ready.'

'It's not a question of being ready, Dad. That may never happen.'

'Well, babies don't ask permission,' her father said, raising his glass so they could toast. 'After all, this was your original plan.'

Her original plan, she thought. That plan had been to grow up beautiful and smart and wealthy. To make her parents proud and to inspire men to great heights of passion. To do something beyond anyone's expectations and yet to remain very much a friend to the little people. She had practised accepting Academy Awards, Nobel Prizes, kissing her hands to large crowds, accepting bouquets from tongue-tied children. She looked down at her stomach and taking her father's hand in her own, guided it to where, if one touched the right spot, a tiny foot was kicking.

When she called Vincent's house the message on his answering machine said he was in Minneapolis. The tour had begun. When the beep sounded, she swallowed and almost began to say something but then she stopped and hung up. Hearing his voice had made her knees weak.

She was fast asleep, the new dress hanging on the door, when the buzzer sounded. It was a few minutes after eleven. She hastily pulled on a pair of leggings underneath one of Vincent's huge 'The Ramones In Dusseldorf' T-shirts.

'Yes?'

'It's Matthew. Lillian?'

'What?'

'It's Matthew. Can I come up?'

She pushed the door buzzer and then looked at herself in the mirror above her dresser and laughed. She hastily ran a brush through her almost waist-length hair and pinched her cheeks.

Matthew was smiling and holding a bouquet of roses when she answered the door. As she took the flowers, his eyes dropped and he gasped at the sight of her stomach.

'You're pregnant!' he said.

'Yup,' she answered. He was still wonderful to look at, tall and slender, but muscular. He was wearing a black T-shirt and jeans, a cotton jacket slung over his shoulder.

'Are you all right?'

'I'm fine,' Lillian said, laughing at the curious, almost frightened expression he had on his face.

'You're having it? I mean, sorry, I guess that's a stupid question.'

'Well, I'm pretty far along.'

'You look beautiful.'

'Matthew!' Lillian made a face. His standards for feminine beauty were ridiculously strict.

'I mean it. You have a wonderful light in your face. I saw that immediately. And your hair – God, it's fabulous! And your body!' He waved his arm.

'Whale-like? Hindenburg disaster?'

'No! God, no! It's—'

'Stop!' Lillian closed the door. 'Let's change the subject. Would you like some tea?'

'Can I make it?'

'That would be lovely.' She started to follow him into the kitchen but then she remembered he knew where to find everything. It seemed like another life when they'd lived together.

He emerged from the kitchen holding her teapot, looking stricken.

'What's the matter?' she asked.

'I have to tell you how sorry I am.' She shook her head but he ignored her. 'You wouldn't believe how sick I was. I hid the cocaine from you.'

'Not really.'

'Most of it. I was free-basing. Cooking it up here after you left for work. Usually I left for the bar just before you got home. Then I'd come back after I knew you'd be asleep. I'd sit in the chair watching you and I felt like such a bastard. I didn't deserve you.'

'Matthew—'

'Let me say this, Lillian! I didn't deserve you. You tried not to worry about me and you tried not to control me, and I completely fucked you over when all you did was love me. You did love me, didn't you?'

'Yes,' Lillian said, 'I did.'

'I wanted you to. I was desperate for it. You were the best thing that ever happened to me and I trashed everything. I left this apartment like a goddamned coward. Like a thief. I fucking abandoned you!'

'Make some tea. Please, Matthew. You don't have to say all this.'

'I was unfaithful to you.'

Lillian flinched. She put her hand on her stomach.

'Oh, you don't have to worry. I used condoms.'

'Don't!' She didn't want to hear this now. 'I'm sorry you feel guilty,' she told him gently, 'but I'm not sure it's fair to tell me this now. You should only make amends if it doesn't harm the other person.'

They drank tea. He told her a bit about his work. There was a feeling about him, a hesitancy that she'd failed to notice before. When she told him about selling the short story, he seemed very happy for her. Relieved, almost. She recognized that he'd never thought her capable of changing. They didn't really know each other. She remembered how he used to abandon her at parties after making sure she had a club soda. She had spent so much of her time making excuses for him, explaining his behaviour. No-one ever cared. He was the perfect bad-boyfriend. It was sad to sit with him now. She felt the weight of his regret and sorrow without accepting any of it. He had ceased to matter. After a while, she sensed he was feeling less miserable. He stretched his legs out the way he used to and glanced around the apartment.

'Where's T.W.?' he asked. 'Was he too much after all?'

'No,' she said. 'I loaned him to the baby's father.'

'Is he in the picture?'

'Maybe.'

'Lizbeth said he's a musician.'

'Yes.'

'You love this guy?' Matthew was looking at his feet.

'Very much.'

'Are you getting married?'

'I don't know. I'm going to ask him.'

'Ah.' Matthew put down his mug and picked up Lillian's hands. 'Can I come and see you again? You'll need a friend if things don't work out.' He stopped.

Lillian shook her head. 'No.' She gently removed her hands and stood up. 'I'm glad you came to see me, though. We never said goodbye properly.'

'I wanted to come back.'

She remembered. His white throat in the streetlight.

'I tried to be different, Lillian.'

'I know.' She stood holding her hands around her stomach.

He picked up his jacket. At the door he took her hand again and kissed it, turned it over and kissed the palm, pressed it against his cheek for a moment and then let it go.

'You're going to be a wonderful mother,' he said. 'I can't imagine anyone with more love to offer.'

'You should forgive yourself, Matthew. It's not your fault you couldn't love me.'

He gave her a startled, almost hurt look. She smiled and closed the door quietly behind him.

Her mother arrived with a bassinet full of vitamins and baby books. 'I'm going to cook you a month's worth of frozen dinners,' she told Lillian, sitting in her living-room-cum-hallway drinking coffee. 'We'll treat you to a new refrigerator. You don't have enough freezer space. And I think you should consider buying a condo in New Jersey.'

'I'm going to have the baby in Maine, Mom. My friend Steven, Helen's son-in-law, is a midwife. I want to marry Vincent.'

'Oh,' said Mrs Jordan, setting down her cup and inhaling deeply, 'are you planning to live in the same town as Mrs Carter?'

'I'm not sure. Vincent talked about a place in Stonington. It's close.'

'Will she be the official grandparent?'

'Mom!'

'How much do you think I'm capable of tolerating, Lillian?'

'I have no idea,' Lillian remarked quietly. 'I seem to have an infinite capacity for allowing other people to push me around.' Mrs Jordan shut her mouth. They both looked around the room.

'We can't change the past,' her mother said.

'Helen told me the silence was her decision. She said it was part of the adoption-agreement because of her alcoholism. She told me you both cried when you saw me.'

'That was noble of her. Did she tell you about your father's suicide?'

'Yes. Look Mother . . . most things I've done for our family I've done out of loyalty. I've never questioned how you chose to conduct your life but I'm starting my own family now. It may just be the baby and I, or it might include Vincent. If it does, Vincent has parents too.'

'I'm sure we'll get on fine with them.'

'I'm sure you won't. They're born-again Christians and they're very bonkers. They live in a trailer and his mother's extremely fat and you don't approve of fat people. But he loves them and they adore him and I'll have as much as an obligation to them as I do to you.'

'What makes you think he'll still marry you?' The instant Mrs Jordan spoke, she blushed deeply.

Lillian counted to ten. All her life she had allowed her mother to make this sort of comment.

'I'm sorry, Lillian.'

'Why are you so afraid?'

'Afraid? What does that mean?'

'Hostility is a by-product of terror, Mum.'

'I'm not hostile.'

'I love Daddy. You've stood in front of him, between us, since I was a little girl. I need him as much as I need you. You should stop trying to keep us apart.'

Mrs Jordan stood up. 'What makes you think I have any control over your father? He does exactly as he pleases! Maybe *he* chooses to keep his distance from you! Obviously you've figured everyone out. What's wrong with your brother? Latent homosexuality? Is that my fault, also?'

'This isn't about you.'

'Oh, yes it is! You're feeling all-powerful because you're pregnant. Well, just wait, Madonna! You go up to that godforsaken town with that ridiculous woman and see how long you can survive without our help!'

Lillian stood up and faced her mother. 'I stopped drinking without your help!'

'What did you expect us to do?'

'Ask some questions! Remember the anniversary of my sobriety and mention it! Be willing to come to counselling.'

'Why should we? It was that woman's fault you turned out like that.'

'Like what? Afraid to love anyone? Filled with fear and self-doubt and unable to connect with men because my own father feels guilty every time he looks at me too closely? Is that Helen's fault, Mother? If I had a feeling which upset you, it was my job to spend hours convincing you I never had it! My dearest fantasy was of dying so you would finally understand I wasn't happy or OK!'

'She's done this to you,' Mrs Jordan said, her eyes filling with tears. 'That woman poisoned your mind against me.'

'Get out!' Lillian crossed to her front door and flung it open, her whole body was shaking.

'Honey!'

'Get out of here, Mother. Just get out.'

Mrs Jordan left, crying. Lillian's phone rang at midnight. She heard the soft tones of her father's voice on her machine.

'—didn't mean to hurt your feelings.'

'Daddy?'

'Honey, it's Dad.'

'I know.'

'You're mother's very upset.'

Lillian didn't say anything. Her father cleared his throat. 'Could you talk to her?'

'No.'

'Can I tell her everything's OK?'

'No.'

'Lillian?'

'Tell her anything's possible. I won't be bullied by anyone, any more. Tell her to go see a therapist.'

'All right. We'll see. Go back to sleep now.'

'Bye, Dad.'

She lay on her back trying to see the sky through the solid plaster of her ceiling. She felt the baby gently moving inside and imagined the two of them floating through Outer Space together with T.W., like a cartoon, each with their own air bubble. She thought it was a good thing she was learning to protect herself. She practised proposing to Vincent.

'Vincent, will you marry us? Vincent, our unborn child and I, we need you. Vincent, I'm having your baby. Marry me! I love you, Vincent. Be my husband.' She began to laugh. 'Yo, Vinnie! A bun's in the oven! Vicenzo . . . *comme si dice*? *Bambino-eccolo che viene!*' She had to get out of bed for a glass of water. Laughing hysterically, flat on her back, had given her hiccups.

21

What first struck her about Minneapolis was how kind everyone was. People offered her their seats, persuaded her to take their place in line, smiled and nodded with an unnatural degree of warmth. It wasn't until she entered the ladies' room of Vincent's hotel that she made the connection: the kind treatment she was receiving was inspired by the largeness of her belly. She stopped in front of a full-length mirror and inhaled sharply. While her face had not changed much, it was undeniably fuller. The distinct lines of her cheekbones had softened.

'You got a little girl, there,' the bathroom attendant said, 'I can tell by the way you're carrying her.'

Lillian smiled. 'I hope so,' she said, putting on some lipstick.

'Well, of course you do, honey! Boys are nothing but heartbreak and bad cheques. You get a little girl and send her to school. She's the one who can take care of Mama!'

At the reception desk they looked at her identification and then told her Vincent's room number. As she walked towards the elevators, it occurred to her that he might have company and she felt it would be wrong to arrive without warning. She asked the receptionist to ring his room.

'He's coming down,' she was told.

He has a woman in his room, Lillian thought. Otherwise, he'd have told her to go up. She looked at herself in the mirror and flinched.

When the elevator doors opened he stepped out, his hair damp. They must have been making love, Lillian thought, he's taken a shower. Looking around the lobby, Vincent saw her and began to cross the carpet towards where she was sitting. Quickly, with difficulty, she stood. As he took her in, the smile disappeared, the expression on his face was one of shock, a look she had never seen.

'Wow,' he said to no-one, 'she's pregnant.' He stepped forward and tried to pull her into his arms.

'Vincent,' Lillian said, 'is there a girl in your room?'

He let go of her and stepped back. 'Great. So who knocked you up?'

'Who do you think?'

'I wouldn't know.' He sat down on the edge of the table while she started to pick up her bag.

'Where are you going?'

'Back to New York.'

'Oh for fuck's sake.'

Several people glared at Vincent and a man stopped on his way out of the door.

'Are you all right, miss?' he asked kindly.

'Of course she's all right,' Vincent snapped. 'It's my baby, jerk.'

'How do you know that?' Lillian tried to pick up her bag again but Vincent put his foot on it.

'Because it is,' Vincent responded weakly.

'There's a girl in your room.'

'Yes,' Vincent snapped, 'there is! A low-IQ blonde who never gives me a bad time.'

'I'm going back to New York,' Lillian sobbed, starting for the door, leaving her bag behind.

'Don't,' Vincent said, his voice low but with a ferocity that froze her. 'If you leave me again, we're finished.'

She turned her face towards him. 'I don't know where to go,' she said, tears running down her face.

'Come here.' Vincent held out his arms and finally she went. Burying her face on his chest, she sagged into his arms. 'I love you, Lillian,' Vincent whispered. 'I love our baby.'

Vincent's suite was filled with music equipment, baskets of fruit and flowers. While he was in the bathroom, Lillian picked up a magazine and several photographs of a naked woman sitting on a huge motorcycle fell out. 'Shit,' she muttered, trying to put them back.

'Honey, you want a shower?' Vincent came out of the bathroom and frowned when he saw what she had in her hand. 'Where'd that garbage come from?'

'It fell out of the magazine. I'm sorry. I wasn't snooping.'

'I know that.' Vincent took the pictures out of her hand and ripped them to shreds, throwing the pieces into the garbage.

'Who sent those?'

'Some dumb cunt.'

'Vincent!'

'A fan, then! Look, she thinks if she sends me pictures of her straddling a Harley, I'll call her.'

'Why do you keep them?'

'I don't. I thought I'd gotten rid of these. One of the maids probably decided to put them in there as a joke.'

'Is this going to work?'

'What?' Vincent asked.

'Us.'

'You tell me, Lillian.'

Lillian sighed. 'I don't know.'

'Do you want it to work?'

'Yes. But I don't understand stuff like this.'

'Naked women? Come on. Sometimes you act like you're a visitor from some third-world country where *Hustler* isn't available. Don't pretend not to get it. *Power*. People like to fuck with power.'

'It's more than that.'

'What do you mean?'

'Women see more than your power. That's normal. You're this guy that plays the guitar and still calls his mother and doesn't fuck around.' She picked up an earring she had found on the bureau. 'Much.'

'So what?'

'Look at me!' Lillian shouted miserably.

'I haven't stopped doing that since you got here!'

'I look like something a child would draw.'

'You're pregnant.'

'I know I'm pregnant! But even when I'm not, we aren't alike.'

'Thank God!'

'Are you sure you want to do this?'

'Did I leave you?'

'No,' Lillian muttered sadly. 'No.'

'Take your clothes off.' He was sitting on the edge of the bed, watching her finish the glass of milk which room service had brought up. She pulled off her leg-warmers and hesitated.

'My body frightens me. I'm really big.'

'It's wonderful,' Vincent said, crossing to where she sat, putting his hands on either side of her face and kissing her mouth. He gently unbuttoned her shirt and unclasped her bra, holding her breasts and then letting them go. He began to massage Lillian's skin. She slid to the floor and he touched her everywhere with long, hard strokes, his lips following the path of his hands, then his tongue. He pulled her to her knees and took off his own clothes. They knelt, facing each other and then he put his hand against her breasts and gently pushed her backwards, burying his face between her thighs. He turned her around and entered her from behind, she felt his arms around her, encircling her completely, as in her dreams. His face was pressed against her back. She sighed with tiredness, relief.

'You missed me, didn't you, babe?' he whispered, kissing the nape of her neck softly.

'Yes,' Lillian moaned.

He moved against her again, touching in front so they both came together. She could feel his heart beating against her back.

'Yes, Lillian,' he whispered, kissing the length of her spine. 'I'll marry you.'

For most of the afternoon they slept, waking up to take a shower and order ice cream and cookies from room service. Lillian showed Vincent her diet and he promised to support her efforts to stop eating junk food.

'We'll go macro tomorrow,' he said, patting her stomach.

The record company was throwing a party for Vincent at a club in the old part of Minneapolis, a section of town that was suddenly very trendy. Beforehand they watched a videotape of Vincent's last local performance in a small club in Cambridge, Mass. She noticed he seemed unusually terse and slightly uncomfortable on stage. When requests for 'Lillian' were shouted, Vincent drank from a bottle of beer and then, bending into the microphone said, 'Don't ask for that song, man. I'll sing anything else.'

'I love you, Vinnie!' a woman screamed from the audience.

'No you don't,' he said, drinking more beer. 'But it's a nice thing to say.'

'What's the matter with you, man?' an audience member shouted. 'Did the bitch burn you?'

Vincent laughed. 'Blame it on the blues,' he said, beginning to play an old tune that was about drinking, gambling, taking drugs, loving and losing. The audience was rapt, touched by his misery.

'When did you play this gig?' Lillian asked, standing behind Vincent, her arms around his neck.

'About a week after you split.'

'Were you that miserable?'

Vincent thought for a moment. 'Well, sure. But hey, I never performed so well! This tape lit a bonfire under Jupiter. They saw I wasn't just a pretty boy. Depth and maturity. It helped push them further towards signing me.'

'How nice for you,' Lillian said, pulling her hands out of his grasp.

Vincent turned around to look at her. 'What's wrong with that?'

'It just amazes me how you use your life for material.'

'That's called being an artist, babe.'

'Don't call me *babe*!'

'For Christ's sake. What do you write about?'

'Me.'

'And?'

'My parents, Edward, Anthony, Lizbeth.'

'Ah hah! What about me?'

'No.'

'Why not?'

'I don't have any perspective.'

'Oh.'

The door buzzer sounded.

'Who's that?'

'Frank. He's coming with us to the party.'

'That nut from Jupiter Records? The one who kept informing me I was "happening"?'

'Yup. Come on Lillian – babe – this is show biz!'

She threw a pillow at Vincent.

'Don't stand up. He has a weak heart.'

She ran into the bedroom while Vincent answered the door. The bed was covered with clothes, books and newspapers. In the bathroom, she carefully applied lipstick and brushed her hair. From the neck up she looked very nice.

'Hey,' Frank said, as she walked back into the living-room. His mouth stayed open as he absorbed the sight of her stomach.

Vincent stood and put his arm around her shoulder. 'You like babies, Frank?' he asked, laughing.

'No,' Frank said automatically. Lillian watched his Adam's apple quiver. 'I mean, sure! Some of them. Quiet ones. You know – quiet babies.'

'We're not going to have a quiet baby, Frank.'

Frank smiled. 'This is great. You look great, Lillian. I mean the hair's great. And so's the rest of it.' He vaguely indicated her body. 'How ya feel?'

'Great,' Lillian said, sitting down.

The party began at eleven, after a short performance by another Jupiter-label band called The Sick Weasels. There was no food and Lillian felt out of place in her linen dress and pumps. The other guests were all thin, dressed in black, and looked stoned. Their ages were hard to determine. Vincent kept bringing people up to meet her, introducing them and then leaving her alone to make hopeless conversation about New York or music. She was hungry and tired. She noticed several women giving her strange looks until she finally encountered one of them in the ladies' room and decided to make an attempt at meeting someone.

'Do you work for Jupiter?' she asked the thin brunette who was wearing black leather.

'No,' the woman said, finishing her lipstick and then carefully (her nails were very long) lighting a cigarette. 'I'm a back-up singer.'

'Oh,' Lillian sat down on the couch and felt she would never get up. 'Who do you sing with?'

'Local bands, mostly. I did a tour with Tom Petty. You're Lillian, right?'

'Yeah.'

'It's a great song. When's the baby due?'

'Late December or early January.'

'You guys getting married?'

'I hope so. What's your name?'

'Audrey.' Audrey sat down next to Lillian. 'How old do you think I am?'

'Twenty-five?'

'Thirty-four.'

Lillian looked more closely at Audrey. 'You look much younger than that.'

'I don't drink or do drugs. It keeps you looking young. If I could just quit these.' She waved her cigarette in the air.

'Did you do it on your own?'

'Get straight? Nah. I'm in AA.'

'Me too!'

'No kidding? That's great!' The two women beamed at each other. 'I guess that's why we're sitting in the bathroom. This party is such a drag.'

'There's no food! I hate parties without food.'

'You want part of a Mars bar?'

'Yes!'

Audrey fished a half-eaten chocolate bar out of her purse. Lillian broke it in two and gave Audrey half.

'Where'd you meet Vincent?'

'In Maine. At a bar.'

'Are you happy?' Audrey asked wistfully.

'I don't know,' Lillian said slowly. 'I think so.'

'I wish I was pregnant,' Audrey said, looking at Lillian's stomach.

'Do you have a boyfriend?'

'I have two boyfriends. They're both losers. I collect losers like little porcelain figurines. It's a habit I'm trying to break. Hey, you want to go to a meeting with me tomorrow?' Audrey took out her AA schedule book. 'There's this great step-meeting at noon tomorrow.'

'Really?' Lillian said. She rested her head on Audrey's naked shoulder for a moment. 'I feel overwhelmed at the moment.'

'Don't worry,' Audrey said, patting her forehead. 'You're safe.'

                    ★   ★   ★

'So,' Vincent asked her as they leaned against each other in the back of the Limo. 'Did you have a good time?'

'Uh huh,' Lillian said sleepily.

'Where were you?'

'In the bathroom.'

'Getting sick?'

'No! Talking to that girl Audrey.'

'The singer? Good. She's a nice person. What were you talking about? Me?'

Lillian laughed. 'No.' She snuggled up against Vincent's shoulder. 'Would you love me if I was always this big?' she asked him as she drifted off to sleep.

'No,' Vincent whispered in her ear. 'I'd send you to a fat-camp.'

With her remaining strength, she grabbed the tiny roll of flesh around his waist. 'And what's your excuse?' she mumbled.

22

On the way home to Maine, they stopped in Boston to buy Lillian's wedding dress. After spending seven hours searching through racks of antique dresses, she found what she wanted: a white embroidered dress with long full sleeves and a dropped waist. Lizbeth had recommended a designer who let out all the seams and restyled the dress to flatter and minimize Lillian's pregnancy.

'He specializes in pregnant brides,' Lizbeth had told her. 'He'll make you look less like an overdressed marshmallow.'

When Lillian returned to their hotel room, Vincent was sitting in the alcove which overlooked a walled garden, playing his acoustic guitar.

'What are you doing?' she asked, putting her packages down.

'Thinking.'

'About what?'

'About you.'

'Yes?'

'How much I want us to be a family. After you left I didn't care about whether all this shit happened with the record deal. That came as a nasty shock. I've never been indifferent to playing music before.'

'Vincent . . . ' she started towards him.

'Why didn't you tell me you were pregnant sooner?'

'I was afraid.'

'That I wouldn't want the baby?'

'No. That I wouldn't. I didn't know how I felt about anything.'

'Is that true now?'

'No.' She sat down at his feet and he slowly began to massage her shoulders.

'It's not enough for us to try and be good to each other. Both of us are pretty selfish. We're going to have to grow up.'

'What if I'm a terrible mother?'

'How can you be a terrible mother?'

'Easy!'

'Hey, it's a baby. We'll do our best. You're sort of a bitch and I'm a manipulative hypocrite. We can balance each other out.'

'Couple counselling.'

'Group therapy.'

She laughed and leaned against his knee. A wooden box dropped into her lap. Inside was a ring, an emerald surrounded by diamonds. It was old and obviously very expensive. The stone was a perfect green. It reminded her of a child's crayon.

'Oh my God! Vincent!'

'Look, we had to get a ring. We're getting married by a radical lesbian.'

'The minister's a lesbian?'

'Of course she's a lesbian!'

'Oh. Well, that's nice.'

'Yes, but it's not traditional. Something has to make the old folks feel like this is a real wedding.'

When Lillian called to invite her parents to the wedding, her mother had been very polite, cool and distant.

'How nice,' she said, as if Lillian had just offered her a trial subscription to *Time*. 'We'll try to make it.'

'Mother, please come.'

'Are you sure you want us there?'

'Yes. Edward's coming. Please. It will give everyone a chance to meet each other. Before the baby's born. The ceremony is going to be short.'

'I hope it's not too short.'

'No, it's the perfect length.'

'Are you having a civil ceremony?'

'No, Vincent went to school with an Episcopal minister.'

'You're not a Protestant.'

'It doesn't matter.'

'What's his name?'

'Her name is Constance Morgan.'

'A woman?'

'Yes. In fact, a lesbian.' Lillian heard her mother exhale like the noise a tyre makes after being punctured. 'Mom, call us with the flight information, OK?'

Someone, one of the guys in Vincent's band, would later describe the wedding as being like 'an acid trip that just kept getting weirder'. On the morning of her marriage, Lillian came downstairs wearing one of Vincent's T-shirts slit up the side, a pair of pregnancy exercise tights, and sweat socks. Her hair was twisted off her face and anchored on top of her head with a knitting needle. When she walked into the kitchen she was greeted by the sight of her parents drinking coffee with Edward.

'Here she is,' Edward said, laughing. 'A fashion statement is being made, ladies and gentlemen. We aren't sure what it is, but she's definitely saying something.'

'What are you doing here?' Lillian asked her parents. 'We expected you at eleven-thirty. It's eight.'

'They got an earlier flight, honey,' Vincent explained. 'You were asleep when they called last night.'

'And I just happened to get in from Montreal last night,' Edward said, beaming at his furious sister. 'Why are you marrying this woman?' he asked Vincent. 'I have never encountered anyone who wakes up with more unconditional hate and rage in her heart.'

'Stop it, Edward!' Mrs Jordan said, glaring at her son. 'I'm sorry honey, but the flight was direct instead of stopping in Boston.'

Lillian shrugged and smiled. 'Welcome to Maine,' she said. Vincent handed her a cup of herb tea. The sink was full of dishes and there were dust balls everywhere she looked. Helen's car pulled into the driveway. 'Oh my God,' she said.

'Hey, it's your real mother!' Edward exclaimed. Lillian kicked him hard under the table. 'What's that for?'

'For being such a creep,' Lillian hissed.

'Give her some coffee, Vinnie. Herb tea does not soothe our savage little mother-to-be.'

Lillian noticed her parents stiffen slightly as Helen opened the door. Her hair had been cut severely and she was wearing an elegant black wool coat. Helen had sounded very happy to hear about the wedding. When Lillian had told her she was eight months pregnant, there'd been a short silence.

'Oh darling,' Helen whispered, her voice breaking. 'Why didn't you let me know?'

'It's OK.'

'How do you feel?'

'Great. Large with child.'

'I have wonderful baby toys in the attic.' Both women were silent.

'It's going to be fun,' Lillian said, her voice shaking.

'We will not regret the past nor will we wish to close the door on it . . . ' Helen quoted from one of the Promises in Alcoholics Anonymous.

'Right,' Lillian said. 'Exactly.'

'How do you do?' Helen said to Mr and Mrs Jordan.

'Fine,' they both replied, their voices slightly shrill. 'We're fine.'

'And how are you, Cary Grant?' Helen asked, turning towards Edward.

'I'm fine, too,' he answered, kissing her. 'Fabulous hair. So, we're the fine family. Personally, I think this is the weirdest configuration I've ever seen, definite talk-show material. All we need is Lillian's ex-husband, an abused child and a few incest victims.'

'Edward,' Mrs Jordan said. 'Don't be so—' she struggled for a word.

'Obnoxious?' Helen suggested.

'Exactly,' Mrs Jordan said, smiling.

'Did you see her dress yet?' Helen asked her.

'No,' Mrs Jordan said. 'We just arrived.'

'Come on,' Helen stood, unbuttoning her coat. 'It's gorgeous.'

'Considering it's cut to fit that.' Edward pointed at his sister.

Vincent leaned over and pulled the knitting needle out of Lillian's hair, which tumbled down below her shoulders. He kissed the tip of her nose. 'Leave her alone,' he said. 'She's my delicate little petal.'

Mr Jordan beamed at his future son-in-law. 'I liked your song, Vincent.'

'Would you like to see the garden, Walter?' Vincent put his arm around Mr Jordan's shoulder. 'I'm trying to get a vegetable patch together. Lillian said you have a green thumb.'

'Yes I would,' Mr Jordan said, picking up his coat. 'I can recommend some excellent natural pesticides.'

When the two men went out, Lillian poured herself a cup of coffee, replaced the knitting needle and sat down.

'Should you drink that?' Edward asked.

'I'm not talking to you.'

'Caffeine's a no-no.'

'Leave me alone.'

'So, what gum machine spat that out?' Edward gestured towards Lillian's ring.

'It's a perfect emerald.'

'Nothing's perfect.'

'I'm not talking to you.'

'So, are you happy?'

'I have a headache.'

'You always have a headache.'

'No I don't.'

'Yes you do.'

There was a long silence. Edward began to whistle but stopped when Lillian pressed the tines of a fork into the back of his hand.

'Is this minister really a radical Lesbian feminist who's having her companion inseminated with a turkey baster?'

Lillian nodded.

'Neat. You never thought of that turkey-baster idea, did you?'

Lillian threw a muffin at Edward which missed him and landed on the floor. The baby kicked hard enough to cause her coffee cup to jump.

'He feels the caffeine,' Edward said fondly.

'She approves of our politics,' Lillian replied.

'She? Oh God, don't have a girl! Girls are a complete disaster! I mean, give Vincent some sort of pleasure.'

'Vincent likes girls more than boys. Anyway, we don't know what it will be. It may be a hermaphrodite.'

'It's gonna be a boy I can take to the ball game. What could I do with a girl?'

'You could torture and belittle her and undermine her self-confidence. You're very good at doing that.'

'Hmm,' Edward said, brightening, leaning over to pinch Lillian's cheek. 'Thanks, sis. I feel a whole lot better. You're really cool even if you are fat.'

* * *

After the wedding, Mildred, Helen and Mrs Jordan cooked enough food to last the entire winter in Stonington. Vincent stayed at home writing music and reading medical textbooks. He was convinced Lillian should go to hospital to have their child. His conversation became full of descriptions of breech births and the importance of having a surgical team present while the mother was in labour. Lillian tried to write and found herself obsessed with reading terrible novels which featured feisty heroines who ran major corporations and had married lovers and then married the boy next door. Her only other reading material consisted of books with titles like *How To Get Your Baby Into An Ivy League College* and *How To Raise A Bilingual Infant*. It seemed impossible to maintain any sort of autonomy. If she wasn't waiting for Vincent to come home with ice cream, she was talking to her stomach. She wandered around her house smiling like a horribly sentimental advertisement for electricity.

The concept of 'natural' childbirth began to seem ridiculous. But when Lillian went into labour, they had Steven beeped. She was very calm. Vincent had an anxiety attack which only ended upon Steven's arrival. He circled his pregnant wife as if she were some sort of explosive object until Lillian ordered him to take T.W. for a walk. During the eighth hour of labour, Lillian made a speech accusing Steven of being a 'quack jerk-off' who enjoyed watching women suffer. Her cervix wasn't dilated enough and she began to wonder if any result would make the process worthwhile. When Vincent suggested she breathe through the pain, she told him she wanted a divorce. 'Life is nothing but pain!' she screamed at both men. 'When this baby is born, you'll have nothing to do with her! I've done everything!'

Vincent gave her a fudgesicle and a back rub and she took most of her words back. Edward flew in from the set of his new movie and amused the in-laws and Mildred with out-takes from *Desert Aliens From Hell*. When he tried to video part of the birth, Lillian called him a 'voyeuristic worm'. He retreated to drink Earl Gray tea and filmed everyone waiting – with the sound of Lillian shouting and breathing as the soundtrack. Everyone was having fun at Lillian's delivery except the madonna herself.

'Go away!' she screamed at Vincent in the eleventh hour of her labour.

'No,' he said, wiping her face with a cold cloth. 'Just get used to it.'

She was, after all, a baby girl. She was called Lydia and there was no way that Lillian could tell by staring into her grey-green kitten eyes whether her life was going to be more difficult or easier than anyone else's. Lillian knew that her life had been changed irreparably and she welcomed that transformation. It seemed perfect that her relationship with this alien creature should commence at such a fever pitch. When Lydia was put down on her mother's belly by Steven, Lillian laughed. Vincent stood looking down at them both. He had deep, purple shadows under his eyes, his hair was pulled back and he looked absurdly young to be a father.

'Nice,' he said, touching Lydia's back and then Lillian's cheek. 'You done good, babe.'

'Don't call us babe,' Lillian whispered. Lydia put her head up like an excited turtle and this time both parents laughed weakly. At that moment Lillian found it trivial to recall the pain that had seemed so unbearable.

Matthew sent them a silver christening set which was first used when T.W. swallowed the spoon. He was taken to the vet and pronounced idiotic, but surgery was not advised and eventually the spoon turned up, tarnished and bent, at the bottom of the garden.

A package arrived from an exclusive French boutique containing matching mother/daughter dresses. Lillian's dress was a size she had not worn since junior school. 'For when you're back to normal,' Lizbeth had written. Lydia's dress was a great success until she threw up on it and Lillian ignored the 'Dry Clean Only' tag and shrank it beyond recognition.

'Imagine buying a new baby a dress that has to be dry cleaned,' she said, lying next to Vincent, reading an article about the feminist backlash.

'You can wear yours, I think it's pretty.'

'It's a size six,' Lillian said. 'I was never a size six.'

'You could be if you wanted to be.'

Lillian put down the magazine. 'I don't want to be.'

'OK.'

'Would you prefer I was?'

'No.' Vincent yawned. 'You're perfect.'

'What's that supposed to mean?'

'What I said.'

'You think I'm too fat.' She stood up and faced him, her arms crossed in front of her. 'I know the kind of anorexic groupie blonde sluts you like.'

'Great. Tell me so I'll know the next time one's offered.'

'Offered? God, how could I have married such a stereotypical masculine personification of female debasement?'

'Who else would have you?' Vincent asked, picking up her magazine and beginning to read an article about day care.

'Matthew for one.'

'The junkie? Well, what a shame I kept you from that.'

'I'm a junkie too, you insensitive creep!'

'Yeah, well . . . ' Vincent looked baffled. 'How did this start?'

'You implied I should be a size six.'

'Oh. Can we stop now?'

Lillian returned to her place and picked up the magazine. 'You hurt my feelings,' she said.

'Never mind,' Vincent murmured, putting his head on her stomach.

'I don't think you'd like Lizbeth,' Lillian said, stroking Vincent's head.

'Why not?'

'She's so intense. Quite neurotic.'

'What makes you think I don't like neurotic women?' Vincent asked, his hand creeping under her nightgown.

'I'm not that intense,' Lillian said sharply. 'And leave my tits alone. They're sore.'

'Shall I kiss them better?'

'No. I'm *not* neurotic.'

'Shall I kiss them all better?'

'Yes. And say I'm not like Lizbeth.'

'I've never met Lizbeth.'

'Well, I don't care. I'm not like her.'

'Good.'

During Lydia's first year, several more of Lillian's short stories were purchased. When the ideas stopped coming, she assumed it was a temporary lull and used the time to start running again, to learn how to 'put up' fruit and when things were really slow, she joined a quilting group and began to work on a massive fabric commemorating some obscure battle that had been fought on the outskirts of Bangor. The group consisted of five other women with babies of Lydia's age, and the sole topic of conversation was the care and feeding of their children.

'I'm not Tolstoy,' Lillian announced one sunny morning as Lydia was feeding her oatmeal to T.W., who waited patiently as the toddler dropped globs of cereal into his open mouth.

'Good,' Vincent replied, looking at her over the *Bangor Daily News*. 'I'm not fond of gloomy Russians. Should we get a new lawn-mower?'

Lillian frowned. 'But I'm an artist,' she continued,

taking Lydia's spoon away and pushing Thomas Wolfe out from under the table. 'What do I care about grass? How can we allow such trivial matters to occupy space in our brains?' Lydia poured her juice over her head and began to scream.

Lillian waited for Vincent to react but he didn't look up from his paper until Lillian leaned over and snatched it from his hands.

'Would you pretend to consider yourself equally responsible,' she hissed like an enraged cobra.

'Your daughter's a nutter,' Vincent said, leaning over with his napkin to wipe Lydia's eyes. 'Just like Mom.'

She went to an AA meeting and shared about her lousy husband. The other alcoholics nodded sympathetically. Almost everyone identified their own spouse as insensitive and stupid. One woman said she hadn't spoken to her husband for nearly two years.

'Tax time. That's when we have a little chat. He asks me to sign the form, I sign the form and then he goes to see his friends at the post office.'

Instead of returning home, Lillian walked down to the harbour and stood looking out across the water. From a distance she could hear the low, slow moan of a fog horn. After two years of marriage, and the birth of a child, she often felt more alone than ever. Many times she reached out to Vincent and found he could not provide her with the answers she needed. In fact he rarely understood the question. To blame him for not viewing things as she did was rarely possible. It was their differences which made them compatible and their differences which underscored her isolation.

Lillian had been born hungry. Her two emotions as a child were anticipation and disappointment: looking forward to everything and feeling let down by it all. The circus had given her a headache; her birthdays invariably ended with her being sent to bed for bad behaviour; chocolate mousse was too guilty a pleasure to enjoy properly.

When Lydia entered her terrible twos, sometimes Lillian noticed her daughter watching her tenderly, looking to be sure her mother was happy. This smote her to the heart. But Lydia could not shoulder the responsibility of her mother's happiness. And Vincent seemed incapable of separating his own wishes from those of anyone else around him. Because he was raised to regard himself as nothing less than a miracle, it was impossible for him to consider other people when he made decisions. As long as everyone was given equal time with him, he assumed they would be happy.

For the first time in her life, Lillian did not react to another person's hurting her by withdrawing. Despite the fear which seemed to grip her by the throat when she tried to express her feelings to Vincent, she persevered. Loving him, loving Lydia, had changed her completely. She would die for either of them without a single regret. The rôle of the sacrificial virgin had never looked so attractive. Lacking such an extreme sacrifice, she tried her best to feel like a woman who was responsible for her own happiness.

23

Vincent's career was the most important one in their family. Since signing with Jupiter, one of his songs had been nominated for a Grammy and several major artists had recorded his music. The most lucrative part of his business was writing and recording jingles. He was the voice and music behind a chain of Texas Barbecue joints called 'Good Eats'. He sang to parents about children's aspirin and crooned a tune about blondes on a commercial for hair colour.

Vincent believed he had sacrificed rock superstardom for his family, a version of his life that Lillian viewed as distorted. In her opinion he was doing exactly what he wanted while she assumed the rôle of the responsible parent. Except for writing an occasional article for the *Boston Globe* and helping to edit an anthology of short fiction which included one of her own stories, she had put her most ambitious career plans on the shelf. It was hard to explain to Lydia why she couldn't play if she was only in the study staring at her computer screen. Her daughter would stand outside murmuring 'Mama' over and over again, ignoring the pleas of the baby-sitter, until the door opened and her mother emerged, furious and guilt-stricken yet secretly relieved.

A prestigious Arts Festival invited Lillian to read her work the summer that Lydia was two. Vincent volunteered to stay home, insisting he would welcome the opportunity to spend time with his daughter. During the previous year he had been away more than he was at home. His band had toured Canada, a film producer had asked him to help score a new movie and he had gone to Europe to play bass guitar with an old buddy from school.

'We'll be fine,' Vincent said, kissing her goodbye at the airport. 'See you in five days.'

The Arts Festival was held in a small town in North Carolina. During the day there were readings of poetry and fiction, workshops with famous writers and the opportunity to swim, run and sit in the sun. At night, people met for dinner and then went dancing. As much as she missed Vincent and Lydia, Lillian found herself having a wonderful time. She wore clothes that had been hanging in her closet for a year, the labels still attached. Instead of ordering food that she knew Lydia would enjoy, she feasted on lobster, oysters and spicy cajun stews. On the third night she was there, she received a message with Helen's telephone number. Vincent had forbidden her to call home, insisting he would contact her if there were any problems.

'Are you having fun?'

Lillian could hear Lydia in the background begging for the phone. 'Sure. What's wrong?'

'Nothing. Everything's fine. Do you want to talk to Lydia?'

'In a second. Where's Vincent?'

'Oh, he had a gig in Boston. Some important contact.'

'This was supposed to be a free week.'

'That's what he said. It's probably for the best, dear. I think he was a little overwhelmed.'

'*Overwhelmed?* Two days alone with his own daughter and he loses it?'

Helen cleared her throat. 'Well, you are a wonderful mother.'

'What does that have to do with anything? He had nothing more challenging to do than feed the dog and play with his kid. Is T.W. there with you, too?'

'Of course he is. Here's your little darling.'

When Lydia was nearly one, Vincent had been hired to write the score for a new television series about three widowers living in Asbury Park. He'd taken his family and they had spent five months living in a bungalow outside Los Angeles. Vincent worked at the studio every morning and usually stayed late into the night. It was impossible to walk anywhere, so Lillian found herself driving up and down the freeway with Lydia strapped into the baby seat, searching for a park in which to exercise Thomas Wolfe. The car began to resemble some sort of prison. Lydia and Thomas Wolfe didn't like being stuck in the back seat while Lillian tried to navigate the LA freeways. On the few occasions she decided to walk anywhere, the baby in her stroller, T.W. on a leash, she felt like an alien from another planet whose ignorance of Earth behaviour would cause her to be hunted down and killed.

She began to crave oblivion, to fantasize about asking her doctor for a Valium prescription so the days might pass with less clarity, the edges rounded. The local AA meetings were filled with celebrities who kept complaining about their lack of credibility. Glimpsing such insecurity in people she recognized as famous only increased Lillian's sense of herself as unsuccessful. Finally, she'd found an office space in Hollywood and rented a computer. But baby-sitters were scarce. After they had hired several unsuitable Valley Girls who put Lydia in front of the huge television set with MTV blaring, the child began to have nightmares. One morning Lillian woke Vincent up by announcing she wanted a divorce. They went to see a famous psychiatrist in Sherman Oaks who was most interested in discussing Vincent's feelings about playing guitar.

'I always wanted to be a rock musician,' he said, leaning back to light his pipe. 'I can't tell you how much I admire you.'

The rest of the session centred upon Lydia's feeling of abandonment when Lillian left her with a baby-sitter and went to the office to write. Lydia illustrated her position well by sucking her thumb (a rare occurrence), clutching a very worn Eeyore doll and clinging to Lillian like a small kangaroo.

Los Angeles taught Lillian what it meant to be married. She had to try and explain her position to Vincent without considering the possibility that their differences were irreconcilable. Negotiation was crucial. She didn't deny that she felt frightened by what was happening to them. They rarely had sex without arguing about the reasons for its infrequency. Each accused the other of using intimacy as a weapon. The responsibility for their domestic life had landed squarely in her lap. Although Vincent made an attempt to be available, he was never out of touch with his record company. There were telephones in their cars, a cellular phone in the bathroom and a fax machine in every place they rented. Lydia cried at the sound of a phone ringing because it invariably represented her daddy's imminent departure.

'She'll have to go to phone therapy,' Lillian told Vincent. 'It's gone beyond sibling rivalry.'

The two years which followed their Los Angeles period were relatively quiet. Vincent had built a studio and worked with local Boston musicians so there was no reason for long trips to California. Lillian was writing a column on books for the *Bangor Daily News*. Lydia graduated from nursery school and began to read much too early. They had the Stonington house renovated, adding an apartment over the garage for visitors and knocking down the walls which divided the dining-room and kitchen. Lillian began to believe marriage was quite an uncomplicated business.

Three days after Lydia's fourth birthday, Vincent's agent called and told him he was needed in Los Angeles to score a major picture for 'at least three months'.

'I'm not coming,' Lillian had announced when Vincent told her of the plan.

'What?' he asked, a portable phone glued to his ear while he lifted a ten-pound weight in his right hand.

'Lydia loves Dorothy and I'm not going to break in another sitter. I hate the AA meetings out there.'

Vincent put down the weight. 'Call me back,' he said into the receiver and dropped the phone on the couch. 'You have to come,' he told Lillian flatly, 'I'm not leaving without you.'

'So don't leave. Why can't you record here? I'm working on a short-story collection.' Lillian picked up one of Lydia's sneakers and put it on the stairs. 'They finally gave me a contract at the paper. I have projects in the thresher which I can't take to California.'

'They want Lydia to be in the video.'

Vincent's new song was about Lydia and an independent record label had signed him to record it. Edward had a friend in Boston, willing to shoot the film for nothing but expenses. While Lillian was happy that her husband was finally being given the opportunity to perform his own music, she believed the ballad wasn't about Lydia at all. It was about children and fatherhood. It was about Vincent's own feelings. Lydia was just a visual cue. She was not the subject of this song any more than her mother was of 'Lillian'. A song might hang upon certain themes but in the end it existed to make the musician lots of money and spotlight him as a sensitive, tortured genius.

'I don't want her being filmed.'

'Why not?'

'Are you crazy? What kind of disassociation would her own video produce?'

'We'll go see Dr Wagner again.'

'That schmuck in Sherman Oaks? He wants to be in your band, Vincent! He wants to be you! If Lydia understood the process, it might be different but she's too young. Anyway, people don't need to know what she looks like.'

'Lillian—'

'I don't want my daughter on television!'

'She's not just your daughter!'

'It's unhealthy, all this attention! Look at you.'

Vincent looked hurt. 'What's that supposed to mean?'

'It means I'd prefer you not to cause our child to be confronted with her own perfection every time she turns around.'

'That's a reference to my parents, isn't it?'

'*Some* people don't save all their children's baby teeth and cassettes of them babbling and files of their refrigerator art . . . '

'So my mother wasn't objective.'

'That house is a shrine.'

'At least my parents wanted me.'

They both froze and looked at the floor. In the years they'd been together, only once had this issue been raised – when Vincent had suggested her paranoia about secrets might have something to do with her concealed adoption. This time, both of them were speechless. What had seemed like bad timing suddenly took on the feeling of a major crisis.

Lillian had found Lydia's other sneaker which she flung to the ground. 'That's unforgivable, Vincent,' she said slowly. 'Would you like it if I attributed your parents' behaviour to their lack of intelligence?'

'We'd better stop now.'

She nodded.

'Can you give me a reason why you won't come to Los Angeles?'

'Vincent, I tell you things and you never remember them. Last week I warned you I couldn't go anywhere for at least six months.'

'What did I say?'

'You said "Great! Fuck me." '

'And you probably said "*No*"! Or you complained about how tired you were.'

'Actually, I fucked you.'

They were both silent. After a moment, Vincent spoke. 'Can't you leave her with my parents?'

'For how long?'

He shrugged. 'Just a couple of weeks.'

'No! God, you don't really want to do that either. Children are arch-conservatives. They want their own beds and blankets and plastic Donald Duck bowls. We've taken her on so many trips. I can't be apart from her that long. Anyway, your mother feeds her Ding-Dongs like they were carrot sticks.'

'So what?'

'They're bad for her.'

'I was raised on Ding-Dongs.'

'Enough said.'

'You'd better lay off my parents.'

He leaned forward and she laughed. 'Or what? You'll hit me?'

He looked at her as if she were a stranger. 'I don't deserve that.'

'Vincent, *we aren't coming*.'

After a moment he raised his hands, a gesture she resented for its implication that she was unreasonable. What constituted reason in this sort of conflict?

'Do you want me to tell you what's happening here? If I'm the one who's ultimately responsible for everything: for keeping track of our doctor's appointments, making sure Lydia is dressed properly, planning the menus and shopping – what are you doing?'

'I'm making a life for us.'

'No, you aren't. You're trying to become some sort of rock star. It's a completely selfish goal, Vincent. The dream of a teenager.'

'So why did you marry me?' His face was closed to her, the mouth set hard and the eyes hooded.

She shook her head. 'I don't understand that question.'

'You married me partly because I was going to be famous. And don't pretend that's not true. You'd had a loser husband and a bunch of loser boyfriends, and a father who wouldn't look up to notice how much you needed him. None of the men in your life gave you anything but a sense of yourself as something without value.'

'What *are* you talking about?'

'Being married to you forced me into reading about dysfunctional families. You're some kind of crazy sober alcoholic. I didn't get it at first. Every time we have a meaningless argument I have to convince you I'm not leaving. You view abandonment as a natural development in any intimate relationship.'

'I never thought you were going to be famous,' she said weakly. 'I would have married you if you were a carpenter. In fact, I hated you being in this stupid business. This is about *my* work.'

'What work?'

'My writing.'

'I didn't tell you to stop writing.'

'That is my work.'

'You made less than two thousand dollars last year.'

'I'm a full-time mother!'

'So what? You once thought you could do it alone!'

'I could have.'

'Oh yeah? So why did you come and get me if everything was working out peachy-keen? There was only your bitch of a mother telling you no-one else was ever going to marry you.'

'Don't call my mother a bitch!'

'Fine. She's not a bitch. It's no big deal to tell your hugely pregnant daughter she's a loser. You want to be alone? Will that make you happy? Maybe this is why I have to go to LA right now. So you can finally write your masterpiece.'

Lillian went over to the desk and found a cigarette pack

with a single cigarette left inside. When she turned back, Vincent was picking up the phone.

'Vincent—'

'I have to call this guy back before he goes into the studio.'

'I'm serious about this.'

'Yeah, well . . . I guess that's the way it goes.'

The house was quiet. Lydia had flung her covers off and was sleeping bum-upwards, all her fingers in her mouth. Lillian put the blanket back over her and kissed her warm cheek. She had been so afraid of not knowing how to be a mother. But there was no mystery to what she was doing. Lydia was impossible to complicate. When she was angry or frustrated she normally went to someone and told them exactly what was wrong. She had a logical mind and delighted in things other children found less attractive. Like going to bed. Lillian wondered if it had anything to do with her being an only child. Her own childhood had seemed full of conflicting desires and fights with her brother that she always lost.

He was asleep when she went into their bedroom. T.W. was curled up on the easy chair, eyes half-closed. Vincent was sleeping on his side, clutching his pillow as if it were something living, capable of providing comfort. His hair fanned out against the sheet. Lillian wished it were possible to give in, to agree to leave Maine again. She lay down next to her sleeping husband and tried to feel something. Compromise had become increasingly difficult for them. When she was angry with him she allowed herself to sink into the feeling she had of being right, of being misunderstood and unappreciated. When he came to her full of desire she turned away, blind to his willingness to forget their differences. And then she'd wake him up in the middle of the night, the sheets wet with her tears, full of terror and contrition. Expecting punishment or, far worse, indifference. And he always forgave her. No, he denied the need to forgive. He'd stop her mouth with the frenzied 'I'm sorry'. He'd hold her as if she were a child and she'd sink into a love she'd never believed in, denied needing, feared missing.

But it wasn't that simple because she was the one who was held responsible for the success of their marriage. Despite the changes in the rôle of women, Vincent's lack of domestic interest was silently condoned. Her refusal to relocate would be interpreted as disloyalty. Vincent would not be condemned unless he were publicly abusive or unfaithful. He knew this. He was the centre of their universe and he counted on public opinion to force Lillian into behaving as if there were nothing wrong.

What did it mean to love someone unconditionally? Fairness probably didn't matter then. You simply transformed what seemed grim and difficult into a lovely place to be. The way she made her daughter's bedroom into a magic cave when Lydia felt sick. But that was how one loved a child. To recreate her husband's childhood meant becoming an acolyte. She pictured her mother-in-law, hugely fat, dusting one of Vincent's old instruments and shuddered.

When she came out of the bathroom, brushing her hair, he was sitting up in bed, reading the Financial Section of the Sunday paper.

'What are we going to do, Lillian?'

'I don't know.' She sensed that he was afraid of her leaving him. 'I'm not leaving you, Vincent.'

'Then what's happening?'

'It's just . . . I don't know.'

'My parents never did this.'

'Your parents have never considered their lives as real. They're waiting for the glory of what's to follow. We don't have that sort of faith.'

'I have faith in us.'

'That may not be enough.' Dropping her sweater on a chair, she pulled on one of his clean white T-shirts and pulled off her jeans.

'AA has taught me not to live exclusively for any person in case that person fails you and that then becomes an excuse to drink. It works even if you're not a drunk.'

'I'd give up my music for you. Is that what you want?'

'No! Don't try to manipulate me. I recognize how much you're willing to put up with. A wife and a toddler is not so great for a rock star. I realize how much you've given up.'

'Do you, Lillian? Maybe I'm not good enough for you.'

'Oh Vincent.' She lay down next to him. 'This sounds like a badly conceived soap opera. Nobody's "good enough" for anyone else. Thomas Wolfe is probably the only perfect thing I know and he's totally useless.' At the sound of his name, the dog raised his head and yawned. Lillian put her pillow over her face and screamed quietly. Vincent took it off and raising himself up on his elbow, he leaned above her, gently tracing her lips with his fingers.

'There are things I don't pay attention to that I know you miss,' he said. 'When you and Steve talk, I see a spark between you.'

'First of all, when was the last time we saw Steven Woodruff? A year at least. You notice a spark because we fight about everything.'

'No, it's more than that. It's the same rapport you have with Edward. Maybe you should have ended up with someone like your brother.'

Lillian felt her anger returning. She put her head against his chest. 'My brother can't love. Marriage and Edward is an oxymoronic coupling. Those sort of men were the sort I always pursued. You love me and I'm learning to accept that. Don't talk to me like this. If you want something different, admit it. I don't know what we're doing. This doesn't seem like a small thing any more.'

'You never thought you married the wrong person?'

'No!' She began to cry. Kneeling next to him, she kissed each vertebra along his spine.

'I would die without you,' he whispered.

She sat astride him and massaged his shoulders and arms with hard, practised strokes. The muscles were beautiful, defined, yet smooth. She kissed his skin with lips that moved as quickly as her fingers. Removing her shirt, she pressed herself hard against him, her body flat along his back. She sank her teeth gently into his skin.

He moaned and, reaching around, rolled her over so she was on her back and then over again so she was on top, facing him. 'What's going to happen?' he asked her softly, his hand moving inside her panties, parting her thighs open for him. She moaned and arched up, he took a breast into his mouth and continued to rub until he lifted her slightly and then she was on top of him. He was buried deep, clutching her waist, while she rode, her head flung back, their movements slowed to keep the other from going too far. She rose and fell and then, pulling away, took him in her mouth and allowed him to twist her body so he could touch her with his tongue. He pulled her down so that he could reach every part of her, so she was unable to move away. As she was about to begin her orgasm, he quickly moved her, her legs spread-eagled, a pillow raising her up to him. Vincent held himself above her.

'Tell me you want me to fuck you, baby,' he whispered.

'I want you to fuck me,' Lillian moaned.

'When?'

'Now!'

'When?'

'All the time!'

'What do you want all the time?'

'I want you to fuck me.'

'How?'

'Hard!'

'Like this?' He entered her with a single thrust and holding both her hands above her head, came into her deeper and deeper, so she was pushed up completely against the headboard, nearly sitting. He kept caressing between her legs while he continued his strokes, making her come while he was inside her, coming at the same time, the two of them in such a frenzy they rolled off the bed and finished on the floor, moaning and biting each other with a vague intent to cause pain. He held her down hard by the shoulders and stared into her face. 'You bitch,' he said. 'You impossible bitch.' And she was angry with him. Angry that he would not stop and reconsider going to Los Angeles, angry that she would do almost anything to be sure of his love. Her anger filled her.

Afterwards, wrapped up around each other, they were silent. She could feel his eyes watching her in the dark.

'What are you thinking?' he asked quietly.

I don't love you any more, she thought. 'Nothing,' she whispered.

He held her as if he feared she might disappear into the night. Each time she shifted, his grip tightened.

They drove to the airport with Lydia strapped into her child's seat. It had a fake dashboard and she loved yelling directions at her mother. They didn't speak. The only sound was that of Lydia's dangerous advice. 'Turn left. No, stop. OK, go right! No. Beep, beep! Mommy and Daddy are very important.' The last was whispered to herself but Lillian and Vincent heard.

'What's that, buttercrunch?' her father asked, turning around in the passenger seat.

'I said you and Mommy are very important.'

'Who told you that?'

'Nobody.' She smiled her radiant smile. 'I figured it out.'

'Well, you're very important also, sweetie,' Vincent said, leaning forward to tweak his daughter's nose.

'I'm just a baby,' Lydia said in a baby voice. 'I'm just a tiny little baby.'

Vincent sat back, glanced at Lillian who was paying strict attention to the road, switched on the radio but turned it off when Lillian winced. The next step had not been discussed. It seemed as if they had already agreed to separate.

As she watched him board the plane, chatting to a giggling stewardess, she detected a look of relief on his face and she felt herself harden to him. But when she turned around for a last look, the expression she saw was that of sheer misery, a man who was being forced to leave his family behind because his wife was tired of living in his shadow.

The pain manifested itself as a stab in the stomach. She sat down in the departure lounge and tried to breathe through the cramps while Lydia pretended to be a rabbit underneath one of the plastic chairs. She put her head between her knees and sat in that position until someone touched her shoulder and she looked up to meet the concerned glance of an airport manager.

'Madam?' the man asked her. 'Are you ill?'

He was younger than she was but it didn't seem possible to be so formal with anyone in the Bangor Airport Lounge.

'Thank you,' Lillian said, standing up, looking for Lydia, 'I was just a bit dizzy.'

They had bought the Stonington house after Lydia's birth, with the money Vincent earned on his first album. Solar panels had been installed on the roof and a new boiler installed to ensure heat through the long, bitter Maine winter. They had used one half of the basement to install a small gym, complete with a sauna and jacuzzi and the other half was Vincent's studio. Otherwise, it was largely the same as it always had been. It was a white house with black shutters and green window-boxes full of flowers which Lillian was forbidden to tend after she managed to exterminate an entire generation of geraniums. Among avid gardeners she was known as 'The black thumb' or 'The Angel of Death'. Plants did not respond well to zealous overwatering accompanied by prolonged and severe periods of drought.

After Lydia had finally agreed to sleep, Lillian wandered from room to room, floor to floor, turning on lights, sitting on pieces of furniture she rarely noticed. We are such creatures of habit, she thought as she saw how Vincent's chair was the perfect distance from the centre table so that he could rest his feet while he watched television. And how had it become 'Vincent's' chair?

The recording studio contained six of Vincent's prize guitars. When she saw them gleaming in the half-light of the hallway, she began to cry. His instruments were an expression of his devotion to his art. Some of them had names, female names he murmured occasionally when he was polishing or tuning them. She had banished him from the source of his inspiration.

She took out the cassette of 'Lillian'. As she listened to the song, it occurred to her that the song was about a woman who was unable to trust, who kept walking away from a man who was clearly devoted to her, who couldn't decide what to do or how to live. Her rôle wasn't that of an independent woman but rather of someone who was unwilling to allow anyone close to her. 'You never knew who I really was,' she said to herself.

'Hi.'

'Hi Vincent.'

'I love you, Lillian.' There was a long pause.

'And I love you.'

'Get on a plane tomorrow.'

'I can't.'

'What the hell's wrong?'

'I don't know. I was just listening to "Lillian"—'

'Christ!'

'That song implies this woman is really damaged because of some man. I'm this icon for the conflicted bitch—'

'You give people what they want and they give you what you need. I used what I needed to sell it. When are you coming out here?'

'You once warned me you were ruthless—'

'Fuck it, Lillian—'

'I don't know!'

'What sort of answer is "I don't know"?'

'Do you want me to lie? Next week! How's that sound?'

'You mean that?'

'No.'

'What the fuck do you need me to do? Beg?'

'I think we should stop talking to each other now.'

'Why don't you call your sponsor and ask her how to handle this? Didn't you tell me the majority of sober women were divorced?'

'Vincent—'

'I don't understand you, Lillian. It's making me crazy. I've been to Al-Anon. They said to leave the person you love alone. I can't do that.'

'That's not what that phrase means. It means to stop trying to control someone.'

'Do you think I control you?' She could hear the tears in his voice. She felt her own throat closing.

'God, Vincent,' she whispered, 'I love you so much. Sometimes it doesn't seem possible to live without you.

I want us to be together for ever, but there's something wrong.'

'Why? Were you born under a cloud?'

'So it's my fault? Who decided to go to California?' When he didn't answer, she considered hanging up. Wouldn't it be less painful just to finish, a clean break, a razor-edge ending instead of what promised to be full of complicated and uncomfortable truths? As she opened her mouth to suggest flying out for a short visit and to ask him if they might arrange to visit the marriage counsellor again, she realized the phone was dead and Vincent had hung up.

She dreamed she was trying to climb stairs with Lydia on her hip. She could hear Thomas Wolfe barking in the distance. And the sound of Vincent's guitar. Her mother appeared at the top of the stairs, her hands on her hips, the face blurry. She was angry.

'You shouldn't have bothered coming,' her mother said, 'you're not needed.'

'But I'm a mother, too,' she screamed, clutching Lydia to herself tightly.

'Things never change,' the woman at the top of the stairs hissed, 'they only get worse.'

The last thing she felt was the child missing from her arms.

24

As the weeks passed she returned to a routine sacrificed to her marriage. She got up at six-thirty and had a cup of coffee while doing half of an aerobic tape, all she could manage before Lydia's cry of 'Momee!' While the morning news was on television, she made them both breakfast: steel-cut oatmeal, a chopped apple, an English muffin for Lydia spread with peanut-butter. They both read after breakfast. Lydia was engrossed in a book that allowed you to 'pat the bunny' and 'poke the pig', Lillian devoured the *New York Times*. When Dorothy arrived, she was given charge of Lydia and Lillian would sit down in her study with a pot of herbal tea to write until lunch. The house was always very quiet. Vincent's absence meant nothing was out of place, the schedule was followed: no-one suggested a trip to the local movie house; no-one tried to convince Lillian to take off her clothes and join him in the sauna.

On one occasion, just before lunch, Dorothy stuck her head in Lillian's study. 'I want to tell you something, Lillian,' she said slowly, her round face looking unusually serious.

'What?' Lillian asked, stretching her arms above her head and turning away from the glowing screen of her computer.

'This house feels empty without that man. I mean the guy's better-looking than Mel Gibson and nicer than any person has a right to be.'

'I know,' Lillian said, frowning.

'So what's the problem?' Dorothy asked, leaning against the door, her arms crossed.

'I don't know,' Lillian said. 'When did you know you didn't love Dirk?'

'When I found him in our bed with my sister and her Pomeranian.'

Both women laughed. 'You never had nothing like that with Vincent, did you?'

'No. Never.'

'He still loves you, right?'

'Yes. But it doesn't feel right.'

'That's because you got intimacy problems.' Dorothy opened the door.

'What?'

'You don't like anybody close to you. Except Lydia.'

'How do you know that?'

'Hey, I watch Oprah. That's all they ever talk about. Sex and intimacy problems. From the three-hour naps you guys used to take, I surmised it wasn't the former.'

Lillian sighed. 'I don't know, Dorothy,' she said.

'Lunch is ready. Why don't you make reservations to Los Angeles. Take the night flight.'

Lillian turned off her computer. 'Not this time,' she said.

After lunch (spaghetti for Lydia, salads for Dorothy and Lillian), Lydia took a nap while Dorothy went grocery-shopping and Lillian went back to writing. At three she put Lydia in the infant seat on the back of her bicycle, both of them wearing special hi-tech helmets that Vincent had found in Boston, and cycled to a women's AA meeting that had a nursery. When she tried to explain her reasons for refusing to go with Vincent, Lillian realized she was glad he had gone, glad in the way one is glad when the most terrible event finally occurs and you are liberated by the shockwaves. 'He would have left me anyway,' she told herself, 'it was only a matter of time.' But she cried in front of the women in her group and when her sponsor took her outside, she sobbed against the woman's shoulder repeating over and over again, 'Tell him to come back. Tell him I'm sorry.' The woman soothed her like a hurt child and when she asked: 'Is that what you really want to say to him?' Lillian shook her head.

Helen had been sick often that winter. Her body was changed. She was somehow insubstantial. When Lillian commented on this, Helen had shrugged and said: 'Age, my dear. I'm an old lady.' But she didn't seem old at all. Her eyes were bright and there was a strange sort of restless energy that suggested someone decades younger.

'When do you go to Los Angeles?' Helen asked her after Vincent had been gone for ten days.

'We're not,' Lillian answered, removing a black olive from her mouth which immediately found a home in Lydia's but then caused tears because of it's salty, unfamiliar taste. Removing the olive from her daughter's mouth, she shrugged.

'Isn't he committed to staying there through the summer?'

'Probably.'

'Are you separated?'

'Not officially.'

'Did something happen?' Helen's gaze stayed steady, making it difficult for Lillian to avoid her eyes.

'No. Yes. I'm not sure. He's not sharing the responsibility of raising Lyd.'

'What's your definition of his job?'

'To assume half the burden. I can't keep track of everything.'

'Why not?'

'It's too much!'

'Isn't Vincent the main breadwinner?'

'That's just because he has more time to work.' She noticed Helen's expression. 'And he's in a more commercial field.'

'Umm.' Helen absently removed a fork from her granddaughter's fist. Lydia picked up a spoon and started banging her water glass. 'You'd better go out there.'

'Why?'

'I can't imagine there aren't several women who'd love to replace you.'

'I don't care. If Vincent wants to boff a groupie, which by the way he never seems very interested in, why should I be concerned? As long as he practises safe sex, he can screw all of Robert Palmer's back-up singers.' Helen looked puzzled. 'Those are the women with the tiny heads and the huge lips who pretend to play guitars . . . never mind. The point is, Vincent and I are two different people. I want to be able to write and take care of my daughter.'

'What about your husband?'

'I hate that word.' Lillian nodded at Lydia, who immediately went under the table in hot pursuit of Helen's cat.

'What word?'

'*Husband.* It sounds incredibly ancient. Medieval. Like something out of *Tess of the D'Urbervilles*.'

'That's not medieval. But look what happened to Tess.'

'She married Roman Polanski.'

'Who did?'

'Nastassia Kinski. She posed nude with a snake and then . . . no, actually she didn't marry him. Anyway, she played Tess in the movie.'

'Isn't he the one whose wife was murdered?'

'Yup. Sharon Tate. The end of the love generation.' Helen put her hand on Lillian's shoulder. 'Maybe I shouldn't be married to anyone,' Lillian said.

Helen sighed and shook her head. 'Don't assume you can't love, darling,' she said tenderly. 'Face your fear.

Tell him what you think is wrong. Talk to him. He'll do anything for you.'

'He hung up on me,' Lillian said, her head held high.

'Then call him back,' her mother said, handing Lydia a cookie.

'Call him back,' Lydia echoed her grandmother, smiling with pleasure at her own brilliance.

'There's nothing to be done,' Lillian said to herself as she drove home. 'I want my own life back.'

When she ran into Steven Woodruff in the Stonington 7–11, Lillian pretended not to recognize him. Lydia had been diverted and bribed with a cherry slurpee that covered most of her face and neck, while her mother had almost finished a package of Pepperidge Farm Milano cookies. It was only eleven-thirty. Steven waved and smiled, motioning that he'd speak to her when they were both through the check-out line. To hide her embarrassment, Lillian picked up a copy of *People* and then found herself staring at a picture of Vincent, his arms around a woman she recognized as an actress from one of the night-time soap operas. Lydia reached up to pull the magazine out of her hand.

'Daddy,' she observed, neatly ripping the entire page from the magazine.

'Bad girl!' Lillian said, tapping her on the back.

'Daddy!' Lydia screamed, her big grey eyes filling with tears at her mother's meanness.

The check-out girl smiled kindly at Lillian. 'You don't have to buy it,' she whispered.

'I guess we'd better,' Lillian replied, nodding at her daughter who was alternately hiding the picture under her shirt or waving it at anyone who appeared interested.

'My daddy,' Lydia kept announcing proudly. The rest of the people in the line seemed unimpressed. For once Lillian was grateful for the famous North-eastern reserve.

She hadn't seen Steven for nearly a year. Every time Helen had mentioned him, he seemed to be camping or attending a medical conference in a foreign country. He looked thinner and his hair had more grey in it than she'd remembered.

'There's my masterpiece,' he said, stooping over to pick up Lydia. 'Remember me, bunny?'

Lydia shook her head. 'Daddy,' she said, thrusting the crumpled page into Steven's face. He shifted her to his hip and then glanced at Lillian who was leaning against the car.

'Well,' he said softly, 'how's the famous writer?'

'Great,' she said, shutting her eyes, trying to breathe. 'Fat.'

'You don't look fat to me.'

'I'm fat.'

'OK, you're fat. Other than that?'

'Fine.'

'Where's Vincent?'

'Oh—' she reached out to Lydia who was happily pouring the rest of her cherry slurpee on the steaming tar of the 7–11 parking lot. Steven put the child down carefully, still holding the torn page from the magazine.

'What's happened, Lillian?'

'I'm not sure. He's in Los Angeles.'

'When did he leave?'

'Nearly six months ago.'

'Were you invited?'

'Of course.'

'And?'

'Oh, I don't know. And . . . he's in LA. And . . . well, fuck it. Looks like he's found some female companionship. That's good. He's a sociable person. And . . . he hates to sleep alone. So . . . how are you?'

'Just fine. I've been meaning to drop in.'

'We should have called.' They looked at each other and laughed. Both of them knew why he had stayed away.

'What are you doing in Stonington?'

'Had to get Bessie overhauled.' Steven indicated his ancient pick-up. 'Best mechanic I know lives here.'

'Really? We should get his name. I mean, I should. Well—' She stared down at the asphalt, the slurpee had dried in the sun. She felt sick.

'Are you busy now?' Steven looked down at Lillian's feet. She was wearing a pair of Vincent's thongs, twice as long as her own feet.

'Yup,' she answered sarcastically. 'I'm having lunch with my personal shopper in an hour.'

'What about a lobster roll?'

'OK.' Lillian bent over to pick up her daughter who was clinging to her knees. In doing so, she stumbled back slightly and put her hand on the car.

'Do you feel faint?' Steven asked.

Lillian nodded.

'Can you drive?'

'No. I think I need to be sick.'

'Come on.' Steven picked up Lydia and while Lillian threw up behind a tree, he taught the little girl how to flip a coin. He then gave Lillian some water from a thermos under his seat and a stick of gum. They drove in silence for several miles.

'So . . . ' Steven stopped. Lydia leaned forward and opened his glove compartment, extracting a woman's bra which she solemnly presented to her mother.

'It's not my size, honeybunch,' she said laughing. 'Oh God, what am I going to do?'

'Go get him.'

'I did that already.'

'Do it again.'

'No.'

'Then do what he's doing. Have an affair. What's good for the goose—'

'Phsaw . . . that's terrible advice. Anyway, who with? Bill? Lydia's pediatrician? My gynaecologist with hands of ice?' Lillian had unclasped the bra and was staring at the tag. '32C'. What kind of woman would fit into a bra that size? Steven grabbed it and stuffed it into his pocket.

'My sister's,' he offered.

'You don't have a sister.' After a moment she sighed. 'Men,' she said bitterly. 'Bastards.'

'Wait a minute! What's that mean?'

'They're always doing it to someone.'

'So what? It's healthy. Why do you think you feel fat?'

'Because I devoured nearly half a cheesecake last night.'

'Why?'

'Boredom.'

'Frustration.'

'Bullshit.'

'If you'd had sex last night you wouldn't have been interested in that cheesecake.'

'That cheesecake was perfect. Sex isn't. Anyway, leave me alone, Steven. Food loves me.'

'I've left you alone. I've left you alone for four years.'

'That's what I like about you. We have a perfect relationship.'

'So now I'm going to come on strong.'

'You'd better not.'

'Why? Vincent's in LA.'

'I don't care where he is. I don't care what you want. I don't even care to know what sort of woman would leave her bra in your glove compartment.'

Steven laughed which made Lydia laugh, which made Lillian kiss her, which made Lydia kiss Steven – which was dangerous since he was driving. They stopped to let Lydia use the bathroom in a rest area off the highway. Before Lillian could follow her out, Steven caught her wrist.

'I think it would be good for you,' he said, pulling her next to him. He pressed his lips against her collarbone and kissed along the line of her neck until he reached her lips at which her head dropped back and his hands were all over her. But she pulled away.

'Why do you always come after me in times of personal weakness?' she asked him pompously.

Steven laughed and shook his head. 'Touché,' he said. 'I'm a toad.'

'My daughter has given you an enormous hickey,' Lillian said, wiping the mark with a tissue. He grabbed her hand and slowly kissed each finger.

'Give it up, Steven,' she said shakily, her skin tingling where he touched her.

'We need to see what this is,' he whispered.

'This is unresolved anger pretending to be raw sexual-desire.'

He dropped her hand in disgust. 'You watch too much daytime TV.'

Lillian frowned and followed her daughter into the bathroom.

25

When Vincent first left, they'd both pretended everything
was going to be fine, that they had decided to create
a temporary bicoastal family situation. After a month,
when Vincent made it clear he found it unacceptable
to be alone, Lillian suggested he return to Maine. He
reminded her of his new recording contract and she,
hating herself for doing it, put Lydia on the phone.
Hearing Lydia's delight at talking to her father made
Lillian feel evil, sexless and ice-blooded, like some sort
of mythological creature, a Harpy perhaps.

'My God,' Vincent said, when Lillian had taken
the phone back. 'Why the hell did you ever come to
Minneapolis?'

'She was your child. I married you because I wanted
to. I still want to be your wife. I just can't keep letting
the other things go—'

'You're letting go of me, for fuck's sake!' The phone
went dead in her hands. She called back and the line
was busy. When she tried again, the phone rang for
ten minutes, no-one answered.

'I still don't get what kept you from going with him,
Lillian.' They were sitting at a picnic table drinking iced
tea. Lydia had found a sandbox and a group of children
young enough for her to boss.

'Dorothy, Lydia's baby-sitter, is wonderful and she
wouldn't go to LA. I've got this book to write. The house
is still being renovated and I've finally got a group of real
friends. Women friends.' Steven gave her a look of utter

disbelief. 'What? Why are you looking at me like that?'

'You let your husband go to California alone because of a baby-sitter, sheet rock and a bunch of bags you like to gossip with?'

'No! Maybe I just don't know how to be anyone's wife. Basically, I hate people.' She put a French fry in her mouth but remembering the ten extra pounds, took it out again.

Steven flattened out the *People* page. Lillian looked away.

'Vincent isn't nailing this broad,' he said slowly.

'How do you know?'

'He was hanging out at some party and they took a picture.'

'Maybe.'

'But let's pretend he is doing the beast with two backs with the bimbo. What's your next move?'

'I'm not sure.'

'So what's your strategy?'

Lillian shrugged.

'It's important to have your pieces lined up.'

'What pieces?'

'Don't you play chess?'

'This is a marriage!'

Steven snorted. 'Right. It's not a fucking board-game . . . it's real life! Well, welcome to the world, Little Bo Peep!'

'Steven, even if it is a chess match, I don't want to play. Chess is boring.'

'Chess is the greatest game in the world.'

Lillian yawned. Lydia appeared to be making a speech in the sandbox, her hands were on her hips and the other children's faces were attentive. One little girl looked very unhappy. 'I think it's boring.'

'No wonder you drive him around the woodshed.'

'What do you mean I "drive him around the woodshed"!

Is that some quaint down-eastern metaphor for a crazy bitch?'

'I'm not interested in your being faithful to Vincent, Lillian. But you got to admit, the guy really loves you. I've never had a better father on a delivery. And you were a real pain in the neck.'

Lillian remembered how Vincent had held her hand and rubbed her back and smiled when she told him she wanted to die, and then kissed her when she'd ordered him to leave her because she was so ugly. He'd said: 'You're all I ever wanted.' She watched as her daughter attempted to feed sand to a small, pink-cheeked boy wearing Osh-Kosh By-Gosh blue jean overalls. One of the straps was undone and he was spitting out the sand, trying to get his mouth empty long enough to start crying.

'Oh God,' she said, pointing at Lydia, 'hereditary man abuse.'

On their way back to the 7-11, she took one of Steven's cigarettes. Lydia was asleep, slumped into the car seat in the back.

'I thought you quit smoking.'

'No. Just drinking. I still smoke. I mean I don't really, but I could if I wanted to. Which I do at the moment.'

'I've missed you,' Steven said, pushing in the lighter. 'There's been such a lack of lucidity in my life.'

'I've been avoiding you.'

'Why?'

'You're dangerous.'

'Am I?' Steven looked pleased and surprised. He glanced at himself in the rear-view mirror and fluffed his hair. 'Dangerous-sexy or dangerous-creepy?' Lillian rolled her eyes. She inhaled deeply and was shocked by the effect.

'Why don't you gals come to the beach with me tomorrow?'

She thought for a moment and then nodded. Only after he drove away, did she realize the magazine was still in his car. She bought another copy and a pint of ice milk. Lydia was in a horrible mood and had to be given another cherry slurpee before she'd agree to go home. 'I am losing control,' Lillian thought as she allowed her daughter's lower lip to intimidate her.

That evening their dinner was so healthy – skinless broiled chicken, boiled potatoes, green beans and salad – that Lydia went into junk-food withdrawal symptoms and kept asking for a 'Happy Meal' instead.

'Do you want me to stuff it into a styrofoam container and nuke it in the microwave?' her mother snapped. 'I'm not pleased with this food thing, Lydia. You have gross eating habits!' Finally she added a small portion of taco chips and Lydia relented. They read *Goodnight Moon* together. Lydia was curled into her mother's arms, whispering the words she had memorized like a timid little echo. She said her garbled prayers and allowed her mother to tuck her in. As Lillian leaned over to kiss her a final goodnight, Lydia put her arms around her mother's neck and pulled her closer to whisper in her ear.

'Mommy?'

'Yes, sugar lump.'

'Would you like to live with me for ever?'

'Well, someday you're going to grow up and want your own family.'

'Why?'

'Uh, because that's what happens.'

'Does Daddy have a mommy?'

'Yes! You know that. Granpop and Granma. They live in the trailer with all the junk food.'

Lydia smiled.

'Honey, go to sleep now.'

'Bye. I told Daddy we were coming to see him.'

'When?'

'In my prayers.'

'Good. Good night muffin.'

'Good night banana,' Lydia answered, shrieking at her own wit.

Thomas Wolfe had divided loyalties. Although he acknowledged Lillian as the ultimate authority, it was always Vincent whom he sought when something was caught in his paw or when he was in the mood to play wild thing out in the woods. Vincent was his buddy who'd taught him how to catch a frisbee in his mouth. Lillian had accepted this man/dog thing as a biological reality. Since Vincent's departure she had sensed T.W.'s disapproval of her without questioning whether it was ridiculous to grant an animal a moral imperative. He seemed to be quietly disappointed in her, as if he wondered when she might realize how good she'd had things and settle down to her real job of providing unlimited snacks and hugs for the three most important beings in her life. Of course, Lillian recognized this nagging voice as her own. The dog merely seemed to agree when Lillian asked him questions like: 'You think I'm a lousy wife, don't you?' or 'You think I made Vincent leave, don't you?' or 'You think I'll always be unhappy and alone, don't you?'

She found the number of Vincent's sublet apartment and picking up the phone, allowed it to ring until the receiver was lifted.

'Hello?' It was a woman with a thick Australian accent.

'Yes. Is Vincent there?'

'Actually, yes. But he's in the shower.'

Lillian thought hard for a moment. 'Can you tell me who you are?'

'This is Mandy Bassett.'

'Is Lillian there?'

'His wife? No. They are separated. I think she's in Maine.'

Lillian sat down on the edge of the bed. Her throat was very dry. 'Mandy?'

'Yes?'

'Would you tell my husband something for me after he dries off?'

'What? Oh shit!'

'It's OK. Just tell him . . . tell him we'd better talk about Lydia soon. She needs to see him. She misses him a great deal and arrangements should be made. Lawyers I guess. Lots of lawyers.'

Mandy sniffed. 'Wait, Lillian. Let me go and get him. This isn't what you think.'

'No. I don't want to talk to him now.'

Sometimes it seemed odd to be connected to other human beings. People were capable of inflicting such pain on one another. People that claimed to love you.

'Mandy?'

'Yes?'

'Do yourself a favour and latch on to someone else. Someone who's free. Vincent still loves me. He may not someday but now's a bad time to go after him. You won't survive any of this.' Then she hung up.

When Steven arrived the next morning to take them to the beach, she was sitting at the kitchen table drinking a third cup of lukewarm coffee, eating a burned piece of pitta bread. Lydia was in the living-room watching cartoons, still in her pyjamas and a fairy-princess crown.

'Nice crown,' Steven said. He was rewarded by the princess opening her mouth to reveal a half-chewed piece of toast. 'Ready?' he asked in the kitchen, despite the mess and the sight of Lillian in her bathrobe, hunched over, smoking. He wore cut-off jeans and sandals, a straw hat was perched on his head.

'Oh,' she said, putting down her mug. 'Oh no. *No*.'

'So, go get ready,' he picked up a dish. 'I'll clean.'

'Did I really say I'd come?' she asked wearily, arranging the crumbs on her plate in a semi-circular pattern.

'Yup.'

'I didn't mean to.'

'Too bad.'

'Can I change my mind?'

Lydia entered from the living-room, her hair in modified dreadlocks (done the previous evening by her devoted mother), wearing one of Vincent's Iron Maiden T-shirts over a G-string he had brought her back from France and which Lillian had reluctantly allowed after her daughter had staged a major temper tantrum. In her right hand was clutched a plastic bucket containing a spade and a headless doll named Sally.

'Kiss Sally,' she ordered Steven.

'Is Sally ready for the beach, sugar-plum fairy?' Steven asked, picking her up.

Lydia nodded and pointed the shovel towards Heaven.

'That's princess sign-language for: "Go get dressed, Mommy".'

'I don't want to wear a bathing suit,' Lillian said, slowly standing. 'This has not been a good week for food.'

'Oh come on,' Steven said laughing. He put Lydia down. 'Let's show Mommy our bellies!' Lydia and Steven pushed out their stomachs until Lillian gasped. 'I was your midwife. Remember? I knew you when you were really a whale!'

'I was never a whale,' Lillian said as she went up the stairs. 'Dolphin-like, perhaps, but definitely not Moby Dick.'

As they were pulling out of the driveway, Thomas Wolfe burst through the woods to join them. He spent the day barking at seagulls, swimming a frantic dog-paddle, chasing whatever Lydia managed to fling and shaking himself dry near warm human flesh.

The beach in Stonington consisted of rocks which gradually grew smaller until becoming almost sand at the very edge of the icy, clear water. Watching Lydia patiently fill her pail with pebbles made Lillian feel somewhat guilty for the absence of actual sand. But she loved the wildness of the Maine coast. The jagged silhouette of the rocks, and the pools filled with exotic underwater creatures, thrilled her. She remembered when she had gone on a whale-watching cruise: Vincent had shot a video of his wife and child watching a whale come up to the side of their boat. They had both seen his eye and Lydia, unable to qualify her sense of wonder, had gasped simply, 'Oh, it's God.'

Steven spread a blanket on a flat rock. As soon as Lillian felt the sun on her shoulders, she fell asleep. Sleeping without Vincent was difficult. Dawn came too early, many times she was aware of never really having fallen asleep. The night sounds: an owl in the woods, the moan and creak of the house settling, would gradually give way to dawn noises; a bird that sang while the sun rose, the rattle of bottles on the front porch which meant the milkman had come, the sound of the paper hitting the door. She had got into the habit of getting up as soon as light streaked across the eastern horizon. The morning was her best time to write. Sometimes she would listen to Vincent's music and for the first time she paid attention to his lyrics. Most of his songs were about their relationship. Vincent said he wrote about her because she was so interesting. Lillian believed it was a form of exerting control. His songs were all about a man who offered a woman unconditional love and how the woman found ways to disappoint and fail him.

His last big hit was called 'Ever After' and was recorded by a new young singer from Seattle. When the video was premiered on MTV, Lizbeth had called. After talking about the latest scandal in the fashion industry, she'd abruptly changed the subject.

'Is something wrong between you and Vincent?' she asked.

Lillian laughed. 'Smooth transition. Why?'

'That new song is pretty grim in a very romantic sort of way.'

'It's a fantasy, Lizbeth.'

'I have a very keen eye, Lillian. You told me Vincent wrote your lives.'

'I don't know,' Lillian had said quietly, 'maybe we can't do it.'

'Do what?'

'Stay married.'

'Why not? I thought you guys were more in love every day.'

'Love doesn't have much to do with this.'

'Oh God, Lillian! Don't fuck this up. See a shrink. See a dozen shrinks. Get a trainer and a nutritionist. It's probably a food thing.'

'It's always a food thing.'

'So? Go off sugar or salt or meat or whatever it is that's doing this to you. See a psychic. Get in touch with your real father. Didn't he commit suicide?'

'Yes.'

'So get the psychic to ask why he did that. Or see a channeller and do it yourself. Go to a rebirther and be rebirthed.'

'Lizbeth!'

'Listen to me, Lillian. You don't know how to have an intimate relationship with anyone! Look how long it took you to trust that stupid dog.'

'That's because he was Matthew's dog.'

'Bullshit. You're afraid of anything that breathes. You treated that dog like he was wired to blow up.'

'T.W. likes Vincent more than me, anyway.'

'Lillian, Vincent's easier to like. He's simple and uncomplicated.'

'He's very selfish.'

'So what? Don't you want to stay married to him?'

'Yes,' Lillian said quietly, looking out of the window.

'Then you'd better tell *him* that. How's Helen?'

'Oh, better, I think. She's very thin but she says she likes it that way. Did you get the promotion?'

'Of course. I am now Director of Publicity for L'image Cosmetics.'

'Bravo!'

'We have a line of make-up for little girls . . . '

'No, Lizbeth! You almost ruined her with those god-damned pearls. She turns her nose up at plastic now.'

'That's my little princess.'

'Has he left his wife yet?'

'No!' Lizbeth laughed shrilly. 'If he left her, he'd be poor. That would be terrible for all three of us. And he has gruesome children I don't want to be connected with. Being a mistress is simply peachy. You're different. You get to wear lingerie and eat truffles on those long, cold nights that he spends in Darien. Lillian, I feel absolutely panicked when I consider the possibility of your not staying with Vincent. It's almost as if you were my parents. I need stability.'

'Stability?'

'Well, I don't know what else to call it. I'd better go. *Ciao, bella.*'

'*Ciao.*'

Standing in the pre-dawn light of the kitchen, she remembered what she had thought on the day of her marriage. 'This won't last,' had flashed across her mind like a neon sign and a cold shiver had gone down her spine, causing Vincent to whisper: 'What's wrong?' But as always she had answered, 'Nothing.'

'Time to turn over. Your shoulders look medium rare.'

She awoke abruptly and when Lydia was not immediately visible, let out a cry and stood up.

'She's right over there. A family of spineless children arrived and she's put them all to work.'

She saw her daughter in a small rock formation which formed a natural play area. She was shouting directions at two giggling girls and a smaller boy. All four of them were vigorously piling up stones.

'My little Mussolini,' Lillian murmured fondly, turning over to face the sun, shielding her eyes to look up at Steven.

'Tired?' he asked.

'A bit.'

'You were snoring.'

'No I wasn't.'

'Yup. I love the sound of a woman snoring. It's so discreet.'

'Steven, why is it important to you that you observe me in compromising positions? Labour, fat, snoring, angry?'

'Demystification. I'm tired of goddesses. You aren't the easiest woman to get a handle on.'

'A handle? Where would you like that handle to be attached? My ass?'

'Hey!' He gave her a look of such kind forbearance, she was stopped cold. Lydia ran over towing a small crying girl.

'Mommy, I fired her and she won't go home.'

'Lydia! Why did you fire her?'

'Because I wouldn't dig a hole,' the little girl said, wiping her eyes.

'Lydia, I'm in charge and there's to be no more bossing around or firing. Everybody works together and has fun like *Sesame Street*. That's how friends get things done.'

'She didn't dig a hole!' Lydia yelled, sticking out her lower lip and stomping her foot.

'I don't care,' Lillian said sternly. 'She doesn't have to dig a hole.' Lillian reached into her bag. 'Would you girls like to split an orange?'

'No!' Lydia said.

The little girl nodded shyly. Lillian peeled the orange

and gave her half. When she offered the other half to Lydia, she shook her head.

'I'll have that yummy orange,' Steven said. The little girl ran off and Lydia threw a pebble at Steven.

'Stop it!' Lillian said, standing up and getting off the rock. Lydia threw another pebble at Steven who put his towel over his head. Lydia burst into tears. Lillian picked her up and sat down with Lydia in her lap, her small warm body wrapped around her mother like an animal clinging to a tree. Lillian stroked her back and smoothed down her wild hair.

'What's wrong, butterfly?' she whispered into her daughter's ear. 'Tell Mommy what's wrong?' She began to walk slowly down the beach, her child in her arms.

Lydia buried her face in Lillian's hair. 'When's Daddy coming home?' she finally whispered.

'Soon,' Lillian answered. 'Or you'll go see him. He has a swimming pool in his yard. And oranges grow on trees out there.'

'Are you coming?'

'I don't know, Lyd.'

'Are we getting divorced?'

'No! Who told you about divorce?'

'Three kids in play-school are divorced: Emma, Natalie and Jason.'

'Umm.' Lillian sat down on the pebbles with Lydia on her lap. 'Your daddy loves you more than anything in the world.'

'I think he should come home.'

'You can tell him that,' Lillian said. 'Now go back and dig some more holes with your nice friends. And don't be a bossy-boots.'

Steven had moved closer to Lillian's blanket and when she sat down, he began to rub an oiled finger up and down the outside of her leg.

'Is she OK?'

'Yeah, she just misses her father.'

'You're a great mother.'

'Thank you.'

'It's not an easy thing to be. There's a level of mothering that many people reach and they never go any further. The kid's perfectly cared for but there's a certain lack of something. But you're totally with her and she can feel that, and if she's a little high-spirited that's just a reflection of how good she feels about herself.'

Lillian glowed. She had wondered if they were raising Lydia too permissively. Instead of stating when it was time to eat or go to bed, Lillian usually suggested such an activity and Lydia agreed because she understood the logic of good behaviour. She and Vincent allowed their daughter to make decisions. Mrs Jordan thought it was ridiculous to give a three-year old so much room for independent thought. She'd criticized her daughter until Vincent had finally spoken up.

'I don't understand why you find this so unacceptable, Anne. Lydia's well behaved because it's her choice.'

'I think that it's absurd to allow a child not to take her nap because she doesn't feel tired.'

'Why?' Lillian had demanded. 'Isn't she supposed to know what she needs? If she gets tired, she'll lie down and fall asleep. I don't want her shut up in a room somewhere – crying because we think it's time for her to rest!'

Now she said to Steven, 'My mother doesn't think I'm particularly gifted in the maternal department.'

'They never do.'

'Helen does.'

'Helen's different.'

With a shiver, Lillian realized how good Steven's hand felt on her leg. She caught it on the trip from her hip to her knee and put it back on his chest.

'There's an awful lot of perfect skin being wasted here, sugar,' he muttered, leaning over to bite her thigh lightly.

Lillian saw that Lydia and her crew were fetching buckets of water from a rock pool to fill up their moat.

'Steven . . . '

'We've avoided this fuck for so long it's become bigger than both of us.'

Lillian sighed, sat up and reached for a cookie. He caught her hand.

'You want something much less sugary with much more energy,' he said, biting her knuckle.

'I want a cookie,' Lillian said, pulling out of his grasp. 'An innocent, unadulterous cookie.'

The mother of Lydia's playmates approached their rock smiling. 'I'm making hamburgers for the children,' she said, 'would your little girl like to come for lunch?' Lillian recognized the woman from an adult class she taught on writing fiction.

'It's Doris, isn't it?'

'Oh, Lillian,' the woman said smiling. 'How nice to see you. I enjoyed your story in *Redbook*. It was wonderful. That's our house.' Doris pointed to a cottage overlooking the beach.

'This is Steven Woodruff,' Lillian said. 'My doctor,' she added unnecessarily.

'Her personal physician,' Steven elaborated, shaking Doris's hand.

'An old family friend,' Lillian added, blushing furiously. She wondered if Doris had a subscription to *People* magazine. There was an awkward pause which Lillian filled. 'Are you writing?' she asked Doris. 'Did you submit your story?'

'Well, only to one magazine. I haven't heard anything yet.'

'Call me. I know a few editors you can contact.'

'That would be great. How's your handsome husband?'

'He's recording in Los Angeles. Film work.' She drew a deep breath. 'We're OK.'

Lydia ran up clutching the hand of the formerly reluctant hole-digger, and reported, 'She doesn't have to dig. She's the one who gets the water.'

'Are you sure you want to feed this little fascist dictator?' Lillian asked, poking Lydia in the belly.

'Absolutely,' Doris said, taking the children's hands.

Lillian watched her daughter skipping happily away from her, until the group reached the path towards the house and then Lydia turned around and waved. Lillian felt her eyes fill with tears and she waved back, leaping to her feet to jump up and down so that Lydia did the same thing until she disappeared into the house. She sat down and saw that Steven was staring at her.

'What?' she asked, sucking in her stomach.

'I'm just looking at you,' Steven said, putting his hands on her ankles.

'Well, stop,' she said, putting her face against her knees.

'So,' he said, leaning forward. 'Let's do it.'

'Do it?'

'Yeah.'

'Is that what you did with the owner of that bra? *It?*'

'Ah come on, Lillian. Be a sport!'

'A sport?'

'Yeah, a sport.'

'Is that what sex is?'

'Nope. Sex is sex.' He ran a hand up her leg reaching the knee before her own hand held his wrist.

'Get real,' she snapped.

'I'm real,' he answered quietly, picking up her feet and putting them in his lap. As he massaged her instep, cracked her toes and gently stroked her heels, she began to relax. The pressure was perfect until she felt him harden under her big toe and she pulled her feet back and sat on them.

'You aren't being a friend right now,' she said unhappily.

'Don't be so rigid.'

'Is this why you offered to take us to the beach?'

He thought for a moment. 'No. I've missed Lydia. She's almost like my niece.'

'Which makes me nearly your sister.'

'But you're not. I actually missed you, too. In fact, I missed Vincent in a weird sort of way. And I love Helen.'

Lillian took a deep breath, steadying herself against the rock. 'Does Helen have cancer?' She had repeated that question in her own mind so many times that it came out as if rehearsed, with a natural raising of her voice at the end. As the words formed in the air, she shivered. Goose flesh sprang across her skin.

Steven's face grew dark. 'I can't tell you that, honey,' he said slowly.

'Are you her doctor?'

'No. But I've talked to him.'

Lillian felt her stomach begin to ache. She wrapped her arms around herself. 'She's been losing weight. I know what cancer looks like. A friend of mine's mother had it. She kept getting smaller and smaller. I want you to tell me the truth. I think I know already.'

Steven leaned forward and took Lillian's hand. 'Yes,' he said.

'Yes?' She grabbed his arm so hard she felt the flesh contract under her fingers. 'Oh my God.' She jumped up. 'Why didn't she tell me?'

'Helen isn't a talker. She doesn't share much with people.'

'I'm not people! I'm her only living daughter. Why doesn't anyone tell me about things?' She walked towards the ocean. 'Why do I get lied to constantly? I'm sick of it. I'm not the selfish one! Edward is. I'm a good mother!' She was screaming through her tears.

Steven followed her and putting his arms around her,

drew her close. 'Don't be so self-centred. What difference does it make? She's the one who's sick.'

'I just found her,' Lillian sobbed. 'We like being together. My other mother makes me feel incompetent. Helen is what I wanted.'

'I know,' Steven said kindly, stroking her back. 'I'm sorry.'

'When is she going to die?' Lillian asked, blowing her nose on the tissues Steven brought her.

'That's a bit pessimistic, isn't it?'

'She would have told me if it were minor, Steven. How long does she have?'

'I don't know.'

When Lydia returned after lunch, trailing an uprooted sunflower, she was picked up by her mother and kissed with such passion that Lydia held Lillian's face, looked deep into her eyes and murmured 'poor Mommy'.

Doris seemed unphased by the murder of her plant. 'I hated that thing,' she told Steven. 'I always felt like it was watching me while I tried to write. Judging, like a one-eyed editor.'

26

Steven invited himself to dinner after the day at the beach.
When they drove into the driveway, he scooped up the
passed-out Lydia and followed Lillian up the path to the
door. While he took her daughter upstairs, Lillian stood in
the dark hallway, limp with misery. Visions of disaster – the
impending death of her real mother, the general instability
and difficulty of life – filled her mind. She sat down on the
bottom step and put her head between her knees. Steven
yelled down to say he was reading Lydia a story. She went
into the kitchen and called several women in AA, leaving
polite but urgent messages on their answering machines.

When she opened the refrigerator door to put away the
leftover juice, her eyes were drawn to the shiny bottles of
imported beer, Vincent's beer, that were still on the bottom
shelf. Why were men always leaving her with their beer?
she wondered. When Steven spoke, she jumped.

'The kid's out cold again,' he said quietly. 'Do you
often bond with your refrigerator?'

She shut the door with a bang.

'I was admiring Vincent's Dutch beer,' she snapped. 'It
occurred to me how nice it would taste.'

Steven's face grew pale. 'I'm kidding,' she said hastily.
'I wouldn't drink a beer after all these years. It would
have to be opiated heroin or something. I'd want to see
the centre of the universe before I died. It would have to
be something that would kill me.'

'Come here,' Steven said, holding out his arms.

He was leaning against the kitchen table, waiting. She
shut her eyes for a moment, saw someone else, pushed that

image away. As she crossed the kitchen towards him, she accepted their coming together as inevitable. It had always been between them, this unexpressed desire. At first he was simply affectionate, kissing her brows and rubbing his cheeks against hers. But when his mouth finally found her own and his tongue pushed between her lips, she let go, felt her body relax and when he pushed her against the counter, pressing his body against hers, she fitted herself to him easily. She returned his pressure with equal force, pulling her sweatshirt over her head so that he could feel the ridged length of her spine and caress her breasts. His hands untied her sweatpants while she unbuttoned his shirt, her nails tracing circles on his chest.

He bent her backwards across the kitchen counter, a woman with a husband and a child, a woman with a dying mother, having sex with a man in the middle of her kitchen, in the late afternoon, a woman who believed that everything simple became difficult, all good things eventually turned sour. Steven's kisses continuing while he pulled off her trousers and underwear. He managed to kick off his own jeans and paused briefly to pull on a rubber. Did he know this would happen? wondered Lillian, her bare skin against the cool Formica. She had a moment to think – 'What am I doing?' – but her eyes remained closed and she waited, hungry for him. When he pulled her forward and thrust himself inside her she knew the answer. And when he wrapped her legs around him and took her breast in his mouth she forgot the question. It was simple to allow herself to fall into her sensations: the dark pleasure, the unconscious-ness that reminded her of taking drugs, of drinking, of escape.

As he carried her into the living-room, she hid her face in his neck, with its skin that had such a different scent from Vincent's, and she allowed him to put her down on the thick grey rug, to place a pillow under her hips so that he could come inside her again as deeply as possible.

Lillian and Vincent always tried to make love in the middle of the afternoon, no matter how busy their schedules. One of them would find the other and announce 'nap time'. They had had sex in every corner of the house including the basement. Sometimes Vincent pretended to be the meter man and insisted Lillian show him where the meter was. Once she had laughed until he'd backed her up against the cold stone wall, put his hand across her mouth and told her she was a 'hot bitch' and that he was going to fuck her. When she described this episode to Lizbeth, Lizbeth had been terribly impressed. 'I can't believe you married someone who turns you on that much.' Her voice was filled with admiration and Lillian stopped feeling guilty.

They had taught Lydia not to leave her room when she woke up from her nap. There were intercoms in every room of the house and Lydia knew how to call her parents. Lillian was on top of Steven, raising herself up and down, making him harder and harder until he gripped her hips in both hands and thrust himself up and then pushed her away until he was ready again. Both of them were covered with a sheen of sweat. Lillian was very close to an intense orgasm when they heard 'Mommy?' over the intercom. Steven stopped. She returned his hand to where it had been and called out in a calm and sweet voice: 'Ten more minutes, honey.'

'Whore,' Steven gasped.

'Not at all,' Lillian replied slowly, her breath becoming shorter. 'Our pediatrician recommended this. The first one is always a false alarm.'

When she came she thought of Vincent. The feel of his arms around her urging her towards more pleasure, how he buried his face in her breasts and how when he came he always told her he loved her, held her face, kissed her lips and said her name. And so she cried. And Steven was embarrassed but also pleased because he thought it had something to do with his consummate skill as a lover. She saw this, and didn't care.

They ate dinner around the kitchen table in a comfortable quiet. Lydia was still sleepy and a bit sunburned. She fed her doll and Thomas Wolfe, sensing her mother wasn't in the mood to enforce the rules properly. Steven read the evening paper while Lillian took down a book she had bought months earlier and never opened, a book called *Facing Cancer*. The first chapter was 'Acceptance'. The author's mother had died of cancer. Lillian looked at the back cover and the photograph was a black and white picture of both women smiling into the camera. The older one's eyes looked far into the distance and the younger one's smile seemed forced. Lydia asked Steven to read her another book and announced she was tired and wanted to go to bed.

'You amazing girl,' her mother said, kissing her sweet-smelling hair. 'Why are you such a smartie-pants?'

'I am ready for Freddie,' Lydia announced, giggling. Freddie was the code name for bed.

Lillian took a long, hot bath. She lay in the tub and prayed for acceptance. When she came downstairs wearing a T-shirt and sweatpants, Steven was standing in the living-room, looking at the pictures that covered one wall: pictures of her and Vincent; Lydia and her father; Lydia and both her parents; Lillian looking unglamorous; Vincent looking gorgeous.

'You have a beautiful family,' Steven said.

'I know,' Lillian replied, laughing. 'It's hard being the smart one.'

'You are a beautiful woman,' he said looking at her hard.

'Thank you.'

'I'd better push off,' he said awkwardly, not meeting her eyes.

'Oh yeah?' Lillian asked, sitting cross-legged on the couch, her arms folded.

'I've got some paperwork to catch up on.'

'Are you busy?'

'Oh sure. These days having babies is very hip.'

'That's fine.' As she said it, she realized it was the truth.

'Well—'

'Was that all you expected?' she asked, watching him closely. 'I mean, we've known each other for a long time.'

'I'm not sure what you mean.'

'Oh, I'm not sure either.' There was a long pause. 'I love Vincent.'

'Yeah, I know.'

'But you were neat. I mean, this was neat.'

'Oh yeah?'

'Yeah! It felt . . . neat.' Steven smiled. 'Did you need to hear that?' He shrugged and sat down on the edge of the couch. She tried not to think bad thoughts about men. Sometimes it was a difficult struggle.

'Not really. I mean, I sort of figured . . . It's sort of awkward.' He put down his jacket and began to look as if he wanted to stay.

Lillian stood, yawned and smiled. She walked towards the front door. 'Well, don't work too hard,' she said.

He picked up his jacket. 'Are you going to speak to Helen?'

'I'm not sure. I guess someone will have to say something eventually.' She thought for a moment. 'If we act the way we usually do it will probably be around her deathbed. She'll say: "By the way, I'm dying of cancer." And I'll say, "Thanks for sharing, Mom. It's been real." Nice and alcoholic. When the monster's eaten all the furniture and threatened your children, you mention its presence.'

'Can I do anything?'

'Can you make her well?'

Steven shook his head. 'No. But something could change. Are you OK?'

'Uh huh. This won't ruin our friendship or anything, will it?'

'Of course not.' He pulled her into his arms and kissed her lightly on the mouth. Everything felt different.

As she closed the door, she knew it would be a long time before she saw him again. 'My mother's dying and my husband's left me,' she thought. 'Nothing like a little intimacy to ruin a friendship.'

Standing in the doorway of her daughter's bedroom, she watched the slow, steady movement of Lydia's breath, the small, perfect lines of her body underneath the cotton sheet. Lillian recognized that motherhood had altered so much of her own behaviour. The selfishness that seemed intrinsic to her personality had been replaced by something else. Now she was Lydia's guardian angel. She had to accept her place in the world so that she could survive to protect her daughter.

Vincent was much more of an optimist. He believed there was no reason to anticipate misery. He assumed that given the proper amount of love and air, good times and accurate information, Lydia would grow like some sort of wild flower, beautiful but not fragile. No matter how many times Lillian reminded Vincent of man's inhumanity to man, of the historical precedents for catastrophe, he continued to view the world as a wonderful place and his music as a gift from God. He saw his wife and daughter as something he deserved, given his talent, his looks and his nice personality. One day he might be proven wrong. But she hoped he was right.

She wanted to tell him about Helen. There were so many things she didn't understand.

★   ★   ★

In the middle of the night a small hand shook her awake. Lydia stood by her pillow, her hair in wild curls around her face. Her cheeks were wet.

'Ducky,' Lillian murmured sleepily, 'what's the matter?'

'I had a bad dream,' Lydia wailed, climbing under the blanket that Lillian held up, snuggling into her mother's body, putting her cold little feet against Lillian's warm shins.

'What about, bunny?'

'Trees,' Lydia whispered.

'Trees?' Lillian repeated sleepily. 'What sort of trees?'

'I don't know.' Lydia began to cry again.

'Shh. Mommy's here. What were the trees doing?'

'Looking at me.'

'Just looking at you?'

'Looking at me and making tree noises.'

Lillian pulled Lydia out of her burrow under the blanket. 'Feel better, squirrel?'

'Yes,' Lydia said, yawning.

'No more trees?'

'No.'

'Back to sleep?'

'Yes.'

'I love you.'

'Mommy?'

'Yes?'

'Is Daddy coming home soon?'

'Well, I don't know yet, sweetie. But you'll visit him soon no matter what. Now go to sleep.'

She breathed with her daughter. Their two breaths were perfectly matched, a synchronicity which always lulled Lydia to sleep. Vincent used to love to breathe with Lydia, loved to hold her close and feel the heartbeat of his daughter. Lillian usually had to wake him up so that he would come back to her, come to her with his strong arms and his beautiful eyes. At night they lay together, her ass against his stomach, curled up tight in the cold Maine winter and he would whisper secrets in her ear, sing her poems he remembered from childhood, old Beatles tunes, Shakespearean sonnets. As Lillian felt the absence of that her heart froze in her chest, and seemed to stop cold when she considered the possibility of their separation being permanent.

At breakfast the next morning, she realized she'd neglected to clear the answering machine. A vague sense of doom lingered around the breakfast table. Lydia drooped like an ailing blossom. Thomas Wolfe kept moaning in his sleep. There were three red lights flashing and she was sure the messages would all say the same thing. 'Our marriage is finished. I don't love you any more.'

The nightmare she'd had was fresh in her mind. She was in a small, oppressive white room, watching her husband make love to another woman. Carefully, with a great amount of concentration, he brought the woman to a climax while he looked at his wife, blank-eyed, grim-faced. She had woken up shaking, covered with a fine sheen of sweat. She felt hung-over, guilty, full of fear. In the bathroom she studied her reflection, the dark circles beneath her eyes. She saw Helen, whose features she had inherited, whose face she was beginning to recognize as her own. She felt old. Yet older women had always made her feel guilty for being young herself. She saw a pattern. Her Jordan parents were so distant with one another. And Helen was always alone. She would also be alone. She stepped on the scales and was surprised to find her weight the same. Lillian felt huge with misery.

27

'Lillian. Call me back.'

'Lillian, it's me again. Mandy's a temp with Jupiter. I wish you'd check this effing machine. Are you OK for money? Call me. Use the car number if no-one answers at the apartment.'

'Ma called about the picture in *People*. That was this Special Olympics gig I did for nothing. I don't even know that woman's name. Ma asked me if we'd taken God into our marriage. Whattya think? I really need to talk to you. I spend all my time in meetings with people wearing Ray Bans talking about "perceived reality". Reality is: 1. Tell Lydia her daddy loves her and to tell her mother the same thing. 2. Why are you such a neurotic bitch sometimes?'

The vision of herself and Steven fucking in the kitchen returned. Here was Vincent defending himself against an imaginary flirtation while she was guilty of flagrant adultery. When she tried to send a fax ('Vincent, I love you too. Come home soon!') the machine made a series of unpromising noises and then flashed a message which translated as 'Failure to transmit'. God hates me, she thought.

'Mommy?' Lydia was standing at the top of the steps, her hair sticking out in spikes all over her head, wearing a sweater over her Mickey-Mouse underpants and mismatched socks. She wore that slightly bruised, sensitive expression children have when they first wake up.

'Yes, Ladybird?'

'You wanna take a shower with me?'

'Before breakfast?' The fax machine was still flashing its negative message. Lillian pulled the plug.

'We could have a cookie.'

'A cookie before breakfast?' Lillian walked slowly up the stairs, her arms outstretched.

Lydia giggled and jumped up and down. 'No! Before our shower!'

'Let me get this straight: First a cookie, then a shower, then breakfast?'

'Yes! And then *Sesame Street* and then swimming and then stories and . . . ' Lydia ran out of her favourite things.

'When do we feed Thomas Wolfe? After our shower and before breakfast or after breakfast and before *Sesame Street* or after *Sesame Street* and then before stories?'

Lydia screamed. Like her mother, she couldn't handle the complications of modern life. Lillian sat down on the steps and Lydia climbed into her lap, putting her face against her breasts.

'Daddy called. He said to tell you he loves you. You can listen to him say that on the machine.' Lillian rubbed her daughter's back. 'OK?'

'OK.'

They went into the kitchen and opened a can of dog food. In the bathroom, Lydia picked out all her father's shampoos for the two of them to use. They rubbed soap and pine-smelling hair conditioner on each other. Lillian shaved her legs in the bath while Lydia made a convoy of boats and sunk an alien spaceship. They took very short saunas, rubbed cream into one another and Lillian ran on the treadmill while they listened to one of Vincent's songs.

'Is Daddy a good singer?' Lydia asked as Lillian was doing sit-ups on the rug.

'What do you think?'

'I like Big Bird more.'

Lillian tried not to laugh. Lydia looked concerned about her critical dilemma.

'That's fine. Big Bird and Daddy don't sing like each other anyway. You can like both of them.'

They decided to dress alike in blue jeans and black sweatshirts with the logo from Vincent's last tour, a star outlined in bright fuchsia-pink. While Lydia set the table, Lillian poured muesli into their wooden bowls. When she looked at the date on the newspaper, she realized it was her mother's birthday. 'Let's call Grandma Jordan and wish her a happy birthday,' she suggested.

When the phone was answered, Lydia screamed 'This is Lydia. Happy Birthday!' and handed the receiver back to Lillian.

'Mom?'

'Was that my perfect grandchild? What a voice she has!'

'Umm. Maybe opera. Happy birthday, Mother.'

'Thank you, darling.'

'There's something in the mail for you.' Lillian looked around the kitchen. 'A microwave oven.'

'Honey, that's much too extravagant.'

'Mother, we're rich.'

'No you aren't. How is Vincent?'

'Fine. He's in Los Angeles.'

'And you're joining him there?'

'I don't know.'

'Ah.'

There was a long pause. Lillian could tell her mother had seen the *People* item. Lydia began to bang her spoon on the table.

'Wait a second, Mom.' Lillian put her hand over the receiver. 'Lydia, you want to watch *Mr Rogers' Neighborhood* until I'm done?' Lydia nodded. Lillian turned on the television set and put Lydia's bowl of cereal on the coffee table.

'We might not make it.'

'What?'

'Vincent and me. We're having major problems.'

'Oh sweetie—'

'I'd like to visit,' Lillian found herself saying. 'Lydia wants to see you.'

'What a wonderful idea!' Mrs Jordan sounded very happy.

Lillian leaned against the refrigerator. She had to tell someone about Helen. What she heard herself saying was, 'How's Edward?'

Her mother sighed. 'Sometimes I think it would be better if your brother was a little less attractive.'

Lillian laughed. 'That's a funny thing for a mother to say! Isn't he meant to be your love object, Mom? How can you resent those dimples, those long lashes, that cherry-red mouth?'

'Don't be nasty, Lillian.'

'You know I love Edward.'

'Everyone loves Edward.' Her mother sighed.

'Everyone loves Vincent,' Lillian gasped. 'God, Mother! I married my brother.'

'Are you still in therapy?' her mother asked.

'Yes. Why do people keep asking me that? Are you afraid I'll stop going and have to wear a Medic-Alert bracelet?'

Mrs Jordan sighed. 'I'll call you tomorrow, dear.'

'Happy Birthday, Mom.'

'Don't worry. Everything will work out.'

The previous winter, the woman Edward had waited for had finally decided to leave her husband. Only to conclude after a month, that it was impossible not to be rich and married to someone with a Lear jet. She left Edward, describing herself as 'shallow, without any depth'.

'Redundant,' Edward said, slurring his words slightly over the phone. 'The woman had the vocabulary of a model.' He was calling from a pay phone in a bar in Tijuana.

'I spent eight years waiting for that bitch to choose me,' he moaned. 'Nobody told me I wouldn't win.'

'Edward,' Lillian said, her tone of voice soft yet firm. 'Go back to your hotel. Get a good night's sleep. Call the airport in the morning and reserve a flight to Bangor. You'll probably have to change in Boston. Then call me and tell me when you're arriving. OK?'

'OK.'

'Tell me what I just said.'

'I'm a drunken clown.'

'No! Come on. What are you going to do?'

'Kill myself.'

'Edward—'

'Go to bed. Alone. Make a reservation. Come to Bangor. Bangor? Why would I visit Maine in January? Who wants to leave Mexico for Maine?'

'You do. I'm hanging up now.'

'Can I talk to my fairy godchild?'

'She's asleep, Eddie. It's three in the morning.'

'Sorry. Is Vinnie there?'

'You want me to wake him up?'

'I need to talk to a guy.'

'For God's sake! Wait a second.' Lillian had shaken Vincent awake.

'Hey bro—' Vincent said sleepily. 'What? Oh yeah? Yeah. That's true. No, I got to disagree with you there. Your sister for one. When? Well, that's great. Of course I'm glad you're coming. Listen, Ed, go to sleep. Call her in the morning. Right. I love you too, man.'

Vincent started to go back to sleep immediately. Lillian poked him in the ribs.

'What did he say?'

'He said all women were whores and bitches.'

'Nice.'

'He's a hurtin' guy, Lil. He's a mess.'

'I know.' Lillian sighed. 'Would you be upset if we broke up?'

Vincent snorted. 'We don't break up, babe. That's for high school. We get divorced. We get lawyers. You take all my money.'

'Let's not.'

'OK. Go to sleep.'

Edward had arrived two days later. Lydia was very excited. Although Edward had only seen his niece twice since her birth, he'd mailed an unending stream of expensive presents found in Beverly Hills boutiques. He was responsible for Lydia's leather fetish, brought on by his purchasing a tiny motorcycle jacket, authentic in every detail and custom-decorated with silver studs.

He looked worn-out. His skin under its usual tan, was grey and muddy. When he took off his dark glasses, she noticed the deep purple circles and kissed him tenderly.

'Hi sweetie,' she said, taking his second bag. When they hugged, she felt his shoulders shaking. 'Never mind,' she whispered in his ear, 'everything's going to get better.'

Vincent had fixed up the attic as a sort of private guest-quarters with a bathroom and a small kitchenette. They gave Edward plenty of privacy but he got up for breakfast every morning and delighted in Lydia's company. She decided he was her special friend and didn't understand why he wouldn't take a bath with her or go to bed at eight. Edward and Vincent spent hours in Vincent's studio or driving around town on mysterious errands. Seeing Edward so sad and quiet, Lillian longed for her arrogant older brother. She took him to an AA meeting and he made nasty comments about the way people dressed. She introduced him to a woman named Myrtle who had seen several of his movies.

'How do you remember all your lines?' she asked him after they were introduced.

'Uhh.' Edward paused. He looked at Myrtle with a dazzling smile. 'What a great question,' he said. 'I have no idea.'

As they drove towards Stonington, Lillian glanced at his wonderful profile.

'You could get a house here, you know. Lots of nice women like Myrtle.'

Edward laughed. 'You'd like me to live in a trailer, wouldn't you. It would finally balance things.'

'Myrtle would never leave you for a man with a Lear jet.' They were both quiet for a second. 'Myrtle would never leave you!'

Edward was still there when they celebrated Easter with Helen. He carved the leg of lamb and they all hunted for dyed eggs. Vincent was dressed up as the Easter bunny and the neighbourhood kids came over for a second, wilder hunt.

'How did you make such a beautiful family?' Edward asked his sister as they stood watching Vincent patiently demonstrate the bunny hop (he had removed the top part of his costume) to all the children. Lydia already knew the steps and was being extremely bossy about which foot to start with. Helen was sitting with a group of people from AA arguing about whether cocaine was worse than gin.

'I don't know. Sometimes I don't see it that way.' She put her arm through his. 'We're not perfect or anything. You've stumbled on a relatively peaceful period.'

Edward laughed. 'Honey, you don't have to tell me that! You forget how many times you called last year to hiss about your – let me see – selfish, insensitive, vain, creep of a husband. But still . . . how do you manage not to cut and run?'

She drew a deep breath. 'One day at a time – sort of like not drinking. Some mornings I wake up and I look at Vincent and he seems like a total stranger. He doesn't get like that about me. But I still can't believe he actually wants to be here, that marriage isn't some sort of jail sentence for him. I think I put this ten-year spell on him and when the time's up – poof! He'll disappear. He'll find a real wife.'

'What are you? Synthetic? Don't confuse that guy, Lillian. He's not like you. I understand what sort of maze your mind is because we grew up together. He sees things very clearly. He wants to understand your feelings but there's a limit. There's always a limit.' Edward's face darkened.

She looked at him closely. 'Did he say anything to you? Is he unhappy? Am I making him crazy?'

'No, honey. I just . . . you want to know what he said? We were driving around in the pick-up truck. Just a couple of guys, a couple of guys talking.'

'I wish you'd stop this male-bonding guy garbage.'

'There's a compliment for you, so listen. Anyway, we were driving along listening to Van Halen. You know, guy music.' Lillian punched his arm. 'Drinking a beer.'

She punched him again.

'Just one. Vincent was going on about his new power-mower. I leaned forward and opened the glove compartment. There's this picture of you and Lydia taped to the door. Lydia's in some sort of ugly hat, that thing Mom knitted her and you're smiling. "Let me tell you something, Ed," he says. "All I ever cared about was music. With music I could be smart without being a jerk and I didn't have to beat anybody up. Women never mattered much. Certainly I'd never think more about a woman than my guitar. Then your sister turned up. When

I saw her it was like my eyes had filtered out all the colour and the depth in the world. She stopped my heart from nearly the first minute I saw her."'

Lillian hugged Edward. He lit a cigarette and they passed it back and forth while they watched Vincent lead the bunny-hop line, his daughter in his arms.

'You know what I said?'

She shook her head. 'No doubt something very spontaneous yet profound.'

'I said: "Vinnie – I like to call him that – Vinnie, you're the best thing that ever happened to that screwed-up little sister of mine. You be good to her or I'll infect your guitars with a superbreed of Japanese termites."' Edward picked up some hard-boiled eggs and began to juggle them. 'I didn't realize I was a loser. Did you know it?'

'You aren't a loser.'

'Sure I am.' His smile disappeared. 'I was just something to keep her from getting old.'

'Edward!'

'I know. So what? It makes me crazy. I feel like my entire life is meaningless. I've wasted so much time on nothing. I should have gone to Law School.'

'Law School?'

'Half my high-school class went to Law School.'

'You're an actor.'

'I could have been a lawyer, or a doctor or a teacher.'

'A teacher? What sort of teacher?'

Edward glared at his sister. 'I don't know what sort! Clown College! What kind of question is that?'

'Well, you sound like Brando at the end of "On the Waterfront". It's pathetic.'

'Do I?'

'Yes.'

'I've been working on that. They're talking about doing a remake. Guess who's up for the lead?'

'Not my big brother!'

'That stupid bitch will regret the day she told Edward Jordan her husband was a more viable commodity.'

'Is that what she said?'

'Yup. A moron. Mom was the one who brought up Law School, by the way. I told her I'd broken up with Cassidy and she said: "Why didn't you go to Law School?"'

'Makes perfect sense to me. How could you fall in love with a woman named Cassidy? Let me introduce you to someone nice, Edward. I think you could get used to trailer life.'

'Nah.' He picked up a spare pair of blue bunny ears and stuck them on his head. The hopping children shrieked at the sight and Vincent relinquished his place to walk over to where Lillian stood holding three eggs.

'Is there a symbolic significance to those?' Vincent asked, pulling her into his arms.

'No,' Lillian whispered in his ear. 'Are you naked under that costume?'

'How could you tell?'

'Never mind. I love you,' she said, putting her hands on both sides of his face.

'You do?' His eyes grew softer. 'What's wrong, baby?'

'Nothing,' she replied, kissing him on each eye. 'I just love you and I can't remember when I last said it.'

'Three weeks ago. After I fixed your printer.'

'Oh.' Lillian put her head on his shoulder. 'Am I difficult?'

'Terribly.'

'Why?'

'You have an acid tongue and a big brain and your moods don't seem connected with things that are happening on Earth.'

'What else?'

'You're cranky and irrational and unpredictable.'

'Vincent—' He was holding her from behind, his chin resting between her shoulder blades.

'Your energy is amazing. You are a wonderful mother. You are the sexiest, funniest woman I've ever known. I love you more than myself, more than my music, and that's probably unhealthy but who gives a fuck?'

Lillian turned around so she was facing him. Her eyes were full of tears. 'Don't,' she whispered. Vincent held her close against him. Deep in her brain a message flashed. *Beware*, was what it said, *dangerous journey ahead*.

28

'Helen?'

The house was extremely clean. The walls looked freshly painted and the wood floors gleamed. Helen was sitting in a chair which faced the picture window that framed the back yard. She turned towards Lillian and putting her finger to her lips, motioned her over.

There was a red fox delicately sniffing at a clump of *pachysandra*. Its coat was an astonishing colour, a film-maker's fantasy of fluffy golden red. His ears were pricked, and slightly forward. His clever, cruel face was very human, almost feminine in its delicate beauty.

'He's waiting for the rabbit,' Helen whispered.

From their position, the entire yard was clearly visible. Helen pointed towards the back fence where a twitching pair of white ears edged in pink were visible.

'Why do I constantly witness rabbit executions?' Lillian sighed. The rabbit continued to hop towards Helen's lettuce patch.

'Kill!' Helen hissed under her breath. She met Lillian's look of reproach with a shrug. 'That little pest has eaten all my new carrots. At least this isn't poison, it's nice and natural.'

Helen looked extremely thin. Her skin was very pale and translucent. Lillian put a hand on her shoulder and felt there was less of her. The fox streaked across the garden as if shot from a cannon. The rabbit was snatched from the ground, tossed in the air and then caught again. There was a streak of gleaming red, a vision of the rabbit caught in the fox's jaws like a piece of laundry.

'Coffee?'

'I'll get it.'

'It's just brewed. Take some bread.'

The kitchen was also freshly painted. There was a new set of cabinets installed over the stove and the floors were buffed. She wondered if this were Steven's work.

'Who's been doing all this fixing up?'

'Steven.'

'That's nice of him.'

'Umm.' Helen sounded doubtful.

'Isn't it?'

'I find his guilt oppressive.'

'Why does he feel guilty?'

'It's genetic in a Catholic. And of course, he's a doctor – more or less.'

Lillian paused in the living-room doorway. 'Why would his being a doctor make him feel guilty?'

'He can't accept there's nothing to be done.'

'What do you mean?'

'Ah.' Helen twisted around to look at Lillian who stood in the doorway, her eyes looking down, her arms twisted around herself. 'Come here,' she said softly, holding out her arms.

'No,' Lillian replied. 'I'm afraid.'

'Don't be. Come here.'

'Oh God!' She began to cry. Large childish tears which rolled down her cheeks and splashed on the hardwood floor as she crossed the room to where her mother sat, and got down on her knees, putting her head in Helen's lap.

Helen gently stroked her hair. 'I need you to help me,' she said softly.

'Helen—'

'Shh. Just listen for a second. The cancer's inoperable. I knew that before the tests were finished and I'm glad because the treatments are terrible.'

'Oh no,' Lillian moaned. 'Don't.'

'I want to stay here in my house. And I want to die sober. Those are the two things that really matter to me. Do you understand?'

'Yes.' She was gasping for air but Helen kept stroking her back and her breath calmed down.

'Good.' There was a long silence.

Lillian heard the birds fighting outside and the sound of the children next door playing softball. She couldn't move. There was such a huge weight pressing down on her she felt she would be flattened by it. All of the things she had failed to accomplish passed through her mind. She saw her own daughter trying to stay happy while she herself allowed their family to fall apart.

'Does it hurt?'

'Not much. I have the medication. The worst is over. Lillian?'

'What?'

'You know I've missed Emily terribly.' Helen stroked her daughter's hair. 'I have this strange, silly feeling we're going to be together. You know, I don't believe in God but I think there's something and I've felt Emily out there, waiting for me.'

Go away, Lillian wanted to scream at her stepsister. 'That's good,' she said, raising her face from Helen's lap. 'And my father? Is there some sort of cocktail party taking place on a cloud?'

'Of course,' Helen said smiling, 'always, he's there.'

At that moment she saw how beautiful her mother must have been when she was in love with him. Yet Lillian could scarcely stand to look at her because there was death in that face, the skull gleaming through the pale skin. Acceptance and death.

'I'll move in with Lydia,' Lillian said quietly. 'She loves it here with you. I love it too.'

Helen smiled. 'Are you sure?'

'Yes.'

'Where's Vincent?'

'Los Angeles still. I don't know whether we're going to stay married. I guess things are in pretty bad shape.'

'Steven showed me the *People* picture. Have you discussed it?'

'No. He left messages on the machine and then I missed him and the fax machine in his office wasn't working.'

'Why don't you try to call him now?'

She sat down at her mother's feet again and took her hand. 'Do you want to talk about it?'

'What?'

'The cancer. I don't know . . . '

'Dying?'

'Yeah. I guess,' Lillian said faintly.

'No. You want to talk about Vincent?'

'No.' They both laughed. 'You want to see your granddaughter?'

'Yes.' Helen's face lit up. 'Go get her. I finally found that box of toys in the attic, sweetie. There's a whole train set and wood blocks your father made for Emily.'

'John?'

'Yes. He loved to give Emily things he'd made.'

'If you had been able to leave here with him to begin a new life, without hurting anyone, would you have? And do you think it would have lasted until you were old?'

Helen smiled and looked out the window again. 'If that fox hadn't grabbed the rabbit, would it have been caught in my trap or would it have survived to eat all the new lettuce? Do we care? I don't know, Lillian. You leave a certain place and you can't keep looking back, can you?'

'Don't you wonder?'

'Not really. Emily wasn't supposed to go sailing the day she died. We were going to a big linen sale in Ellesworth. She and Steven were thinking about having a baby. Then the car battery died. Steven couldn't find the cables. It was too late to drive to Ellesworth, so they decided to go sailing. He left the life jackets on the dock because Emily made him go below, and then she cast off while he was finding her sunglasses. I remember everything. Steven and I sat here in the dark going over and over every minute of that day. A thousand opportunities to change direction. But we didn't know where we were going. You can spend your entire life regretting things,' Helen said softly, touching Lillian's cheek, 'and that turns out to be the worst mistake of all.'

Lillian went home to pick up Lydia and T.W. and to pack some clothes. The answer machine was blinking again.

'Hey, what's going on there? Is it that stupid *People* thing? Lillian, don't believe something without talking to me. I need to talk to you. Hug the kid. Hug yourself. I miss you so much, I feel sick. I saw a commercial for cotton and it reminded me of both of you. Everything does.'

She called the apartment number again but the machine answered and she hung up without speaking. Opening their closet door, she took out Vincent's faded denim jacket and put it on. She packed two suitcases, found Lydia's stuffed gorilla and T.W.'s rubber mouse. He was lying down in the corner of their bedroom, chewing on one of Vincent's sneakers.

'Come here,' Lillian called from the door. 'Here, boy.' T.W. stood and waggled his rear end. He was now almost eight years old. Lillian kneeled and buried her face in his coat which smelled faintly of smoke.

'Helen's going to die,' she whispered into his shoulder. He waited patiently to be released.

While the car warmed up, she pulled out a small leather case she found in the pocket of Vincent's jacket. Inside was a picture of Lydia taken about five minutes after she was born, lying on Lillian's stomach. Lillian looked as if she had survived combat. Her hair was tangled and soaked with sweat, her face dead white, and she was staring at the creature that had just emerged from her body with total amazement. There was another picture from the Easter when Lydia was a two-year-old yellow chick in the annual Stonington Easter parade. She looked like a little yellow sun. The last picture was one she had never seen, taken just after they had met. She was sitting at the kitchen table in Mildred's house in a shaft of light. Her eyes were shining and she looked very young.

On the way to Helen's she drove to American Express and sent a mailgram to Vincent. 'I love you. Stop. Come back to us. Stop. Call Helen's. Stop.'

When she and Lydia drove into the driveway, Helen came out and took Lydia out of her car seat.

'Hello, love of my life,' she said, nuzzling Lydia's neck. 'Vincent just called. I tried to tell him you were on your way home but he'd called there already. He was pretty abrupt.'

'Is he there now?'

'No. The studio asked him to go to Las Vegas to supervise a studio recording.'

'Damnit! I just sent him a mailgram.'

'He seemed to think you might file for d-i-v-o-r-c-e.'

Lydia picked her head up from her grandmother's shoulder. 'I know letters,' she said proudly.

'What's that spell Miss Smartie-pants?' Lillian asked her, handing over the stuffed gorilla.

'It spells dum-dum doodie head!' Lydia shouted, over-whelmed by her own intelligence.

'Go call him,' Helen said. 'Maybe he is still there.'

Instead she sat in the study smoking a cigarette and listened while Helen put Lydia down for her nap. They played the game Lydia had invented where you call each other every name in a category until you can't think of any other fruit or vegetable or piece of furniture and then you giggle and go to sleep after singing 'I love you. A nickel and a peck. A nickel and a peck and a hug around the neck . . . '

Lillian prayed. 'Please give me time,' she muttered. 'I want more time.' Time for what, she asked herself. Time for whom? She saw herself back on the streets in New York, encased in her own anxiety, running, escaping from the press of the crowds, the constant reminder that she was never alone and always lonely. She put her cigarette out and fell on her knees. 'Help me,' she asked someone. 'Help me accept all of this. My daughter, mother, husband, mother, father, brother.' She put her forehead against her thighs and stayed in the yoga pose of the child. Her body seemed very small, the floor was hard against her knees. Fear gripped her entirely.

'Lil,' it was Helen calling from downstairs, 'you OK?'

'Yes. I'm fine. I'll be down in a second.'

When she walked into the kitchen, Helen was reading a cookbook and asked her, 'What do you say to something really yummy for dinner?'

'Hello, Mr Yummy! A direct quote from my genius daughter. I'd better go to the Shopwell and pick up our fetish objects like peppermint soap and artichoke hearts.'

'Did you reach him?'

'No.'

'Go to a meeting tonight. I'll make dinner with the kid.'

Lillian nodded. She didn't want to do anything but find a small space and fit herself inside.

When she'd first begun attending AA meetings in Maine, she'd felt different from the people she met there. AA in New York was full of celebrities, drug addicts and people who talked to themselves. There were open discussions about sexual preferences, affairs, job disasters and neurotic obsessions with money, food, sex and gambling. Members identified themselves as victims of domestic violence and incest, many of them paid their rent by continuing to deal drugs, practising witchcraft, being prostitutes or call girls and thieves. Of course, most sober New Yorkers were employed, housed and in therapy. But the lunatic fringe was represented in a way that Lillian missed when she left Manhattan.

At first she thought the programme was too religious in Maine. Then she decided there was too little 'real' honesty. After listening to several sober qualifications, she realized it was exactly the same. For an alcoholic, continuing to drink meant insanity or death. When she listened without judgement she heard willingness, acceptance, hope, endurance and faith. No-one mentioned their therapists or how badly an audition had gone. That was all that really distinguished AA in Maine from AA in New York.

When she drove into the driveway again after the meeting, she saw Helen sitting in the corner of the living-room, her lap empty, staring into the fire. The light fell across her so that she appeared one-dimensional, like a portrait. Lillian thought about the first time she had seen her and observed her own eyes in the face of another person, about how much she had wanted to understand. Helen hadn't explained everything but Lillian understood enough.

She rested her head against the steering wheel for a minute. How could she take care of her so that death would appear natural, like another step? You struggled so hard to live and then, when you'd finally learned how to do it properly, it was time to die. This was subject matter for terrible articles which women's magazines would print under titles like, 'How I came to have faith.' Or, 'My mother's death taught me how to feel.'

'Fuck it,' Lillian muttered to herself, opening the car door. T.W. came bounding out of the dark, his coat covered with some kind of thistle. He ran up and buried his nose in her crotch.

'Sit!' she commanded sternly. Thomas Wolfe's bottom trembled an inch away from the ground. She picked some of the weeds out of his coat. His rear quarters slowly moved back and forth. 'Come on,' she said, opening the door. 'You can sleep with me tonight and catch me up on what it is to be a wild thing.'

Helen was asleep by the fire. Lillian sat down on the couch and looked at her. I don't know how to do this, she thought. But wasn't that what she had told Vincent moments before she'd gone into labour? 'I don't know how to have a baby,' she had told him. 'I need summer school.'

'How did you learn to swim?'

Lillian thought for a moment. 'Edward threw me into the middle of a pool without my water wings.'

Vincent beamed. 'That's great,' he said. 'You used your natural ability and started paddling.'

'No,' Lillian gasped as a pain ripped through her abdomen, 'I sank to the bottom like a stone and my entire life flashed before my eyes which took about six seconds since I was only three and then I was rescued by the lifeguard whom I worshipped until he went to Vietnam and stepped on a land mine.'

'Well,' he had said. 'At least you still like swimming.'

Helen was now awake and looking back at Lillian.

'How was the meeting?'

'OK. Debbie's husband is still convinced she can have wine with dinner. Arthur's mother-in-law thinks Arthur's possessed by the devil and wants to have him exorcised.'

'Oh dear. What were you thinking about?'

'Giving birth.'

'Really? I wouldn't imagine that provides a pleasurable memory. Unless you meant afterwards?'

'No, it has something to do with trust I guess.'

'Why don't you try to call Vincent again?'

'I told him in the mailgram I was here.'

Helen stood up and put the screen in front of the fire. The two women stood for a moment in the dark living-room, listening to the silence.

'I love this house,' Helen whispered.

Lillian nodded.

'You're very brave,' Helen said, looking at her. 'I'm extremely proud of you.'

Lillian kissed her mother and, picking up her book, slowly climbed the stairs to her room.

She dreamed her life was a dream. She dreamed that someone came to wake her up and she was a woman who had no past because she had slept and dreamed a life and by waking she lost it all. 'It was a dream,' she kept repeating to herself as she wandered the barren landscape of her 'real' life. And the dreamer cried for the misery of consciousness. When she woke up and heard the sound of her child singing in the other room, her heart was pierced by Lydia's voice.

'Mommy,' Lydia had once told her, 'I dreamed I disappeared.'

'Then what happened?'

'You found me.'

'Then what happened?'

'We were all happy.'

'I'll always find you.'

'How?'

'Call me. I'll hear your voice.'

'What if I'm on the moon?'

'Use your moon phone.'

'What if you don't hear me?'

'Try again.'

29

When the birds outside her window reached a crescendo, Lillian opened her eyes. The ceiling, while familiar, was not her own. The curtains wafted in the cool breeze of the open window. She was sleeping in a hard, single bed. It made her feel like a spinster. She pulled on a pair of jeans and brushed her hair until it stood out around her head like a cloud. 'I need a haircut,' she told her reflection. Finding an elastic band, she pulled her hair away from her face and made a ponytail which stuck up in the air.

'Good morning.' Steven Woodruff was sitting at the kitchen table. 'You look like Pebbles Flintstone.' Lydia, who was sitting at his feet tearing newspapers into shreds, let out a loud laugh.

'What's so funny?' Lillian asked, bending down to kiss her upturned face.

'You look like Pebbles,' Lydia said, laughing harder.

'Do you know who Pebbles is?' Lillian asked her daughter, who slowly shook her head.

'Good morning,' Steven said again, putting down his paper. 'What do we call Mommy?'

'Sleepy dum dum head.'

'How charming.' Lillian sat down and poured herself a cup of coffee from the thermal jug on the table. 'That's a nice way to treat your sweet mother who buys you slurpees and never complains about having to read you *Goodnight Moon* three hundred and sixty-five days a year.'

'Dum dum sleepy head,' Lydia murmured to herself. 'Pebbles.'

Lillian took a banana from the fruit bowl and peeled

it slowly. As she put part of it into her mouth, she saw that Steven was looking at her and she felt her face grow warm.

'Are you delivering in the neighbourhood?' she asked sarcastically.

Steven shook his head. 'I drop in here pretty often. Have you heard from Vin?'

'We keep missing each other. Helen talked to him.'

'Is he coming back?'

'Why would he do that?'

'Because of Helen.'

'He doesn't know yet.' Lillian glanced at him. 'You didn't tell him, did you?'

'Of course not. But something's up.'

'What do you mean?' She stared at Steven, a pain in the pit of her stomach.

'I don't know. I was just surprised to hear from Vin.'

'He called you?'

'Yup.' Steven picked up his paper again.

'Oh my God.' Lillian held her head in her hands. 'He knows.'

'Did you tell him?'

Picking up her knife, she waved it at him. 'Sure. I called him and gave him a blow-by-blow description.'

'So—'

'He just does. Some people can predict the weather. Vincent knows when people are misbehaving.'

Steven shook his head. 'All he asked me was whether I remembered the name of a guy who used to play guitar around here.'

Lillian groaned. 'He'll never forgive me,' she said. 'Never.'

'Did you talk to her?'

'Yes.' Lillian drank some coffee. 'I don't understand anything. I mean, I understand everything but I don't know what it means.'

'You should tell Vincent. Those two have been close for a long time. She sort of sponsored his music career.'

Lillian nodded. She knew how much Vincent loved Helen. He had mowed her lawn every summer. She had always treated him like an adult and encouraged him to visit her whenever he wanted to escape from the oppressive love of his large parents in their small trailer. He took care of the grand piano which Emily never really learned to play. Lillian was secretly glad he was so far away. She wasn't sure how to tell him that Helen was dying. Or how to deny making love to another man in their kitchen.

'I know that, Steven. There's very little about my husband I don't know.'

'Hey, I wasn't trying to imply anything.'

Lillian held up her hand. 'I wake up miserable. I need to be given a cookie and walked around the house and told what a pretty, good baby I am. Vincent had the routine down perfectly. He either agreed with everything I said or he ignored me.'

Lydia put down her tiny scissors and came to stand between Lillian's legs. She put her hand on her mother's forehead.

'You're burning up,' she announced firmly.

'No, I'm not! You little copycat! You quack!'

'Ducks say quack,' Lydia said.

'*Quack, quack,*' went Steven. 'Tell your mother she's a good baby.'

'I'm the baby,' Lydia pouted, her hands on her hips.

'You're my baby,' Lillian said, pulling her onto her lap. 'I need an armful of you,' she whispered into Lydia's ear.

'I have to leave now,' Lydia said, going to the door.

'Where are your clothes?' Lillian asked. Lydia was still wearing her pink fuzzy pyjamas.

'Outside?' Lydia suggested hopefully.

'Upstairs.' Lillian pointed and Lydia began to march.

Lillian took some more coffee and began to peel an orange. Steven resumed the crossword puzzle.

'I don't know what to do,' she said after a moment. 'It's a bad reason for him to come back.'

'What is?'

'This,' Lillian gestured vaguely in the direction of Helen's room. 'That.'

'You mean Helen dying?'

'Steven—'

'She wants us to accept it, Lillian.'

'Fine. *I* understand that. *I* know about acceptance. What should I tell him?'

'Tell him your mother's dying.'

'She's not my mother. I mean, she's like my mother but she's not. I wish I could tell my mother the things I can tell her.'

'Why can't you?'

'It never comes out right. I want to talk about me or her and it's always about my father.' Lillian sighed. 'The endless battle over my father. And he doesn't think about anything but the ozone layer. And his trees.'

'I think you'd better find a way to contact Vince.'

'Umm. He's never going to forgive me.' Lillian began to tear the orange peel into strips. 'How do you feel?'

'Me?' Steven looked at the crossword puzzle. 'Uh . . . I feel stupid.'

'No-one can do that crossword puzzle without a dictionary. Get a dictionary.'

'That's not why I feel like a schmuck.'

'Oh.'

'You love your husband, don't you?' Lillian nodded. 'Actually, I sort of love your husband. I certainly love your daughter. And I'm afraid I love her mother. I've felt this way for a long time but it used to be because you reminded me of Emily. Now it's more like a habit.'

348

'A habit? Like biting your nails?' Lillian offered him a piece of the orange.

He smiled and shook his head. 'No.' His face softened. 'More like expecting Emily to be there when I get home.'

Steven looked haunted. For a moment Lillian imagined herself dead and Vincent grieving, her infidelity forgotten. But then she thought of Lydia with no-one to monitor her cherry-slurpee consumption and her eyes filled with tears.

'I'm going away,' Steven said finally.

'Away?'

'I have an offer to start a birth centre in California. Santa Cruz.'

'Don't,' Lillian said.

'Hey, it's not because of you, honey. Sorry, but you're not that big a deal.' She stuck her tongue out. 'Well, some of it's about you. I need a change. Growing up twenty miles from here, I can't scratch my ass without someone telling someone else.'

'Do you like California?'

'Sure. I spent a year there after I graduated from college. Before medical school. Great salads and women.'

'That's a myth,' Lillian said, 'but the salads are great.'

'Look, Emily's buried up on the hill over there.' Steven pointed in the direction of the Protestant cemetery. 'Helen has a plot on one side of her.' Steven's voice shook slightly. 'I bought the other one.' He rested his head in his hands. 'I'm not sure if you understand . . . I feel like the two people I've loved the most in the world will be waiting for me. There are so many dead,' he said in a strangled voice.

Lillian put her mug down and, going around to the other side of the table, she hugged Steven who pressed his cheek against her stomach.

'We kept each other alive after she drowned,' he

whispered, 'Emily was the centre for both of us. I feel like I'm losing my entire family all over again.'

'What about your other family?'

'This is it. My parents were killed in a car accident when I was in college.'

'Oh, Steven!'

'Their life insurance put me through medical school. But I never wanted to be a doctor. I just wanted to deliver babies. I was the richest kid in the school. I owned a BMW and had a swanky apartment. On holidays I'd hole up with lots of booze and drugs, and stay drunk until those fucking Christmas shows were all over. I was an orphan. Women couldn't resist the combination of my being a bastard and an abandoned child. Many therapists have me to thank for their patients. I was just what the doctor ordered.'

'Steven, you're a good person.'

'Helen thinks I am and that's what matters. Now I understand how I felt when my mother died. The vice-principal, this moron named Mr Herbert, came and took me out of Civics class to tell me. "I'm sorry, son," he said. All I wanted to do was scream at him, "You're not my father!" I left the school and went home and found my dad's whisky. They hardly ever drank anything but a little wine. My aunt found me under the patio table. Like a frightened kid. I was waiting for them to come home. I always thought I'd have time to tell them stuff, you know. My dad was a quiet guy. It was hard sometimes. But he never made me feel lousy. And my mom was really funny. Like Gracie Allen, but not dumb. Sharp and intuitive. I could talk to her. They were only forty-two years old.'

'Oh, Steven,' Lillian said again. 'I'm so sorry. That's the saddest thing I've ever heard.'

'I couldn't feel anything then. It was someone else's life. I've tried to screw up your marriage. And it's not like I'd ever have the patience to tolerate all your neurotic behaviour.'

She let go of his head. 'Who asked you, creep?'

'Well, nobody. But that Vincent's a saint.'

They both laughed weakly.

After Steven had gone home, Helen and Lydia went upstairs to look at family bric-à-brac in the attic. Lillian whistled for T.W. and they headed towards the end of the garden. As they followed the path through the woods, she tried to comprehend how things had gone wrong. Marriage wasn't that different from being single except you were never really alone and you constantly felt responsible for something you had no control over and didn't really understand. Loving Vincent wasn't difficult but she could never believe in return that his love for her was unconditional; she assumed that a limit would be reached. Motherhood had changed the world for her. Now she listened to the news with a sense that the world had to improve, so that her daughter's life would not be lived on a ruined, depleted planet. Lydia's face was always in her mind: she saw the child still connected to her, yet so separate. Would Lydia, too, be addicted to alcohol? Would she make the same mistakes, suffer the same disappointments as her mother and grandmother?

'I want to go back,' Lillian muttered as she walked along. During the year following Lydia's birth, she and Vincent had had nothing much to do but play with their new baby. The success of 'Lillian' had put him in touch with other musicians and he'd started to get steady work writing commercial jingles. They spent their evenings watching movies, cooking elaborate meals, working out (Lillian had a lot of weight to lose) or writing together. Each was eager to make the other happy. They *were* very happy. And Lydia . . . Lydia made them understand why people bothered having families. She was a beautiful, funny, interesting baby.

Their lives became more complicated. Vincent's career accelerated after he was nominated for a Grammy award.

His private life became a subject of attention when his picture was published in *Rolling Stone* and people saw how handsome he was. He flew out to Los Angeles, leaving Lillian alone in the Maine winter with a young baby. She didn't tell Helen that he was going away for so long and Helen assumed he had returned weeks earlier. The car wouldn't start; the furnace broke; Lydia had mysterious raging fevers which required cool baths and steam. Every night Lillian was up, tending to their croupy baby. When Vincent returned, tanned, well-rested, his ego stroked by the attention he'd received, he was surprised by the foul temper of his exhausted new wife and the indifference of the daughter who had forgotten him.

There was little hope of his assuming more responsibility. Each time he performed some 'untraditional' task (feeding the baby, doing the wash, making dinner), he made sure that everyone was aware of his lack of male ego. A women's magazine profiled him as a house-husband, which caused Lillian a huge amount of irritation.

'Who do you think you are?' she screamed at him one day after he had spent ten minutes on the phone with a magazine writer, giving his recipe for home-made babyfood. 'Being a father isn't what it used to be. You are expected to take care of this baby! This is your baby! Why do they consider it such a miracle that you are willing to bathe your own daughter?'

But they did. Increasingly, the planning of their day-to-day lives was completely left up to Lillian. When Lydia was a week away from her second birthday, she fell in the kitchen and bit through her lip. The doctor suggested minor plastic surgery but a major anaesthesia needed to be administered. It took her all day to reach him in Dublin where his band was playing their final gig of a tour around the British Isles. He was rather drunk and couldn't understand her wanting to get his opinion. 'You're my little genius, honey,' he'd told her. 'You decide.'

She was sweating. As they approached the pond she noticed T.W.'s ears prick forward and, leaning down, she patted his damp back. 'Go on,' she said. The dog ran and after pausing for a second, plunged into the water. Lillian slowly unbuttoned her shirt. There were so many times she had feared Vincent would turn on her and tell her to get out. It made no sense. He had never acted as if he were capable of such brutality. But she had always expected it. When Anthony had hit her she hadn't protected herself. Being a drunk had meant she deserved to be punished. She had no rights. She had no boundaries. Her behaviour had always caused deep shame and guilt. How could she have fucked another man in her kitchen while her own daughter had slept on upstairs? Drawing a deep breath, naked at the edge of the water, she muttered a prayer.

'God, grant me the serenity to accept the things I cannot change. I love my family. Help my mother. Protect my child. Forgive me. Vincent, forgive me.' The water was like liquid heat in its freezing impact. Her body felt electric. She did a frenzied crawl across the pond and then back. On the bank, she stretched out in the early morning sun and dried off. As the sun increased in heat, she dozed and thought about Helen. They had begun to hold AA meetings at her house. All she ever talked about when she shared was the future. Her plans for her new organic garden, visiting London with Vincent and Lillian the next Christmas, gratitude for all she had to live for. Lillian was afraid. She didn't want Helen to die. She didn't want anyone to die. *Ever.*

When she was five, her cat had been hit by a car. Edward had dug the grave and they had covered up the shoe box with dirt. When she'd finished throwing rose petals all over the mound of dirt, he had turned to her and said, 'You'll die some day.'

'No I won't,' Lillian had said, her eyes growing larger.

'Yes you will!'

'Not everyone does.' She could feel a certain unsteadiness in her position. 'Not always!'

'Yes they do! God, you are such a retard. Let's go ask Mom.'

They went into the house and into the kitchen where their mother was reading the *New York Times*.

'Everybody dies, don't they Mom?' Edward asked, opening the refrigerator.

'Uh huh,' Mrs Jordan had replied, deeply engrossed in the crossword puzzle.

'Everyone?' Lillian asked, barely daring to breathe. She remembered what it felt like to touch Sasparilla's limp body. Nothing.

'Yes,' her mother said, '*everyone*.'

'See?' her brother sneered. 'See, dummy?'

'Will I die?' Lillian had asked, her eyes filling with tears. 'Will you and Daddy?'

'What a doodie bird,' Edward said, taking an apple and going out of the back door.

Lillian was frozen by the table. 'I'm going to die,' she whispered. 'I don't want to.'

Mrs Jordan at last put down her paper. 'Oh dear,' she said. 'I forgot.' She held out her arms. 'Come here, honey.'

When her father found her under the piano later that afternoon, he got down on the floor next to her.

'What's wrong, Lil?' he asked kindly.

'I don't want to die,' she whispered.

'Don't worry,' he said. 'It will be such a long, long time. You'll have been alive for so long, you'll be ready for a change.'

She believed that was how Helen felt, now. Tired. She would leave Lillian again and nothing would be different. She hit her hands against the solid bank until the fingers were numb, bleeding.

*   *   *

There was a message to call Edward when she got back to the house. Helen had made blueberry pancakes.

'I have had four pancakes,' Lydia informed her as she put her blue-stained lips up for a kiss.

'One for each perfect year, my darling,' Lillian said, tears filling her eyes. Lydia looked disgusted by her mother's excessive emotion. 'No crying,' she said sternly.

Helen looked at her sharply. 'Have you been swimming?'

'Yes.' Lillian sat down and poured herself some coffee.

'Have you spoken to Vincent yet?'

'No. I've done something unforgivable.'

Helen glanced at her sharply. 'Do you have to tell him?'

'I'm afraid so.'

'Make amends. Tell him you're sorry. You are sorry. Marriages are more complicated than this. You have a complicated marriage.'

'He'll leave me.'

'It would kill him.'

'You think he loves me?'

'Oh, Lillian.' Helen shook her head. 'Why is it so hard for you to believe that?'

Edward was on his other line when she called. 'Hold on,' he told her.

She looked out of the window at the garden where Lydia and her grandmother were inspecting their vegetables. Lydia's face was turned towards Helen's as she listened intently. Soon they would have to explain that Helen was sick, and try to define death to a four-year-old. And divorce? Vincent would have to help her. She felt a shiver go down her spine. Vincent's parents had been so Christian he rarely discussed his own beliefs. But she remembered him once telling her he viewed God as a force of love and that terrible things occurred outside that force. She didn't know how he would explain death.

'Lil?'

'Hi, Eddie.'

'How are you?'

'OK.'

'So . . . ' Edward cleared his throat. 'So?'

'I've ruined everything again.'

'Have you? I don't think so.'

'Helen's dying.'

'Oh my God.' Edward's voice grew very tender. 'My poor little sister,' he said quietly. 'What can I do?'

'Nothing. Just don't stop loving me now.'

'OK. I still haven't forgiven you for breaking my burnt-sienna crayon, but I'll try.'

They were both quiet. Out of the window she saw her mother and daughter were still talking, heads very close together. Then they both looked up at the sky and laughed.

'Is it cancer?'

'Yes. It's inoperable. She saw a specialist in Boston who recommended a hospice. But she wants to die here. It's so hard . . . Edward, I don't think I can manage.'

'Yes you can.'

'I want to go back.'

'Back where, darling?'

'Before I knew anything. Why can't we protect people we love?'

'Lillian, dying is part of everything. It means you were alive.'

'I don't want to be part of anything! That's why I used to drink. I can't stand people expecting things from me. I can't be a mother or a daughter or a wife!'

She was sobbing into the phone. Edward began making soothing noises like the sound one would make to calm a baby. 'Stop it!' she said finally, beginning to laugh.

'OK?'

'Yes.'

'Good. When do you see Vince? Does he know about Helen?'

'No.'

'Why don't you tell him?'

'I can't. Not over the phone. He loves her.'

'What about you? She's your mother. One of your mothers, anyway. Work it out, Lillian. You don't have time to break in another husband.'

'I'll try.'

'Mommy?'

'Yes, buttercup?'

'Grandma's going to die.'

'How do you know that?'

'She told me.'

'When you were in the garden?'

'Uh huh.'

'Does that make you feel sad?'

'Nope. She said it would be like she was here. She's going to be in the sky.' Her daughter's eyelids were drooping.

'Did she tell you when, Lydia?'

'Soon. She said I could help you. We can have a party and I can help you do things.'

'Yes,' Lillian said, tucking the quilt around her daughter. 'You can help me do things.'

Helen was sitting on the porch reading *Bleak House*. 'I don't know why I began this,' she said as Lillian sat down in the chair next to her.

'Why?'

'It's so long. I'll be dead before I finish it.'

'Shall I tell you the end?'

Both women began to laugh.

'There's a guy who reads classics at top speed,' Lillian said. 'I think he does *War and Peace* in under an hour.'

'I've read that,' Helen said. 'How about *Moby Dick*?'

'Lydia said you told her you were going to die.'

'Yes. I thought it would be better. Is that all right?'

'Of course, Helen. I mean, why would you ask that?'

'You're her mother. You may have wanted to explain things.'

'No. I think she'll understand better this way.'

'What about you?'

'What?'

'Do you understand?'

Lillian shrugged. 'No.'

'Is there anything I need to explain to you? Something I can tell you about the adoption . . . '

'No.' The night was cool and quiet. They both looked at the Milky Way and then the moon. 'What will I do if Vincent can't forgive me?'

'Go on.'

'Do you think he will?'

'I don't know, dear. You love him. Try to show him that.'

'He knows.'

'Don't assume he does! Or if he does, that he doesn't need you to tell him.'

'How do people learn how to get these things right?'

'From their children if they pay attention. I've learned a great deal from you. Watch Lydia.'

'What did she say when you said you were sick?'

'She shook her head and said it was just too many pancakes. I explained a bit about cancer and she announced her belief that no-one she knew was ever going to die. I went on and told her what the doctor said. She listened and then she started to pat me and say "poor Grandma". Then she went back to digging and advised me to do the same.'

'A survivor,' Lillian said. 'I wonder where that came from.'

'I wonder,' Helen replied, smiling.

*　　*　　*

It was Mrs Jordan's nervousness that broke the ice. Lillian was so afraid of being judged, she had made Lydia wear a ridiculous outfit for travelling – a dirndl dress complete with a matching scarf and little white socks.

'Too hot,' Lydia kept announcing as they dashed through Logan Airport and later through Newark. 'Stupid, hot dress.'

When Mrs Jordan arrived, she brought with her a cooler full of drinks. After kissing her granddaughter and daughter, she began to offer Lydia drinks. 'Do you want juice, sweetie? Or maybe soda or just plain water or chocolate milk or how about a popsicle?'

Lydia, sensing an adult who could be easily bullied, put her finger to her brow and began to speak in a sing-song baby voice. 'Maybe chocolate milk, no! Maybe orange juice, no! Maybe soda, no!'

Lillian ignored this at first but then looked over the seat and said, 'Miss Repulsive better make up her mind or Miss Repulsive's Mommy is going to be very, very cruel.'

Mrs Jordan laughed and patted her daughter's leg. 'We used to call you "Miss Repulsive",' she said. 'That was your favourite word.'

'I know,' Lillian smiled back. 'It's hard to be original sometimes.'

'My dress is repulsive,' Lydia said, displaying her underpants.

'Yes it is,' Lillian agreed, wearily sinking down in the front seat of the car. 'Lizbeth thinks Lydia needs to identify with Heidi.'

'I'll have some beer,' Lydia announced from the back seat. 'Like Daddy.'

'Umm,' Lillian murmured, reaching into the cooler and extracting a carton of cranberry juice. 'No beer for the baby,' she said, watching as Lydia, who had finally had enough of looking like an Alpen maiden, divested herself of most of her clothes and in her white cotton underpants gravely accepted the drink.

'*Merci beaucoup*, Mama,' Lydia said.

Mrs Jordan smiled. 'My, my,' she said, 'who's teaching you French?'

'My Grandma Helen,' Lydia murmured. She sat forward and touched Mrs Jordan's shoulder lightly with her hand. 'She's going to die of cancer,' Lydia whispered.

Lillian gasped. She inhaled deeply and felt her mother's hand on her knee.

'Honey?'

'Yes. I wanted to tell you later.'

'I told her,' Lydia said.

'Yes you did, smartie-pants.' Lillian looked out of the window. As always, gas burned on the New Jersey Turnpike. 'It's stomach and it's inoperable. We've seen everyone. There's a hospice if it gets too difficult but she'd like to die at home.'

Mrs Jordan reached for the Kleenex on the dashboard. 'I don't know what to say.' She touched Lillian's cheek with her hand. 'I'm glad you've come home.'

'I didn't know where else to go.'

'Does Vincent know?'

'We're in a lot of trouble, Mom. I don't want to drop this on him in the middle of a discussion about custody.'

Mrs Jordan looked through the rear-view mirror at her granddaughter who was slumped down, thumb in mouth, fast asleep. 'I can't believe you won't work this out, Lillian. The marriage is stronger than that.'

'It was but I think once there's a break the material tears easily . . . '

Mrs Jordan shook her head. 'You always assume the worst. It's part of your charming perversity.'

Lillian stuck her tongue out at her mother, who reciprocated.

*　　*　　*

Mr Jordan was in the garden pruning the hedge when they arrived. Lydia ran outside in her underpants despite Lillian's offer to put her dress back on.

'Well, well,' Mr Jordan said, squeezing Lillian's arm, 'your daughter appears to be travelling *au naturel*.'

They both watched as Lydia, spotting the sprinkler, shed her remaining article of clothing and ran naked into the water.

'How's the hedge?' Lillian asked after a moment of silence.

Her father glanced at her and laughed. 'Just fine. Is Vincent still in LA?'

'Uh huh.' She looked up at her father. 'Helen's got stomach cancer,' she said quietly. 'They've given her about six months.'

His hand reached out for her and she came into his arms without thinking. How long had it been, she wondered, as she rested her head on his shoulder and felt him brushing the hair away from her brow. The smell of his skin combined with the scent of all the boys and men she had once loved, and yet it was only his scent, the scent of her father.

'My brave daughter,' Mr Jordan murmured. 'How sorry I am for your pain.'

She sank, allowed her weight to settle against him, faintly sensed his heart beating and felt the fear abate slightly.

'Mommy,' Lydia screamed. 'I'm nude.'

'Show Grandpa how you can stand on your head.'

They both watched as Lydia's bottom wavered in the air. For a second, she straightened her legs and then did a forward somersault.

'My God,' Lillian's father said, 'a naked Olympian.'

When the phone rang the next morning, it was Lillian who answered it.

'Lillian?' Vincent's Maine accent sounded more pronounced than usual.

'Hi.'

'Everybody OK there?'

'Yeah. I mean, Lydia's fine. Let me tell her you're on the phone.'

'Great. And then come back on.'

She watched her daughter tell an endless story about their trip to Grandma Jordan's. Lillian had asked her not to tell anyone else that Helen was going to die.

Lydia had agreed and then, squinting at her mother, she'd smiled. 'Is it a surprise?'

'Yes.'

'Like my birthday?'

'Sort of.'

When her mother put down a bowl of oatmeal, Lillian mindlessly began to eat it. Outside, her father was putting fuel in the mower. Lydia was trying to stand on her head while she held the receiver and continued to speak to her father. The only word Lillian could hear clearly was 'nude'.

'You think she's an exhibitionist?' Vincent was still laughing.

'Maybe.' *I love you.*

'Could you get out here immediately?'

'Is that what you want?' *Forgive me.*

'Would you be able to leave Lydia with them?'

'Of course.' *Don't leave me.*

'Call me when you get a flight. Try to be on the red-eye.'

'Vincent—'

'Did you sleep with Steven?'

'Why are you asking me that?' *Yes. Once. Never again.*

'Because he said you did.'

'What!'

'I asked him and the answer was positive.' There was a

long pause. 'Well, baby, this time the man isn't the villain. You really can't imagine how I feel.'

Don't call me baby, Vincent. My mother is dying. 'I'll call you with my flight number.'

'Is that all?'

No. Don't you know that I have accepted the responsibility for raising your daughter largely alone because you, the perfect husband, stay above all mortal concerns on your fucking pink cloud of immortality, autographing 8x10 glossies for all those prepubescent twinkies in the Vinnie Delacroce fan club?

'I guess so.'

Vincent suggested meeting in San Francisco instead of Los Angeles. He was flying up to do business there anyway and they could use the recording studio's apartment in Pacific Heights.

'I'm sick of Los Angeles,' he said on the phone. 'People here don't seem to come out during daylight. The Vampires are starting to depress me.'

30

As Lillian packed, she realized it was nearly six months since he had left. Folding the white nightgown he had given her for their first Christmas together, she imagined the scene that night and the two lovers seemed like strangers. After breakfast, Mrs Jordan suggested a trip to the mall for new underwear. As she stood in the changing-room of a designer-outlet store, wearing a bathing suit that made every part of her body look terrible, Lillian began to wonder if she was really going to lose her wonderful, albeit selfish, husband. After a few moments of hyperventilating, she sunk to her knees, her head resting on the chair. Small, cool hands touched her back and she looked into the anxious face of her daughter.

'That's a beautiful bathing suit,' Lydia said anxiously. 'Like Madonna.'

Lillian gathered Lydia onto her lap. 'I look like Miss Piggy,' she whispered into her daughter's shell-like ear. 'Miss Piggy and I are twins.'

Lillian's mother came in holding a pink dress which was something no self-respecting person, except an ageing, preppie, suburban housewife, would wear.

'I thought it was sweet,' she said as Lillian and Lydia held their noses.

Just before reaching the house, with Lydia asleep in the car seat, Mrs Jordan drew a deep breath. 'I want to tell you something,' she said.

'I'm adopted. You told me already.'

'Something else.'

'Don't Mom.' Lillian glanced out of the window and

watched two teenagers smoking cigarettes with major attitude. 'Family secrets are unbearable.'

'I had an affair.'

Lillian groaned. She banged her head against the window.

'It was a long time ago.' Mrs Jordan turned into their driveway. Mr Jordan was weeding the rose beds. Both women waved.

'Do I know the person?'

'Joe Tulliver.' Mrs Jordan smiled.

'Why are you smiling?' Lillian asked in horror. Joe Tulliver had been the vice-principal at Lillian's school. He combed his hair over his bald spot and seemed to be in a perpetual panic.

'I don't know what possessed me.'

Lillian groaned again. 'Is that why he always let me off detention?'

Mrs Jordan nodded. Her eyes looked slightly dreamy.

'That's disgusting,' Lillian said vehemently, 'totally repulsive.'

'Don't be so judgemental,' Mrs Jordan snapped.

'Repulsive,' Lydia murmured sleepily from the back. 'I'm repulsive.'

'No you're not,' Lillian said, her tone heavy with moral indignation. 'You are my perfect child.' She gave her mother a mock horrified look. 'And Grandma is a s-l-u-t,' she whispered.

'Afraid of flying?' her seatmate on the Newark–San Francisco flight was a young businessman reading Machiavelli.

'Not really.' They both looked down to where Lillian's hands were clutching the armrests so tightly, her fingers were completely white. She let go.

'I hope you don't mind me asking you this,' the businessman said, 'but are you someone famous?'

'No,' Lillian said.

'An actress, maybe?'

'No.'

'Were you ever an actress?'

Lillian shook her head. 'What do you do?' she asked, hoping this would alter his line of questioning.

'I'm in metal.'

'Heavy metal?' she couldn't help asking, assuming he'd catch the reference.

'No. Sheet metal.'

Lillian smiled and took her Walkman out of her bag. She seldom used it for anything but self-defence. Men like this made her want to kiss the ground that Vincent walked upon. She thought about her mother and Mr Tulliver. The image of Joe Tulliver in his underwear seemed absolutely surrealistic. He probably wore boxer shorts with black socks until he got under the covers. How could her mother have allowed that man to touch her? Did Mr Jordan even notice his wife's fading attention? For some reason she thought of Vincent again and a list of possible affairs. Lizbeth's face kept drifting into her consciousness. The previous winter Vincent had been stuck in New York with nowhere to stay and Lizbeth had offered him her apartment for a weekend when she was meant to be with her married lover in the Hamptons. The lover's wife had needed surgery and Lizbeth had stayed in town.

Lillian remembered having received an odd phone call from Vincent that afternoon, Sunday afternoon, before he'd caught the shuttle to Boston. 'I love you,' he had told her as soon as she picked up the phone. He'd sounded miserable and said he didn't want to play gigs out of town any more.

'Something happened,' Lillian thought, the words written across her mind in fire. 'Those two did something.' Suddenly, unexpectedly, she felt much better. Her best friend had done something with her husband and neither of them had had the decency to confess or even to suffer noticeably. Although she knew there was a possibility that it had never happened, the fact of Mr Tulliver and her mother made it seem definite.

'Fidelity is a state of mind,' she told herself as she drifted off to sleep.

When she came into the arrival area, there was no-one to meet her. She stood and watched the other passengers being spirited away by their friends and relatives. Her baggage was carry-on. As she was about to find the ladies, a young man came up to her elbow.

'Lillian?'

'Yes?'

'I'm Sam. Vin's driver. He's waiting in the car.'

'His driver?'

'The studio has a fleet of limos.' Sam winked. 'Nice perk.'

'Great. I just need to use the bathroom.'

'Let me take your bag. We're parked right in front.'

She stood looking at herself in the full-length mirror and wondered what sort of women Vincent had been spending time with. He'd always had a penchant for tiny, sloe-eyed blondes. Her opposite. She was tall and slender and well-dressed, and so afraid of seeing her husband she looked like someone in an ad for headache remedies. She tried to smile but the effect was worse than the neutral expression she'd had previously. The expression on her face was one of guilt. She smoked three puffs of her last cigarette, rinsed out her mouth and left the bathroom.

The limousine was silver-grey and the windows were smoked. When Sam opened the door she heard a Beethoven concerto playing on a perfectly balanced sound system.

'Hello!' She sounded like a stewardess. Absurdly perky. She sat down on the jump seat across from Vincent, her handbag clutched in her cold, stiff hands. 'Hello!' she said again.

'*Hello?*' Vincent took off his sunglasses. 'What's this? This is what you say to your husband after six months?'

'You could get out and greet me in person.'

'I thought you liked this,' he waved his hand in the air, 'stuff.'

'Me?' Lillian shook her head. 'I'm your first wife. The one who never enjoyed the trappings of luxury.'

'My first wife?'

'Did you sleep with Lizbeth last year?'

Vincent blinked. He exhaled a large amount of air. 'Where did that come from?' he asked slowly.

'My mother had an affair.'

'Interesting logic. Your mother committed adultery and I'm implicated?'

'I began to rethink the impossible,' Lillian replied primly, her hands folded in her lap.

'What about you?' Vincent was looking at her steadily. The limousine was travelling fast on the way to San Francisco.

'I asked first,' Lillian said, sounding, she realized, remarkably like Lydia.

'How did you find out about your mother?'

'She told me.'

Vincent made a face. 'Ah. Because you told her about yours and she wanted to make you feel less like a whore.'

'A what?'

'A whore! Bitch! Did you really fuck that new-age, midwife bastard?'

'You fucked Lizbeth, didn't you?'

'I knew he would get in there sooner or later, always hanging around like a dog sniffing at you, trying to find a hole in the fence.'

'Don't you talk to me about dogs! My best friend!'

They looked at one another in horror, recognizing

in these words, the possibility of irreparable damage. The silence which ensued seemed endless. When Lillian looked at Vincent, his face was averted, tears running down his cheeks. She landed in his lap, kissing his eyes, his cheeks and then his mouth.

He buried his face in her hair. 'Oh baby,' Vincent murmured. 'Where have you been?'

'In Maine,' Lillian whispered, covering his face with kisses.

'I want you now,' Vincent said, unbuttoning her shirt and unsnapping the black bra she'd bought for their reunion. The limousine kept moving smoothly along the freeway. The smoked windows made it seem as if they were in a large, comfortable closet. Vincent had her naked in two minutes. He pushed her back on the leather seat and looked at her. 'This is too much for me,' he said, his hands stroking her outer thigh.

Lillian reached her arms out. 'Come here,' she said.

Vincent took off his clothes. He held himself above her, his incredible eyes staring at her. 'You want me?' he asked softly, his teeth sinking into her shoulder.

'Yes,' she said, wrapping her legs around his waist and pulling him inside, down, hard, deep inside so that she groaned and arched her back. And he bit her lips, holding her hair in one hand and pulling her closer, hard so that it hurt but felt good. And the car kept moving, Beethoven continued while Vincent fucked his wife and his wife fucked him back. They knew each other's bodies but everything was different. The distance had made them more aware of the miracle they could create with their love-making and he told her over and over again, as he came, hard, his fingers digging deep into the skin of her ass, that she was his wife, his lover, his bitch . . . and he would never love anyone else as much as he loved her and if she ever made love to another man he would never forgive her.

Afterwards, they put their clothes back on and found sodas and fruit in the icebox. Vincent peeled an orange and fed the pieces to her, and then he began all over again, sucking her tits and touching her. He kneeled between her legs and, parting her thighs, his tongue probed and licked; his teeth nibbled as if he were consuming the sweetest fruit in the world, making her come, although she could tell by the way the car was slowing down they were almost there. But he kept going, whispering, 'come', until she did.

The apartment didn't feel intimate like home but it wasn't neutral like a hotel. The furniture was quite expensive and tacky, but they had a wonderful view of the bay from the bedroom window, which is where they spent most of their time. They fucked and they fought over the reasons for their infidelity. Vincent refused to accept Lillian's theory that his betrayal was the greater.

'Just because you can't keep a secret doesn't mean you're less guilty than me,' Vincent said. 'You run off to those meetings and tell a roomful of strangers things that are private and personal and I never complain, so don't try and make me out to be evil and devious.'

'You are evil and devious,' was Lillian's response. But since they were in the bathtub and Vincent's hand was inside her and she was kissing him, her head bent back to receive all of his tongue and about to have yet another orgasm, her fourth or fifth that evening, the discussion was derailed. And later, when she had him on his back and was sucking his erect cock she stopped and whispered, 'Admit you were wrong.'

He didn't hesitate to admit to everything, including his being self-centred and chauvinistic about pulling his weight with domestic chores, so she continued until he was whispering, 'God, I love you!' and pulling her hair, thrusting his pelvis hard into her face. She took all of him inside her mouth and then, for a few hours, they slept.

There was something very erotic about fucking in a

stranger's bed. They got carried away and tore the sheets and then Vincent decided it was a good thing because he wanted to tie her up and Lillian was always reluctant to sacrifice percale to bondage. He ripped them into long strips and bound her hands above her head and around the brass railing of the bed. They played these games quite frequently. He liked her tied-up. It was all very sexy but there was an edge to the rôles they played. He wrote a song called 'Little Blue Boy' which she considered an indictment of their marriage.

> Little Blue Boy, left on his own.
> His wife's got a migraine
> She's writing a poem.
> Where is the boy who loved her so deep?
> He's alone in the night-time, trying to sleep.
> He can't reach her, she's never at home,
> Little Blue Boy, who left you alone?

When he played the song for her she felt betrayed.

'I don't get migraines,' she had muttered under her breath.

'What?' Vincent made a face. 'This isn't about us.'

'Who is it about? The neighbours?'

'Hey! Don't think I believed you when you claimed that short story about the woman married to the Elvis impersonator was fiction.'

'You think everything's about you even if it's not, so what's the point?'

They used one another ruthlessly as subjects of their art and neither really felt the other was guilty since they each knew themselves to be equally culpable. And when they could no longer talk they fucked and sometimes Vincent tied her up as if to say, 'Don't think there's such a thing as equality.' And Lillian felt too unsure of her own feelings to tell him how angry she was.

She woke up one morning with Vincent's arms wrapped around her. Their view of the bay was panoramic, the buildings gleamed white as the San Francisco fog burned off. As she tried to slip out of bed, his grip tightened.

'Don't,' he mumbled.

'I'm awake.'

'Go back.'

She brushed the long hair away from his brow and kissed it. His skin was a lovely golden colour, weight-training sessions had toned his muscles and his entire body was lean and smooth.

'What are you thinking, Lillian?'

'How beautiful you are.'

'Let's not get divorced, baby.'

She drew a deep breath. 'Can you forgive me?'

'I have no choice. The thing between Lizbeth and me isn't what you think, but I did cheat on you out here.'

She tried to pull out of his arms but he held her tightly against his chest. After a moment, she relaxed again.

Vincent kissed her breast. 'I was furious with you for not coming with me.'

'That's not why you screwed a bimbo.'

'You assume it's a bimbo?'

'If she wasn't, I do want a divorce.'

'How come you get to boink doctors, then? And practically commit incest?'

She raised her fist but Vincent caught her hand and gently kissed each knuckle. 'Truce,' he murmured. 'You're my wife and I deserve loyalty. But it's also true that I wasn't doing shit about Lydia or the house or the bank or the cars. You had all the responsibility while I acted like a visiting celebrity.'

She sat up. 'Did you find God or something?'

'I've changed. It's important that people stop repeating the same mistakes.'

'Vincent, what's happened to you?'

'A lot of stuff. I saw a shrink out here who helped me see what kind of a nutty family I grew up in. My parents worshipped me, every day was like my birthday, and I was ashamed of them. So I pretended to be indifferent. Helen's probably responsible for any healthy attitudes I possess. She kept me from being an insufferable prick.'

'You're a good man.'

'I miss my daughter. Lillian, I'm a lousy father.'

'No you aren't!'

'Come on. She never comes to me for anything important. I'm her playmate. It's all seduction and good times. Mommy provides stability and all the rules. That isn't fair. And she'll hate me when she finds out how little she knows about men.'

'She knows what it is to be loved.' Lillian put her hand on Vincent's cheek.

'But when she's frightened or hurt, it's always Mommy.'

Lillian drew a deep breath. 'I have something to tell you about Helen.'

'She's terminal.'

Lillian looked startled.

'Steve told me. He didn't think you should be doing everything alone. I'm so sorry, Lil. I'm so sorry.'

So that was that. He still loved her and he didn't want a divorce. It felt as if someone had removed a yoke from around her shoulders. She rolled the tension from her neck and felt her breath finally deepen. The sense of foreboding and dread evaporated. They stayed in the apartment for three more days. Vincent had borrowed a jeep from a friend and they drove it up into the mountains and then had a cook-out on the beach. But Vincent was tired and anxious to come home. He had spent day and night in the studio, missing Lydia, angry at Lillian and upset about Helen. While she listened to her husband describe some of the projects he'd completed, Lillian noticed that he really had changed. During the past six months he had grown up. There was now a quieter, less cocky man sitting across from her, someone who finally seemed rooted in the present. One reason Lillian had felt alone was because while she'd been the one to attend PTA meetings, call the local newspaper to complain about the cuts in the hours of the Public Library and wear socks to bed, Vincent still had hair long enough to braid down his back, suggested trips to Bombay as a suitable holiday and remained ridiculously youthful. But now there were faint lines in his skin and among the gleaming mass of his hair, she noticed silver threads. They had promised to take care of each other but Lillian's burden had been the heavier one.

They visited museums, saw several movies and a terrible musical comedy about Yuppies. The weather was perfect: hot and clear during the day, cool at night. The apartment was large and had a sunken bathtub big enough for two where they made love and discussed whether to take Lydia to Paris the following winter. Neither of them said 'After Helen dies . . . ', but both heard it in the other's voice.

She refused to return to Maine without him.

'I should see some people in Los Angeles,' he'd told her when she announced she'd made return reservations for both of them to Bangor, 'I can get out by the end of the week.'

'No, Vincent,' she said, sitting on his lap, crushing his Filofax. 'I want you at home now. I'm not letting you go back there.'

They went home. Bill met them at the airport.

'Vin,' Bill shook his head, overcome with emotion. 'You're all grown-up.'

Vincent punched him softly on the arm. 'Give us some local dirt, pal.'

'The Weedens bought the lot next to their house,' Bill told them as they drove home. 'They're digging a pool.'

'Who got the contract?' Vincent asked, rolling his eyes at Lillian.

'Whattya mean? The same people who get all the pool contracts! Peterson's Pools!'

'Right,' Vincent said, again rolling his eyes towards Lillian, who frowned. 'How could I have forgotten that?' He bit Lillian's ear.

'Hey, no necking in my car,' Bill said, nudging Lillian with his elbow.

'She's attacking me!'

'You two never change,' Bill said. 'I remember when you first set eyes on each other in the restaurant.'

'Like a firestorm, wasn't it, Bill?'

'Sure was. You told me she was too stuck-up for you, too New York. But I could tell you were a goner. It doesn't look like you're gonna split up again.'

'Never,' Lillian said fervently.

'Next time she'll come to LA,' Vincent said, pulling Lillian's hair.

'Vincent's spending the winter in Maine, taking care of the plumbing so I can write.'

Bill smiled at them fondly. 'Just a couple of crazy kids,' he said.

Lillian stared out the window. She was about to say something cynical and funny, but words failed her. They were on their way home.

When Helen saw Vincent she held her arms out and said, 'Come here you gorgeous thing!'

He held her in his arms for a moment and then let go.

'Good Lord,' he said. 'Your daughter's a tub of lard, compared to you!' His voice was light but his face reflected shock and grief. Lillian realized she had been refusing to acknowledge how sick Helen looked. When she saw Vincent bending over her mother, she realized death was extremely close. It seemed to exist just outside the frame of the photograph, a cloud which moved inexorably towards the sun. Soon they would all be bathed in shadows.

When Dorothy drove in with Lydia, Lillian ran outside and opened the door. 'Guess what, snookums,' she said, unfastening the car seat-straps, kissing the child.

'What did you bring me?'

'Daddy!'

Lydia screamed and ran towards the house but when her father appeared on the porch, she froze and stared at him without moving.

Vincent stooped and held his arms out. 'Who's my bunny?' he said. 'Where's Flopsy Cottontail?' And Lydia, her hands creating bunny ears, hopped into her father's arms.

Helen and Vincent sat outside on the porch talking until after midnight. He held both her hands. Helen took out the photo albums and they looked at images of Vincent with his first guitar and Beatle boots, Helen bringing Emily home from the hospital. They laughed a great deal and Helen gave him the envelope with her will in it. Lillian had asked her to go over the details with Vincent. She hadn't been able to listen when Helen had tried to explain how she was disposing of her property. In her head there was a phrase that just kept repeating itself: *Don't die, don't die, don't die.* She watched her husband and mother sitting together on the porch swing, Helen leaning against Vincent's shoulder. Lillian tasted something bitter in her mouth. Her chest hurt. It was difficult to breathe. She looked down and saw she had scratched the knuckles of her hands until they were bleeding.

Standing in the doorway of her daughter's bedroom, she considered the fate of her real father. How had he lost the will to survive, the strength to swim another stroke? Would he have been able to love his only daughter or would the fact of his sin, against the Church and his wife, poison everything?

'Mommy?' Lydia was sitting up in bed, a patch of

moonlight lightening her hair until it gleamed like silver.

'Yes?'

'I dreamed Daddy came home.'

'That wasn't a dream, honey. He's downstairs talking to Grandma. He'll come up in a second.'

'Did he bring me a pony?'

Lillian laughed and crossed to sit on Lydia's bed. 'That was a dream.'

'A black pony?'

'Nope.'

'With a white star on his forehead?'

'Black Beauty. Nope. No pony.'

'Oh. I dreamed that.'

Lillian leaned over and kissed Lydia's cool skin. 'Well, you do get Daddy.'

'*And* a black pony,' Lydia murmured as she turned over, inserting her thumb in her mouth.

Lillian took Thomas Wolfe's leash and left the house with her dog. They walked down to the lake and while Lillian counted shooting stars, T.W. swam back and forth, his body barely visible in the moonlight. Why did she feel so thwarted, she wondered. Did she really believe the people she chose to love should remain immune, immutable, untouched? While she moved among them, reaching out only to them, avoiding contact with the rest of the world?

Children insisted on that sort of order. Their parents firmly in place; their best friend at the desk next to them in school; their stuffed animals arranged in perfect rows. It was something you were meant to outgrow. As a child, her favourite game had been statues. You twirled someone around and then made them freeze in the position they stopped in. Then you attempted to make the 'statues' move or laugh. Lillian rarely lost. The game would never end if left to her because she could remain motionless. Edward often left her when he was sick of the game, hungry for his dinner. She would wait for him to come back, motionless, a prisoner of her own will.

She had always hated things ending. As a drunk she would stay after the end of parties. She didn't accept the closing of bars, the coming of dawn as a signal that the night was over, time for sleep, time to go home. The end of things frightened her. If you stayed awake, people wouldn't disappear. But things changed. She taught her daughter that bed-time was lovely, that the morning always came, holidays returned, the future was full of delights.

'Hey.' Vincent sat down next to her, his feet crossed in front of him.

'Hi.'

'Are we getting daisy-face a black pony?'

'No.'

'You sure?' Vincent looked slightly worried.

'Did you tell her we were?'

'Umm . . . maybe.'

'Jerk!'

'I want her to like me.'

They both stared into the water. Vincent reached out and gently kneaded her shoulders. 'You OK?'

'Yeah.'

'Where's the hound?'

She pointed towards the lake. Thomas Wolfe's snout was visible, glowing silver in the moonlight.

He laughed. 'What's he doing? Impersonating an otter?' He pulled her close, into the circle of his arms. 'It's almost time, Lillian.'

'I know. I can see her skull through the skin. I can see her somewhere else. She's so tired.' Looking up at Orion's Belt, Lillian swallowed hard. 'My mother.'

'You should talk to her. She wants to tell you stuff.'

'I will.'

'Do it tomorrow.' He looked at her. 'What's the matter, sweetheart?'

'I'm so afraid.'

He pushed the hair away from her forehead, kissed each brow and the eyelids. 'What are you afraid of?'

'I don't know what's going to happen.' She held up her empty hands. 'I don't know what's going to happen.'

'Helen's going to die.'

'What does that mean, Vincent?'

He shook his head. 'You tell me, Lillian. You were close to it once.'

'What about us?'

'Us? We're going to live. We're going camping. I want to climb a mountain. I want to watch you make breakfast over a fire.'

'I have to make breakfast?'

'Who else?'

'You could.'

'I have to make the fire.'

'Who said?'

'Jesus, you suck at building fires. It will be fine. We're going camping.'

'Who is?'

'You and me and Lyd. And that stupid dog, I guess.'

'Oh.' Lillian breathed deeply. 'Why can't Lizbeth find someone who loves her? Why doesn't she marry Edward?'

'Everybody will be OK.'

'Bill said he was feeling depressed.'

'Bill's going to be fine.'

'Did you know Steven was an orphan?'

'Yup.' Vincent nudged her. 'Was that why you slept with him?'

She pinched him and was happy to find an inch of extra flesh.

'Is this what it feels like?'

'What?' Vincent pulled her hair back and held it, heavy in his hands.

'Living.'

'Is it a good feeling?'

She thought for a moment. 'Yes.'

'Then, this is it.'

'This is it?'

'Well, this is part of it.'

'The good part?'

'I don't know.'

'I thought you knew everything.'

'I don't know shit.'

'So I'm still the smart one?'

'You knew that already. I'm pretty and you're smart.'

'You *are* pretty, Vincent. My beautiful husband.'

'You want to take off all your clothes?'

'Yes.'

They stripped naked. Admired each other in the moonlight. Kissed passionately and then, holding hands, leapt off the bank into the cold, clean, dark water, shouting and laughing at the shock of it, the dog swimming towards them both, his head raised above the water, barking at the moon. Up on the porch, Helen Carter held her granddaughter in her arms. They watched a star shoot across the clear night sky.

'I wished for a pony,' Lydia shrieked, reaching to hold one of those bright planets in her hands.

'So did I,' Helen whispered, sitting down to rock the child back to sleep.

THE END

PARTING IS ALL WE KNOW OF HEAVEN

'Contains more real energy, passion, humour and drama than half a dozen restrained and overwritten yuppie novels'

Alison Lurie

'Full of anger and compassion'
Madison Smartt Bell

Cordelia Cavanagh is a twenty-nine-year-old aspiring actress living in Manhattan whose oldest sister, an aspiring saint, is brutally murdered. The event turns Cordelia's life – until now the average maze of small triumphs, big disappointments, and casual, trendy attitudes – into a battleground where grief and guilt vie for control. Inner strength ultimately prevails after experiments with sex, anorexia, and drugs do not allow her to escape from the pain of her loss.

With hypnotizing clarity we see a privileged family's struggle to come to grips with the loss of its number-one daughter, and a woman's denial of her feelings to the point of self-abuse.

0553 40366 4

LONG DISTANCE LIFE

'In intense, luminous prose, Golden deftly blends the experiences of the black family into the tapestry of 20th-century black history . . .'
Publishers Weekly

Naomi Johnson is the spiritual and emotional centre of her family. After marrying to get away from her father's home, and in spite of expectations that she stay in a deadening marriage with no future, she leaves Spring Hope, North Carolina, in the 1920s and becomes part of the Black migration North.

Naomi finds success in the new world, and marries a man of passion and intelligence. But Rayford dies early leaving Naomi to raise her daughter, Esther, alone.

Despite her mother's opposition, Esther drops out of university after falling in love with Randolph Spenser, a married man. Fleeing the confines of her mother's dreams and her lover's weaknesses, Esther heads South to join the civil rights movement. When she returns, she brings freedom and renewed hope for her life and that of her family.

0553 40362 1

A WAY THROUGH THE WOODS

'Crisp amd engaging'
The Times

Beside the River Needle is a willow and beyond the willow are the Tunnel Woods, a meeting place for generations of Needlewick girls.

The Tunnel Woods provide a haven of secret joy for Helen – a sensitive and lonely child who lives in a private world of imagination. But in 1909, when her cousin Sophia is sent from London to stay, Helen experiences new joy – the joy of friendship.

Years later, Sophia is engaged to be married. She has lost much in the intervening time, but not her ambition for a rich and secure future. When she receives news of a strange legacy, she returns to Needlewick and seeks out the people and hidden places of her girlhood – a time and place she would rather forget.

0553 40431 8